D1453630

Bloody Murder

Bloody Murder

*The Homicide Tradition in
Children's Literature*

Michelle Ann Abate

The Johns Hopkins University Press

Baltimore

The Johns Hopkins University Press
2715 North Charles Street
Baltimore, Maryland 21218-4363
www.press.jhu.edu

Library of Congress Cataloging-in-Publication Data
Abate, Michelle Ann, 1975–
    Bloody murder : the homicide tradition in children's literature /
Michelle Ann Abate.
        p. cm.
    Includes bibliographical references and index.
    ISBN 978-1-4214-0840-8 (hdbk. : alk. paper) — ISBN 978-1-4214-0841-5
(electronic) — ISBN 1-4214-0840-6 (hdbk. : alk. paper) —
ISBN 1-4214-0841-4 (electronic)
    1. Children's literature, English—History and criticism. 2. Children's
literature, American—History and criticism. 3. Homicide in literature.
4. Crime in popular culture—United States—History. 5. Literature
and society—United States—History. 6. Social values in literature.
7. Murder in literature. I. Title.
    PN1009.5.H66A23 2010
    820.9′9282—dc23   2012025276

A catalog record for this book is available from the British Library.

*Special discounts are available for bulk purchases of this book. For more
information, please contact Special Sales at 410-516-6936 or
specialsales@press.jhu.edu.*

The Johns Hopkins University Press uses environmentally friendly book
materials, including recycled text paper that is composed of at least
30 percent post-consumer waste, whenever possible.

Dear Reader,

If you have picked up this book with the hope of finding a simple and cheery tale, I'm afraid you have picked up the wrong book altogether.

—Lemony Snicket, *The Reptile Room* (1999)

Contents

Acknowledgments

Russian novelist Vladimir Nabokov once wrote, "You can always count on a murderer for a fancy prose style" (9).

This book examines a variety of homicide-themed narratives that possess, if not a "fancy prose style," then certainly gripping plots and interesting characters. Accordingly, it seems appropriate to begin by thanking the individuals whose support, encouragement, and assistance have influenced me along with these pages.

First, I am greatly indebted to Hollins University librarian Joan Ruelle and her incredible staff: Luke Vilelle, Maryke Barber, Katy Baum, Jonathan Overturf, Erin Gordon, Josephine Collins, Lee Rose, Lilla Thompson, and Beth Harris. Their skillful, speedy, and truly tireless efforts in tracking down references that were not only obscure but often grisly were nothing short of astounding. I am equally grateful for their cheerful camaraderie that made my work on even the most thematically dark and intellectually difficult sections of this book bearable.

I would like to extend my thanks to several colleagues who provided valuable assistance: Pauline Kaldas and T. J. Anderson, whose personal and professional friendship has been an asset in every way; Nancy Gray, Jeanine Stewart, and Hollins University for several travel and research grants that helped offset the costs of research materials; Philip Nel, Kenneth B. Kidd, and Roberta Seelinger Trites for their sage advice during a crucial turning point in the project; Rhonda Brock-Servais and Pauline Kaldas, whose sharp editorial eyes and equally astute critical comments greatly improved this manuscript; Matt McAdam, my wonderful editor at the Johns Hopkins University Press, MJ Devaney for her fine copyediting work, and the anonymous outside readers for their encouragement and insight; and, finally, to the members of the Children's Literature Association, who formed the audience for conference paper versions of some of this material and offered many compelling comments.

Likewise, many individuals outside of academia provided invaluable support that made both the experience of writing this book more enjoyable and its completion possible. I am especially grateful for the love, encouragement and understanding of my grandmother, Lorraine B. Hunt. This book focuses on issues involving death, but I have benefited enormously from her sage advice about life. I am also indebted to Joan Ruelle, Todd Ristau, Michelle Sheridan Bennett, Alice Burlinson, Jonathan Overturf, Beth Larkee Kumar, Max Bowman, Pauline Kaldas, and Emily Faye Jewett for their many kindnesses over the years and especially during a trying personal period as this manuscript neared completion. Your much needed help and equally needed good humor will not be forgotten.

A version of chapter 1, titled " 'You Must Kill Her': The Fact and Fantasy of Filicide in 'Snow White,' " appeared in *Marvels and Tales: Journal of Fairy-Tale Studies* 26.2 (2012) (© 2012 Wayne State University Press, reprinted with the permission of Wayne State University Press). Likewise, a rendering of chapter 3, called " 'The Queen Had Only One Way of Settling All Difficulties . . . Off With His Head!': *Alice's Adventures in Wonderland* and the Anti-Gallows Movement," was published in *Papers: Explorations into Children's Literature* 21.1 (2011): 33–56. I would like to thank both the editors of these journals and their publishers for permission to reprint.

Finally, I'd like to dedicate this book to C., a high school classmate whose tragic and brutal death unfortunately gave me my first personal experience with homicide. Sadly, it would not be my last—I was also walking through London's West End the night of the 1996 bombing and riding the subway into lower Manhattan the morning of the September 11 terrorist attacks. This volume is in honor of the memory of C. and dedicated to the lives—and deaths—of murder victims everywhere.

Bloody Murder

Once upon a Crime

Homicide in American Culture and Popular Children's Literature from "Bluebeard" to Harry Potter

> Every child is born a criminal. All children are murderers.
>
> G. STANLEY HALL, *West Virginia School Journal* (1899)

In 2007, David F. Schmid, a professor of English and author of *Natural Born Celebrities: Serial Killers in American Culture* (2005), told a journalist that "most societies, perhaps all, find murder and murderers of compelling interest, but Americans have taken this fascination to another level entirely" (qtd. in Donovan, par. 8). Patricia Donovan, the journalist, agreed: "Bloody murder has been a quintessentially American preoccupation since John Newcomen sailed on the Mayflower and was whacked by a fellow colonist" (par. 1). As the British-born Schmid went on to observe, "It is not only serial killers, but all kinds of murderers, that Americans find compelling" (Donovan, par. 5). From the colonial period through the twenty-first century, "Americans have consumed murder on a grand scale. It is a diversion that is familiar and comfortable to us" (Donovan, par. 7).

Even a cursory examination of print, visual, and material culture in the United States reveals the veracity of these claims. The American thirst for murder can be traced back to the nation's earliest history. Daniel A. Cohen has written that beginning in the colonial period, sermons delivered on the gallows of individuals being executed for homicide and other crimes were collected and printed to brisk sales. Cotton Mather, who published more than a dozen such volumes during his lifetime, once boasted that a "local bookseller had sold off nearly one thousand copies of his newest execution sermon in just five days" (qtd. in Cohen 6).

By the late 1600s, the captivity narrative emerged as one of the most popular literary forms in British America. Its appeal arose, at least in part, from graphic descriptions of the killings of whites by indigenous tribes and vice versa. For instance, the opening segments to *A Narrative of the Captivity and Restoration of Mrs. Mary White Rowlandson* (1682)—a text that was a best-seller in its day and remained popular through the nineteenth century (Harris 437) —describes the brutal deaths of her neighbors, family and friends at the hands of Narragansett Indians: "They were knockt on the head [with a hatchet]. . . . Another their [sic] who was running along was shot and wounded, and fell down; he begged of them his life, promising them Money (as they told me) but they would not hearken to him but knockt him in the head, and stript him naked, and split open his Bowels" (443).

During the eighteenth century, narratives offering eyewitness accounts of gruesome murders were combined with information about the killers who had committed them. Appearing as chapbooks, broadsides, and pamphlets, these materials typically contained short autobiographies along with the "dying verses" and "last speeches" of the condemned (Cohen 19–21). According to Schmid, "Hundreds of such accounts were published in New England alone" (qtd. in Donovan, par. 12). Increased attention to the criminals who committed murder was accompanied by increased interest in the legal system that had brought them to justice. Karen Halttunen has written that by the mid-1700s, trial reports—either in the form of a narrative account or a court transcript—attracted a wide readership (10).

By the dawn of nineteenth century, murder-related materials had become so popular that entire newspapers and magazines sprung up that were dedicated to them. *The American Bloody Register*, which started in 1784, was perhaps the first such publication. Recounting incidents of true crime in locales around the United States, the periodical was "based on England's *Newgate Calendar*" and "combined moralism with explicit details about various crimes" (Donovan, par. 12). In the 1830s, such individual publications were accompanied by bound collections bearing sensational titles, such as *Murder Most Foul!* (1836) and *Annals of Murder; or, Daring Outrages, Trials, and Confessions, &c.* (1845). Meanwhile, the birth of the penny press and the growing legions of tabloid-style newspapers reveled in the subject. As Roger Lane has written, journalists quickly realized that when it came to selling copy, "nothing beat a juicy murder" (93). Accordingly, the grisly crimes of alleged hatchet-murderer Lizzie Borden and London serial slayer Jack the Ripper fascinated readers around the country.

Homicide was also a staple among the nation's fiction writers. As David Brion Davis has documented, the plots to some of the earliest narratives by American authors—including Charles Brockden Brown's *Wieland* (1798), Washington Irving's *The Sketch Book* (1820), and James Fenimore Cooper's *The Last of the Mohicans* (1826)—feature prominent instances of murder. By the mid-nineteenth century, the wildly popular dime novels often contained homicides; killings and killers appeared in adventure stories and Western tales along with gothic thrillers and mystery narratives. Likewise, the nascent genre of detective fiction—inaugurated in 1841 with the release of Edgar Allan Poe's "The Murders in the Rue Morgue"—made homicide its raison d'être. Throughout the remainder of the nineteenth century, crime-themed narratives like Wilkie Collins's *The Woman in White* (1860) and Sir Arthur Conan Doyle's Sherlock Holmes stories, which debuted in 1887, dominated American best-seller lists.

As Colin Wilson has aptly observed, "With the twentieth century, [the United States] entered the new age of murder" (4). An array of novels, ranging from literary fiction like Theodore Dreiser's *An American Tragedy* (1925) and Richard Wright's *Native Son* (1940) to mass-market narratives, such as Mario Puzo's *The Godfather* (1969) and John Grisham's *A Time to Kill* (1989), showcased homicide as a central plot point. Meanwhile, the 1966 publication of Truman Capote's *In Cold Blood* ushered in a new fictional form: the true crime novel. Finally, the perennially popular genre of murder mysteries remained an audience favorite. Titles like Agatha Christie's *Murder on the Orient Express* (1934), Mickey Spillane's Mike Hammer series (1947–2010), and Sue Grafton's "Alphabet" murder books, beginning with *A Is for Alibi* in 1982, topped best-seller lists.*

Murder was equally pervasive on the silver screen, beginning with early

---

*Although Spillane died in 2006, he left an array of unfinished manuscripts which his editor and friend Max Collins completed and released. In an interview with Chris Wiegand for the *Guardian* Online web site, Collins noted: "Mickey had been creating these half-manuscripts and setting them aside throughout our friendship, and I had a reasonable expectation that I'd be chosen to complete them. Just days before his death, he told his wife Jane, 'When I go, there's going to be a treasure hunt around here. Give everything to Max—he'll know what to do with it'" ("Mickey Spillane").

silent films like *The Great Train Robbery* (1903), continuing through postwar classics, such as *The Big Sleep* (1946), and extending into popular murder-themed thrillers in the closing decade of the century, including *The Silence of the Lambs* (1991), *Seven* (1995), and *The Sixth Sense* (1999). Meanwhile, horror films, which featured the killing sprees of deranged maniacs, were experiencing a golden era amid the release of such now-classic titles as *The Amityville Horror* (1979), *The Shining* (1980), and *A Nightmare on Elm Street* (1984).

Although television operated under greater constraints with regard to the depiction of violence, it, too, routinely portrayed homicide. From the successful adaption of popular radio programs like *Dragnet* (original series 1951–59, remake 1967–70 and 2003–4) and *Perry Mason* (original series 1957–66, remake 1973–74) to the debut of new shows such as *Murder, She Wrote* (1984–96), *Columbo* (original series 1971–78), and *Homicide: Life on the Street* (1993–99), television detectives solving murder cases were perennially popular with American audiences.

Murder also plays a central role in the nation's new media technologies and emerging forms of leisure entertainment, namely, video games. While the object of many arcade, home console, and online games hinges on players killing someone or something, the ones released in the final decade of the twentieth century took this feature to an extreme. *Mortal Kombat*, which made its debut in 1992 and went on to become one of the most commercially successful games of the decade, quickly became infamous for its gruesome killings. During the matches, players can rip the limbs off their opponent's body, decapitate them with axes, and eviscerate them, while blood squirts, intestines spill out, and bone fragments fall to the ground.

The nation's appetite for murder was not simply limited to fictional incidents but embraced factual ones as well. As Lane has observed, the twentieth century was the era of the sensational murder trial in the United States (221–23). The legal proceedings against figures like Nathan Leopold and Richard Loeb in 1924, Ted Bundy in the 1970s, and O. J. Simpson in 1995 sparked a national media frenzy.

The American obsession with homicide continues in the new millennium. Some of the most popular television shows such as *CSI: Crime Scene Investigation* (2000–present), films like *Kill Bill* (2003), and novels such as Alice Sebold's *The Lovely Bones* (2002) have murder as their central theme. Meanwhile, the internet has taken the national fascination with homicide in new directions. Websites like CrimePic.com post photographs from actual crime scenes, including murders, and others go one step further, publishing autopsy images of both killers and their victims. Most infamous among these venues perhaps is CelebrityMorgue.com. The site contains postmortem images featuring an array of well-known murder victims, ranging from Tupac Shakur and John F. Kennedy to Sharon Tate and the Lindbergh baby.

For some individuals, merely looking at crime scene materials online is insufficient; they seek to collect such items themselves. The sale and purchase of authentic homicide photographs, pieces of evidence, and legal documents has become so popular over the past few decades that it has emerged as a new niche market, known as "murderabilia." In a powerful indication of the pervasiveness of this activity, the *Oxford English Dictionary* added this term to its March 2003 edition. Some murder enthusiasts go even further, seeking to obtain objects and items from the killers themselves. As Katherine Ramsland has written, paintings, drawings and collages made by figures like Charles Manson, Patrick Kearney (better-known as "the Freeway Killer"), and Richard "the Night Stalker" Ramirez have sold for hundreds of dollars ("Serial Killer Art"). Artwork by serial killer John Wayne Gacy—who murdered more than thirty boys and young men during the 1970s—has attained even more notoriety. Dozens of his drawings and paintings were exhibited at an antique store in Palm Beach County in 2004, more than a decade after his execution (Associated Press).

Growing public interest in murder and murderabilia over the past few decades contributed to the founding of the Museum of Death in California in 1995. The name of the facility notwithstanding, it focuses mainly on homicides. Indeed, the homepage for the museum touts that the Museum of Death

> houses the world's largest collection of Serial Murderer Artwork, Photos of the Charles Manson Crime Scenes, the Guillotined Severed Head of the Blue Beard of Paris, Henri Landru, Original Crime Scene and Morgue Photos from the Grisly BLACK DAHLIA MURDERS [*sic*], a Body Bag and Coffin collection, replicas of Full Size Execution Devices, Mortician and Autopsy Instruments, Pet Death Taxidermy, and much much more! ("Museum Info")

The opening of the Lizzie Borden Bed and Breakfast at the beginning of the twenty-first century closed the gap between citizens and killers even further. Located in the Borden family home on 92 Second Street in Fall River, Maine, the site of the infamous 1892 hatchet murders, the B&B offers visitors a unique experience. As the website touts, "Now for the first time the public is allowed not only to view the murder scene, but is given an opportunity to spend a night (if you dare) in the actual house where the murders took place" ("Lizzie Borden Bed and Breakfast History" par. 3).

The obsession with violent crime in general and homicide in particular in the United States has led Jeffrey S. Adler to assert that the nation and its populace possess nothing less than a "mania for murder" (253). Indeed, Schmid has noted that American leisure from the seventeenth century through the present day can largely be characterized by what he calls "entertainment by murder" (qtd. in Donovan, par. 2). In spite of the profusion of fictional as well as factual accounts of homicide in books, magazines, films, and television shows, "our appetite . . . cannot be sated" (Donovan, par. 19).

However unexpected and even seemingly unlikely, the American obsession with murder also permeates its literature for children. Whether written by U.S. authors or by individuals from other countries, some of the most well-known and beloved works for young readers in the United States contain instances of killing. This theme is an all-too-common feature of the genre that forms the foundation for much of children's literature: fairy tales. In "Jack and the Beanstalk"—a story that is a mainstay in American childhood, as its ubiquitous presence in bookstores, schools, and home libraries attests—the giant has a reputation for making humans a murderous snack. In a rhyme that is as macabre as it is memorable, he states,

> Fee-fi-fo-fum!
> I smell the blood of an Englishman.
> Be he 'live, or be he dead,
> I'll grind his bones to make my bread. (224)

Charles Perrault's "Bluebeard" presents murder in an even more gruesome manner. When the young bride enters a forbidden room while her husband is away on business, she makes a horrifying discovery: "The floor was covered with clotted blood and the blood reflected the bodies of several dead women hung up on the walls (these were all the women Bluebeard had married and then murdered one after another)" (145). Unsurprisingly, when the husband realizes that his wife has discovered his secret life as a serial killer, his reaction is homicidal: "'Prepare to die.' Then, taking her by the hair with one hand and raising his cutlass with the other, he was about to chop her head off" (147).

These stories are far from anomalous. Many other fairy tales contain instances of murder that are equally grisly. In Charles Perrault's version of

"Little Tom Thumb," for example, an ogre wishes to slit the throats of the title character and his six older brothers so that he may eat them. After being convinced by his wife to postpone killing the boys until she has a chance to fatten them up, he gets drunk on wine and accidentally slits the throats of his own seven daughters, mistaking them for the boys.

Even fairy tales that do not contain instances of actual homicide often depict attempted murders. In the Grimms' "Hansel and Gretel," for example, the Witch feeds a young brother and sister a steady diet of candy, nuts, and pancakes in a failed scheme to fatten them up so that she can bake them in the oven and eat them for supper. Similarly, in Charles Perrault's "Sleeping Beauty," the title character is put under a spell by a wicked witch that will cause her to die rather than merely slip into a long slumber. Finally, in the closing scenes of Hans Christian Anderson's "The Little Mermaid," the eponymous figure is given a knife by the sea witch and instructed to slay the sleeping prince.

Homicide is equally common in boys' adventure books. Among the various noteworthy events that the title character witnesses in Mark Twain's *The Adventures of Tom Sawyer* (1876) is a murder. Similarly, the killing of John Thornton, the kindly owner of the sled dog Buck in Jack London's *The Call of the Wild* (1903), forms a turning point in the story. Finally, as its title implies, Buck Wilson's *The Lone Ranger and the Menace of Murder Valley* (1938), makes homicide—both the act and its setting—the central focus.

Murder, likewise, appears in numerous prose and poetic works for young readers. In the opening pages of L. Frank Baum's *The Wonderful Wizard of Oz* (1900), a house famously falls on and kills the Wicked Witch of the East. Captain James Hook spends the bulk of J. M. Barrie's popular drama *Peter Pan* (1904) trying to murder the title character; the jealous Tinker Bell has similarly homicidal thoughts about Wendy. By contrast, many actual killings— including instances of infanticide and geriatricide—permeate Lois Lowry's Newbery Award–winning novel *The Giver* (1993).* Likewise, a homicide forms the focal point of Lois Duncan's *Killing Mr. Griffin* (1978). The events of Pam Muñoz Ryan's historical novel *Esperanza Rising* (2000) are set into motion by the murder of the title character's father, and many of the books in R. L. Stine's

---

* Admittedly, the characters in Lowry's novel do not see these deaths as homicides. For them, this is just the way life ends. However, for the readers of *The Giver*, these killings are certainly murders, and this normalization of lethal violence is one the most horrifying elements of the fictional society that Lowry portrays. I am indebted to Rhonda Brock-Servais for pointing out this distinction.

wildly popular Goosebumps series and Fear Street series center around a murder, including *Beach House* (1992), *Piano Lessons Can Be Murder* (1993), *Bad Dreams* (1994), and *Call Waiting* (1994). Finally, some verses penned by popular nonsense poet Edward Lear address the subject. His limerick "There Was an Old Man of Peru" (1846) concludes with the eponymous character being put in a pan and baked in an oven by his wife.

Acts of homicide can also be found in the arguably more unlikely venue of picture books. In Claire Huchet Bishop's classic, albeit culturally controversial, *The Five Chinese Brothers* (1938), a group of siblings draw on their superhuman talents in an effort to save their brother from the executioner after he has been sentenced to death for murdering a young boy. Homicide likewise appears in Edward Gorey's *The Gashlycrumb Tinies* (1963). While most of the deaths featured in the alphabet book are the result of an accident or mishap—such as "J is for James who took lye by mistake" and "U is for Una who slipped down a drain"—several are the result of foul play: "H is for Hector done in by a thug," "K is for Kate who was struck with an axe," and "Y is for Yorick whose head was knocked in."*

Murder remains a central theme in picture books released during the new millennium. Lemony Snicket's *The Composer Is Dead* (2008), for example, recounts the unexpected fatality of the titular virtuoso and the effort by the inspector "to find the murderer or murderers and haul them off to jail." In Snicket's signature macabre humor, one of the opening scenes presents the deceased composer lying face down on a table; the page that follows contains a large illustration of a fly and the solitary caption: "This is called decompos-

---

*As Jackie E. Stallcup has observed, *"The Gashlycrumb Tinies* is part of a long tradition in children's literature in which young characters meet violent punishments and even death because they transgress social boundaries and challenge adult authority" (125). By far, the most famous example of such a text is Heinrich Hoffmann's *Struwwelpeter* (1845). A collection of narrative poems accompanied by brightly colored illustrations, each scenario depicts a young boy or girl who does not heed parental advice and thus meets a terrible—and usually lethal—fate. In "The Dreadful Story of Harriet and the Matches," for instance, the title character disobeys her mother's admonition about playing with fire and promptly burns to death: "And see! oh, what dreadful thing! / The fire has caught her apron-string; / Her apron burns, her arms, her hair— / She burns all over everywhere." *Der Struwwelpeter* does feature many acts of violence against children, but the scenarios that it presents are not homicides: rather, they are deaths that result from the child's poor judgment, negligence, and/or stubbornness. Thus, although English translations of Hoffmann's book were popular in the United States for generations—as Rachel McCarthy notes "*Der Struwwelpeter* had a huge following in the States, up until World War I, when anti-German sentiment caused a dip in popularity. But the stories have lived on, influencing cartoon bad boys, the Katzenjammer Kids and later Dennis the Menace"—I do not address it.

ing." By this point, of course, Snicket's interest in the subject of homicide had been well established through his wildly successful A Series of Unfortunate Events books. Not only does the first book in the series, *The Bad Beginning* (1999), commence with the murder of the Baudelaire children's parents by means of a house fire set by an arsonist, but then numerous killings take place in subsequent novels as the villainous Count Olaf attempts to steal the youngsters' inheritance.

Murder is especially endemic to the comparatively new genre of young adult (YA) fiction. Some of the first and most famous novels for adolescent readers, in fact, have their narrative roots in murder. The memorable climax to William Golding's *Lord of the Flies* (1954)—which, while not written by an American author, is a perennially popular title among the nation's juvenile readers—presents a group of boys senselessly attacking and brutally killing a fellow member of their tribe, the youngster Simon. Similarly, at various points throughout John Knowles's *A Separate Peace* (1959), classmates, teachers, and friends wonder whether Finny's fall from the tree was truly accidental or the result of Gene's conscious or unconscious desire to eliminate him.

Narratives for young readers published during the opening decade of the twenty-first century expand on this tradition, presenting murder even more openly and directly. Suzanne Collins's science fiction narrative *The Hunger Games* (2008) depicts a dystopian world in which one girl and one boy from each district are selected by the government to fight to the death in a competition that is broadcast on live television. Jennifer Donnelly's historical novel *A Northern Light* (2003) examines the true-life Big Moose Lake murder case in Upstate New York from 1906 through the eyes of a young girl who stumbles on the investigation. Neil Gaiman, who was born in England but has resided in the United States for several decades, begins his *The Graveyard Book* (2008) with the chilling murder of the central character's entire family by a mysterious man wielding a knife.

These books by Gaiman, Donnelly, and Collins are among the most commercially popular and critically acclaimed. *The Hunger Games* was a fixture on the *New York Times* best-seller list for months after its release. In addition, it was selected as one of *Publisher Weekly*'s Best Books of the Year in 2008, and it was also chosen by the *New York Times* as a Notable Children's Book of 2008. In early 2012, *The Hunger Games* was released as a feature-length film that enjoyed both critical acclaim and commercial success. *A Northern Light* has likewise been widely feted. The book was the recipient of the Carnegie Medal and the 2003 Los Angeles Book Prize for Young Adult Literature and was named an honor book for the Michael L. Printz Award. And perhaps most notably, Neil Gaiman's *The Graveyard Book* was awarded the Newbery Medal, the highest honor that can be bestowed on a book for young readers.

Even the wildly popular Harry Potter series has its genesis in murder. When the title character is just a baby, the villain Voldemort kills his parents in an attempt to consolidate power. While this event occurs before the first book commences, frequent reference is made to it throughout the series. Then, in each of the narratives that comprise the seven-book sequence, Voldemort tries to complete his initial plan by killing the now adolescent-aged Harry. Although the eponymous character survives all of these attempts, many others perish, either directly or indirectly, as a result of the conflict. Of course, J. K. Rowling's books are a worldwide success, attaining best-seller status in their native England as well as in many other English-language-speaking countries. But their popularity in the United States assumes added significance given our culture's long-standing obsession with murder.

As even this brief survey suggests, homicide has formed a beguiling subject and recurring theme in narratives popular with American youth for centuries. In fact, a search for the keyword "murder" in WorldCat, a global category of library holdings, yields over three thousand citations for various novels, stories, plays, and poems intended for a juvenile audience. This topic has become so pervasive, in fact, that "Murder—Juvenile Fiction" is its own classification category in the database. Not surprisingly, many of these listings are either books written by American authors or are titles that have a secure place in the canon of literature for children in the United States.

In spite of the long history and strong presence of homicide in narratives for young readers, little work has been done on the subject. To date, in fact, no full-length exploration of the issue from a literary, historical, psychoanalytic, or criminal justice standpoint has been published. Seminal studies that examine the themes of crime, violence, and death in U.S. literature and culture fail to mention its prevalence in narratives intended for children. David Brion Davis's influential early tome, *Homicide in American Fiction, 1798–1860* (1957), discusses scores of titles depicting murder, but none written for young readers. The topic is similarly omitted from more recent examinations of murder in American life and letters. Scholars seeking information on the tradition of homicide in books enjoyed by U.S. children will find no mention of it in Karen Halttunen's *Murder Most Foul: The Killer and the American Gothic Imagination*

(1998) or Sara L. Knox's *Murder: A Tale of Modern American Life* (1998). Reference works like *The Cambridge Companion to Children's Literature* (2010) and *The Oxford Companion to Children's Literature* (1999) contain entries about gritty issues like drugs and sex but not murder or homicide. Loretta Loach's *The Devil's Children* (2009) purports to offer, as its subtitle announces, "A History of Childhood and Murder." But the book only provides selected portraits of young people who have actually committed the crime over the centuries rather than exploring the wide-ranging literary, visual, and material presence of homicide in Anglo-American childhood culture. Even critical books that examine the presence of death in literature for young readers— such as Kathryn James's *Death, Gender, and Sexuality in Contemporary Adolescent Literature* (2009) and Marianne S. Pyles's *Death and Dying in Children's and Young People's Literature: A Survey and Bibliography* (1988)—do not address the issue of homicide. Finally, and perhaps most surprisingly, a search for the keywords "U.S. children's literature" and "murder" in the Modern Language Association's International Bibliography yields no results. By comparison, an analogous search for this term and the phrase "American literature" generates over three hundred citations. Martin Daly and Margo Wilson have observed that murder is one of the most routinely researched subjects in the United States (ix, x). However, its presence has gone curiously unexamined in the arena of children's literature.

This book offers a long-overdue corrective to this trend. The chapters that follow investigate the pervasive but previously unexplored homicide tradition in narratives for the nation's young readers. In so doing, they demonstrate how murder is not simply an overlooked theme in books for American boys and girls; it is also a productive point of critical entry that yields compelling new insights on an array of literary, social, political, and cultural issues. These topics range from the development of the American criminal justice system, the rise of forensic science, and shifting attitudes about crime and punishment to the birth of sensation fiction, changing cultural conceptions about the nature of evil, and the myriad ways that murder has been popularly presented and socially interpreted. Accordingly, this book stands at the crossroads of literary criticism, American studies, criminal justice, childhood studies, law, psychology, and history, revealing children's literature to be a rich, complex, and previously neglected locus of information regarding the national obsession with violent crime and the ongoing attraction to horror.

In what has become an oft-quoted line from John Webster's *The Duchess of Malfi*, a character opines, "Other sins only speak; murder shrieks out" (4.2.261). This book adds to the cacophony associated with killing, making heard an array of previously silent voices. By including narratives for children in the representation of homicide in the United States, we not only gain a more accurate portrait of the range, depth, and variety of crime literature, but also come to see that our existing conceptions about the politicized purposes of violence, the emotional appeal of fear, and the cultural construction of death and dying need to be revised.

For generations, the tendency of young people to shout, yell, and shriek has caused adults to accuse them of "screaming bloody murder." This phrase, which may reference the sounds made during playing or fighting, has been heard by arguably every boy and girl at some point during his or her childhood. In the chapters the follow, I explore how children in the United States do not reflect merely this one isolated behavior associated with homicide. In narratives ranging from fairy tales to young adult novels, they routinely encounter and even immerse themselves in every conceivable facet of bloody murder.

"The Crime Is Murder": A Social History of Homicide

If prostitution is the "oldest profession," then murder is perhaps the oldest crime. Instances of homicide date back to biblical times, most famously via the story of Cain and Abel. While it might seem that the definition of murder is static, homicide actually has a complex history. How murder has been conceptualized and criminalized by American society, as well as prosecuted and punished by its legal system, has changed dramatically over time.

In the twenty-first century, the killing of one individual by another is considered the most serious crime. Whether the homicide occurs intentionally or accidentally, it is routinely characterized as the worst transgression that can be committed against an individual and, by extension, against society. Accordingly, homicide is subjected to the most severe penalties, including death.

The most surprising facet in the social history of murder in the West is that it has not always been seen as a civic offense. As Lane notes, "Among the Germanic tribes who once overran Europe, assault and even murder were considered matters for the injured individuals or families to settle among themselves, either by killings in revenge or through the payment of wergild, or blood money, as compensation for their lives" (10). By the late Middle Ages, the task of keeping law and order increasingly became the responsibility of the feudal lords. Consequently, homicide came to be criminalized as a "breach of the King's peace" (Lane 11). Since society was personified by the monarch, a crime against one of his subjects was seen a crime against the king himself— and punished accordingly (Lane 11). Even then, however, there were several classes of individuals who were considered exempt from these laws:

> The Roman Catholic Church had established the principle that its own officials, if tried in royal courts, could only be punished by the church itself. This exemption, "benefit of clergy," applied to thousands of people in the Middle Ages, not just parish priests, bishops and monks, and nuns but a host of minor clergymen, wandering friars, and university students, who were not punished physically but made to do penance, at worst losing their positions in the church. (Lane 11)

Furthermore, as Eliza Steelwater has pointed out, lay members of the community could escape punishment via what might be called the "literacy loophole." Through the seventeenth century, "some who were convicted of murder were pardoned with only a brand on the thumb—for one murder only—if they could show they were able to read" (53).

An array of American colonies, including Maryland, Massachusetts, and Virginia, adopted both the benefit of clergy and the practice of granting pardons for literacy. As Thomas G. Blomberg and Karol K. Lucken have observed, "As in Europe, the benefit of clergy, jails, and workhouses existed in colonial America. By 1600, the benefit of clergy had become so relaxed that it protected not only church officials but anyone who could read" (32). Indeed, Jeffrey K. Sawyer has written that two of the soldiers involved in the Boston massacre were acquitted after claiming benefit of clergy; "the court ordered the men 'burnt on the hand' and released" (49).

The colonial and federalist eras were not the only times in America history when various forms of murder were condoned or, at least, overlooked. Well into the nineteenth century, dueling—whether to first shot, first blood, grievous wound, or death (see Baldick)—was often used by men from the upper classes to settle disputes and defend both individual and family honor. Indeed, Andrew Jackson, the seventh president of the United States, boasted of his dueling abilities, framing them as a necessary component both to manhood and a healthy democracy. As he wrote: "To go to the law for redress is to confess publicly that you have been wronged and the demonstration of your vulnerability places your honor in jeopardy, a jeopardy from which the 'satis-faction' of legal compensation in the hands of secular authority hardly re-deems it" (qtd. in Ayers 18). Alexander Hamilton, the first secretary of the Treasury, and Aaron Burr, vice president at the time, participated in an in-famous duel on 11 July 1804. As in other such contests, the incident resulted in the death of one of the participants: Burr fatally wounded Hamilton, who died the next day. This extralegal form of murder, however, was overlooked by society: although the duel took place in broad daylight and was witnessed by many bystanders, the vice president was never charged, let alone convicted of any crime (see Fleming).

While duels were generally small, isolated events, usually limited to just the two men involved and a few witnesses, the lynching of criminals or sus-pected criminals—murderers among them—was a major public spectacle in both the North and the South. In the words of Lane: "Lynchings occurred in every state of the Union outside of New England . . . with more than 3,700 incidents recorded between 1889 and 1930, and victims of every color" (151). As Dora Apel, James Allen, and Jacqueline Denise Goldsby have all written, scores of men, women, and children would often attend the killing; people from the surrounding region knew when a lynching was going to take place; indeed, these executions were often even openly advertised. It was not un-common, for instance, for local railroads to run extra trains to the town where the lynching was scheduled to take place to accommodate the large crowds who wished to witness the spectacle (Brown 217). In addition, bystanders at the event often removed pieces of the victim's clothing, hair, or bone, keeping them as mementos (Apel 136). Local photographers took pictures of the desecrated corpse and sold them later as souvenir postcards (Allen). Steel-water relays the mundane message written on the back of one such image from the early twentieth century: "Dear Em: Have been here a week. Weather hot. George and Sally well" (8). Dueling and lynching thus provide a vivid illustration of Wendy Lesser's observation that "we tend to say that if a killing is justified, it is not murder. But the definition of what is justifiable alters over time" (5).

In many ways, forms of vigilante justice like lynching and dueling were products of an environment that predated formalized systems of public pro-tection. While citizens today rely on local police to investigate crimes and apprehend those responsible, a standing cadre of professional salaried officers has not always been a feature of American civic life. Until the mid-nineteenth century in the United States, "there was no real equivalent of police, detectives, or regular patrol, the closest thing being the night watch that was ordered . . . to look out for fire or other kinds of trouble" (Lane 12). Thus, the task of law enforcement largely fell to members of the community. If individuals witnessed a crime such as murder, they had a responsibility to stop it. If they were unable to do so, or if the suspect eluded their efforts, they were "to raise a 'hue and cry,' calling on all other members of the town or vill to form a posse and chase the killer" (Lane 12). After catching the suspected criminal, the posse was supposed to turn the individual over to the sheriff or constable. That said, calls for a "hue and cry" sometimes resulted in mobs taking matters into their own hands (Lane 11–13).

Surprisingly, as Gini Graham Scott has written, even after most American cities had salaried police officers who walked regular beats, "little priority was given to solving homicides" (1:vii). In marked contrast to today's practice in which murder cases are considered the most important in every precinct— typically assigned to a special group of well-trained and usually elite detectives —few police departments during the mid-nineteenth century had anything resembling a formalized "detective bureau" and those that did were not necessarily appreciated by taxpayers, who often resented the time and money devoted to it (Lane 103). As far as most citizens were concerned, such resources were better used solving property crimes. "Bankers and grocers, visiting farmers who had lost watches and wallets, all had business with the cops. But there was no money in 'solving' murders, and no one assigned to it" (Lane 112).

As a result, until the latter half of the nineteenth century, the investigation of homicides in most American towns fell to the hands of coroners, who "were not usually doctors but low-caliber elected officials" (Lane 112). When a body was discovered lying in a ditch or floating in a river, the coroner was called to examine it. In this era that predated the advent of forensic pathology, "investigation was rarely intense; a doctor might be called for an autopsy, but taxpayers resented the additional expense" (Lane 103). Indeed, as Lane explains, from the colonial era through the eve of the Civil War, "the inquest was generally held near the spot where the body was found, on the same day or the next; it generally lasted no more than a couple of hours" (103). Astounding as it might be to modern sensibilities, "the great majority of homicides that came to the coroner's attention were 'solved' at this level, immediately after the death" (Lane 103). "In a world of most small towns and farms," Scott points out, "a suspect couldn't easily hide" (1:vii–viii). Not only did everyone know each other, but they also knew who had long-standing grudges or recent feuds. Consequently, determining who had killed the victim—or, at least, who was likely to have done so—was a relatively easy task. The coroner would relay the name of the suspect to the magistrate, who would promptly make the arrest (Lane 100–104; Scott 1:vii–viii).

While the prosecution of murderers today falls solely to the district attorney's office, this too is a relatively recent development. For centuries in the United States, families of victims often hired private prosecutors to assist with the case or, in some instances, to adjudicate it exclusively. Robert M. Ireland has observed that "privately funded prosecutors constituted a significant element of the state criminal justice system throughout the nineteenth century" (43). Owing to the numerous deficiencies that plagued district attorneys' offices throughout the nation—including high turnover rates, a preponderance of inexperienced young lawyers, and lack of sufficient material, monetary, or human resources—"privately funded prosecutors most often appeared in murder trials" (Ireland 46). Ireland notes that the use of an attorney who was paid by the family of the victim remained a legal practice in many states well into the twentieth century (55).

Whether adjudicated by a private prosecutor or a publicly funded one, murder trials today are associated with great drama and even theatrics—eloquent opening statements and closing arguments, clever cross-examinations of witnesses, and a sustained battle of wits between the opposing sides. In yet another significant difference, prior to the Revolutionary War, all trials—even murder trials—were not the adversarial contests that we know today. Until the 1730s, in fact, most defendants did not have a right to counsel, could not testify in their own defense, and were not permitted to call witnesses or to cross-examine those brought against them (Halttunen 95). Meanwhile, even for those who had legal representation, courtroom proceedings were more like casual conversations or what John Hostettler, among other legal historians, terms a "rambling altercation" between the two sides (116). Little testimony was heard, a minimal amount of evidence was introduced, and no formal arguments were made by either the prosecution or the defense (Lane 21).

Only during the late eighteenth century, amid the rapid rise in power of the legal profession, did this format change. As Cohen notes, "By the beginning of the nineteenth century, New England's capital cases were typically tried in highly-competitive, lawyer-dominated proceedings that were often entertaining events for both spectators and readers" (29). Indeed, this era saw lawyers become a new type of social celebrity. By the end of the 1800s, "crowds packed the courtrooms to hear their favorite legal orators, while newspapers and journals gave extensive coverage to trials and related legal matters" (Halttunen 96), sometimes even reprinting their complete opening statements and closing arguments.

Such transformations to the adjudication of murder cases were spurred as much by changes in the American political and legislative climate as by its cultural and social one. Nearly half of the amendments to the U.S. Constitution "dealt specifically with criminal procedure and were designed to protect accused criminals from high-handed state action" (Lane 78). The Fourth Amendment protected individuals from unlawful searches and seizures, mandating that the authorities obtain a court-order warrant before entering private property. The Fifth Amendment shielded individuals from self-incrimination, safeguarded them from double jeopardy, and ensured due process of the law. The Eighth Amendment protected even convicted criminals from suffering any "cruel and unusual punishment." In keeping with other constitutional provisions, a "defendant also had the right to be informed of all charges in writing, to subpoena defense witnesses, to have 'the Assistance of Counsel,' and not to pay 'excessive bail'" (Lane 78). Finally, but not insignificantly, "the laws of evidence were carefully and formally elaborated with a care that went well beyond English precedents, with elaborate rules to keep hearsay testimony out of court, for example, and strict guidelines to be followed literally, at every stage, on pain of having convictions overturned on appeal to higher courts" (Lane 79).

The advent of the adversarial trial and the introduction of an array of new regulations guiding legal prosecution added greatly to the length of criminal cases, especially those for murder. According to Lane, during the American colonial era, most trials—even in homicide cases—lasted just a few hours (115–16). Sometimes, deliberations by the jury concluded "in a matter of minutes" (Lane 21). Karen Halttunen has documented that the executions of convicted killers were carried out just as quickly, usually within a few weeks of sentencing, at most within a couple of months (19). Over time, as the number of appeals permitted and—in some cases—even required by law increased, so did the length of time needed to bring criminal proceedings to a close. During the 1820s and 1830s, most murder cases "were settled within ten months from the date of the crime to the sentencing" (Lane 115–16). By the final decade of the twentieth century, the average time between the act of murder and the date of execution had ballooned to ten years (Steelwater 12).

Regardless of how murder is adjudicated in the United States, it has historically been a highly gendered crime. "In comparison to men, homicides committed by women are relatively infrequent. Men commit murder at a significantly higher rate than women, accounting for approximately 87% of all homicides each year" (McKee, Shea, Mogy, and Holden 367). Just as men commit the bulk of all murders, they also account for the majority of those killed. The number of victims who are male has occasionally reached "more than 80 percent" in the United States (Lane 16). Whether male or female, most murderers know, or at least are acquainted with, their victims: as neighbors, friends, or family members. "The answer to 'What was at stake?' is too often, Nothing—except perhaps an alcoholic conception of male honor" (Lane 127). Indeed, as Daly and Wilson have documented, homicide is typically an "altercation of relatively trivial origin": usually sparked by the long-standing feelings of jealousy, anger, and resentment often exacerbated by inebriation (125). Through the nineteenth century, the most common locale for murder was the street, followed closely by the bar or saloon (Lane 126). By the 1950s, this trend had shifted and the home "had become the far most frequent site," accounting for "over half of all cases" (Lane 259). Wherever and whenever a murder takes place, one detail remains constant: "In general, murderous attacks . . . grow wilder as the relationship between victim and killers grew closer, as the fury of betrayal, or years of anger, [are] reflected in the number of shots, blows, or cuts inflicted, often on an already lifeless body" (Lane 259).

The late nineteenth and early twentieth century witnessed the emergence of two new and particularly pernicious forms of homicide: serial killing and mass murder. Grouped under the larger category of "multicide," "serial killing" connotes the periodic killing of many people over a long period of time by an individual, while "mass murder" refers to the murder of a large number of people in one brief episode by one or more individuals, usually culminating in their own deaths, often by suicide. Mass killings had certainly occurred at earlier points in American history, but they were rare. As Jay Robert Nash has noted, "In the deeper past the mass killer was the exception, almost a medieval rarity" (15). The first documented serial killer in the United States did not emerge until the *fin de siècle*, when H. H. Holmes (born Herman Webster

Mudgett) made headlines around the nation for the slayings of more than two dozen people in his carefully constructed "murder castle" in Chicago. A labyrinth-like structure that he had built himself, the abode, which contained a maze, had at least one hundred windowless and soundproof rooms, each fitted with gas lines to asphyxiate his victims and a chute to transport their lifeless bodies to the basement where he variously dismembered, dissected, and incinerated them (Schechter *Depraved* 3–4).

When news first broke about Holmes's horrific killings, he was cast as a freakish anomaly, the likes of which the nation would never see again; time would prove otherwise. Over the course of the twentieth century, as Jane Caputi has noted, "FBI statistics show that this new type of [multicidal] murder . . . increased drastically in the United States" (444). A powerful indication of the relatively new nature of mass homicide is that fact that the term "serial killer" was only coined in the 1970s.* By 1984, though, "the Justice Department estimated that there were at the very least 35 and possibly as many as 100 such [serial] killers roaming the country" (Caputi 444). More- over, unlike previous murderers, "the killings seemed senseless—just done for the sport of it on a grand scale" (Scott 2:5). According to Scott, "These kinds of killers felt no qualms about killing and were typically either moti- vated by a high level of anger against particular people or society in general or by a powerful sex drive that they felt free to express" (2:5). The evolution of chain murders, sex slayings, and shooting sprees from rare and unusual events to common and even typical ones prompted Nash to remark that on the eve of the twenty-first century in the United States, this "lunatic fringe of murder [had] become a ghastly norm" (15).

Whether a serial murderer or the slayer of a single victim, convicted killers today face an array of possible punishments, from the death penalty or life imprisonment to a prescribed period of jail time or, in some cases where there are extenuating circumstances, possibly only a period of probation. Until the late eighteenth century in the United States, though, execution was the only penalty for homicide. While hanging was by far the most common means for carrying out capital punishment through the nineteenth century, in some parts of the country, burning at the stake as well as drawing and quartering

---

*Much controversy exists over who can be credited with inventing this term. Former FBI agent Robert Ressler commonly claims that he was the first to use the word "serial" in connection with murders and killing in 1974 (see Vronsky 328). That said, a search for the phrase "serial murder" in Google Books yields many earlier usages.

were also frequent execution techniques.* Efforts to make executions more humane or, at least, less brutal have led to the adoption of new methods and the invention of new devices: in 1890, the electric chair made its debut (Brandon 7); in 1924, the gas chamber was first used for execution (Christianson 1); and, beginning in 1982, lethal injection was introduced and quickly became the new norm (Elder 191). Such innovations demonstrate what Louis Masur has called "the nation's faith in technological and medical palliatives" for the death penalty (163).

In a landmark decision in 1972, the United States Supreme Court outlawed capital punishment nationwide. Ruling on *Furman v. Georgia*, "the majority—consisting of justices Brennan, Douglas, Marshall, Stewart, and White—held in five separate opinions that capital punishment was contrary to present standards of decency, offered no deterrent over imprisonment, and was applied capriciously and unfairly, especially against minorities" (Steelwater 215). The decision was overturned in 1976, in *Gregg v. Georgia*, when the court ruled that "the punishment of death does not, under all circumstances, violate the Eighth and Fourteenth Amendments," provided that states refashion their execution procedures to satisfy the concerns outlined in the 1972 ruling (see Zimring and Hawkings 51). The first post-*Furman* execution was performed in 1977 in Nevada, when Gary Gilmore was put to death by a firing squad. Execution by firing squad, though rare, has been implemented as recently as 1996, when John Albert Taylor was judicially killed in this manner by the state of Utah.† The use of capital punishment, by whatever means, separates the United States from nations commonly seen as its peers: "The United Kingdom, France, Germany, Spain, Italy and *all* other western European nations" have abolished the practice (Steelwater 4; italics in original). Today, more than thirty U.S. states have capital punishment on their books (see "States with and without the Death Penalty"). Moreover, the practice remains not simply prevalent but popular. "According to a 2007 Gallup poll, about 70% of

---

*A search of the database America's Historical Newspapers for the phrase "at the stake" reveals more than thirty reports about executions via this method, and a search for the phrase "drawn and quartered" yields more than a dozen articles.

†Trina N. Seitz notes that "the firing squad is an all-but-obsolete mode of execution in the modern United States, but two states (Utah and Idaho) still offer it as an option" (358). She also recounts the following macabre detail in relation to Taylor's execution: "Taylor opted for death by firing squad over lethal injection, fearing he would die 'flipping around like a fish out of water' if he chose the latter procedure" (359).

the American population currently supports the death penalty for murder" (Shepard 195).

A desire to reduce or, at least, restrict the use of capital punishment precipitated another major development in the social history of murder in the United States: its division into categories or "degrees." In 1794, Pennsylvania became the first state to differentiate among types of murder. "The statute provided that 'all murder, which shall be perpetuated by means of poison, or by lying in wait, or by any other kind of willful, deliberate, and premeditated killing or which shall be committed in the perpetration, or attempt to perpetrate any arson, rape, robbery or burglary shall be deemed murder in the first degree; and all other kinds of murder shall be deemed murder in the second degree'" (Kadish and Schulhofer 394). As this language indicates, these designations do not signal varying degrees of criminality; rather, they denote different levels of punishment, with certain types being considered more heinous and thus deserving of more severe sentences: given that "all of the varieties of [homicidal] behavior dealt with are crimes of some sort, the only question" is "the determination of what crime is involved, which is to say, what punishment is authorized" (Kadish and Schulhofer 385). While first- and second-degree murder are the most common, some states have third-, fourth-, and even fifth-degree designations, but their usage is increasingly rare.*

Incarceration—for murder or any other crime—is also a relatively recent practice. Prior to the late eighteenth century, jails were used merely for the short-term holding of defendants: they were a place to house arrested criminals temporarily while they awaited arraignment, trial, or sentencing; jail was not the punishment itself. The modification of the Walnut Street Prison in Philadelphia in 1790 led to a radical departure from this practice that forever changed American criminal justice. Designed by Quakers with a Christian mission, the facility was "a place where offenders would be locked in solitary confinement, still at work—work being good for both body and soul—living under harsh conditions, but with plenty of time, alone, to think about and repent for the crimes that had brought them there" (Lane 80). For this reason, Walnut Street Prison, along with the many other facilities that would be modeled after it, was deemed a "penitentiary," from the Latin verb "poenitēre" or "to repent."

---

*For more information on these statutes as well as the states that have them, see R. Perkins.

The birth of the modern-day system of incarceration marked a shift not only in the point or purpose of punishment but in beliefs about the causes or origins of crime. In stark contrast to pre-Enlightenment era views that murder arose from the depravity that was inherent in all humankind, penitentiaries like the Walnut Street Prison demonstrated that crime was the product of free will. Indeed, the whole notion that an individual could repent for his or her wrongdoing, be cleansed of the sinfulness that brought him or her to jail, and return to society as a productive and law-abiding citizen indicated that a new cultural conception about the nature of evil had arisen. As Louis Masur has noted, by the late eighteenth century prevailing opinion held "that social influences, not depravity, caused crime and that reformation, not retribution, should govern punishments" (5).

Compared with many other crimes, determining the rate or frequency of murder is a relatively easy statistical task. Unlike other offenses, homicide is "always taken seriously, almost always subject to law, never common enough to be completely tolerated or overlooked. The legal disposition of murder cases is—usually—a matter of record, whatever records have survived" (Lane 5). That said, as Lane reminds us, "It is never easy to measure the extent of any illegal activity. Even in the most vigilant of modern jurisdictions there is a 'dark figure' representing the unknown and unknowable number of acts that are never discovered, or reported" (5). This phenomenon is complicated further by the fact that the Federal Bureau of Investigation only began assembling a comprehensive account of all the crimes—including murder—that had been reported to police departments across the United States in the 1930s. Called the *Uniform Crime Reports for the United States*, it "was only one symbol of the many ways in which the federal government was becoming more involved in crimes like homicide, which had earlier been left almost entirely to the states" (Lane 242).

Whenever and wherever incidents of murder are recorded, they are expressed as an annual rate per one hundred thousand people. As one might imagine, the murder rate in the United States has varied tremendously both by region and by historical era. Data from the sixteenth century and early seventeenth century, "while fragmentary, shows clearly that the murder rate among white colonials was comparatively low" (Lane 59). Although exact figures are hard to determine—and no records were kept about the killings of black slaves or indigenous peoples—Lane estimates this number "was far less than 1 per 100,000 annually" (Lane 60). The murder rate remained low during the American federalist period. In Richmond, Virginia, for example, "there were some hangings and some homicides, but in the course of the entire thirty-seven years [spanning 1784 to 1820] not one hanging for homicide" (Lane 81)—a statistic that Lane characterizes as representative of many other locales.

Murder rates in the United States would not always be so minuscule. Homicide increased greatly during the antebellum period, fueled by the tensions wrought by rapid urbanization, the massive influx of immigrants, the growing conflict over slavery, the economic disparities precipitated by industrialization, and the introduction of small, cheap, and easily concealable firearms, most famously those manufactured by Samuel Colt and Henry Derringer. Taken collectively, these factors turned the period from the 1830s to the 1840s into "the most disorderly and bloodiest in our history" (Lane 92). In the first three-quarters of the nineteenth century, according to Eric Monkkonen, "New York City shows an average of 25.7 homicides a year" (93).

The twentieth century would see the murder rate in the United States fluctuate sharply. During the 1920s, massive labor protests, upheavals in race relations, widespread youth rebellion, and the passage of Prohibition very quickly and rightly earned it the nickname "the Lawless Decade." Throughout the nation, rates of all kinds of crime, including murder, skyrocketed. "The death toll in some places was appalling: the Chicago Crime Commission estimated that in that city alone, during the Lawless Decade, there were some four hundred gangland killings, virtually all officially unsolved, the killers speeding away in Buicks or dumping bodies into the river or abandoned lots, leaving no witnesses to talk" (Lane 219). Such circumstances pushed the U.S. murder rate to 8.4 per 100,000, but—as a national average—some states were much higher. In Florida, for example, it reached 30 per 100,000 during the 1920s (Lane 229).

The outbreak of World War II rapidly lowered the murder rate nationwide, as economic stressors were eased by an abundance of well-paying wartime jobs, the removal of many pugnacious young men from the domestic population by conscription in the military, and the eradication of family tensions by the physical separation of many husbands and wives. And, "despite a brief upward blip in 1946–47 as the servicemen came home, it kept dropping afterward, and none of the violent developments of the 1920s and 1930s were echoed in the 1940s and 1950s" (Lane 150). By 1960, in fact, the national murder rate had dipped to 4.7, a historic low for any census year (Lane 265).

But, over a ten-year period beginning in 1963, the murder rate would increase sharply. Amid tensions caused by the civil rights movement and the social unrest resulting from U.S. involvement in the Vietnam War, the murder rate more than doubled, reaching 10.2 in 1974 (Lane 303), and by the election year of 1980, it had inched up to 10.7 (Lane 303). That number would dip to 8.3 by 1985, and—with some variation—it would continue to inch downward as the twentieth century drew to a close (Lane 306, 313). By the first decade of the new millennium, the murder rate had leveled off to around 5.5 per 100,000 ("Regional Murder Rates, 2001–2009"). Once again, however, because this number was an average, great variation existed from region to region and state to state. Statistically, more murders take place in the South, while the Northeast has the fewest. In 2007, for example, the South's regional average was 7.0, while the Northeast's was 4.1 ("Nationwide Murder Rates, 1996–2008"). Likewise, tremendous differences exist between states. Louisiana, for example, routinely has one of the highest murder rates—12.7 in 2004—while New Hampshire has one of the lowest—at 1.4 in 2004 ("Nationwide Murder Rates, 1996–2008").

Although roughly five murders for every one hundred thousand U.S. citizens may not seem like a large number, it is scandalously high when compared to statistics from countries commonly considered its peers. Since the late twentieth century, the United States has had the highest murder rate not simply in the West but in the industrialized world—and by a wide margin. "Japanese murder rates have averaged well under 1.0 a year, while German, French, and English have all hovered somewhere close to that figure. Our near neighbor Canada has sometimes broken 2.0, and Italy pushed past 2.5, but no developed nation in recent years has averaged as high as 3.0" (Lane 313). In fact, in December 1993, after the U.S. murder rate had been hovering between nine and ten per one hundred thousand during the previous decade, "the chair of the U.S. Senate Committee, charged with oversight of the several federal agencies devoted to fighting crime, announced that 'the United States is the most dangerous country in the world. No country in the world has a higher per capita murder rate than the United States'" (Lane 304). While theorists speculate about the reasons fueling this condition—citing everything from our frontier history, gun culture, and independent spirit—the grim fact is that "we remain a shamefully murderous nation" (Lane 348).

As Karen Halttunen has written, many attitudes "run so deep in modern liberal culture that they appear to be natural, instinctive, when in fact they are historically contingent" (6). This observation is perhaps most true with regard to murder. Robert Asher, Lawrence B. Goodheart, and Alan Rogers have asserted that, contrary to common conceptions, "legal decisions about the guilt of people accused of murder and the proper punishment of those convicted of murder have not followed automatically any set of principles and procedures" (3). Rather, they continue, "murder jurisprudence has also been affected by the existence of powerful social norms that influenced the way juries, judges, prosecutors, and lawmakers viewed persons accused of criminal homicide" (14). For this reason, while terms like "homicide" and "murder" are commonly expressed in the singular and viewed as stable, they are actually malleable and even multivalent, changing with the social, political, and cultural circumstances of a particular era.

Nearly a century ago, British jurist and historian Frederic William Maitland commented that "if some fairy gave me the power of seeing a scene of one and the same kind in every age of history of every race," he would choose a murder and its accompanying trial "because I think that it would give me so many hints as to a multitude of matters of the first importance" (qtd. in F. Stern 29). How communities respond to the act of murder sheds light on prevailing beliefs about how members of that locale ought to live. In the words of Pieter Spierenburg, "Killing always affects the fundamental values of those who participate in and witness the act, thus providing valuable information about culture, social hierarchy, and gender relations" (1). For this reason, although murder is in many ways the most destructive of acts—what Michel Foucault would classify as dissolution of the social order—it is also one of the most instructive.

"This Wave of Blood in Print": The Homicide Tradition in Narratives for U.S. Children

The chapters that follow contribute to the social history of murder in the United States by tracing the homicide tradition in its popular children's literature. In so doing, they demonstrate that "this wave of blood in print," which Roger Lane identifies as a long-standing feature of U.S. literature for adults (93), includes texts for young readers. Far from existing outside of or even separate from the history of homicide, popular American children's literature is both influenced by it and exerts an influence on it. Murder-themed children's narratives form a significant but hitherto overlooked component of what David Ray Papke characterizes as the nation's "crime-related cultural production" (xiv).

Chapter 1 spotlights one of the most famous fairy tales of all time that is also one of the most widely known narratives among generations of American children: the Grimm Brothers' version of "Snow White." Over the course of the narrative, the title character is murdered not once, but multiple times. While common critical readings of "Snow White" focus on the way in which the story allows child readers to explore taboo feelings concerning inter-familial conflict, I argue that its narrative origins, original audience, and publication history support a different interpretation. The individual attraction and ongoing appeal of "Snow White," I maintain, is not that it allows young people to work through psychological jealousy of their mother but rather that it allows the nation's parents the opportunity to indulge in homicidal fantasies toward their children.

Chapter 2, on Lewis Carroll's *Alice's Adventures in Wonderland* (1865), reveals the new interpretive possibilities that emerge when the character of the Queen of Hearts—along with her murderous mandate "Off with their heads!"—is moved from the background to the forefront. State-sanctioned executions were a vivid social reality and the subject of heated public controversy in England during the period when Carroll conceived and composed *Alice*. Throughout the nineteenth century, but especially during the 1860s, the ethics, efficacy, and even wisdom of the practice was discussed in popular newspapers, among British citizens, and by elected officials. In this chapter, I make a case that in *Alice's Adventures in Wonderland*, Lewis Carroll weighed in on this debate. The Queen of Heart's repeated, impulsive, and usually absurd calls for various individuals to be executed satirize this long-standing civic practice and disclose a new, and previously neglected, area of cultural commentary within the novel: the antigallows movement. Given that judicial execution is still lawful on a federal and, in many regions, a state level in the United States, Carroll's meditation on its merit constitutes an overlooked source of cultural interest in the text. Many of the criticisms raised in *Alice* about the practice—from its cruelty to its capriciousness—mirror both past and present debates about the American practice of capital punishment.

Chapter 3, on Edgar Rice Burroughs's *Tarzan of the Apes* (1912), calls attention to the numerous and often gory murders that permeate this well-known adventure story: humans killing humans, humans killing animals, and animals killing other animals. While Burroughs's book is commonly seen as a product of the Progressive-era interest in cultural anthropology owing to its setting in the remote jungles of Africa and its depiction of indigenous tribal peoples, I demonstrate that its presentation of corporeal violence places it in dialogue with a related discipline: criminal anthropology. Spearheaded by the work of Italian researcher Cesare Lombroso, this new and highly influential field argued that individuals engaged in aggressive violence were evolutionary "throwbacks" to the "lower" races and "lesser" species. *Tarzan of the Apes*, with its depiction of mutinous "swarthy" sailors, killer anthropoid apes, and cannibalistic, indigenous Africans, can be clearly connected to the viewpoints of this discipline. Rereading Burroughs's narrative in light of its engagement with criminal anthropology gives new social meaning and added literary significance to oft-discussed elements such as its engagement with biological determinism, its views on race and eugenics, and its portrayal of Tarzan's physical and intellectual exceptionalism.

Chapter 4, on the Nancy Drew Mystery Stories, demonstrates that while the title character rarely solves cases of murder, the books are filled with numerous threats to the girl sleuth's life as well as to the lives of other characters. To foil these attempted murders, as well as to solve the mysteries with which they are connected, Nancy Drew ostensibly relies on some of the identifying elements of the mystery genre: a legendary intellect, sharp deductive reasoning skills and—with the aid of her signature magnifying glass—the discovery of forensic evidence. However, this chapter offers an additional, and alternative, explanation for the girl sleuth's detective methods: her engagement with parapsychology. As I demonstrate, a central but commonly overlooked feature of the title character's crime-fighting prowess is her psychic ability. In narratives throughout the series, Nancy's famous hunches, her powerful sense of intuition, and her unfailingly accurate gut feelings play as great a role in her ability to solve cases as her use of reason, logic, and material evidence. More than simply constituting a previously neglected source of Nancy's detective prowess, her use of parapsychology may also point to a possible factual inspiration for her fictional character. During the 1920s and 1930s when the original Nancy Drew books were being written, a teenager named Eugenie Dennis made headlines throughout the United States for her psychic sleuthing abilities. Hailing from the Midwest and specializing in cases of stolen jewels, missing wills, and kidnapped children, Dennis's life and career contains an array of uncanny similarities to that of Nancy Drew.

Chapter 5, on S. E. Hinton's *The Outsiders* (1967), rereads both the style and the substance of the numerous physical assaults, gang rumbles, and even outright killings throughout the narrative to suggest a new source of influence on the classic young adult novel. While *The Outsiders* is commonly heralded as a landmark text in the history of children's literature for its presentation of working-class youth living in a world riddled by gang violence, I posit that its tone, characters, and content were not entirely innovative. Far from inventing a completely new style of writing, Hinton's book can be seen as incorporating elements from an already popular one: pulp fiction in general and the growing legions of paperback books about juvenile delinquents in particular. In so doing, *The Outsiders* demonstrates that the YA genre owes at least as much to the lowbrow world of paperback sensationalism as to the more commonly identified highbrow realm of literary realism.

Chapter 6, on Walter Dean Myers's *Monster* (1999), explores shifting views of crime and changing attitudes about criminals as the twentieth century drew to a close. Through the portrayal of alleged murder accomplice Steve Harmon, Myers calls into question a long-standing phenomenon whereby individuals who engage in violent crimes are demonized and even dehumanized. Far from an unfeeling monster, the sixteen-year-old-protagonist reveals himself to be a thoughtful and intelligent—if also flawed and imperfect—individual. By presenting Steve as, essentially, no different from the young men and women reading his story and by spotlighting the many smaller decisions that led him to this large criminal act, Myers's postmodern narrative acquires a premodern component. Although written as a screenplay and released on the eve of the twenty-first century, *Monster* encodes a kinship with an unexpected literary source: colonial American execution sermons.

Finally, the epilogue, on Stacey Jay's *My So-Called Death* (2010), examines the growing genre of zombie-themed narratives for young adults that emerged at the dawn of the twenty-first century. As figures who have died but paradoxically continue to live, the zombies in *My So-Called Death* engage not only with the issue of the posthuman but also with what may be termed "posthomicide." If Jay's zombified characters cannot die, then, by extension, they cannot be murdered. Consequently, *My So-Called Death* can be read as a meditation on the status of murder in a posthuman, posthomicide age.

Together with adding important information to the representation of violent crime in the United States, placing murder at the center rather than the margins of the nation's popular children's literature also upends received notions of the genre as moving—to borrow a well-known phrase from William Blake—from innocence to experience. Anne Scott MacLeod has written that the 1960s marked a sea change in books for young readers: "Political and social changes leaned hard on the crystal cage that had surrounded children's literature for decades. It cracked, and the world flowed in" (59). Whereas subjects like violence, death, and crime were previously viewed as too frightening, serious, and even "adult" for juvenile audiences, they came to be seen as acceptable and even necessary for them. As Maria Tatar explains, "On the theory that children will be better equipped to manage pain and loss in the real world if they encounter plenty of both in fiction, authors such as Paula Fox (*Monkey Island*), Sharon Creech (*Walk Two Moons*), and Paul Zindel (*The Pigman*) took up suffering, trauma, abandonment, and loss" (*Enchanted* 104).

The homicide tradition in U.S. children's literature challenges this common assumption, demonstrating that elements of violence, death, and crime appeared in narratives for young readers far earlier, far more frequently, and far more graphically than critics generally contend. Indeed, these elements have been present in narratives popular among American youth from the beginning.

Lesser has noted that "murder stories are by definition plot-based; in them, literally, 'the end is everything'" (188). That said, while the action of the narratives profiled in the stories I analyze form a crucial component of my discussion, they are not the sole focus. In the words of Roger Lane, "To understand murder is to understand ourselves, in that we all share at least the capacity to destroy ourselves and each other" (4). Echoing this observation, I examine homicide as both a rare anomaly and a powerful commonality. As journalist Janet Malcolm puts it:

> The crime of murder is one we have all committed in our (conscious or unconscious) imaginations. We have all dreamed about the violent deaths of our families; we have all said about people we love: "I could kill him (or her) . . ." And so as we need to be punished and then absolved of our guilt, so do we punish and then absolve those who actually do what we only dream of doing. (43)

At least in part because of own secretive homicidal fantasies, "we feel in regard to our murderers more sympathy, more identification, than most of us can easily admit" (Lesser 46). Murder literature is often cast as mere escapism —fun, exciting, and often mindless "beach reading"—but I explore it as a crucial source of psychological development, social identity, and individual character formation. Indeed, as Gerhard Falk reminds us, "murder is a form of human relationships" (xiii).

Because murder always involves violence to the body, many chapters examine questions of corporeality and bodily integrity. At the same time, they explore what this phenomenon says about a national body politic who produced and published—or, at least, purchased and read—such accounts. After all, "questions about murder are usually questions about identity. The issue is not just who committed the crime and what kind of person one would have to be to do that; it is also who would be interested in such a crime, as either news or entertainment, and what that interest says about us" (Lesser 13).

Given the disturbing nature of many of the murders depicted in these narratives, it will come as no surprise that I draw on contemporary trauma theory along with recent work on affect, melancholy, and remembrance. As Judith Herman notes, "The ordinary response to atrocities is to banish them from consciousness. Certain violations of the social compact are too terrible to utter aloud: this is the meaning of the word *unspeakable*" (1). Individual reactions to traumatic events, however, are neither this simple nor one-sided. As Herman goes on to observe, atrocities like murder "refuse to be buried. . . . The conflict between the will to deny horrible events and the will to proclaim them aloud is the central dialectic of psychological trauma" (1). For this reason, "people who have survived atrocities often tell their stories in a highly emotional, contradictory, and fragmented manner which undermines their credibility and thereby serves the twin imperatives of truth-telling and secrecy" (1). Accordingly, the chapters that follow explore the tension between what may be called "strategic disclosures" and "productive withholdings," paying as much attention to what is revealed as to what remains unspoken. In each case, murder-themed books for young readers echo while they extend Mark Seltzer's observation that "the contemporary public sphere represents itself to itself, from the art and culture scenes to tabloid and talk TV, as a culture of suffering, states of injury, and wounded attachments" (254).

Eric Tribunella, in his book *Melancholia and Maturation*, makes a case for the centrality of trauma in American children's literature. Be it "a dear friend, a beloved dog, a possibility, an ideal," various forms of irrecoverable loss become "a way of representing and promoting the process of becoming a mature adult" (xi). For Tribunella, "It is as if this loss generates the escape velocity of youth. It is the fuel used to achieve the speed necessary for escaping the gravitational force of childhood" (xi). The chapters that follow echo and extend his observation. I, too, trace the recurring presence of various forms of traumatic loss in narratives popular with American youth, but with some understandably differing results. When physical, material, or psychic loss is precipitated by corporeal violence and even brutal murder, the aftereffects are not always so positive or even productive. Instead of helping to propel young protagonists and, by extension, their juvenile readers out of the realm of childhood and into the maturation of adulthood, murder can precipitate arrested psychic development and even regression. Jean-Paul Sartre commented on the disorientating impact of corporeal violence, seeing it as an act that stopped time, distorted reason, and left individuals with powerful feelings of uncertainty and confusion: "A murder. I say, it's so abstract. You pull the trigger and after that you no longer know what goes on" (107). While the incidents of bloody murder featured in these narratives do, on occasion, lead to insight and wisdom—an act that attests to the resiliency of young people—they almost as often result in turmoil and bewilderment, a consequence that attests to the enduring power of trauma. Katharine Capshaw Smith has commented on this duality, writing that "because children are imagined as innocent, they are figured almost iconographically as the ultimate victims of trauma" while, at the same time, "they are also figured as survivors of trauma, those who can offer adults spiritual advice in how to triumph over pain through simple, honest, essential values like love, trust, hope and perseverance" (116).

Not coincidentally, the time period my study covers coincides exactly with both the rise of children's literature as a distinct literary genre and the birth of "murder culture" in the United States. The opening decades of the nineteenth century witnessed the widespread acceptance of childhood as an important new phase of human development worthy of its own literature; likewise, this same historical period also saw homicide emerge as a distinct sociocultural subject that would quickly come to permeate nearly every facet of American print, visual, and popular media. This book sits at the nexus of these phenomena, examining not merely their chronological simultaneity but also, possibly, cross-pollination. While narratives for young people are not commonly associated with issues like the spectatorship of violence, the problem of evil, and the spectacle of the dead body, the chapters that follow demonstrate that they have been engaged with them from the beginning. In so doing, this project adds another important but as-yet overlooked dimension to the ongoing fascination with violent crime in the United States. The homicide tradi-

tion in children's literature locates these narratives in what Pieter Spierenburg has identified as the long-standing disjunction between "official and
popular attitudes to violence" (64). On one hand, Americans publically de-
nounce crimes like murder, elect public officials based on their willingness to
"get tough" with offenders, and support legislation to build more prisons and
institute mandatory minimums for certain crimes. Meanwhile, on the other
hand, those same individuals consume homicide-themed films, books, and
television shows with a seemingly insatiable appetite.

This book thus takes up Lesser's question: "What harm, to the murdered
person or to ourselves, do we do by using someone's murder as the occasion
for our entertainment?" (8). At the same time, it pushes this issue in a new
direction because the intended audience for the narratives under consideration is young people: a group commonly seen as more innocent, naïve, and
impressionable than adults. In the popular movie *You've Got Mail* (1998),
character Kathleen Kelly, who owns a children's bookstore, asserts that "when
you read a book as a child, it becomes a part of your identity in a way that no
other reading in your whole life does." If this observation is correct—and I
believe many parents, teachers, and child psychologists would argue that it is,
at least to some extent—then what does it mean if the text that the young
person is reading features murder? Given the prevalence of homicide in books
popular among American children, to what extent does such violence become
part of their identity? Moreover, what light can this issue shed on perennial
questions like the reason for the consistently high murder rate in the United
States, the origins of the national interest in both fictional and factual blood-
shed, and the basis for the long-standing cultural fascination with crime and
criminals?

My interest in the homicide tradition in American children's literature
goes far beyond mere psychological, anthropological, or sociological concerns, however. As David Ray Papke rightly notes, "Crime is a political subject" (xiii). In the words of Roger Lane, "Fear of criminal violence plagues the
United States today, driving much of our politics, our patterns of settlement,
the relations among our races and social classes" (6–7). This book demonstrates that, far from being cut off from sociopolitical forces, many works for
young readers are products of those forces. Especially in homicide-themed
narratives, questions of race, class, and gender influence plots, shape characters, and even dictate real or imagined readerships. Accordingly, this project
participates in the ongoing efforts, to borrow a phrase from Papke once again,

to "recognize the way crime and the criminals are framed by our cultural experience" (xiii).

An equally powerful but less often discussed detail is that murder also contains an aesthetic component. Joel Black has observed that "instances of violence are regularly presented to us artistically, and routinely experienced by us aesthetically. The very activity by which we represent or 'picture' violence to ourselves is an aesthetic operation whereby we habitually transform brutal actions into art" (5). While he primarily draws on the films by British auteur Alfred Hitchcock to illustrate his point, those by American directors Quentin Tarantino, Sam Peckinpah, or Wes Craven would serve just as well. As Black discusses, in movies like *Psycho*, the attention that Hitchcock gives to the proper lighting, right camera angle, and the amount as well as placement of blood demonstrates the way in which murder can be a work of art. The same could be said of authors when they write homicide scenes: the care with which they select each word and decide on every detail, as well as the way they describe each facet of both the crime and the corpse, offer further proof that "the affinity between art and murder is far greater than all but a few artists and killers have been willing to admit" (Black 103). Thus my exposition explores acts of homicide as "the aesthetic subversion of the beautiful by the sublime, and more generally, the philosophical subversion of ethics by aesthetics" (Black 15).

Of course, while Americans demonstrate a particularly intense fascination with murder and murderers, children's narratives written by authors in other countries do as well. Incidents of lethal violence litter stories, past and present, for young people all over the globe. For example, the traditional Russian folktale "Vasilisa the Beautiful" features a witch who is both a murderer and a cannibal. A version of the story that appears in the volume *Favorite Folktales from Around the World* offers the following terrifying description of this figure's home: "The fence around the hut was made of human bones, and on the spikes were human skulls with staring eyes; the doors had human legs for doorposts, human hands for bolts, and a mouth with sharp teeth stood in place of a lock" (337). Likewise, German writer Otfried Preussler's fantasy novel *Krabat* (1971), which is set at a school for black magic, contains numerous sinister murders. As the eponymous character quickly learns, one student is selected for death each year and then the corpse is put to grisly use in the school's curriculum: "The things lying around the bin floor looked like pebbles at first sight; a second glance showed Krabat that they were teeth—

teeth and splinters of bone" (26). *Krabat* was awarded the Deutscher Jugend-buchpreis—a prize recognizing excellence in literature for young people—in 1972 and has been made into multiple live-action and animated films over the years (see "*Krabat*"). Finally, and perhaps most powerfully, *The Book Thief* (2005), by Australian young adult author Markus Zusak, has murder at its core: the book is not only set in Germany during the World War II but it is narrated by none other than Death himself. The loss of human life during the course of the text—from combat, malnutrition, disease, civilian bombing campaigns, and the concentration camps—affirms Gaston Bouthoul's obser-vation that "war is organized homicide that has been legalized" (31).

The existence of these and other texts underscores the need for an exam-ination of murder-themed children's narratives from an international per-spective. Are the types of murder and murderers depicted in these stories comparable to or dissimilar from those featured in popular American chil-dren's literature? Does homicide function in analogous social, political, and even aesthetic ways in these books for young readers? More specifically, what literary roles and even artistic functions does corporeal violence play in nov-els, stories, and poems for non-U.S. juvenile audiences? Finally, and perhaps most pressingly, what does the presence of homicide in these narratives say about public perceptions of violent crime in these countries and cultures? It is my hope that this project will begin a larger conversation about the textual incidents along with political implications of homicide in literature for chil-dren, inspiring further work on the subject both inside and outside of the United States.

One final note about methodology: although the chapters that follow are arranged chronologically, this sequential arrangement is not meant to suggest a linear progression or even the literary-cultural evolution of murder narra-tives over time. Rather, they are intended, to borrow a phrase from Jay Robert Nash, to map a "geography of murder" (14). By calling attention to the con-nections among and between texts, my discussion casts murder-themed chil-dren's literature in the United States as engaging in an ongoing sociocultural dialogue rather than offering an ahistorical monologue.

Libby Gruner, in an article that appeared in *Inside Higher Education* in October 2009, identifies some recurring themes of children's literature: "re-bellion and obedience, growth and change, dreams and imagination" (par. 4). The pages that follow make a case for adding corporeal violence and murder to this list. Although perhaps not as prevalent as the tropes of "growth and change" or "dreams and imagination," it is a powerful and important theme. Indeed, acknowledging and embracing the homicide tradition in popular children's literature in the United States rather than ignoring or overlooking it changes the way we think about the genre.

At the same time, the representation of murder in narratives for boys and girls says much about current cultural attitudes regarding children in the United States, and, by extension, prevailing perceptions about the purpose of art and literature for young readers. As Maria Tatar has aptly noted, works of juvenile literature "may not offer much insight into the minds of children, but they often document our shifting attitudes toward the child and chart our notions about childrearing in a remarkable way" (*Off* 20). For these reasons, she adds, "it is important to remember that what we produce in our retellings and rereading" of narratives for young readers "discloses more about an adult agenda for children than about what children want to hear" (*Off* 20). As narratives that offer commentary not only about life but also about death, homicide-themed texts form a rich and largely untapped well of information concerning the American cultural mindset.

Wendy Lesser once observed that "murder literature forces us, or lures us, or invites us to identify with the murderer. It is an invitation we readily accept" (55). This book extends this phenomenon, demonstrating how the issue of murder enthralls even the nation's youngest of readers.

CHAPTER ONE

"You Must Kill Her and Bring Me Her Lungs and Liver as Proof"

"Snow White" and the Fact as well as Fantasy of Filicide

No quarrels . . . are so bitter as family quarrels.

WILLIAM ALCOTT, *The Young Husband* (1846)

Psychologists Geoffrey R. McKee and Steven J. Shea assert that "few crimes generate greater public reaction than the intentional murder of children" (678). Given prevailing views about the innocence and defenselessness of young people, the slaying of a boy or girl is seen as particularly heinous. While individuals can imagine an array of reasons why an adult might kill another adult, they cannot fathom what could possibly prompt them to murder a child. As Marianne Szegedy-Maszak remarks, "Both the crime and the motivations defy easy comprehension" (28).

Given the condemnation associated with child murder, it is surprising how commonly this event occurs in classic fairy tales. Many of the homicides depicted in some of the most beloved stories are acts of filicide, neonaticide, or infanticide. The Wolf's consumption of Little Red Riding Hood, the Witch's similar attempt to bake and eat young Hansel and Gretel, and the Ogre's slaughter of his seven daughters in "Little Tom Thumb" constitute just a few examples.

Of all the fairy tales that depict the murder of a child, arguably the most well known is "Snow White." As Linda Dégh has observed, "The common knowledge of the [narrative] is so profound, so deeply ingrained, that, even without the story being told in full, a reference or casual hint is enough" (102). Although the story of Snow White exists in numerous forms, the telling by Jacob and Wilhelm Grimm has risen to prominence. According to Maria Tatar, "Today, adults and children the world over read the Grimms' tales in nearly every shape and form: illustrated and annotated, bowdlerized and abridged, faithful to the original or fractured" (*Hard* xv). Nowhere, perhaps, is this more true than in the United States. Fairy tales by the Grimm Brothers have long been staples of American childhood. For generations, volumes of their narratives have been given to young people as gifts, read to them as bedtime stories, and loaned to them by school and public libraries alike. It is no coincidence, for example, that when Walt Disney sought to bring the story of Snow White to the silver screen in 1937 he chose the version by Jacob and Wilhelm Grimm. While Disney did make modifications to the narrative, the tremendous commercial success of *Snow White and the Seven Dwarfs*—breaking box office records, winning an honorary Academy Award, and being beloved by generations of children to this day (Wasko 14, 129)—solidified its status in the United States. Other editions of the story are still extant, of course, but the Grimms' version is the one that is commonly seen as the "best," and—in the minds of many American children and adults alike—even the "real" or "correct" one.

The Grimm Brothers' "Snow White" is not only the most popular but also, perhaps not surprisingly given the national obsession with violence, the most homicidal one. The jealous stepmother in the tale kills the beautiful title character not once, but three times: first, by suffocating her with staylaces; next, by brushing her hair with an enchanted, lethal comb; and, finally, by feeding her a poisoned apple. Moreover, these murders occur after an initial unsuccessful attempt on Snow White's life. In a passage that is as famous as it is gruesome, the Queen instructs the Huntsman that, after taking Snow White deep into the woods, "you must kill her and bring me her lungs and liver as proof of your deed" (84). Demonstrating the centrality of murder to the story, even in Walt Disney's highly sanitized version of the Grimms' "Snow White," the title character is murdered: after the Huntsman cannot bear to kill the little girl, the evil stepmother draws on her magical powers to disguise her identity, concoct a poisoned apple, and murder the young girl herself.

This chapter seeks to account for the ongoing fascination with the Grimm Brothers' "Snow White." I argue that the story endures not in spite of its depiction of a heinous queen who engages in the horrific act of child murder but because of it. As Bruno Bettelheim famously asserted in *The Uses of Enchantment* (1975), the story of "Snow White" is the representation of the repressed feelings, hidden desires, and forbidden thoughts of its juvenile readers. In his view, the tale is not about a stepmother who is jealous of her stepdaughter but about a daughter who is jealous of her stepmother. In what has become an oft-quoted passage, he explains that

> Snow White, if she were a real child, could not help being intensely jealous of her mother and all her advantages and power.
>
> If a child cannot permit himself to feel his jealousy of a parent (this is very threatening to his security), he projects his feelings onto this parent. Then "I am jealous of all the advantages and prerogatives of Mother" turns into the wishful thought: "Mother is jealous of me." The feeling of inferiority is defensively turned into a feeling of superiority. (204)

Bettelheim contends that "the form and structure of fairy tales suggest images to the child by which he can structure his daydreams and with them give better direction to his life" (7). In the specific case of "Snow White," the story helps the child work through the powerful feelings of filial jealousy, sentiments that Bettelheim identifies as "an age-old phenomenon" (204).*

This chapter offers an alternative assessment that upends critical viewpoints about "Snow White" that have persisted for decades. Building on the work of Sandra Gilbert, Susan Gubar, and Shuli Barzilai concerning the centrality of the character of the stepmother, I argue that the fairy tale is a product of wish fulfillment or fantasy. But, as I demonstrate, this projection is performed by its adult and not child readers. Given that "Snow White" is a story that was originally created by adults, was initially published in a collection by the Grimm Brothers that was not primarily intended for a child audience, and endures because it is continually rewritten, retold, and republished by men and women instead of boys and girls, the murderous impulses in the tale may more accurately be viewed as the result of parental desires rather than of desires belonging to children. An unexplored source of the ongoing appeal of

---

*Although Bettelheim's reading of "Snow White" as the product of the child's projection may be the most influential, it is certainly not the only one. Sigmund Freud, in *The Interpretation of Dreams*, views the story of Snow White as a tale concerning the psychosexual struggles of children. In his estimation, the narrative is about a young person "being in love with one parent and hating the other" (260).

"Snow White" is not that it allows young people to work through the psychological jealousy for their mother; rather, the tale allows parents the opportunity to indulge in homicidal fantasies about their children.

Once upon a Time, There Were Only Grown-Ups: Fairy Tales as Narratives by Adults, for Adults—and about Adults

In the twenty-first century, fairy tales occupy a central place in the canon of
literature for young readers. Routinely read by boys and girls as well as to
them, stories like "Cinderella," "Beauty and the Beast" and "Snow White" are
regarded as having a large juvenile audience.* To be sure, collections of fairy
tales are often shelved in the children's sections of bookstores and libraries.
Similarly, studies about the origins and evolution children's literature routinely begin with a consideration of fairy tales, framing them as foundational
texts of the genre.†

This has not always been the case. Although critics hotly debate whether
fairy tales have their root in an oral or written tradition, few contest that they
began as stories that were initially created by and for adults.‡ Maria Tatar, for
instance, in an argument that supports the origins of fairy tales in orality,
asserts that "traditionally folktales"—including the ones that the Grimm
Brothers would later collect and publish—"were related at adult gatherings
after the children had been put to bed for the night" (*Hard* 23). In this child-

---

*While fairy tales are often read by and to children, they do not of course form their sole
audience; adults also read, write, and enjoy them. Indeed, some fairy tales—such as the retellings of
various classic narratives by Angela Carter in *The Bloody Chamber* (1979)—are intended for adults.

†For a discussion of both past and present examples of this viewpoint, see Kidd (1–2).

‡As Jack Zipes has written, "There are numerous theories about the origins of fairy tales, but
none have provided conclusive proof about the original development of the literary fairy tale"
(introduction xi). In the words of Martha Hixon, for decades "the theory of orality as the womb of
fairy tales" has constituted "an assumption that is an almost sacrosanct tenet of folktale history"
(231). However, in the past few decades, this axiom has been called into question, most recently—as
well as infamously—by Ruth B. Bottigheimer in *Fairy Tales: A New History* (2009). As she asserts,
"The current understanding of the [oral] history of fairy tales is not only built on a flimsy foundation;
its very basis requires an absence of evidence" (2). Bottigheimer goes on to explain that this is
patently not the case; in her book, she makes the case that an abundance of print proof or, at least,
literary antecedents exist for this genre. These claims have proved quite controversial, and her book
has sparked what Martha Hixon describes as nothing less than a scholarly "slugfest" (231). Zipes has
attempted to ease tensions between opposing sides. As Jennifer Howard reports, he "has little
patience for the idea that oralists and print partisans must be at war with each other over fairy tales.
'It's absurd to create a dichotomy' between the two, he says. 'The literary and the oral thrive off one
another and have since literacy became widespread'" (par. 28). In spite of such interventions, the
debate over this issue continues.

free atmosphere, "peasant *racounteurs* could take certain liberties" (*Hard* 23). These freedoms took the form of everything from creating lewd plots and using crass language to featuring taboo subject matters and presenting uncouth characters. Indeed, in the absence of child listeners, storytellers were able to "give free play to their penchant for sexual innuendo or off-color allusions" (*Hard* 23). In *Fairy Tales: A New History* (2009), Ruth B. Bottigheimer adds to this portrait by calling attention to a piece of possible source material whose initial audience was adult and not juvenile: the work of sixteenth-century Italian author Giovan Francesco Straparola.

Whatever their specific sociocultural origins—via print or oral media, among the peasantry or the professional class—folk and fairy tales allowed for the free reign of the imagination. As Jack Zipes has written, "The basic nature of the folk tale was connected to the objective ontological situation and dreams of the narrators and their audiences" (*Breaking* 33). The stories brought amusement at the end of a long work day, and they also gave adults an opportunity to release pent-up feelings. Through the tales that they read, heard, or invented, men and women could give voice to fears, dreams, and fantasies (Tatar *Hard* 20–25).

When the tale of "Snow White" was first published by the Brothers Grimm in *Kinder- und Hausmärchen* (1812), it retained this quality. Alfred David and Mary Elizabeth David have noted that, even though Jacob and Wilhelm Grimm gave their collection the title "Nursery and Household Stories," "they did not mean to imply that they had compiled a volume of stories for the nursery" (181). On the contrary, "For the Grimms, it meant that the stories preserved the simplicity and innocence that their generation—the first generation of romantic writers—associated with childhood and the family hearth" (David and David 181). Giving further credence to this viewpoint is the fact that "in the foreword to the first volume Wilhelm Grimm wrote: 'These stories are pervaded by the same purity that makes children appear so marvelous and so blessed to us'" (David and David 181). As David and David go on to explain, "In other words, it is not that the stories are primarily *for* children (though most children enjoy them), but the stories are *like* children, have lived *among* children, and have been treasured and preserved within the family" (181; italics in original).

Zipes has made similar observations. In "Who's Afraid of the Brothers Grimm?," he states in reference to *Kinder- und Hausmärchen* that "the original publication was not expressly intended for children" (8). On the contrary, "these collections flourished throughout Europe and were read by children and adults but they were not considered the prime or appropriate reading material for them" (*Why* 85). Furthermore, in contrast to contemporary attitudes about the place and purpose of fairy tales, they were not "considered to be 'healthy' for the development of children's minds" (*Why* 85). Indeed, as Frederick Rühs emphasized in his review of *Kinder- und Hausmärchen* in 1815, "This [is] not a book to put into the hands of children" (qtd. in Tatar *Hard* 15).

Over time, such attitudes would change. Maria Tatar has documented that, as the nineteenth century progressed, fairy tales gradually began "being appropriated by parents as bedtime reading for children" (*Hard* xiii). Then, as now, mothers and fathers were drawn to the short lengths, fast pace, and clear morals of the tales. Boys and girls for their part enjoyed the magical happenings, fantastical settings, and spine-tingling plots that are a common feature of many narratives.

This change in the audience for fairy tales necessitated a change in their content. In the words of Tatar, "While parents appreciated the narrative hiss and crackle of the stories in the collection, they were less enthusiastic about the Grimms' efforts to capture the authentic language of the German *Volk*, a roughhewn idiom that often took a vulgar, burlesque turn" (*Hard* xiii). Accordingly, when the Grimms began to revise their collection of fairy tales for child readers beginning in 1819, they made numerous modifications, "adding Christian sentiments and cleansing the narratives of their erotic, cruel, or bawdy passages" (Zipes *Why* 85). In one extant version of "Little Red Riding Hood," for instance, the title character asks the Wolf if she can go outside "to make a load" (see Tatar *Hard* xvii). Similarly, in the Grimms' initial version of "Rapunzel," the title character is perplexed why her belly has gotten plumper after many overnight visits from the prince (see Ashliman). These few examples illustrate John Updike's observation that folk tales functioned as the "television and pornography of their day, the life-lightening trash of preliterate peoples" (662).

Interestingly, while the Grimm Brothers deemed sex, bawdy language, and crass behavior inappropriate for young readers and therefore eliminated passages containing such elements, they did not have a similar view about acts of violence. As Tatar has noted about the brothers' editorial practices, "They had no reservations about including detailed descriptions of children abused or abusers punished; nor did they rush to excise passages that showed heads rolling or fingers flying through the air" (*Hard* 20). If they made any alter-

ations along these lines, in fact, it was "adding or intensifying violent episodes" (*Hard* 5). The passage where the doves systematically peck out the eyes
of Cinderella's stepsisters or the moment when Rumplestiltskin becomes so
enraged that he literally pulls himself apart constitute just a few examples.
These gruesome scenes are not present in other extant versions; they are
unique to the Grimms' telling alone (see Tatar *Hard* 3–10).

Although fairy tales such as "Snow White" are now primarily associated
with children and childhood, they endure not because boys and girls keep
retelling and republishing them but because adults do. Of the more than
twenty-seven hundred different editions of the story of Snow White listed in
WorldCat—an international catalogue of library holdings—at the time of this
writing, none are by juvenile authors.* Moreover, WorldCat also reveals that
over eleven hundred of these retellings are intended for an adult and not child
audience.

Bruno Bettelheim, in sentiments that have been voiced by many other
critics, accounts for the powerful attraction that fairy tales have for boys and
girls by arguing that they "give body to anxieties" (*Uses* 7). Reading narratives
about enchanted castles, magic spells, and evil witches permits young people
to explore forbidden feelings, confront personal demons, and conquer deep-
seated anxieties. In this way, fairy tales form a powerful example of what Jerry
Griswold describes in *Feeling Like a Kid* as the pleasurable nature of being
scared (31–50).

Both the past narrative history and the present print existence of fairy tales
like "Snow White" allow for an alternative analysis. Given that this story was
initially created by adults, the fears, dreams, and anxieties that it gives voice to
may more accurately reflect those of men and women than of boys and girls.
In *Fairy Tales and the Art of Subversion* (2006), Zipes considers "the liberating
potential of the fantastic" (169–91). In the realm of "once upon a time," he
contends, anything is possible: hazelnut trees can bestow beautiful gowns,
mirrors can tell fortunes, and frogs can turn into princes. For this reason, fairy
tales serve a function that is as freeing and empowering as it is cathartic and
therapeutic.

---

*Admittedly, the vast majority of children's books are authored by adults. That said, I believe it is
important to call attention to the fact that this condition is absolute with regard to "Snow White."
There are no published versions of the story composed by children, so it is not that child-authored
versions of it are simply rare—as is the case with other stories and styles for young readers—but
rather nonexistent.

The long-standing adult-centered nature of "Snow White," however, suggests that the emancipating powers of the story are directed at the parent, not the child. Sandra Gilbert and Susan Gubar, in their well-known feminist reading of the tale, foreshadow this argument by calling attention to the importance of the adult rather than the child characters. In *The Madwoman in the Attic* (1979), they argue that the story of Snow White is really a story about the Queen. Snow White and the Queen are not separate and distinct individuals; rather, they are competing forms of female identity imposed on women by patriarchal Western culture: the innocent, beautiful angel and the mean, ugly witch. Viewing the story from this perspective transforms the conflict between the Queen and Snow White. In the words of Gilbert and Gubar, "Shadow fights shadow, image destroys image in the crystal prison, as if the 'fiend' . . . should plot to destroy the 'angel' who is another one of her selves. . . . The Queen, adult and demonic, plainly wants a life of 'significant action.' . . . She wants to kill the Snow White *in herself*, the angel who would keep deeds and dramas out of her own house" (36–37, 39). Thus, they argue that the fairy tale is not about the rivalry between two women but rather about the competing personalities within one woman.*

More than a decade later, Israeli scholar Shuli Barzilai expanded on this viewpoint. Making a case for the centrality of the filial relationship within the tale, she argues that the story of Snow White is really about a mother's struggle with the processes of parenthood, aging, and—ultimately—letting go: "Corresponding to separation anxiety in children, to the fear of being cut off from parental love and protection, there is comparable anxiety in adults: a fear of being cut off from the child's proximity and dependence, a fear of freedom from the thousand and one tasks that structure the life of the mother" (527). Accordingly, she reads the Queen's jealousy as a product of her inability to accept Snow White's physical and intellectual maturation and especially her increased independence: "Since pain as well as pleasure may be part of the maternal experience of a child's growing autonomy, 'mothers engage in practices other than and often conflicting with mothering.' It is the Queen's radical attempt to perpetuate primary intimacy and identification with her (step)-daughter that marks the specific pathology of her story" (529).

While I echo the observations by Barzilai along with Gilbert and Gubar

---

*Given my focus on the place and purpose of "Snow White" in the United States, it is worth noting that not only are Gilbert and Gubar both American critics but their argument concerns the Anglo-American readership of the story.

about the centrality of the figure of the Queen, I also extend their readings of "Snow White" by refracting them through the lens of the American obsession with homicide. I argue that the Grimms' tale has been so powerful and so popular for so many generations in the United States because it taps into a grim reality: whether out of jealousy, anger, or simple frustration and exhaustion, mothers and fathers have all fantasized—at some time, in some place, during some moment—about murdering their children.

A Grim Truth: The Factual Basis for Fairy-Tale Filicide

In the apt words of Terri Windling, "The term *fairy tale*, like the word *myth*, can be used, in modern parlance, to mean a lie or an untruth" (4; italics in original). Echoing this observation, Eugen Weber has noted that the classic "once upon a time" opening of many narratives announces that the story is not rooted in "everyday reality"; the phrase "warns us that we're not going to hear about real persons and places" (96). For these reasons, both past and present readers have often insisted on the innocuous nature of fairy tales, "dismissing them as nonsensical, irrational and trivial" (Zipes *Breaking* 31).

Umberto Eco reminds us, however, "there is nothing more meaningful than a text which asserts that there is no meaning" (7). The Grimm Brothers' "Snow White" can be viewed in this way. Although the tale commences with the classic "once upon a time" opening, it is far from a vacuous work that is devoid of real-world significance. Together with engaging the oft-discussed feminist issues of motherhood, aging, and beauty, "Snow White" addresses the sociological subjects of child abuse, neglect, and mistreatment. Indeed, at its core, the story is a meditation on the horrific, persistent, and even lethal forms of violence that children are often subjected to by adults. As the Queen's persecution of Snow White reveals, this mistreatment commonly comes at the hands of the individuals who are supposed to love, nurture, and protect young people the most: their parents or guardians. Moreover, while not all parental figures are as cruel as the one in this story, the character of the Queen reflects another dire historical reality. The grim truth of the Grimm Brothers' "Snow White" is that, both in past times and during the present day, stepparents are far more likely to murder their nonbiological children than any other individual, be they adult or child, stranger or family member, friend or foe.

The lethal jealousy that the Queen in the Grimm Brothers' "Snow White" harbors for her charge emerges within the first few paragraphs of the tale. In a detail that has prompted feminist readings of the story as an example of "the competition between . . . two women [which] results from a patriarchal culture that pits woman against woman for the favor of a male" (Zipes *Why* 134), the Queen asks her enchanted mirror, "Mirror, mirror on the wall, / Who's the fairest one of all?" (83), and she is shocked by the response: "My queen, you are the fairest one here, / But Snow White is a thousand times more fair than you!" (83). As Gilbert and Gubar note, in the Queen's patriarchal society, women's social value and personal worth emanate from their beauty (36–37). Thus, her loss of the title "the fairest one of all" constitutes not simply a threat to her ego but a threat to her power, agency, and even socioeconomic means of survival. Accordingly, the text reveals, "Envy and pride grew like weeds in her heart. Day and night, she never had a moment's peace" (84). Given what is at stake, the Queen decides that the only way she can eliminate this threat to her cultural standing is by eliminating Snow White.

In spite of the Queen's firm resolve to murder Snow White, she does not initially wish to perform the deed herself; instead, she instructs the Huntsman to kill Snow White for her. However, echoing the taboo against child murder, he is ultimately unable to carry out this task. Taking pity on the defenseless girl, he tells Snow White, "Just run away, you poor child" (84). Rather than being afraid because he has failed to carry out a royal order, the Huntsman is relieved: "He felt as if a great weight had been lifted from his heart, for at least he did not have to kill her" (84). To satisfy the Queen's request for proof of the slaying, the Huntsman kills a wild boar, removes its "lungs and liver and [brings] them to the queen" (84).*

Soon enough, however, the magic mirror reveals the Huntsman's ruse.

---

* Readers quickly learn that the Queen does not want the organs as mere physical proof that Snow White is dead. Instead, she intends to combine her transgression of one powerful social taboo—child murder—with another that is equally strong: cannibalism. Upon receiving the organs from the Huntsman, "The cook was told to boil them in brine, and the wicked woman ate them up, thinking she had eaten Snow White's lungs and liver" (84). The Queen's decision to consume the internal organs of the young girl is commonly seen as further evidence of her inhumanity. But, as the work of N. J. Giradot has suggested, it may also be linked with primitive desires to acquire the youth's power and beauty by ingesting her body (290). In *Totem and Taboo*, Sigmund Freud cites this rationale as a part of what motivates some sons to commit patricide: "The violent primal father had doubtless been the feared and envied model of each one of the company of brothers: and in the act of devouring him they accomplished their identification with him, and each one of them acquired a portion of his strength" (142). Giradot argues that "Snow White" reflects this process even as it reconfigures it in the form of an older, jealous woman ingesting the organs of a young, beautiful girl.

Snow White remains alive and thus is still "the fairest one of all." This news reignites the Queen's desire to kill Snow White, thus suggesting that her plan to murder the young girl was not an impulsive act sparked by a momentary loss of reason. Rather than entrusting another person to perform this task for her, the Queen elects to murder Snow White herself. Disguising herself as an old peddler woman and offering the young girl a pretty corset string "made of silk lace woven of many colors," the evil queen "laces her up so quickly and so tightly that Snow White's breath was cut off," and she falls to the floor (86).

Reflecting the enchanted nature of fairy tales, Snow White is not actually dead; or, perhaps more accurately, her death does not mean that she cannot be brought back to life. When the dwarfs return home, they are miraculously able to revive her: "They lifted her up, and when they saw that she had been laced too tightly, they cut the staylace in two. Snow White began to breathe, and little by little she came back to life" (86).

The Queen learns of Snow White's resurrection from her magic mirror, and she immediately plots to kill her again: "Using all the witchcraft in her power, she made a poisoned comb. She then changed her clothes and disguised herself as another old woman" peddling goods (87). After arriving at the forest cottage and settling on a price for the object, the Queen offers to give Snow White's hair a thorough combing. In a passage that reflects prevailing societal beliefs about the innocence and even naiveté of children, the narrator notes that "poor Snow White suspected nothing and let the woman go ahead, but no sooner had the comb touched her hair when the poison took effect, and the girl fell senseless to the ground" (87).

As before, Snow White's death is not permanent. When the dwarfs return home, they are once again able to resuscitate her. Predictably, when the Queen learns of this event, she becomes enraged and commences work on her most lethal plot to date: concocting the poison apple.

Accordingly, "no sooner had [Snow White] taken a bite when she fell down on the ground dead" (88). This time, in spite of the dwarfs' ardent efforts upon returning home, they are unable to bring her back to life: "Not a breath of air was coming from her lips. She was dead" (88).

While the Queen's homicidal designs for Snow White may seem extreme and even absurd—a product of the fantasy world to which fairy tales belong—they are, sadly, not so. Although few crimes are viewed with such shock, horror and repugnance as filicide, George B. Palermo reports the harsh reality: "The murder of one's children is ubiquitous and is not limited to any specific social class. The poor and the wealthy have both committed such unconscionable offenses throughout history" (123). So, too have individuals from different races, regions, and historical time periods. Mark Koenen and John W. Thompson illuminate the tragic fact: "Filicide is ubiquitous throughout history and across cultures" (62). While men and women today tend to romanticize an earlier, bygone era when children were cherished and protected rather than exploited and even "adultified," Lloyd deMause reminds us that such perceptions are often just that: personal perceptions, not historical facts. "The further back in history one goes the lower the level of child care, and the more likely children are to be killed, abandoned, beaten, terrorized, and sexually abused" (1). Palermo notes that "the practice of infanticide was common in England, France, and Russia. In 1600 England [*sic*], smothering, strangling, neck breaking, or throat cutting and drowning were frequent methods used to kill babies" (126). In Victorian England, rather than killing unwanted infants, some mothers surrendered them to what were known as "baby farms," private orphanages that ostensibly adopted children for a one-time fee but were commonly known to maximize their profits by killing the youngsters either immediately after receiving payment or over time through lack of care (Knelman 157–80). Meanwhile, older children, especially in times of famine or financial hardship, were often abandoned, hired out to work, or subject to fatal neglect (Schwartz and Isser 5–6).

In spite of claims by politicians, parents, and media figures in the twenty-first century that children are the nation's most important asset, conditions for many young people in the United States are, arguably, not much better now than they were before. Beverly Lyon Clark asserted in 2003 that for all our eagerness to proclaim the sanctity of childhood, "the position of the country's children provides little cause for jubilation" (2). As she explains, "For many years children in the United States have been overrepresented among those living in poverty, at a rate almost 50 percent higher than the national norm" (Clark 2). This low socioeconomic status makes boys and girls vulnerable to an array of hazards ranging from malnutrition and disease to abuse and even death. To be sure, in a detail that is surprising given the pervasiveness of national rhetoric concerning "family values," Janine Jason, Jeanne C. Gilliland, and Carl W. Tyler reveal that "homicide is a major cause of pediatric mortality" (191). According to the Uniform Crime Reports maintained by the FBI, in 2008, individuals under the age of eighteen constituted 10.5 percent of all homicide victims ("Murder Victims by Age, Sex and Race,

2008"). This figure gives the United States the dubious distinction of being the country where filicidal murder "occurs more frequently . . . than in other developed nations" (Friedman, Horowitz, and Resnick 1578). Moreover, as Janna Haapasalo and Sonja Petäjä have documented, "the rates of child homicide have been on the increase" during the past few decades (219). In 2004, for example, according to the FBI, the murder of individuals under the age of eighteen accounted for 10.3 percent of all homicides in the United States ("Murder Victims by Age, Sex and Race, 2004"). In 2000, it was 9.9 percent ("Murder Victims by Age, Sex and Race, 2000") and in 1995 8.25 percent ("Murder Victims by Age, Sex and Race, 1995"). Geoffrey R. McKee, using information tabulated by the U.S. Department of Health and Human Services' Office on Child Abuse and Neglect, translates these abstract statistics into more concrete numbers. In 2001, he observes "approximately 1,300 children under 18 died as a result of abuse and neglect—a rate of more than three deaths per day, or one child death every 7 hours" (McKee 9).

"Snow White" reflects the strong past presence as well as powerful current reality of child murder. Far from a fictive tale about an imaginary situation, it relays an all-too-common factual occurrence. Indeed, even the methods the evil queen employs to kill Snow White reflect the common ones by which women kill, especially when they commit filicide. Psychologists Koenen and Thompson reveal that while men commonly employ brute physical force or a weapon—usually in the form of a knife or gun—women typically murder through less violent means, namely, suffocation and poison (70). For poisoning, as Roger Lane remarks, "arsenic was the potion of choice, in both real and fictional incidents, trailed at some distance by cyanide or mercury" (202). Judith Knelman notes that until the mid-nineteenth century, arsenic was "easy to acquire," available over the counter at most druggist shops (52). In addition, it was "cheap, colourless, odourless, soluble in hot water, and hard to detect" (52). Moreover, since women were most often responsible for the preparation of meals, they had ample opportunity to place it in a child's food or drink.

Karen Rowe, Marcia Lieberman, and Gilbert and Gubar have written that the Queen's selection of staylaces, a comb, and an apple with which to murder Snow White are stereotypically feminine items. All of these objects reflect the importance placed on women's physical appearance as well as relate to their role in feeding, nurturing, and caring for others. At the same time, the suffocating staylaces along with the poisoned comb and apple also accurately represent the manner, and even the specific methods, by which women commit filicide.

By whatever means, one group of individuals has attained historical infamy for its presumed mistreatment of children: stepparents and especially stepmothers. As Eugen Weber has documented, before the twentieth century, "deaths in childhood and after made for high female mortality between the ages of 20 and 39" (qtd. in Tatar *Off* 222). Many widowers remarried not only out of a desire for love and companionship but, given the division of labor between men and women, "so that there would be someone to run the household" (Knelman 131). Weber estimates that "during the seventeenth and eighteenth centuries," when many fairy tales were either conceived or recorded, "between 20% and 80% of widowers remarried within the year of their spouse's death" (112).

For this reason, Knelman asserts that "the wicked stepmother did not live only in fairy tales" (131). According to Martin Daly and Margo Wilson, "Stepparents do not, on average, feel the same child-specific love and commitment as genetic parents, and therefore do not reap the same emotional rewards from unreciprocated 'parental' investment" (38). This emotional indifference often escalates to active dislike and occasionally even open contempt. "That stepmothers treated the children of their husbands' first marriages badly—in part because they wished to preserve the patrimony for their own children, in part because they resented the idea of becoming enslaved to a previous wife's children—was more or less a fact of life in the era that gave shape to the tales recorded in Grimms' collection" (Tatar *Off* 222). At times, as Daly and Wilson note, such mistreatment took physical forms. "Enormous differentials in the risk of violence are just one, particularly dramatic, consequence of this predictable difference in feelings" between biological and nonbiological parents (38–39). Daly and Wilson further reveal that children living with an unrelated, nongenetic guardian are a hundred times more likely to be the victims of fatal abuse than those who reside with their biological parents (28).

The Grimm Brothers' "Snow White" likewise reflects this historical and contemporary reality. The opening paragraph of the story makes clear that the Queen is the title character's stepmother. Readers learn that Snow White's biological mother "died after the child was born" and that "a year later the king married another woman" (83). In both past and present criticism, the murderous Queen in Snow White has been regarded as a hyperbolic—or, as Dave Kehr asserts, a "wildly excessive"—character (AR12). Seen as too cruel to be real or even believable, she has been viewed symbolically, as either a psychological manifestation or a monstrous aberration. In short, as anything but an actual person. The long-standing historical reality of filicide ought to change our view of this murderous figure. While she may be dismissed as a horrific anomaly, her behavior is more common than many readers realize— or perhaps care to acknowledge.

"Mommy Dearest": The Original Manuscript—and the Original Murderess

Although the murderous stepmother has become as integral to "Snow White" as the title character herself, she was not always a part of the Grimms' tale. In the original 1812 publication of the narrative, it is the young girl's mother who is trying to kill her. As the narrator reports near the middle of the story: "When Snow White awoke, they asked her who she was and how she happened to get into the house. Then she told them how her mother wanted to have her put to death" (qtd. in Zipes *Subversion* 66).* In the second edition of *Kinder- und Hausmärchen* that appeared in 1819, the Grimm Brothers made various changes to the story. As Zipes has documented, they added more descriptive passages, elaborated on the title character's domestic arrangements with the dwarfs, and included more information about the types of metals that the figures mined (see *Subversion* 66–72). In addition, in a detail that has been the subject of extensive critical discussion, the brothers changed the evil mother to a stepmother.†

In the nearly two hundred years since this version of "Snow White" made its debut, critics have offered varying explanations for why the Grimm Brothers altered the protagonist's familial relationship with her murderer. Valerie Paradiž, among others, has suggested a biographical reason, citing the strong affection that Wilhelm Grimm—who was responsible for the bulk of the revisions—had for his mother. Consequently, she sees the change as a product of his desire not to offend her (1–9). Tatar, on the other hand, offers a more

---

*It is worth noting that both the number and the sequence of murderous acts committed against Snow White in this version remain the same (see Zipes *Subversion* 65–68).

† As I have noted, the opening paragraph to the revised edition reveals that "the queen died after the child [Snow White] was born" (83). Meanwhile, the sentence that follows introduces the king's new wife, Snow White's stepmother, along with her vanity and obduracy: "A year later the king married another woman. She was a beautiful lady, but proud and arrogant and could not bear being second to anyone in beauty" (83).

sociocultural explanation, calling attention to the historical reality that many mothers died in childbirth, many fathers remarried, and thus many children were raised by a stepmother (*Off* 222). Finally, and perhaps most famously, Bettelheim proposes a psychological reason. Reading the story as a product of the child's projection of the murderous jealousy that she feels toward her mother, he sees this transformation as a further manifestation of the story's psychosexual dynamics. Bettelheim argues that in "Snow White," along with other fairy tales that contain cruel stepparents, the

> splitting of the mother into good (usually dead) mother and an evil stepmother serves the child well. It is not only a means of preserving an internal all-good mother when the real mother is not all-good, but it also permits anger at this bad "stepmother" without endangering the goodwill of the true mother, who is viewed as a different person. (69)

According to Bettelheim's reading, the stepmother is not really a stepmother at all; rather, she is a manifestation of the child's actual mother.

While the presence of the biological mother in "Snow White" may seem to lessen the likelihood of her harboring murderous feelings toward the title character, it does not. Stepparents are statistically more likely to commit filicide, but biological parents—especially mothers—also kill their offspring. Szegedy-Maszak comments that "this most baffling of crime is as old as humanity itself, and shockingly common today" (23). Psychologists Catherine F. Lewis, Madelon V. Baranoski, Josephine A. Buchanan, and Elissa P. Benedek have observed that "maternal filicide, defined as the murder of a child by its mother, has been reported for centuries in many different cultures" (613). While the answer to "the troubling question: Why would a mother ever kill her child?" varies widely, the fact remains that the crime occurs with what Szegedy-Maszak calls "surprising frequency" (23). For example, Knelman provides a statistic that upends perceptions of the Victorian period as a time of reverence for and even adoration of children: "In nineteenth-century England babies and children were the most common murder victims of women" (123). She goes on to note that a study examining inmates in a London prison during the mid-nineteenth century found a high incidence of maternal filicide: "The victims of male murderers (32 percent) were most commonly their wives, but those of murderesses (91 percent) were most often babies and children" (7). According to Robyn Anderson, 44 percent of all indictments for murder at Old Bailey jail between 1856 and 1875 were for child homicide

(172). Such statistics were not limited to this one locale. "In Victorian Kent, for example, only one woman killed her husband, but 71 per cent of the victims of murderesses were children" (Knelman 123). As even this brief sample suggests, "historically filicide has been recognized as a crime predominantly committed by women" (Liem and Koentaadt 167).

Once again, this observation holds true today. As mentioned previously, the United States ranks highest among Western, industrial nations in the overall rate of child murder. An article published in 2005 revealed: "Child murder by mothers occurs . . . more frequently in the United States than in other developed nations" (Friedman, Horowitz, and Resnick 1578). Moreover, "studies have estimated that up to 10% of cases of sudden infant death syndrome might actually be murder" (Koenen and Thompson 63), a claim that if true would push the child murder rate even higher.

As with any other crime, the motives fueling infanticide are as numerous as they are diverse. Carol E. Holden, Andrea Stepheson Burland, and Craig A. Lemmen summarize a research study pertaining to motives conducted in the United States:

> Resnick (1969, 1970) provided the first comprehensive review of 155 existing case reports of child murder by parents. He proposed a classification system for these murders based on the parent's (generally, mother's) motives for committing the act, and suggested five categories: *altruistic filicide*, in which the murder was committed to relieve suffering or to avoid abandoning a child by suicide; *acutely psychotic filicide*, in which parents killed under the influence of hallucination, epilepsy or delirium; *unwanted child filicide*, in which the murder was committed simply because the child was not wanted by the murderer; *accidental filicide*, in which the murder occurred in the course of a beating or other violent outburst toward the child; *spouse revenge filicide*, in which the murder was committed in a deliberate attempt to torment the spouse. (25; italics in original)

Whatever the specific classification, one characteristic about the murderer remains constant. As Christine M. Alder and June Baker state, "An image emerges of a woman extremely 'stressed,' whose frustration and anger build to the point where she explodes in a highly emotional, uncontrolled moment of violence against her children" (21). In some instances, the child serves as a proxy for anger that the mother feels for another figure or family member. "In these cases, homicidal behavior is usually precipitated by the child's behavior eliciting aggression in the mother, or the child becomes a vicarious object of aggression felt toward a husband or some other person" (Haapasalo and Petäjä 220). Finally, in a few cases, such as with the much-publicized cases of Susan Smith in 1994 and Andrea Yates in 2001, mothers kill their children because they desire personal freedom, because they feel overwhelmed by domestic responsibilities, or because they are clinically depressed. Whatever the cause, one sobering fact remains: "Filicide is relatively common, with estimates that it comprises 4 percent to 20 percent of all homicides in various populations" (Holden et al. 25).

The past fact of maternal filicide offers a different reason for why the Grimms decided to change the familial relationship between Snow White and her killer. Given that the second edition of *Kinder- und Hausmärchen* was reworked to make it more suitable for a juvenile audience, the brothers may have felt that leaving reference to the murderous acts that mothers sometimes commit against their offspring would be too frightening for child readers. As Maria Tatar has observed about the United States, "The need to deny adult evil—whether it takes the form of infanticide, abandonment, physical abuse, or verbal assault—has been a pervasive feature of our culture" (*Off* xxv). This desire may have been equally strong in Jacob and Wilhelm Grimm.

The Unspeakable Spoken: Filicidal Fantasies and the Enduring Popularity of "Snow White"

As Anna Motz asserts, "We are all guilty of the wish to murder, all subject to thoughts of killing, and all capable of extreme violence in fantasy" (51). We may be able to accept the veracity of this observation when it involves adults contemplating murdering other adults, but we are less comfortable when it involves adults ruminating about killing children. And while a relatively small percentage of parents in the United States actually kill a son or daughter—or even attempt to do so—psychologists, anthropologists, and sociologists reveal that nearly all fantasize about murdering them at some point. What fuels such fantasies varies—from momentary frustration and long-suffering exhaustion to a desire for more personal freedom and even clinical postpartum depression—but the sentiment does not.

Psychologist Beatrice Weinstein has written about filicidal fantasies among women based on research that she conducted in the United States: "While it is vital to society as a whole as well as to individuals to retain the image of the good mother, infanticidal wishes may be universal in mothers and mothers-to-be" (286). As she goes on to note, "These wishes vary in strength, length of time, and degree of awareness for each woman" (286). Nonetheless, they are present, either on the conscious or unconscious level. Many others agree. Harold Blum—whose work is also based on psychological studies performed in the United States—has pointed out that "conflicts between the maternal ego ideal and infanticidal impulses are ubiquitous and clinically significant" (189). Susan Levitsky and Robin Cooper recorded similar sentiments in their research with mothers in New York City who were caring for colicky infants: "One mother's fantasy took the form of dropping the infant out of the window. Another mother stated: 'If I just smothered him with the pillow, I could sleep.' Also, one mother reported, 'it makes me realize that's why mothers and fathers kill them'" (398). Indeed, as one woman admitted after a colicky episode with her infant, "I hate him. I wanted to throw him on the bed. I thought the baby was vicious and evil-tempered. I understand child abuse. I felt like throttling him" (398).

Levitsky and Cooper emphasize that these mothers fantasized about harming or even murdering their babies not because they were evil or even uncaring but simply because they were human: "Sleep deprivation and physical exhaustion experienced by the mothers attempting to care for their colicky infants often contributed to feelings of depression, anger, anxiety, and agitation. Mothers also expressed their feelings of resentment, frustration, helplessness, fear, and loneliness" (398).

Even parents who do not have a colicky child often share such sentiments. After all, boys and girls who are generally well behaved can at times be obstinate, exasperating, and draining. According to British psychologist Dorothy Rowe, filicidal fantasies are quite common among mothers with children of all temperaments precisely because all children can be trying. During a radio broadcast, Rowe reassured women who had fearful flashes that they might hurt or even murder their children that they were not alone and should not worry; such thoughts, she asserted, "were simply the manifestations of a tired mind" (see Robinson 582). Echoing such claims, an article that appeared in the September 2005 issue of the prestigious *American Journal of Psychiatry* offered the following blunt pronouncement: "Mothers thinking about harming their children is not rare" (Friedman, Horowitz, and Resnick 106).

Although filicide fantasies are common, they are seldom expressed or even acknowledged. As Jean Robinson has documented, out of personal shame, concerns about public judgment, or fear of legal consequences, most mothers and fathers keep these thoughts "from doctors and health visitors" (582)— and often even from one another. Although homicidal feelings may seem alarming, Robinson contends that they usually "represent no real risk" (582). On the contrary, they are a perfectly normal and even healthy way for parents to vent frustration, cope with stress, and relieve tension. For these reasons, Robinson urges social workers, members of the legal community as well as family members and friends of parents to stop "over-reacting" to such disclosures and "start supporting mothers instead" (582).

"Snow White" has retained its popularity, at least in part, because it breaks the silence surrounding filicide. The story allows the nation's parents a venue in which to safely indulge murderous fantasies toward their children.* When the Queen learns that her stepdaughter is the now "the fairest of them all," she is incensed: "She trembled and turned green with envy. From that moment on, she hated Snow White, and whenever she set eyes on her, her heart turned cold as stone" (84). This resentment quickly turns homicidal, as the Queen orders the murder of her stepdaughter. In a comment that echoes the sentiments of many of the exasperated mothers in Levitsky and Cooper's study, she tells the Huntsman that she does not "want to have to lay eyes on her ever again" (84).

---

*The ubiquity of child murder—in fact as well as in fantasy—may also be an unconscious reason for the long-standing popularity of Disney's film version of the fairy tale both inside and outside of the United States. As various critics, biographers, and film historians have documented, when *Snow White and the Seven Dwarfs* was initially released in 1937, it was an immediate sensation. Kevin Shortsleeve, for instance, notes that "*Snow White* was the most successful feature-length film of 1938," breaking box office records in the United States and receiving an honorary Oscar for "significant screen innovation" (6). Meanwhile, as Neal Gabler has commented, "Europe was equally rapturous. The film played for twenty-eight weeks in London, grossing over $500,000 in one theater alone, and when it was released to the seaside towns that summer, the theaters were forced to take reservations three weeks in advance, eventually instituting special morning performances to satisfy demand" (277). *Snow White* received similarly enthusiastic receptions in other nations. "It grossed $155,000 at one first-run theater in Paris and over $1 million when it had completed its second run in the city. In twenty-one weeks at one Sydney, Australia theater, it took in $132,000. When censors in Holland forbade children under fourteen from seeing it because they thought it too gruesome, the youngsters staged an impromptu nationwide boycott of a Dutch Snow White chocolate bar, and the censors relented" (277). According to Gabler, "By the time it had finished its run in 1939, it had played in forty-nine-countries and been dubbed into ten languages" (277). *Snow White and the Seven Dwarfs* remains just as popular with national and international audiences today. As Janet Wasko points out, the film is consistently identified as one of the all-time top-selling Disney titles both in the United States and abroad (45, 64). While adult fans of *Snow White and the Seven Dwarfs* tend to cite reasons such as the beauty of the animation or their love for Disney storytelling, another, and more sinister, reason may also be fueling their enthusiasm for the film.

As the story progresses—and the Queen's attempts to murder her step-daughter successively fail—she grows increasingly angry. Upon realizing that the Huntsman has deceived her and that Snow White is alive, "she was horrified" (86). Consequently, "she thought long and hard about how she could kill Snow White. Unless she herself was the fairest in the land, she would never be able to feel anything but envy" (86).

When the magic mirror reports that the staylaces have not suffocated Snow White, she is enraged: "The blood froze in her veins" (87). Not surprisingly, her aggressive feelings toward the young girl grow even stronger: "'But this time,' she said, 'I will dream up something that will destroy you'" (87). After brushing her stepdaughter's hair with the lethal comb, she once again expresses murderous delight: "'There, my beauty,' said the wicked woman, 'now you're finished,' and she rushed away" (87). When the mirror informs her that Snow White has been resuscitated once again, she snaps: "She began trembling with rage. 'Snow White must die!' she cried out. 'Even if it costs me my life'" (87). Her demonic glee after feeding Snow White the poisoned apple reaches a frenzied level: "The queen stared at her with savage eyes and burst out laughing: 'White as snow, red as blood, black as ebony! This time the dwarfs won't be able to bring you back to life!'" (88). On returning home and learning from the magic mirror that she has regained her status as "the fairest of the land," the Queen is clearly relieved. In a passage that highlights the cathartic nature of the murder, the narrator notes that "her envious heart was finally at peace" (88).

Viewing "Snow White" as a product of the homicidal fantasies on the part of adult authors rather than as reflecting child readers' matricidal fantasies also allows for a more satisfying explanation of the sadistic violence at the end of the story. Tatar has observed that in many fairy tales "'happily ever after' [often] means witnessing the bodily torture of villains" (*Hard* xviii). The same is true for the finale of the Grimm Brothers' "Snow White." In what has become a much-discussed ending, when the wicked Queen arrives at Snow White's wedding to the prince, a tragic fate befalls her: "Iron slippers had already been heated up over a fire of coals. They were brought in with tongs and set right in front of her. . . . She had to put on the red hot iron shoes and dance in them until she dropped to the ground dead" (89).

If the story of Snow White functions as a safety valve for adult fantasies about filicide, then the need for the evil Queen to be not simply chastised but punished horrifically is all the more important. Her fate of being forced to dance to her death in shoes made of hot iron is a death so terrible that it forms a powerful preventative. Giving further credence to this reading, Zipes points out that the Grimm Brothers added this finale to the story; it was not in the original version that they had gathered. "In the 1810 [manuscript] version, the father comes with doctors and saves his daughter. He arranges a marriage for his daughter and punishes the wicked Queen. In the margin of their manuscript, the Grimms remarked: 'This ending is not quite right and is lacking something'" ("Who's" 14). The Queen herself seems cognizant of her guilt, as well as of the terrible fate that awaits her. When she receives her invitation to Snow White's wedding—and thus realizes that the young girl has been revived once again— she lets "loose a curse" and becomes "so petrified with fear" that she doesn't "know what to do" (89).

Significantly, fairy tales like "Snow White" are not the only genre of children's literature that embody adult frustrations with and even rage toward young people. Nicholas Tucker, in his examination of lullabies, characterizes the lyrics to some of these songs as nothing less than "exercises in controlled hatred" (21). Unable to soothe their children to sleep with gentle lyrics and calming melodies, exasperated mothers turn to threats. The following British lullaby stands as a poignant example:

Baby, baby, naughty baby,
Hush, you squalling thing, I say.
Peace this moment, peace, or maybe
Bonaparte will pass this way.

Baby, baby, he's a giant,
Tall and black as Rouen steeple,
And he breakfasts, dines, rely on't,
Every day on naughty people.

Baby, baby, if he hears you,
As he gallops past the house,
Limb from limb at once he'll tear you,
Just as pussy tears a mouse.

And he'll beat you, beat you, beat you,
And he'll beat you all to pap,
And he'll eat you, eat you, eat you,
Every morsel snap, snap, snap. (Opie and Opie 59)

As Tucker observes, "given that no other audience is intended for these occasions, a mother on her own can be fairly uninhibited in what she croons to her infant in the combination of hushed voice and personal privacy most appropriate to singing a baby to sleep" (18). Moreover, he continues, "whether a baby actually understands such threats is not the point; it is the vicarious relief to the mother, putting her anger into such punitive phrases, that is important here" (21).

This phenomenon is far from unusual. The lyrics of many other common bedtime songs often voice hostile wishes or even speak of physical violence toward children. These elements form the basis for what Lucy Rollin characterizes as "the single most transmitted [lullaby] rhyme in the canon, offered by mother to infant, generation after generation, for centuries" in both England and the United States: "Rock-a-bye baby" (107). The lyrics recount an infant plummeting if not to its death, then surely to some gross bodily harm:

> Rock-a-bye baby, on the treetop,
> When the wind blows, the cradle will rock,
> When the bough breaks, the cradle will fall,
> And down will come baby, cradle and all. (McCaskey 67)

Echoing Tucker's conclusions, Rollin asserts that "the aggressive words of many lullabies help the beleaguered mother vent her frustration" (107). Such lyrics, along with their counterparts in print and visual culture, "reassure artist and spectator alike that healthy people can contemplate their anxieties without losing control of them" (106).

In Kate DiCamillo's novel *The Tale of Desperaux*, a character observes that "stories are light"; they are told to "save you from the darkness" (270). In the case of "Snow White," this comment may be more accurate than we realized. As Zipes notes, fairy tales were one of the myriad ways of teaching children that "society conditioned and punished young people if they did not conform to proper rules" (*Subversion* 120). The harsh reality of child murder, however, suggests that the psychological attraction, transgressive appeal, and cautionary messages of "Snow White" may be directed more at men and women than boys and girls.

On the opening page of *I Could a Tale Unfold: Violence, Horror and Sensa-*

tionalism in Stories for Children, P. M. Pickard poses the provocative question: "Do children need horror stories? If so, how much and how soon?" (1). While Pickard never offers a definitive answer to this question, the high incidence of filicide in both fact and fantasy, coupled with the adult origins of "Snow White," suggests that whether or not American children need horror stories depicting violence and even homicide, their mothers and fathers do.

CHAPTER TWO

"The Queen Had Only One Way of Settling All Difficulties . . . 'Off with His Head!'"

Alice's Adventures in Wonderland *and the Antigallows Movement*

> What have I done that you think it such fun
> To indulge in the pleasure of slaughter.
> CHARLES LUTWIDGE DODGSON, "The Two Brothers" (1853)

Of all the villainous characters in children's literature, the Queen of Hearts from Lewis Carroll's *Alice's Adventures in Wonderland* (1865) is one the most infamous. With her haughty attitude, volatile mood, and tempestuous personality, she has become arguably as well known as the book's title character. Even those who have never read Carroll's novel are likely familiar with her murderous refrain "off with their heads!"

Like "Snow White," *Alice's Adventures in Wonderland* is not an American narrative. As most readers are aware, it was written by an English author, intended for a British audience, and released by a London-based press. Almost immediately on the book's initial publication in 1865, however, it became an international success. As Donald Rackin notes, "Numerous North American editions and translations into a host of foreign languages during Carroll's lifetime" of both *Alice* and its sequel, *Through the Looking-Glass* (1871), "attest to the books' immediate popularity abroad. By the end of the Victorian age they were international classics" (20).

The following for *Alice's Adventures in Wonderland* in the United States remains among the most fanatical. A search of WorldCat reveals that hundreds of different editions of the book have been issued by American publishers over the years. In addition to being reprinted in its original form, Carroll's narrative has appeared in a myriad of alternative literary formats, including picture books, pop-ups, and annotated editions. There have also been sound recordings, dramatic renditions, and even musical scores encompassing styles from jazz to orchestral.* Finally, the tremendous success of feature-length film adaptations of Carroll's story—most notably, the animated version by Walt Disney in 1951 and, more recently, the live-action feature by Tim Burton in 2010—attest to the secure status of *Alice's Adventure in Wonderland* in the nation's popular culture. As American critic Roni Natov asserts in an article aptly titled "The Persistence of Alice," "Lewis Carroll's children's epics have been written about, dramatized, and illustrated from so many points of view that they are obviously among the great classics of all times" (38).

As readers both inside the United States and throughout the world are aware, the Queen's calls for various individuals to be put to death throughout *Alice's Adventures in Wonderland* inspires terror in the book's characters: the Hatter flees the courtroom without even stopping for his shoes in order to avoid her henchmen, the three playing-card gardeners paint white roses red in a futile attempt to assuage her anger, and the royal soldiers immediately cease whatever they are doing whenever she give an order, lest their execution be next. To be sure, when the Queen shouts at one point: " 'Now, I give you fair warning,' . . . stamping on the ground as she spoke; 'either you or your head must be off, and that in about half no time! Take your choice!' " (93), no characters question the veracity of this vow.

Far from a detail that is unique to Carroll's imaginary Wonderland, state-sanctioned executions were a vivid social reality and the subject of heated public controversy in England during the period when he composed *Alice*. Throughout the nineteenth century but especially during the 1860s, the efficacy and humanity of the practice were discussed in popular newspapers, by British citizens, and among elected officials. While some made a case for retaining this long-standing practice as an appropriate punishment for serious offenders, others argued for its abolition. To those who comprised what became known as the antigallows movement, execution was barbaric: it was a relic from Great Britain's less-enlightened past whose presence in contemporary culture was unwarranted. The debate over the death penalty was not

---

* For more information on this general phenomenon as well as for specific examples of the forms mentioned, see Brooker.

merely a fringe social subject; it occupied the sociopolitical center stage throughout the mid-nineteenth century, with individuals ranging from lawyers and judges to clergy and even writers weighing in on the issue. Literary celebrities Charles Dickens, William Makepeace Thackeray, and Coventry Patmore all wrote about capital punishment during their careers, condemning its brutality, chastising its capriciousness, and calling attention to its overall futility in deterring crime.

This chapter makes a case that, in *Alice's Adventures in Wonderland*, Lewis Carroll did so as well. State-sanctioned death sentences are a prominent feature of the narrative. The Queen may be the character who is most well known for ordering beheadings, but she is not the only one to do so: the Duchess, the King, and the dog, Fury, all call for executions at various points. Being condemned to death is so common a fate for the figures in Wonderland that, at one point, Alice notes how nearly everyone except herself and the King and Queen "were in custody and under sentences of execution" (94).

While hanging and not beheading "was by far the most common form of execution" in England, according to Richard Clark (11), the Queen's cry "off with their heads" evokes the linguistic roots of the term "capital punishment."* As the *Oxford English Dictionary* reveals, the word "capital" comes from the Latin "capitalis" for "regarding the head." Hence, the phrase "capital punishment" literally means "affecting, or involving loss of, the head or life" (*OED*). This etymology assumes added significance given Carroll's lifelong interest in word play, puns, and philology—elements that figure prominently in *Alice*.

Another level of cultural commentary can thus be elicited from Carroll's already rich text by rereading it in light of contemporaneous debates surrounding capital punishment. As Richard Kelly points out, ever since its initial publication, the narrative has been "the treasure of philosophers, literary critics, biographers, clergymen, psychoanalysts, and linguists, not to mention mathematicians, theologians, and logicians" (78). Given the variety of subjects addressed in the text, Kelly aptly concludes that "there appears to be

---

*As Clark goes on to reveal, the reason that this means was preferred over others was simple: "It became the normal method because it was convenient, not excessively cruel and could be carried out anywhere upon either individual prisoners or groups by unskilled executioners" (11). Clark speculates that hanging was introduced to the region that would become Great Britain by the Saxons in the sixth century (11).

something in *Alice* for everyone, and there are almost as many explanations of the work as there are commentators" (78). This chapter uncovers the presence of yet another topic: criminal law. Through the characters of the King, Queen and Duchess, Carroll does not simply matter-of-factly present capital punishment; as with the other facets of Victorian life that he addresses, he offers a satirical portrayal of it. The frequent, impulsive, and often unfounded calls for various individuals to be executed throughout the narrative lampoon this long-standing British legal policy and civic practice. Rather than presenting the death penalty as sage and serious, *Alice* portrays it as ridiculous and unreasonable. In so doing, Carroll reveals that elements of nonsense are not limited to the seemingly socially vacuous realm of literature for children; they permeate even the most sober and serious facets of adult society.

These details complicate common historical views about Carroll's engagement with Victorian views of children and childhood. As Marah Gubar remarks, critics have long argued that *Alice's Adventures in Wonderland* subscribes to the era's emerging conception of young people as pure, innocent, and blissfully ignorant of the problems in the adult world and to the idea that it is the responsibility of children's literature to maintain this state (vii). The centrality of capital punishment in *Alice*, however, calls such beliefs into question. Instead of seeking to shelter his juvenile readers from adult issues like state-sanctioned execution, Carroll introduces them to it, educates them about it, and even calls them into action on its behalf. In so doing, *Alice's Adventures in Wonderland* demonstrates the desirability of fully acculturating children and the powerful social agency that they can possess as a result of being politically aware. Alice's outburst in the final few moments of the story, "Stuff and Nonsense!," that eradicates the murderous Queen of Hearts reveals that far from protecting children from the problem of capital punishment Carroll positions them as a vital part of the solution. Moreover, in the United States where judicial execution is still lawful on a federal and, in many regions, a state level, Carroll's meditation on its merit forms a possible and previously overlooked locus of national interest in the text. Many of the criticisms raised in *Alice* about the practice—from its cruelty to its capriciousness—mirror both past and present debates about capital punishment in the United States.

"Every Page of Our Statute-Book Smelt of Blood": Capital Punishment, the Bloody Code, and the Antigallows Movement in England

With a lifetime spanning from 1832 to 1898, Charles Lutwidge Dodgson—better known by his pen name Lewis Carroll—witnessed one of the most bloody, controversial, and transformative periods in the history of capital punishment in Great Britain. Challenging perceptions of Georgian and Victorian England as a demure and even decorous place, "execution remained a central fact of English life during the late eighteenth and early nineteenth centuries" (Meranze 374). The death penalty was not only imposed frequently but it was also carried out publicly, with executions taking place in the town square, at the scene of the crime, or outside the walls of the local jail.

Such gruesome events were an all-too-common occurrence throughout Britain. According to V. A. C. Gatrell, in England and Wales alone between 1770 and 1830, citizens witnessed "between 6,322 and 7,713 executions—probably nearer the higher total than the lower" (618). Conventional wisdom might suggest that as British society progressed its use of brutal practices like the death penalty would decrease, but the opposite was actually true. "From 1805 to 1830, prosecutions for capital crimes in England and Wales increased almost 300 percent" (Meranze 374). As such statistics suggest, the death penalty was anything but a marginal social practice. According to historian Harry Potter, "capital punishment was a constant and growing part of English criminal justice" (2). Indeed, in one form or another throughout Carroll's life "execution loomed over England" (Meranze 374).

Great Britain did not witness so many men and women put to death during the Georgian and Victorian periods because its population was exceptionally criminal; rather, the death penalty flourished because of the penal code at the time was particularly harsh. As Potter relates, "In 1688 there had been only fifty capital offenses in England, over forty of which were statutory additions to the small common law quota of treason, murder, arson, robbery, and grand larceny" (4). With the passage of the Waltham Black Act in 1723, however, the number of crimes punishable by death increased exponentially. In the words of Auberon Waugh, the new legislation "made practically everything a capital offense" (19). For example, "all felonies except petty larceny and mayhem (maiming) were capital" (Potter 4). In addition, many property offenses, including stealing sheep, horses, or cattle, as well as poaching one of the king's deer or rabbits, were subject to the death penalty (Hay 51; Waugh 19; Potter 4).

Over time, more crimes were added to this list. By 1815, in fact, the number had ballooned to "over two hundred and twenty" (Potter 4). Many of these offenses were minor. Capital crimes in late Georgian and early Victorian England included such relatively harmless acts as the following: cutting down trees; stealing a loaf of bread; keeping the company of gypsies for one month; being out all night with a blackened face; damaging the Westminster Bridge; impersonating a Chelsea pensioner; stealing gathered or harvested fruit; pick-pocketing; forging birth, marriage, or baptism certificates; and shoplifting goods worth five shillings or more (Potter 6; Jacobson 11).

Given the sheer number of acts deemed capital offenses, "the end result was that the courts could hang anyone they felt like hanging" (Waugh 19). Waugh explains how this was usually accomplished: "If theft of a handker-chief was not specifically listed as a capital offense, they could charge the wretched felon with robbery after dark, or in a public place, or conspiracy to rob, and string him up just the same" (19). And "string people up" they did. In the words of Gatrell, "In theory, a Londoner growing up in the 1780s could by 1840 have attended some four hundred execution days outside Newgate alone, discounting other locations. If he was unimaginably diligent he could have watched 1,200 people hang (and there were such obsessives)" (32). By the 1820s, a decade before Carroll's birth, death sentences had become so common that British officials calculated that "if you hanged all of the con-demned, you would have to hang four people every day of the year, excluding Sundays" (Gatrell 21). In light of the large number of crimes punishable by death and the thousands of men and women executed for them, the criminal laws during this era earned the pejorative nickname "the Bloody Code." Sam-uel Johnson wrote that these statutes gave rise to an "indiscriminate judicial massacre" (qtd. in Potter 10). Indeed, in a observation that was as macabre as it was true, Charles Philips declared in 1857 that "every page of our statute-book smelt of blood" (qtd. in Gatrell 11).

After generations of operating under what Phil Handler calls this "mono-lithic mass of draconian measures" ("Forging" 250), English law in the decade of Lewis Carroll's birth gradually saw the repeal of the Bloody Code: "Piece-meal reform gave way to a series of sweeping measures that removed the death penalty from the vast majority of felonies" (Handler "Law" 195). The Punishment of Death Act, passed the year Carroll was born, marked the first major turning point. The act reduced the number of capital offenses from over two hundred to around sixty (R. Clark). In its wake, an array of additional statutes were enacted that limited the application of the death penalty even further. By 1861, capital offenses had been reduced to a mere four: "murder, treason, piracy with violence, and arson in Her Majesty's dockyards" (Potter 43).

In spite of this vast reduction in capital crimes, executions still numbered well into the hundreds. According to Gatrell, between 1837 and 1868 in England and Wales, more than 340 men and women were hanged for the crime of murder alone (594). Although representing only a fraction of the total put to death during the height of the Bloody Code, he observes that "this number was enough to ensure that executions remained a familiar urban spectacle" (594).

British citizens were doing more than simply reconsidering the broad issue of which offenses ought to be punishable by death during the Victorian era; they were also reexamining the practice of public execution itself. For centuries, the rationale for hanging individuals in full view of the community was that their deaths would serve as a powerful deterrent to others who might be contemplating similar crimes. As Sir Francis Buller infamously informed one thief in the late eighteenth century, "You are to be hanged not for stealing horses, but that horses may not be stolen" (qtd. in Potter 1). Capital punishment was a means to showcase the power of the state, inspire terror in the individuals who witnessed the execution, and thus promote good civic behavior. As Michel Foucault has remarked on the subject, "The public execution is a ceremonial by which a momentarily injured sovereign is reconstituted" (9). Capital punishment called attention to "the dissymmetry between the subject who has dared to violate the law and the all-powerful sovereign who displays his strength" (23). For this reason, Foucault asserts that "the public execution did not re-establish justice; it reactivated power" (48–49).

Victorian Britons would have agreed. "A Tory solicitor general said in 1830 that 'he thought the appalling punishment of death, executed as it was with so much ignominy in the public streets, where criminals were suspended before a gazing populace, was greatly calculated to deter men from the commission of crime'" (McGowen "Powerful" 316). A powerful indication of the era's overarching belief in the positive influence of hangings, was the fact that "people took their children to see the criminal executed and learn a moral lesson" ("Victorian England" 336).

The actual atmosphere at most executions, however, was markedly different. Far from somber and serious moments, "they were scenes of carnival and public holiday, where the most extravagant and ostentatious villains were cheered and toasted, and only certain categories of offenders were booed. More particularly, they were traditionally the favourite hunting ground of pickpockets and footpads" (Waugh 19). By the mid-nineteenth century, such drunken, unruly, and irreverent behavior had become a widespread cause for concern. In July 1840, for example, novelist Charles Dickens was appalled by the behavior of the crowd at the execution of Francois Courvoisier. As a consequence, Gatrell reports,

> Dickens recommended ending public execution not out of pity for the victim but to deny the crowd occasion for its "odious" levity. Attending Courvoisier's hanging in 1840, he saw in the audience no "emotion suitable to the occasion. . . . No sorrow, no salutary terror, no abhorrence, no seriousness; nothing but ribaldry, debauchery, levity, drunkenness, and flaunting vice in fifty other shapes." (59–60)

A few years later, poet and critic Coventry Patmore went even further. He argued that, far from deterring the crowd from crime, witnessing an execution actually inspired delinquent and often violent behavior. In a poem called "The Murderer's Sacrament" (1845), he offered the following unflattering description of the scaffold audience:

> Mother held up their babes to see
> Who spread their hands, and crow'd for glee; . . .
>
> .   .   .   .
>
> A baby strung its doll to a stick
> A mother raised the pretty trick
> Two children caught and hanged a cat
> Two friends walk'd on, in lively chat;
> And two, who had disputed places,
> Went forth to fight, with murderous faces. (qtd. in Gatrell 56–57)

In light of the numerous problems associated with public hangings, critics like Patmore and Dickens argued that they should be conducted privately. By moving executions behind prison walls, officials could dictate the composition of the audience and, more importantly, the atmosphere surrounding the event. As Annulla Linders has written, "The construction of private audiences became a matter of not only controlling the class and gender composition of those invited to watch, but also of producing appropriate emotional responses to the execution" (626). "Professional men," for example, could be invited specifically because "they could be trusted not to defile the moment with coarseness, laughter, and eagerness" (Linders 629).

For some British subjects, however, the problem with capital punishment was not rooted in the composition of the audience; it lay with the practice itself. As Gatrell reports, whether the scaffold was used publically or placed behind the confines of the prison walls, "People did not die on it neatly . . . they urinated, defecated, screamed, kicked, fainted, and choked as they died" (vii). Mistakes and mishaps were also common: "Sometimes the rope snapped or the cross-beam fell loose" (Gatrell 50). In such cases, the condemned had to endure an agonizing wait while repairs were made and they could be hanged for a second time. Other problems were more serious. For example, if the length of rope used to hang them was too long, the jerking force on the noose would be strong enough to cause decapitation, a gruesome and bloody scene. Conversely, if the length of rope was too short, the drop would not break their neck and cause instant death. Instead, the condemned would die slowly and painfully by strangulation, a process that "could take up to 30 minutes" (R. Clark 20). During the course of this slow asphyxiation, it was not uncommon for the condemned to thrash violently around, gasping for air and even desperately trying to hook their legs on the scaffold, hoist themselves up, and obtain some relief. Clark documents the case of one condemned woman who did not die instantly when the trap door released: "People in the crowd, her friends perhaps, hung on her legs to shorten her sufferings, a not unusual occurrence" (20).

Even when an execution went according to plan, it was a ghastly sight. Although the prisoners wore hoods to cover their faces, attempts to shield those viewing the execution from the horror were futile. As a newspaper account reported after one hanging, the condemned man's "protruding tongue and swollen distorted features [were] discernible under their thin white cotton covering, as if they were part of some hideous masquerade" (qtd. in Gatrell 46).

Such gruesome sights prompted many men and women to conclude that judicial murder was no different from criminal murder. As a consequence, they made a case for the complete abolition of capital punishment and alternative means of punishing offenders: via monetary fines, property forfeiture, or—echoing the newest idea in criminal justice—a period of incarceration.

As Louis Masur has argued, these proposals signaled the beginning of a shift in societal attitudes about both the causes of crime and the purpose of punishment. Whereas civic transgressions had formerly been seen as resulting from an individual's innate depravity, they were now being viewed as the product of free will. Similarly, while the primary purpose of punishment had long been retributive—a means for the state to reassert its authority—it was now being recast as rehabilitative, as a method to reform the individual and restore him or her to society as a law-abiding citizen (Masur 5). Capital punishment stood in contradistinction to both of these sentiments; state-sanctioned executions sent the message that some citizens were either beyond rehabilitation or were not worth the effort. For those in the antigallows movement, neither standpoint was acceptable. As McGowen puts it, "In their minds, death was quite simply inconsistent with the values of a humane civilization" ("Civilizing" 259).

While Enlightenment-inspired beliefs in proportionality, humanity, and even mercy formed the foundation of the revised penal code in Great Britain, those who subscribed to them remained in the minority for the duration of the nineteenth century. As the Victorian era progressed, the antigallows movement steadily lost members and, as a result, cultural momentum. McGowen records this shift: "Whereas in the 1840s the abolition of the gallows had been a popular cause with intellectuals, by the 1860s most writers supported capital punishment" ("Civilizing" 258). So, too, did the bulk of the British public. In fact, antigallows sentiments grew so low that "in 1862 the Society for the Abolition of Capital Punishment was so diminished that it had to suspend its operations several times owing to lack of support" (Potter 88). Great Britain would not abolish the death penalty until more than a century later, in 1968. Meanwhile, it would permit public execution until 1868.

As a consequence, capital punishment remained a central facet of Victorian life. V. A. C. Gatrell has written that the practice was not simply an integral part of British criminal law; it was "also embedded in the collective imagination, the subject of anxiety, defence, and denial, of jokes, ballads, images, and satire" among its citizens (32). In this way, while the scaffold may have physically constituted a simple wooden structure, it culturally embodied a far more powerful sociopolitical institution.

"A Stern Critic of Personal Behavior and Social Conduct": Lewis Carroll on Current Events, Religious Convictions, and Moral Debates

While Lewis Carroll never explicitly wrote about capital punishment in any of his extant poems, diaries, letters, essays, or books, it seems likely that he was aware of the issue and the debates surrounding it. The author had sustained interest in current social, political, and cultural events. As biographer Morton Cohen has recounted, "Although [Carroll] worked hard at his profession, he did not altogether neglect the larger world, as most Oxford academics were inclined to do" (71). On the contrary, letters and diary entries from the time he was a young man are filled with commentary about happenings both at home and abroad. Derek Hudson, for instance, has discussed Carroll's various comments concerning the Crimean War. Likewise, Cohen has documented the way in which the question of Irish independence preoccupied him throughout his life. Some matters even inspired Carroll to compose an editorial for the local newspaper or write a letter to Parliament.* Through these and other actions, he developed a reputation as having an "uncompromising moral stance" (Cohen 308). As Cohen puts it, Carroll "kept a critical eye on the life of his college, his university, his society, and the world. When he uncovered ugliness or injustice, he put his pen to paper and wrote scathing attacks and proposed reasonable remedies" (386).

Another equally probable point of contact with contemporaneous debates concerning capital punishment was Lewis Carroll's voracious reading. At the time of his death, a catalogue of his library revealed hundreds of volumes ranging from works of literature, history, geography, philosophy, linguistics, and religion to politics, biology, philology, natural science, classics, and economics (J. Stern 17–44). Significantly, one of his favorite novelists was also one of the most outspoken critics of the death penalty: Charles Dickens (Kelly 19; Arnoldi 91).

Carroll's love for Dickens was rivaled only by his love for the British humor

---

*In March 1882, for example, Carroll's essay on parliamentary cloture appeared in the *St. James Gazette* (Cohen 425). Meanwhile, in the 1880s and 1890s, he wrote various members of Parliament about issues ranging from the best method for curbing the outbreak of fires in London and the need for legislation establishing an eight-hour work day to his views on how officials ought to structure the rules for a major lawn tennis tournament and his firm belief that "'Members of the Government of either House be allowed to appear in the other, to answer questions, and join in discussion'" (Cohen 425, 483–84).

magazine *Punch*. Founded in 1841, the weekly publication contained articles, essays, and cartoons that offered comic and often satirical commentary on current events. As Frankie Morris has documented, "Carroll had been a *Punch* reader since his teens" (139); he would remain one for the rest of his life. Of course, when Carroll was looking for an artist to illustrate *Alice's Adventures in Wonderland*, he turned to a member of the *Punch* staff, John Tenniel. As Morris notes, "In a letter in late 1863 [Carroll] asked *Punch* writer Tom Taylor to see if the famed cartoonist would be open to drawing 'a dozen wood-cuts' for him, acknowledging, 'Of all artists on wood I should prefer Mr. Tenniel'" (139).

Over the years, *Punch* published numerous articles addressing the issue of capital punishment. In an antigallows piece from 26 July 1856, for example, the magazine asserted that a bishop officiating at a recent hanging would be "better employed in the vineyard of his master, than in the ropeyard of the Judges" (qtd. in Potter 85). Another essay that appeared the following year ridiculed the role of the clergy and its confidence in being able to reform the condemned, concluding that "the attention paid by the convict to the discourses of his spiritual advisor 'was about equal to the pleasure which he derived from them'" (Potter 53). And in 1849 illustrator John Leech penned a cartoon for *Punch* after accompanying Charles Dickens to the hanging of husband-and-wife killers Mr. and Mrs. Manning that satirized the common belief that public executions served as a solemn object lesson. Leech's illustration, titled "The Great Moral Lesson at Horsemonger Gaol, Nov 13," did not even depict the gallows; instead, it showcased the disorderly conduct, disrespectful manner, and drunken merrymaking of the audience (see Gatrell 607). Morris has commented about the powerful influence that the humor magazine had on Lewis Carroll's views: "A devotee of *Punch* from his teens, Carroll would come to agree with many of the paper's positions" (206).

Carroll's viewpoint on any social issue was also always powerfully influenced by his profound Christian faith. The eldest son of an archdeacon in the Anglican Church, the famed children's author was a devout man.* In fact, in late 1861, he even took deacon's orders.† Carroll's letters and diaries are filled with passages documenting his ongoing struggle with sin, his ardent desire to

---

* For an informative overview of the secular life, religious views and ministerial career of the elder Charles Dodson, see I. Davis.

† Admittedly, ordination was a requirement for all Oxford dons during this time. But it is clear that taking holy orders was more than merely a professional obligation for Carroll; it was also an act that he took both willingly and very seriously. As Martin Gardner has written "There is no doubt about the depth and sincerity of his Church of England views" (xvi).

do God's will, and his earnest ruminations about the true meaning of scrip-
ture. These personal qualities were vividly evident in his sermons. "'Under-
graduates flocked to hear him . . . ,' Michael Sadler, Christ Church steward,
wrote. 'He wept when he came to the more serious parts of the sermons'"
(Cohen 293). Another student echoed such sentiments: "'His sermons were
picturesque in style,' wrote T. B. Strong, 'and strongly emotional. . . . They
came from real and sincere devotion'" (qtd. in Cohen 294).

Lewis Carroll, however, did not blindly absorb Christian dogma. Instead,
as he explained in a letter to friend Mary Brown in December 1889, he
believed that individuals must carefully consider questions of right and wrong
and conduct themselves in accordance with their convictions, even if those
beliefs differed from convention (Cohen 373). At numerous points throughout his life, Carroll made comments about the nature of Christianity and the
proper deportment of its followers that could be extrapolated to the question
of capital punishment. In a letter from June 1889, for example, he passionately
argued against the Anglican Church's belief in eternal punishment (Cohen
362). Carroll believed that the essence of Christian thought and practice was
simple: "He detest[ed] theological controversy most of all because it goes
contrary to Christ's teaching and his own belief that instead of contending,
Christians should practice self-denial and love" (Cohen 352).

Years earlier, Carroll had articulated his conviction about the sanctity of all
life and his equally strong repugnance for cruelty toward any living thing. In
the 1870s, he fact, he wrote a series of editorials denouncing the practice of
vivisection. One of Carroll's central points in these articles was whether
"vivisection, if practiced on animals, will not, in time, lead to experiments
with human beings" (qtd. in Cohen 391). Significantly, among the various
classes of individuals that the author identified as being particularly vulnerable to such inhumane treatment were criminals (Cohen 391–92). Mirroring
a common critique of capital punishment at the time, Carroll was concerned
that vivisection had a corrupting influence, desensitizing individuals to the
suffering of others. In his view, mankind "is constructed with enough of the
'wild beast' in him to enable vivisectors to grow accustomed to inflicting pain
without qualms, to become ensnared in the process, and ultimately to take
pleasure in it" (qtd. in Cohen 392). In a powerful indication of how deeply
concerned Carroll was about the practice of vivisection, Stuart Dodgson Col-
lingworth noted that his normally shy uncle who shrank from the public

spotlight and often even vociferously denied that he was the famous children's author signed the article with his well-known pseudonym "in order that whatever influence or power his writings had gained him might tell in the controversy" (166).

Although this overview is brief, it affirms Cohen's characterization of Carroll as a "stern critic of personal behavior and social conduct, especially in matters concerning religion" (370). Even when it was unpopular or even socially unacceptable, he was "a man who thought carefully, deeply, and constantly about what is right and wrong, who asked all the crucial questions about life and death, good and evil, seeking answers from congenial guides, and ultimately tested and shaped his faith and destiny" (Cohen 372).

"Come, I'll Take No Denial: We Must Have the Trial": Lampooning the Law in *Alice*

As Martin Gardner once pointed out, "No other books written for children are more in need of explication than the *Alice* books. Much of their wit is interwoven with Victorian events and customs unfamiliar to American readers today, and even to readers in England. Many jokes in the book could be appreciated only by Oxford residents and others were private jokes intended solely for Alice" (xxiii). References to real people, places, or events in Carroll's life are often embedded in character names, plot details, and poems and songs.* Given the prevalence of allusions, Jan Susina has asserted that *Alice's Adventures in Wonderland* "is a text firmly rooted in the codes and conventions of the Victorian period" (33). Indeed, in the words of Gardner, Carroll's narrative was "written

---

*For example, the names that Carroll chose for his central characters were coded references to participants on the rowing expedition on 4 July 1862 during which he first told the tale: Alice, of course, for Alice Liddell, the story's muse and dedicatee; Lory, for her older sister, Lorinda Liddell; the Eagle, for the younger sibling Edith Liddell; the Duck, for Reverend Robinson Duckworth; and the Dodo for the Carroll himself, whose stutter often caused him to pronounce his real surname "Do-Do-Dodgson." Likewise, most of the poems and songs that appear throughout the narrative "are parodies of poems or popular songs that were well known to Carroll's contemporary readers" (Gardner 23n5). For example, when Alice recites "How doth the little crocodile / . . . How cheerfully he seems to grin, / How neatly he spreads his claws, / And welcomes little fishes in, / With gently smiling jaws!" (23) she is parodying a then well-known verse by Isaac Watts: "How doth the busy bee / Improve each shining hour, / And gather honey all the day / From every opening flower!" Finally, the chapter title "The Lobster-Quadrille" "is a play on 'Lancer's Quadrille,' a walking squared dance for eight to sixteen couples that was enormously popular in English ballrooms at the time" (Gardner 100n1). Similarly the simile "grin like a Cheshire cat" "was a common phrase in Carroll's day," appearing on signboards and even rounds of cheese (Gardner 61n3).

for British readers of another century, and we need to know a great many things that are not part of the text if we wish to capture its full wit and flavor" (xiii).

The book's discussion of criminal offenses and jury trials also benefit from such contextual decoding. *Alice* contains two formal judicial hearings, and—echoing many of the criticisms levied against Victorian legal system—both are farcical. The first hearing appears in the third chapter of the narrative, and it recounts the playtime prosecution of the Mouse by a dog named Fury. The trial begins casually and even capriciously. As the narrator reveals, it is spurred more by the dog's boredom than the rodent's misbehavior: "Fury said to a mouse, That he met in the house, 'Let us both go to law: I will prosecute you.— Come, I'll take no denial: We must have the trial; For really this morning I've nothing to do'" (34). The manner in which the hearing is conducted is even more ludicrous. As the Mouse points out to his canine accuser, "'Such a trial, dear sir, With no jury or judge, would be wasting our breath'" (34). The dog is undeterred, however, offering an easy if grossly unfair and inappropriate solution to this situation: "'I'll be judge, I'll be jury,' said cunning old Fury" (34).

Like other other scenes in *Alice*, this seemingly silly scenario reflects Victorian social reality. British criminal law had long been seen as fickle and flawed. Echoing the predicament of Carroll's Mouse, men and women were often sentenced "to the scaffolds or exile for puny as well as casually tried crimes" (Gatrell vi).*

This brief legal scenario foreshadows the lengthy trial that occupies the final two chapters of the book: the prosecution of the Knave for his alleged theft of the Queen's tarts. As Morris observes, from the very beginning, the proceeding "is a total travesty" (213):

> The twelve jurors were all writing very busily on slates. "What are they doing?" Alice whispered to the Gryphon. "They ca'n't have anything to put down yet, before the trial's begun."
>
> "They're putting down their names," the Gryphon whispered in reply, "for fear they should forget them before the end of the trial."
>
> "Stupid things!" Alice began in a loud indignant voice. (111)

---

*The trial segments are not the only ones that satirize judicial authority in Carroll's narrative. As Frankie Morris has written, Tenniel's illustration of the Caterpillar is evocative of a judge: "The Caterpillar's segmented back seems to separate from the shaded 'face' to form the curls of a full-bottomed wig such as Tenniel had frequently drawn for *Punch*" (213–14). Morris continues: "The creature's ample sleeve, falling back to show another sleeve beneath, suggests judicial raiment. In fact, our squint has revealed a veritable robed judge who interrogates Alice from the heights of a mushroom bench—'Who are *you*?' . . . 'What do you mean by that?' . . . 'Explain yourself'" (214).

Even worse, the jurors display a complete inability to distinguish relevant information from unimportant occurrences: "Alice could see, as well as if she were looking over their shoulders, that all of the jurors were writing down 'Stupid things!' on their slates, and she could even make out that one of them didn't know how to spell 'stupid,' and that he had to ask his neighbor to tell him. 'A nice muddle their slates'll be in, before the trial's over!' thought Alice" (111). When Alice takes a pencil away from one of the jurors because he is using it to make an annoying noise, he is both baffled and undeterred. The lizard "could not make out what had become of [the pencil]; so, after hunting all about for it, he was obliged to write with one finger for the rest of the day; and this was of very little use, as it left no mark on the slate" (112).

Rather than becoming more competent as the trial progresses, the jurors seemingly become more incompetent. When the Hatter, March Hare, and Dormouse debate the day on which the tea party commenced—citing the fourteenth, fifteenth, and sixteenth of March, respectively—the King has to order them to make a note of these important dates. Even so, the reason for keeping this record continues to elude them. As the narrator notes, "the jury eagerly wrote down all three dates on their slates, and then added them up, and reduced the answer to shillings and pence" (113).

Once again, these details reflect various criticisms levied against the British legal system during the nineteenth century. Sally Lloyd-Bostock and Cheryl Thomas explain that while the sanctity of trial by jury was "burnt into the consciousness of every Englishman" (10), the fitness of jurors was often called into question. "In 1848, for example, the editors of the *Times* commented that at the Assizes held at Monmouth 'the composition of common jury lists seems to be conducted on the principle of selecting the most uneducated and incompetent persons to be found in the respective counties with the requisite qualifications'" (qtd. in Hanly 265). Such sentiments were echoed by various legal experts. An article that appeared in the serial *Jurist* "regretted that juries were usually composed of 'persons with scarcely sufficient education to understand the ordinary conversational language of educated men, and quite incapable of any close or acute reasoning'" (qtd. in Hanly 265).* In light of the absurdist nature of the jury in *Alice*, Michael

---

* As Conor Hanley records, some articles went even further in their criticisms. An editorial that was printed in the *Law Times* in 1848 compared the jury to "a quack doctor" (265). Meanwhile, a journalistic piece that appeared that same year in the *Times* railed against the "'blunder-headed stupidity' of juries" (qtd. in Hanley 265n87).

Hancher has commented on the seeming symbolism encoded in the specific animals that Tenniel chose to represent the jurors. As he points out, one of them is a parrot (37).

The incompetence of the jurors in *Alice* is exceeded only by that of the judge. First, reflecting the historical reality that "until the Revolution of 1688–89, judges held their offices at the pleasure of the Crown, and were regarded as Crown servants" (Hanly 255), it is the King himself who officiates at the Knave's trial. Carroll details the many legal, ethical, and procedural problems that arise when the monarch is also the adjudicator. Lacking any formal legal training, the King commits many gaffes. For instance, immediately after the White Rabbit finishes reading the accusation, he asks the jury to render their decision: "'Consider your verdict,' the King said to the jury" (112). Luckily, the White Rabbit intervenes: "'Not yet, not yet!' the Rabbit hastily interrupted. 'There's a great deal to come before that!'" (112).

One essential aspect of any trial, of course, is the hearing of testimony. Throughout this process in *Alice*, however, the King repeatedly interrupts, insults, and even intimidates the witnesses. As the narrator notes, after numerous such threats, "the wretched Hatter trembled so, that he shook off both shoes" (114). The following chapter, when Alice herself is called to testify, builds on such criticisms. Before taking the stand, the young girl is informed that she is in violation of "Rule Forty-Two," which dictates height limitations for witnesses. Alice protests the rule and, in so doing, reveals its contrived nature:

> "Well, I sha'n't go [out of the courtroom], at any rate," said Alice: "besides: that's not a regular rule: you invented it just now."
>
> "It's the oldest rule in the book," said the King.
>
> "Then it ought to be Number One," said Alice.
>
> The King turned pale, and shut his note-book. (120)

As before, the points Alice makes reflect common criticisms of the bench at the time. Conor Hanly documents the battles over what he calls "judicial amateurism" (264), noting that "legal education was in a poor state in the first third of the nineteenth century" and that many judges lacked formal training (263). As a result, magistrates consciously or unconsciously committed various mishandlings of justice. Commenting on such abuses, an article that appeared in the *Times* in 1850 lamented how the "mere pantomimical expression of disgust or incredulity on the part of the presiding magistrate will be sufficient to neutralize the hypothesis of an advocate or to shake the testimony of a witness" (qtd. in Hanly 259). In some courtrooms, such behavior became so egregious that the atmosphere was likened to a "petty tyranny" (Hanly 268)—a characterization that aptly describes the environment created by the judge-King in *Alice*.

Before the trial of the Knave concludes, *Alice* lampoons other aspects of the legal system. For instance, when one of the guinea pig jurors erupts in an inappropriate cheer, the creature is "immediately suppressed by the court" (115). With typical Carrollian humor, the author includes the following parenthetical aside: "As this is a rather hard word, I will just explain to you how it is done. They had a large canvas bag, which tied up at the mouth with strings: into this they slipped the guinea-pig, head first, and then sat upon it" (115). Underscoring the way in which the fictional narrative parodies factual elements of Victorian life, Carroll provides a rare reference to the world outside of Wonderland:

> "I'm glad I've seen that done," thought Alice. "I've so often read in the newspapers, at the end of trials, 'There was some attempt at applause, which was immediately suppressed by the officers of the court,' and I never understood what it meant until now." (115)

In 1857, Charles Philips proclaimed that the "sanguinary system" of criminal justice in Great Britain "is sure to exasperate the popular patience" (qtd. in Gatrell 11). Whether or not Lewis Carroll was "exasperated" by the failings of English jury trial, the satiric humor in *Alice* certainly suggests that he was amused by them.

"They're Dreadfully Fond of Beheading People Here": Critiquing Capital Punishment Inside— and Outside—of Wonderland

The two trials presented in *Alice* are more than simply criminal cases; they are capital ones. As Fury informs the Mouse: "I'll be judge, I'll be jury. . . . I'll try the whole cause, and condemn you to death" (34). Moreover, that the Knave of Hearts is facing execution for the theft of the Queen's tarts seems to be an allusion to the fact that many petty property crimes carried the penalty of death during the height of the Bloody Code.

Far from being limited to these two legal scenarios, capital punishment as both a legal policy and civic practice permeates *Alice's Adventures in Wonder-*

land. For example, in chapter 4, Alice learns why the White Rabbit is so frantically searching for his missing gloves. She overhears the harried hare "muttering to itself, 'The Duchess! The Duchess! Oh my dear paws! Oh my fur and whiskers! She'll get me executed, as sure as ferrets are ferrets!'" (37). The expression "as sure as ferrets are ferrets" gives this remark an added criminal innuendo. As the *Oxford English Dictionary* reveals, the term "ferret" was slang during the nineteenth century for a "dunning tradesman," a "pawnbroker" or, more bluntly, a "thief."

When Alice finally meets the Duchess, she discovers that the White Rabbit has good cause to be alarmed, for the noblewoman is fond of commanding that individuals be put to death. After the young girl points out the astronomical fact that "the earth takes twenty-four hours to turn round on its axis," the sound of her final word prompts the Duchess to threaten her life. For seemingly no reason whatsoever, she erupts, screaming, "Talking of axes . . . chop off her head!" (61).

The King is likewise fond of threatening individuals with execution. When the Hatter is testifying during the trial of the Knave of Hearts, the male monarch barks, "Give your evidence, . . . and don't be nervous, or I'll have you executed on the spot" (113). This threat is reiterated several times. Shortly after this first confrontation with the Hatter, for example, the King repeats his demand: "'Give your evidence . . . or I'll have you executed, whether you're nervous or not'" (114). Then, a few moments later, when the Hatter is unable to recall a conversation he had with the Dormouse, the King warns: "You *must* remember . . . or I'll have you executed" (115; italics in original).

Of all the characters who order executions, however, the Queen of Hearts is the most infamous. As the narrator says of Her Majesty, "The Queen had only one way of settling all difficulties, great or small. 'Off with his head!' she said without even looking round" (87). The narrator's remark is far from hyperbole. When Alice is unable to identify some members in the royal procession, the monarch becomes incensed: "The Queen turned crimson with fury, and after glaring at her for a moment like a wild beast, began screaming 'Off with her head!'" (82). Then when Her Majesty learns that the playing-card gardeners have mistakenly planted white roses when she requested red, she decides that death is the only appropriate penalty for this blunder: "Off with their heads!" (83). During the croquet match, this pronouncement becomes even more common. As the narrator reveals, "in a very short time the Queen was in a furious passion, and went stamping about, and shouting 'Off with his head!' or "Off with her head!' about once a minute" (85). Carroll's narrative takes historical critiques of the overly expansive list of capital crimes even further, since the offenses that the condemned have allegedly committed are not merely trivial but often purely imaginary, existing as crimes only in the Queen's mind.* For example, Alice hears the monarch "sentence three of the players to be executed for having missed their turns" (87). Likewise, she threatens the Duchess with execution for simply commenting that it is a nice day (93). Finally, she orders the Cheshire Cat to be executed for seemingly no reason whatsoever; perhaps for simply appearing in her line of sight.

Although the King serves as the officiating judge during the trial of the Knave, the Queen does not relinquish her authority to order executions. The Hatter avoids being beheaded by His Majesty while testifying, but he is quickly sentenced to death by *Her* Majesty upon being dismissed: "'You may go,' said the King. . . . '—and just take off his head outside,' the Queen added to one of the officers" (116). Similarly, when the Dormouse comments during the testimony of the Cook, he too ignites the monarch's ire: "'Collar that Dormouse!' the Queen shrieked out. 'Behead the Dormouse! Turn that Dormouse out of court! Suppress him! Pinch him! Off with his whiskers!'" (117).

Together with these explicit references, capital punishment also appears in more subtle and coded ways in Carroll's narrative. When Alice first arrives in Wonderland, the White Rabbit mistakes her for his servant girl. The hare calls "out to her, in an angry tone, 'Why Mary Ann, what *are* you doing out here?'" (37–38; italics in original). "Mary Ann" was both a widely known British euphemism for a "servant girl" and—as *Brewer's Dictionary of Phrase and Fable* notes—a slang term for the guillotine (674). The name acquired this meaning around the time of the French Revolution and, given the frequent calls for beheadings in the text, this association would likely have come to mind for Carroll's original readership.

Given the fondness for ordering executions in Wonderland, it comes as no surprise that roughly thirty minutes from the start of the croquet match, "all the players, except the King, the Queen and Alice, were in custody and under sentences of execution" (94). This situation affirms the young protagonist's

---

*The one exception to this phenomenon is the Duchess being placed under sentence of death for, as the White Rabbit reveals to Alice, "boxing the Queen's ears" (84). Given that the noblewoman assaulted the monarch, this act of insubordination could be viewed as treason.

previous observation, "They're dreadfully fond of beheading people here: the great wonder is, that there's any one left alive!" (87).

The repeated reference to state-sanctioned executions gives new meaning to the age that Carroll chose for his title character. Peter Heath has called Alice "the best-known seven-year-old in literature" (3). The author's decision to make his protagonist seven when the real-life Alice Liddell was ten at the time he wrote the story has been the source of much speculation by critics and biographers. Gardner, for example, points out that "the number forty-two held a special meaning for Carroll. . . . [A]nd seven is a factor of forty-two" (120). Meanwhile, the entry for the author in *The Oxford Companion to Fairy Tales* suggests that "perhaps Dodgson wistfully regarded [seven years old] as the perfect age in Alice Liddell" ("Lewis Carroll" 88).

Rereading the story in light of the history of capital punishment in Great Britain offers another possible explanation for this decision. Richard Clark explains that throughout the late eighteenth and into the nineteenth centuries "there was a different concept of the criminal responsibility of children and at this time the age of criminal responsibility of children was originally just seven. The law did not see children as distinct from adults until much later (1933) and . . . still mandated the death sentence for children above the age of seven convicted of a capital felony" (106). While the lives of many juveniles were spared through pardons or commuted sentences, they were nonetheless *eligible* for the gallows. Clark recounts numerous cases of adolescents who were executed during the Victorian period for crimes ranging from murder and rape to arson and discharging a firearm (106–17). Moreover, given that the "legal requirement to register a birth" was not mandated in Great Britain until 1837—coupled with the fact that many jails did not record the age of those hanged on the gallows—it seems likely that many more young people were executed than history is aware (107).

In what has become an oft-discussed issue in Carroll criticism, the published version of *Alice's Adventures in Wonderland* differs significantly from the original gift version that he presented to Alice Liddell. As Derek Hudson relays, the author "enlarged the 18,000 words of *Alice's Adventures Under Ground* into the 35,000 words of his famous book" (118). Carroll offered the following explanation for his lengthening the story: "In writing it out, I added many fresh ideas, which seemed to grow of themselves upon the original stock; and many more added themselves when, years afterward, I wrote it all over again for publication" (qtd. in Cohen 90).

While changes were made to Britain's capital code throughout the nine-teenth century, quite a number were effected during the early 1860s when Carroll was conceiving and composing *Alice*. As noted, in 1861, the year before the mathematics don created the story for the Liddell sisters, the Criminal Law Consolidation Act that drastically reduced the number of capital crimes was enacted, and 1864, when Carroll was rewriting and expanding the tale for commercial publication, "was an unusually busy one for hangings at New-gate" (Clark 134). Although Carroll lived in Oxford, he made frequent trips to London—where the infamous jail was located—to visit friends, hear lectures, and attend the theater (Cohen 261). Martin J. Wiener notes that one capital case of the time especially captured the public's imagination: that of con-victed wife murderer George Hall. In 1864, "a large campaign that for several weeks attracted an immense amount of public attention" was carried out in an effort to save this man, whom many believed had acted justifiably, from the noose (175). An array of popular newspapers covered this issue, and it was the subject of widespread public debate.

Growing antipathy toward the death penalty prompted Queen Victoria to convene the Royal Commission on Capital Punishment in May 1864. Chaired by the Duke of Richmond, the committee was asked "to inquire into the Provisions and Operation of the Laws now in force in the United Kingdom, under and by virtue of which the Punishment of Death may be inflicted upon persons convicted of certain crimes, and also into the manner in which Capital Sentences are carried into execution, and to report whether any, and if any what alteration is desirable in such Laws, or any of them, or in the manner in which such sentences are carried into execution" (Royal Commission 2). For two years, the commission reviewed existing research and conducted interviews with judges, lawyers, chaplains, and prison officials to determine the efficacy of capital punishment in Great Britain.

The commission published its report in 1866, and the more than six-hundred-page document proposed an array of modifications to the legal code from dividing the crime of murder into degrees and clarifying the meaning of "malice aforethought" to adding the crime of infanticide and permitting judges, not juries, to determine sentences (Royal Commission xlviii–li). The change the commission is most well-known for, however, was ironically one of the last ones listed: "the abolition of the present system of public execu-tions" (Royal Commission l). While not all of the recommendations made by the commission were adopted, this one became law. The Capital Punishment

Amendment Act, enacted in 1868, decreed that "judgment of death to be executed on any prisoner sentenced on any indictment or inquisition for murder shall be carried into effect within the walls of the prison in which the offender is confined at the time of execution."

Given the widespread public debate over capital punishment in general and the work of the commission in particular, it comes as no surprise that among those "many fresh ideas" that Carroll mentioned adding to *Alice* are ones concerning the criminal code and state-sanctioned execution. While *Alice's Adventures Under Ground* contains calls for characters to be put to death—by the Queen of Hearts and by the Marchioness (who is renamed the Duchess in the revised version)—the elements related to the penal code are greatly expanded in the published text. The original gift edition, for instance, does not contain the Mouse's comic, corrupt, and capricious trial by the dog Fury. Instead, the rodent's "long sad, tale" concerns his family's troubles with a local feline and the feline's problems, in turn, with a neighborhood dog. The Mouse begins his story thus: "We lived beneath the mat / Warm and smug and fat / But one woe & that / Was the *cat!*" (22; italics in original). The poem does mention the deaths of many members of the Mouse's family, but judicial execution is not the cause. Rather, his siblings perish by accident, as a result of residing in the unfortunate locale of under the mat:

> But alas!
>> one day, (*So* they say)
>>> Came the dog and
>>>> cat, Hunting
>>>>> for a
>>>>>> rat,
>>> Crushed
>> the mice
> all flat. (22; italics in original)

Even more noticeable, the trial of the Knave of Hearts in the gift edition of *Alice* is extremely short. It consists merely of the White Rabbit reading the accusation about the stolen tarts and then the Queen demanding that the sentence be delivered before the evidence is presented. Unlike in the published version, there is no testimony by the Hatter, Cook, Dormouse, or Alice and thus no repeated demands by Her Majesty or the King for beheadings.

Taking the public debates concerning the death penalty during the period in which Lewis Carroll composed *Alice's Adventures in Wonderland* into consideration gives new literary meaning and added social significance to the Knave of Hearts' trial. Carroll's decision to expand this section of all the sections in the book is significant. By presenting criminal law, jury trials, and state-sanction death sentences as silly and even ridiculous, Carroll extends his exploration of nonsense from songs, poems, and games intended for children to some of the most serious, solemn, and seemingly sacrosanct aspects of adult society. Indeed, the Queen of Hearts' cry "Off with their heads" not only evokes the etymology of the word "capital" in "capital punishment" but also refers to a form of execution commonly considered the most dignified. Steve Fielding has documented that hanging "was the usual punishment of commoners, noblemen being given a more honourable death by beheading" (1). The fact that all the calls for execution in *Alice* take the form of a demand for beheading has the effect of demonstrating how even this allegedly esteemed form of capital punishment is cruel and absurd. Instead of debating whether executions should be held in public or private, *Alice* pushes the issue one step further, questioning—to use the words of Ann Widdecombe—"the very validity of the State's taking life" (7).

In what has become an oft-quoted line from *Alice*, the Cheshire Cat comments on prevalence of insanity in Wonderland, stating, "We're all mad here" (66). Viewing the 1865 narrative in light of contemporaneous debates concerning capital punishment leads one to conclude that this quality of lunacy was not limited to the fictional residents of Wonderland but encompassed factual inhabitants of British society. In this way, while Carroll would title the 1871 sequel to Alice's adventures *Through the Looking-Glass*, it is clear that the initial narrative also functions as a mirror of Victorian society, reflecting its ideology, institutions, and injustices back to readers.

Evidence of Alice's Activism: Juvenile Agency and the Fully Acculturated Victorian Child

Although nearly every character is sentenced to death at some point in *Alice*, none are actually executed. As Nina Demurova has observed, the individuals in Carroll's novel are "always hitting, banging, beating, kicking, teasing, threatening, scolding, or killing (but not quite)" (82). Through various means, every condemned figure is able to avoid the gallows: the gardeners hide from the axman in a flowerpot, the Hatter runs out of the courtroom

before the royal henchman can catch him, and the Cheshire Cat slowly van-
ishes while the Queen is distracted. Even those characters who do not actively
evade the executioner are spared. When the Duchess commands her servants
to chop off Alice's head and when the Queen demands that nearly everyone in
the croquet game be put to death, their orders are forgotten almost as quickly
as they are uttered.

As with numerous other details in *Alice*, this disjunction between the
number of death sentences imposed and executions carried out reflects another prominent criticism of capital punishment during Carroll's time. Michael Meranze has documented how at the same time as prosecutions for
capital crimes were on the increase, executions remained stagnant, ensuring
that "the actual numbers of executions did not grow apace and the sheer
arbitrariness of the system became impossible to hide" (374). Capital law was
not enforced fairly or applied uniformly. Individuals from powerful, wealthy,
or well-connected families were often able to avoid prosecution, while others
escaped charges or even punishment by claiming the benefit of clergy, demonstrating proof of literacy, or enjoying "the discretionary power of prosecutors" (Masur 3). Richard Clark has explained how these elements both operated and expanded over time:

> Initially to get the benefit [of clergy] the accused had to appear in court wearing
> ecclesiastical regalia, but over time this provision was removed and they had to
> read a passage from the Bible instead. Obviously this extended the benefit to
> anyone who was literate, not just priests. In fact it could be extended to the
> illiterate as in most cases the passage to be read was from the 51st Psalm and
> could be memorized. It became known as "the neck verse" as it saved many a
> neck from the noose. (13)

These abuses created what Gatrell has characterized as a system of "slap-
happy justice" (vi). In a comment that could be applied to almost all of the
calls for execution in *Alice*, by the Victorian era in Great Britain "capital law
had come to look randomly cruel and terminally silly" (Gatrell 21).

Even if a prisoner was ineligible for protections like the benefit of clergy,
juries often spared his or her life by returning what was known as a partial
verdict: they found the accused guilty but refused to order the person put to
death. As a result, "scores of crimes were considered capital offenses, but
execution rates for those convicted of capital crimes generally remained well
below 50 percent" (Masur 3). During the late eighteenth and into the nine-

teenth century, such provisions in "criminal law enabled hundreds of condemned prisoners to sidestep the gallows" (Masur 3).

This phenomenon was even true for those who had been sentenced to death. Echoing the situation in Wonderland, Potter notes that, as English history progressed, "only a small and declining proportion of those capitally condemned were actually executed. Between 1749 and 1758 more than two-thirds of the capitally convicted were executed. Less than a third died in the last decade of the century. By 1810 it was about one in seven, and half that proportion again by the mid 1830s" (9).

Alice satirizes this real-world situation in which capital convictions had been rendered almost meaningless. The Gryphon points out to the title character in the wake of one of the Queen's calls for mass beheadings that "they never executes nobody, you know" (95). While readers never see an accused claim the benefit of clergy, a prosecutor exercise discretionary power, or a jury return a partial verdict to spare an individual from the gallows, they do witnesses a royal pardon. At the end of the croquet match, when all of the players except the title character and monarchs have been sentenced to death, Alice hears "the King say in a low voice, to the company generally, 'You are all pardoned.' 'Come, *that's* a good thing!' she said to herself, for she had felt quite unhappy at the number of executions the Queen had ordered" (94; italics in original).

Given that capital punishment is merely an empty threat in Wonderland, the policy—along with the individuals who invoke it—loses its power. Contrary to arguments by defenders of the practice that executions inspire fear and thus good behavior in citizens, the Gryphon finds the beheading-loving Queen entertaining rather than terrifying:

> The Gryphon sat up and rubbed its eyes: then it watched the Queen till she was out of sight: then it chuckled. "What fun!" said the Gryphon, half to itself, half to Alice.
>
> "What *is* the fun?" said Alice.
>
> "Why, *she*," said the Gryphon. (95; italics in original)

The Queen's frequent calls for execution thus function more as an amusing pastime than an effective means of social control.

Alice's Adventures in Wonderland may incorporate many of the contemporaneous criticisms of capital punishment, but it offers another, more original, and by far more powerful argument against it: an individual's ability to openly defy the practice along with the authority of those who order it. The first of these acts of rebellion occurs when the Queen asks Alice the names of the three playing-card gardeners. Aware that if Her Majesty realizes that they are the ones who planted the wrong color roses she will order their execution, the young girl engages in a bold act of defiance to protect them. "'And who are all these?,' said the Queen, pointing to the three gardeners. . . . 'How should *I* know?' said Alice, surprised at her own courage. 'It's no business of *mine*'" (82; italics in original). Not surprisingly, the monarch is incensed by the youth's insolence: "The Queen turned crimson with fury, and, after glaring at her for a moment like a wild beast, began screaming 'Off with her head!'" (82). Alice rebels, and it is once again effective: "'Nonsense!' said Alice, very loudly and decidedly and the Queen was silent" (82).

Seemingly emboldened by this victory, when the Queen discovers the gardeners' efforts to paint the white roses red and predictably cries "Off with their heads!" Alice intervenes even more directly on their behalf: "'You shan't be beheaded!' said Alice, and she put them into a large flower-pot that stood near" (83). As before, her actions prove effective. The narrator notes that "the three soldiers wandered about for a minute or two, looking for [the condemned cards], and then quietly marched off after the others" (83).

Possibly as a result of seeing that Alice has been able to defy the Queen in her calls for execution, other characters begin doing the same. A group of soldiers uses a clever play on words to avoid executing the three playing-card gardeners whom Alice has hidden in the flowerpot. When Her Majesty inquires about whether the heads of the three playing-cards gardener are off—that is, whether they have been beheaded—they respond by saying "their heads are gone, if it please your Majesty!," meaning, of course, that they are nowhere to be found (83). Later, the executioner himself is even more defiant. When the Queen orders the beheading of the Cheshire Cat—whose body has disappeared—he protests. "The executioner's argument was, that you couldn't cut off a head unless there was a body to cut it off from: that he had never done such a thing before, and he wasn't going to begin at *his* time of life" (88; italics in original). A debate ensues, and Alice intercedes. She tells the Queen that the Cheshire Cat belongs to the Duchess who will be able to settle the dispute. As the young girl undoubtedly planned, in the midst of the confusion while the Duchess is summoned, the feline is able to fade away and thus escape the ax.

Of course, Alice's boldest work of activism occurs in the final chapter. In yet another absurd moment during the trial of the Knave of Hearts, the Queen insists "Sentence first—verdict afterwards!" (124). Having already endured jurors who cannot remember their own names and a judge who intimidates witnesses by threatening them with execution among other travesties of justice, Alice can take no more. The exasperated young girl erupts. "Stuff and nonsense! . . . The idea of having the sentence first!'" (124). When an enraged Queen orders her to be silent, she refuses: "'I won't!' said Alice" (124). At this point, Her Majesty predictably orders that the young girl be beheaded and the entire courtroom realizes they are witnessing if not a full-fledged coup d'etat at least a dramatic power struggle between the two figures. Indeed, unlike the other times when soldiers sprang into action after the Queen shouted "Off with her head!" this time Carroll's narrator notes: "Nobody moved" (124). Possibly sensing this support, the young girl is even more daring. In a derisive tone, she asks the Queen, "Who cares for *you*? . . . You're nothing but a pack of cards!" (124). This announcement trounces not only Her Majesty but Wonderland itself. Alice's comment ends the dream that gave life to this world and the characters in it:

> At this the whole pack rose up into the air, and came flying down upon her, she gave a little scream, half of fright and half of anger, and tried to beat them off, and found herself lying on the bank, with her head in the lap of her sister, who was gently brushing away some dead leaves that had fluttered down from the trees upon her face. (124)

In this way, the young girl's activism saves not only a handful of characters from annihilation, but, ultimately, herself. Rather than relying on outside forces—like parents, tutors, governesses, judges, or even the monarchy itself—to protect and defend her, she uses her own agency.

These details call into question commonly held assumptions concerning changing conceptions of childhood during the Victorian era and the role that they played in Carroll's construction of *Alice*. Marah Gubar, in her book about children's literature from the period commonly referred to as the "golden age," aptly summarizes this viewpoint. She argues that in narratives for young readers published from the late nineteenth century through the early decades of the twentieth century various "political, social, and religious crises led Victorian and Edwardian authors to construct childhood itself as a golden age, a refuge from the painful complexities of modern life" (4). Drawing on highly romanticized views, Victorian society painted children as the antithesis of adults in many ways: whereas men and women were worldly, boys and girls were innocent; while adults were corrupt, children were pure; where grown-ups were aware of injustice, juveniles were blissfully ignorant. As Judith Plotz notes, this dichotomy located children "outside of the context . . . of schools, of the state, and especially of their families" (14). Of course, in order for children to maintain this state of unsullied purity, adults needed to actively shield them from the unsettling aspects of the world. For these reasons, Gubar argues that "when children's authors whisk child characters away to Wonder-lands, secret gardens, or uninhabited islands," it is often viewed as a testament "to their 'regressive desire for a preindustrial, rural world,' as well as their longing to believe in the existence of a natural, autonomous self, free from the imprint of culture" (4).

Such views about the inherent innocence of children and the need for adults to protect it played a significant role in arguments calling for the abolition of public execution. According to Annulla Linders, as children in-creasingly came to be seen as "separate and innocent beings, the stern warn-ing of the gallows, having previously provided the justification for parading school children in front of it, could no longer be defended" (623). Members of the antigallows movement argued that public execution was a corruptive influence not only on adult witnesses but—even worse—on their more im-pressionable juvenile counterparts. Because children were viewed "as vulner-able and in need of protection, [they] were to be spared the horrors of the gallows rather than being intentionally frightened by it" (623). For these reasons, by the mid-nineteenth century, "an outward veneer of respectability, the hallmark of the Victorian age, was to apply also to hanging: not in front of the children" (Potter 79). Thus, while hangings continued, they were no longer seen as appropriate spectacles for young eyes.

Lewis Carroll is commonly seen as having subscribed to these views about the inherent innocence, purity, and even naivety of children—and about the responsibility of adults to protect these qualities. As Cohen has documented, Carroll lamented that Alice Liddell, along with the many other young girls he befriended over the course of his life, had to grow up. In various letters and diary entries, he wished that these prepubescent girls could stay young, pure, and innocent forever (102–3, 156, 172, 181, 187). As Jan Susina argues, critics and biographers routinely extrapolate these beliefs to the author's view about all children and to the period of childhood as a whole (7).

The recurrence of references to capital punishment, the frequency of jury trials, and the persistence of criminal violations throughout *Alice's Adventures in Wonderland* call this belief into question. Far from trying to shield his child audience from the problems, debates, and controversies of the adult world, Carroll was seeking to educate them about such issues. The numerous facets of British criminal law incorporated into the narrative suggest Carroll's belief that young people need to be informed about rather than sheltered from the world. Indeed, Richard Kelly has remarked that "as a man who considered to his dying day that life was a puzzle, Carroll always held the art of teaching to be an essential part of his work" (19). Moreover, given the success of Alice's verbal activism, the book demonstrates that boys and girls whom Victorian culture had classified as socially weak, personally defenseless, and even politically impotent actually have the power to effect change. Ernest Dowson, in what has become an oft-quoted remark from his 1889 essay, asserts that "there is no more distinctive feature of the age than the enormous importance which children have assumed" ("Cult of the Child" 434). Carroll would have agreed but perhaps for a different reason than critics and biographers have commonly imagined.

While Lewis Carroll's home country of England ultimately outlawed judicial execution, the practice is still legal in the United States on both a federal and, in many areas, a state level. As I discuss in the introduction to this book, the nation did briefly prohibit capital punishment—via the 1972 Supreme Court ruling in *Furman v. Georgia*—but the decision was overturned only four years later. In the decades since, the United States has put to death hundreds of men and women.*

Far from a universally approved practice, judicial execution remains one of the most controversial topics. Opponents of the practice cite many of the same criticisms that Carroll uses to rebuke it in *Alice*. As Eliza Steelwater has written, for example, capital punishment is applied unevenly and, often, arbitrarily: "Currently, of the 300 murderers per year sentenced to death, more than two-thirds of those who have their sentences reviewed are given a new trial, have their sentence commuted, or are pardoned. Capital punish-

---

* Eliza Steelwater, in *The Hangman's Knot: Lynching, Legal Execution, and America's Struggle with the Death Penalty*, offers the following general statistics: "The number executed each from 1976 to 2003 has varied even over the last decade—from a low of 31 in 1993 and 1995 to a high of 98 in 1999" (12). Thus, even if only the minimum number of individuals were put to death each year in the United States since capital punishment was reinstated in 1976, the total figure would still be well over one thousand.

ment today is tokenism. Some even say it's a lottery" (12). In another equally common critique, the practice is regarded as inhumane. Even the various medical and technological advances—such as the invention of the gas chamber or the adoption of lethal injection—that are intended to minimize the condemned's pain and suffering are viewed as abhorrent. Not only do these devices fail to address the moral objection that many have to the taking of another human life but they can also malfunction. As Chris McGreal reported about an incident involving convicted child rapist and murderer Romell Broom in September 2009, "Ohio is to try again to execute a man convicted of murder after his death by lethal injection was botched earlier this week when technicians spent two hours in a futile hunt for a vein able to take a needle" (par. 1). McGreal offered the following details:

> Prison officers described how, after about an hour of hunting for a suitable vein, Broom helped them by turning on to his side, by moving rubber tubing along his arm and by flexing his hand and muscles. At one point, technicians found what appeared to be a suitable vein but it collapsed as they inserted a needle, apparently because of past drug use.
>
> Broom . . . became so distressed that he lay on his back and covered his face with both hands. One of the execution team handed him a toilet roll to wipe away tears. (pars. 4–5)

Even in cases where the procedure is successful, lethal injection is still seen as a violation of the Eighth Amendment. As journalist Ashley Fantz reported in an article for CNN, "Thirty years after it was developed, the practice is drawing protest as cruel and unusual punishment, a claim supported by recent medical studies that say the mixture of chemicals used may cause a slow and excruciating death" (par. 11).

Problems with the American legal system form a final reason for opposition. While the nation's lawyers, jurors, and judges are not as incompetent or corrupt as in Carroll's *Alice*, they are far from flawless. As Steelwater remarks of American trial law, "Good conquers evil—unless evil happens to have a team of skilled attorneys and/or something to trade with the prosecutor" (12). Not only are men more commonly sentenced to death than women but other vectors of identity play an equally significant deciding role. "African-American men convicted of murdering someone who is not black" and especially those "who can't defend themselves financially" are far more likely to receive the death penalty (Steelwater 12). Demographic issues aside, the accused are sometimes wrongfully convicted. According to the Death Penalty Information Center, a nonprofit research organization, "Since 1973, 138 people in 26 states have been released from death row with evidence of their innocence" ("Innocence and the Death Penalty"). At least in part because of the many legal, moral, and logistical problems with judicial execution, "every other developed Western nation has ceased to use the taking of life as a legal punishment" (Zimring ix).

Given that capital punishment is still both lawfully practiced and hotly debated in the United States, the role that it plays in *Alice's Adventures in Wonderland* may contribute to the narrative's ongoing appeal. Lewis Carroll's story engaged in dialogue with contemporaneous debates concerning judicial execution in England in 1865, when it was first published. Now, more than a century later, I would argue that the locus of this engagement has shifted. For U.S. readers, *Alice's Adventures in Wonderland* speaks, consciously or unconsciously, to national controversies concerning capital punishment and what such debates reveal about America's understanding of itself.

In what has become an influential discussion, Achille Mbembe proposes the concept "necropolitics," a neologism that he defines as "the power and the capacity to dictate who may live and who may die" (11). As Mbembe points out, "To kill or to allow to live constitute[s] the limits of sovereignty, its fundamental attributes. To exercise sovereignty is to exercise control over mortality and to define life as the deployment and manifestation of power" (11–12). Whether this power is exacted by the government or by an individual, it is the supreme display of authority. For this reason, while Mbembe draws on Foucault's concept of "biopower" (12), he also posits a new and even more potent concept: what he terms "necropower" (40): "What place is given to life, death, and the human body (in particular the wounded or slain body)? How are they inscribed in the order of power?" (12). For both its original English audience and its contemporary American readership, *Alice's Adventures in Wonderland* provides a rich and formerly overlooked venue where such questions are asked—as well as answered.

CHAPTER THREE

"Swarthy, Sun-Tanned, Villainous Looking Fellows"

Tarzan of the Apes *and Criminal Anthropology*

> I will not go into all the reasons for these cranial abnormalities in criminals, but I cannot avoid pointing out how closely they correspond to characteristics observed in normal skulls of the colored and inferior races.
>
> CESARE LOMBROSO, *Criminal Man* (1876)

Perhaps more than any other author of boys' adventure novels, Edgar Rice Burroughs is known for the gory violence of his narratives. As biographer Richard A. Lupoff observes, "There is the unquestioned sanguinary tone of the great bulk of Burroughs' tales" (193). Whether it is "John Carter or Carson Napier slashing his way across an alien world, or some other Burroughs hero slaughtering foemen by the score, there is hardly a Burroughs book without a liberal drenching, somewhere in its pages, in freshly spilled blood" (193).

His classic tale *Tarzan of the Apes* is no different. First appearing in *All-Story Magazine* in 1912 and published in book form in 1914, the narrative not only has its genesis in murderous violence but its plot is propelled by subsequent acts of homicide. First, in what has become an oft-recounted beginning, the parents of the title character are caught in a bloody coup d'etat aboard the ship that is conveying them to Africa: "'You mean, my man, that the crew contemplates mutiny?' asked Clayton. 'Mutiny!,' exclaimed the old fellow. 'Mutiny! They means murder, sir'" (7). His words are far from hyperbole. Burroughs provides a graphic description of the mutineers' assassination of the captain and his crew: "Before the officers had taken a dozen backward steps the men were upon them. An axe in the hands of a burly negro cleft the captain from forehead to chin, and an instant later the others were down; dead or wounded from dozens of blows and bullet wounds" (13).

Numerous other slayings are carried out over the course of the story. From humans killing other humans and humans killing animals to animals killing humans and animals killing other animals, these deaths assume many forms. Moreover, each is described with the author's characteristic brutality. For instance, a quarrel between two sailors is only settled when one murders the other with a pickax: "He raised his pick above his head, and, with a mighty blow, buried the point in Snipes' brain" (154). In another scene, Tarzan watches as a group of Africans drag a prisoner into their village, tie him to the stake, and begin torturing him to death: "Eyes, ears, arms and legs were pierced; every inch of the poor writhing body that did not cover a vital organ became the target of the cruel lancers" (90). As if this scene were not suffi-ciently gruesome, readers quickly learn that these individuals are also can-nibals. As Tarzan observes upon his first visit to their village: "Several human skulls lay on the floor," and "a necklace of dried human hands" hung from the neck of Mbonga, their chief (84, 85).

Such homicidal cruelty is not limited to the human world. When readers first meet Kerchak, the leader of the gang of anthropoid apes who murder the title character's parents, he is engaged in a deadly "rampage of rage among his people" (29). Burroughs describes the fate of one unfortunate female who is the target of his fury: "With a wild scream he was upon her, tearing a great piece from her side with his mighty teeth, and striking her viscously upon her head and shoulders with a broken tree limb until her skull was crushed to jelly" (29). Before Kerchak's "uncontrolled anger" is spent (Burroughs 29), more innocent apes die by his hand. One young male who is caught by Kerchak while trying to flee meets an especially grisly end. In details that recount the death from Kerchak's point of view, the narrator notes that "the infuriated brute had felt the vertebra of one snap between his great foaming jaws" (29).

Tarzan takes part in many bloody fights with ferocious apes like Kerchak and other equally fierce animals of the jungle. During a battle with a bull gorilla, for example, Burroughs recounts how the animal "struck terrific blows with his open hand, and tore the flesh at the boy's throat and chest with its mighty tusks" (49). When his ape foster mother, Kala, finds him after the skirmish, he is unconscious and seriously injured: "A portion of his chest was laid bare to the ribs, three of which had been broken by the mighty blows of the gorilla. One arm was nearly severed by the giant fangs, and a great piece had been torn from his neck, exposing his jugular" (51).

In spite of the numerous killings featured in the novel, *Tarzan of the Apes* is not commonly viewed through the lens of violence or even criminality. Rather, critics have tended to examine the story about an aristocratic white boy raised in the jungle by a band of wild apes from the perspectives of gender, race, class, and empire. Given both the frequency and the centrality of murder in the novel, however, it is clear that the narrative is concerned with exploring the issue of crime and the characteristics of those who commit it. Either explicitly or implicitly in numerous passages, Burroughs contemplates several questions. Who kills? What motivates them to do so? What rewards are attained by engaging in lethal violence? Conversely, what penalties are incurred?

This chapter examines the answers that Burroughs's novel provides to these and other questions. In so doing, it demonstrates that murderous violence is far from a merely sensational element in the narrative—a means to attract juvenile male readers and hold their attention, as several previous critics have asserted.* On the contrary, these episodes play a crucial role in the book's formulation of its title character, the development of its plot, and the construction of its themes. Tarzan of the Apes is presented as a superior being, and he is never more physically powerful or socially impressive than when he is engaged in the act of murder. Whether he is taking the life of a human or an animal, his status as a great man is predicated on his ability as a fierce killer.

Moving the incidents of murder from the background to the forefront of *Tarzan of the Apes* yields another, arguably even more valuable, insight. Burroughs's book is commonly seen as being informed by the Progressive-era interest in cultural anthropology, given its setting in the remote jungles of Africa and its depiction of indigenous tribal peoples. But, I demonstrate that the narrative is also in dialogue with a related discipline: criminal anthropology. As its name implies, this new field applied scientific methodologies like empirical observation, careful measurement, and detailed classification to the exploration of crime and criminals. While many early cultural anthropologists used their findings to justify existing racial hierarchies, their counterparts in the arena of criminal anthropology engaged in a variation on this practice.

* See, for example, Mandel.

Heavily influenced by the evolutionary theories of Charles Darwin, they of-fered atavistic explanations for men and women who committed offenses like murder. This thesis was first articulated by Italian researcher Cesare Lom-broso in his landmark 1876 book *Criminal Anthropology* (*L'uomo delinquente*), and it made a case that individuals who engaged in aggressive violence were evolutionary "throwbacks" to the "lower" races and "lesser" species.

In everything from its depiction of mutinous sailors and killer anthropoid apes to its portrayal of cannibalistic indigenous Africans and the oft-murderous title character himself, *Tarzan of the Apes* alludes to these influential theories. Rereading Burroughs's narrative in light of its sustained interest in criminality and suggestive engagement with criminal anthropology gives new meaning to oft-discussed elements like its espousal of Darwinism and biological deter-minism, its views on race and eugenics, and its portrayal of Tarzan's excep-tionalism. In Burroughs's text, the title character is a superior being not simply because he is a white man who hails from one of the "high" races but because he does not possess any of the atavistic elements that criminal anthropologists like Cesare Lombroso associated with chronic thieves and habitual murderers. Accordingly, this chapter reveals how Tarzan may be popularly known as the "ape-man," yet his prowess is determined in an equally real and recoverable way by his embodiment of what might be called the anti-Lombrosian man.

"A Very Likable Murderer": Tarzan as Killer and Thus *Übermensch*

Although Edgar Rice Burroughs died in 1950 having never set foot on the continent of Africa where he situated *Tarzan of the Apes*, he did meet several murderers during the course of his lifetime. In 1928, the novelist accepted an assignment from the *Los Angeles Examiner* to cover the trial of William Ed-ward Hickman. Hickman was charged with the bold kidnapping and grue-some murder of twelve-year-old Marian Parker.* As Bill Hillman notes, the

---

*Bill Hillman provides a brief overview of the case. On 15 December 1927, the defendant kidnapped the adolescent girl from her school and then sent her family a series of ransom notes, demanding the surprisingly small sum of $1,500. Four days later, Parker's family paid the ransom, but Hickman had already killed the girl. So, he left a satchel containing her dismembered body in return. Hickman eluded capture for more than a week, and, as a nationwide manhunt ensued, the case made headlines around the country. For more information on the Hickman case as well as Burroughs's journalistic coverage of it, see Hillman's "Introduction: Edgar Rice Burroughs Reports on the Noto-rious William Edward Hickman Trial" (*ERBzine*, http://www.erbzine.com/mag17/1767.html).

Examiner hired Burroughs, who was then living just outside of Los Angeles, "to attend the sessions and write a syndicated column giving his personal reactions. The column, appearing January 26 to February 10, presented Burroughs in his most irascible and opinionated mood" (par. 1).*

The Hickman case, however, was not the first time the author had come face-to-face with a killer. In 1890, Burroughs spent the summer in Idaho, where his two older brothers operated a ranch. While there, the fifteen-year-old future writer met a wide array of interesting individuals, some of them criminals. As biographer Irwin Porges has documented, while Burroughs was chatting one day with a follow ranch hand, "his friend described how he had killed a man named Paxton" (23). Burroughs would later learn that the homicide was not the result of a foolish drunken brawl; it was an act of murder for hire. Later in life, Burroughs recounted the episode in language that revealed his relative comfort with the crime: "It was perfectly all right because each of the two men had been hired to kill the other and though Paxton got the drop on him across the dinner table, my friend came out alive and Paxton didn't" (qtd. in Porges 23). Later in life, the author would often remark how this man was a "very likable murderer" (Taliaferro 31).

Burroughs's King of the Apes is likewise a congenial man. Tarzan is not commonly described in terms suggesting criminal conduct but rather is presented throughout the novel as a "very likeable murderer" in many ways. From the time that the protagonist is a young boy, he is an astute and accomplished killer. His ape foster mother marvels at his ability to render a large male gorilla "stone dead" when he is only ten years old (50). Later, Tarzan slays his arch nemesis, Kerchak: "A muscular hand shot out and grasped the hairy throat, and another plunged a keen hunting knife a dozen times into the broad breast. Like lightning the blows fell, and only ceased when Tarzan felt the limp form crumple beneath him" (63). Similarly, in an oft-referenced scene, he kills the ape Terkoz. Burroughs describes the brutal hand-to-hand contest: "Like two charging bulls they came together, and like two wolves sought each other's throat. Against the long canines of the ape was pitted the thin blade of the man's knife" (175). Finally, not once but twice in the novel, Tarzan slays a lion: "His right arm encircled the lion's neck, while the left

---

ERBzine has made available all thirteen of Burroughs's columns about the trial (http://www.erbzine.com/mag17/1767.html).

hand plunged the knife time and again into the unprotected side behind the left shoulder" (126).

Tarzan is a killer not only of beasts but of humans as well. The first man that Tarzan sees is also the first one that he murders. When Kulonga, the son of the leader of the local tribe, slays Kala, the King of the Jungle kills him to avenge her death. Tarzan does not murder this man by simply stabbing him, as he had done with many other victims. Instead, he employs another weapon: a noose. As a young boy, Tarzan had discovered both how to tie a slip-knot and the lethal effect that the loop had when placed around the throat of jungle creature. As the narrator relays, "Many were the smaller animals that fell into the snare of the quick thrown noose" (67). Tarzan elects to use this method to kill Kulonga, and this decision places the murder in dialogue with the numerous lynchings of blacks in the United States during the opening decades of the twentieth century. As a study released by the National Association for the Advancement of Colored People (NAACP) reports, the period from 1889 to 1918 witnessed the height of white mob violence against African Americans, during which at least one lynching took place nearly every week. The NAACP study notes that "the United States is the only advanced nation whose government has tolerated lynching. The facts are well known to students of public affairs . . . and they are the common shame of all Americans" (5).

Especially for the original audience of *Tarzan of the Apes*—but also for its current readers—it would be difficult to encounter Tarzan's lynching of Kulonga and not be reminded of this historical reality. Burroughs provides a detailed description of the event:

> So it was that as Kulonga emerged from the shadow of the jungle a slender coil of rope sped sinuously above him from the lowest branch of a mighty tree directly upon the edge of the fields of Mbonga, and ere the king's son had taken a half dozen steps into the clearing a quick noose tightened about his neck.
>
> So quickly did Tarzan of the Apes drag back his prey that Kulonga's cry of alarm was throttled in his windpipe. Hand over hand Tarzan drew the struggling black until he had him hanging by his neck in midair; then Tarzan climbed to a larger branch drawing the still threshing victim well up into the sheltering verdure of the tree.
>
> Here he fastened the rope securely to a stout branch, and then, descending, plunging his hunting knife into Kulonga's heart. Kala was avenged. (79)

Emboldened by this success, Tarzan goes on to kill many other members of Kulonga's tribe, "picking up solitary hunters with his long, deadly noose, stripping them of weapons and ornaments and dropping their bodies from a high tree into the village street during the still watches of the night" (100). Burroughs's title character engages in this practice so often that Gail Bederman characterizes him as nothing less than "a one-man lynch mob" (223).

Given Tarzan's penchant for killing, it comes as no surprise that he adopts a murderous identity. As the title character confidently announces to the other apes after one of slayings, "'I am Tarzan,' he cried. 'I am a great killer. Let all respect Tarzan of the Apes and Kala, his mother. There be none among you as mighty as Tarzan. Let his enemies beware'" (63). Such statements are far from mere posturing; Burroughs's King of the Jungle is feared by both apes and humans in large part because of his appetite for lethal violence.

Admittedly, Tarzan has been reared in an environment where such behavior is necessary for survival. As the narrator notes, "To kill was the law of the world he knew" (81). However, the King of the Apes does not engage in such murderous violence reluctantly. As Burroughs says of his title character, "Few were his primitive pleasures, but the greatest of these was to hunt and kill" (81). In a comment that likens Tarzan in many ways to sadistic serial killers who murder compulsively, Burroughs says of his title character that the "desire to kill burned fiercely in his wild breast" (77).

In spite of the murderous nature of his protagonist, Burroughs does not want his readers to view Tarzan as a criminal or even a villain. The author frames Tarzan's homicidal actions as not only appropriate and justified but admirable and even enviable. The title character's primitive upbringing in the jungles of Africa do not make him an "inferior" or "lesser" figure. As Bederman suggests, his life among a band of wild apes has molded him into "a powerfully appealing fantasy of perfect, invincible manhood" (219). Although Tarzan is not as brawny as the apes, his active, outdoor existence has rendered him more robust than the typical white man. For instance, the narrator notes that when Tarzan is only ten years old "he was fully as strong as the average man of thirty, and far more agile than the most practiced athlete ever becomes. And day by day his strength was increasing" (39). For these reasons, both Richard Dyer and John F. Kassan have argued that Burroughs's King of the Apes constitutes a defining cultural symbol of white male muscularity. In a passage that typifies descriptions, readers are informed that by the time he is a full grown man, "the immense muscles of Tarzan's shoulders and biceps leap into corded knots beneath the silver moonlight" (136).

Tarzan's homicidal actions provide the ultimate proof of his manly superiority. When the King of the Apes battles a lion to save the life of his cousin William Cecil Clayton, the narrator offers the following awe-inspiring description: "With lightning speed an arm that was banded layers of iron muscle encircled the huge neck, and the great beast was raised from behind, roaring and pawing the air—raised as easily as Clayton would have lifted a pet dog" (126). After Tarzan kills the big cat, Clayton concludes that "the man before him was the embodiment of physical perfection and giant strength" (126). Later, when Tarzan is engaged in another bloody battle, the narrator reveals that "from the first sensation of chilling fear Clayton passed to one of keen admiration and envy of those giant muscles" (133).

Perhaps no other character marvels at Tarzan's homicidal abilities more than love interest Jane Porter. After being abducted by the sadistic ape Terkoz, who carries her off into the jungle where he hopes to satisfy his base sexual desires, Tarzan comes to her rescue. While the ape-man engages his longtime foe in a fight to the death, Jane marvels at his physical prowess: "The great muscles of the man's back and shoulders knotted beneath the tension of his efforts, and the huge biceps and forearm held at bay those mighty tusks" (175). As the bloody battle continues, she grows erotically entranced by Tarzan's brute strength: "Her lithe, young form [was] flattened against the trunk of a great tree, her hands [were] tight pressed against her rising and falling bosom, and her eyes [were] mingled with horror, fascination, fear, and admiration" (175). Not surprisingly, given such attitudes, Jane deems him nothing less than "a perfectly god-like white man" (164).

Such accolades place Tarzan in dialogue with another phenomenon contemporaneous with Burroughs's novel: Friedrich Nietzsche's *Übermensch*. First presented in Nietzsche's four-part philosophical novel *Thus Spoke Zarathustra: A Book for All and None* (1883–85) and translated literally as the "overman," the *Übermensch* "transcends the boundaries of classes, creeds, and nationalities; he overcomes human nature itself and maintains a lordly superiority to the normal shackles and conventions of social life" ("Ubermensch" 385). Indeed, as the *Routledge Encyclopedia of Philosophy* notes, he is a figure who actualizes his full potential and refuses to take a passive approach to life ("Nietzsche" 856–57).

Although Nietzsche would later remark that only "scholarly oxen" (qtd. in Kaufmann 511) could view his idea of the *Übermensch* as Darwinian, many saw his views as advocating for the separation of mankind into superior and inferior beings. Walter Kaufmann argues that, despite Nietzsche's protestations to the contrary, "Darwin did influence [his] conception of the overman, and at times Nietzsche did approximate a bifurcation of humanity" into greater and lesser individuals. As the *Routledge Encyclopedia of Philosophy* aptly puts it, "The idea of becoming a higher kind of being by overcoming one's humanity can seem frightening. For some, it calls up images of Nazi storm troopers seeking out 'inferior' human beings to annihilate" ("Nietzsche" 856). To be sure, the philosophical views of Nietzsche in general and his concept of the *Übermensch* in particular have been used to justify the so-called superiority of certain groups and, conversely, to rationalize the subjugation—and even murder—of those they deemed inferior. For instance, the actions of Chicago "thrill killers" Nathan Leopold and Richard Loeb were fueled, at least in part, by their belief in the *Übermensch*. As Katherine Ramsland explains,

> Leopold was an avid reader of the nineteenth-century German philosopher Friedrich Nietzsche, and was especially taken with the idea that superior men are not bound by social moral codes. He considered himself to be superior, and Nietzsche gave a name to his arrogance by proposing the idea of the *Übermensch* ("overman" or super man) and the privileged class of aristocrats who made and lived by their own moral rules. ("Existential" par. 2)

In a letter that Leopold wrote to Loeb shortly before their kidnapping and murder of fourteen-year-old Bobby Franks in May 1924, he asserted that "a superman . . . is, on account of certain superior qualities inherent in him, exempted from the ordinary laws which govern men. He is not liable for anything he may do" (qtd. in Lief, Caldwell, and Bycel 198).

Such viewpoints were in place by the time Edgar Rice Burroughs wrote and released *Tarzan of the Apes*. Crane Brinton has documented that Nietzsche "had been since about 1900 a favorite subject for the erudite and the literary" (132). One feature that especially attracted individuals to German philosopher's work was his reputation for being one of the foremost "preachers of the creed of race and power" (132)—issues that were at the forefront of Progressive-era thought and politics. In fact, as Briton has suggested, Nietzsche's writings provided a powerful, though commonly overlooked, catalyst for World War I (131).

The year 1914, of course, also saw Burroughs's tale about a white ape-man appear in book form. *Tarzan of the Apes* made its debut in the serial publication *All-Story* in 1912, but it was released two years later as a single-volume hardback by A. C. McClurg. Although Burroughs never overtly likens his title character to an *Übermensch*—nor does he explicitly address Nietzschean concepts of power, privilege, and race superiority—numerous passages reflect these ideas. Especially to the book's original World War I–era readership, statements like "he lost no particle of that self-confidence and resourcefulness which were the badges of his superior being" (41) and "in his veins . . . flowed the blood of the best race of mighty fighters" (48) about Burroughs's ape-man could have as easily been ascribed to Nietzsche's overman. Indeed, by creating a figure who is physically and intellectually superior, who is a member of the "high race," and who kills both inferior beasts and inferior humans with no sense of remorse, Tarzan's status as "King of the Apes" differs little from the *Übermensch*'s standing as what might be characterized as "king of the white men."

"The Born Criminal with His Apish Stigmata": Lombrosian Criminal Anthropology and Edgar Rice Burroughs's Criminals

The writings of Friedrich Nietzsche were not the only ones exerting cultural influence during the time that Edgar Rice Burroughs composed *Tarzan of the Apes*. So too was the work of an Italian psychologist named Cesare Lombroso (1835–1909). Trained in forensic medicine and holding one of his first professional posts at a psychiatric institution, Lombroso was interested in the nature of crime and the character of criminals: what compels some individuals to commit robbery, rape, or murder, and do criminals share any psychological, intellectual, or emotional characteristics?

Lombroso's forays into these areas helped constitute a new interdisciplinary subspecialty: what came to be known as criminal anthropology. As Stephen Jay Gould explains, this field offered "a specific evolutionary hypothesis for the biological nature of human criminal behavior" (142) and combined the sociological aims of criminology with the empirical approaches of anthropology. Its "basic methodology . . . comprised anthropometric measurements of the cranium and the description of anomalies of the face and of peculiarities of the bodily structure" (Savitz x). As Lombroso and his followers asserted, criminals could be studied, calibrated, and categorized just like anthropologists at the time were doing with foreign peoples and cultures. In this way, "Lombroso promised to turn the study of criminals into an empirical science" (Gibson and Rafter 1). Indeed, by the time of the Italian researcher's death in 1909, "criminal anthropology had become world famous for its elaborate classification of criminals" (Gibson and Rafter 9). Lombroso's major work, *Criminal Man* (*L'uomo delinquente*), was first released in 1876. The book covered offenders ranging from prostitutes and arsonists to rapists and murderers. It sorted them into various categories by the type of offense they had committed as well as by the physical and psychological traits that they possessed, outlining what soon came to be called an "etiology of deviance" (Gibson and Rafter 12). Over the next twenty years, Lombroso would revise, edit, and expand on this system, ultimately publishing five different editions of *Criminal Man*; the final one, released between 1896 and 1897, comprises four volumes.

As Leonard Savitz has rightly observed, "The importance of Lombrosianism to the field of criminology was enormous" (xvii). Mary Gibson and Nicole Hahn Rafter remark that his ideas achieved "iconic status" and caused him to be identified as "the father of modern criminology" (3, 4). In the words of Savitz once again, "While . . . there is still contention about the earliest 'sources' of criminology, one must admit that modern criminology stems directly from the activities and dedication of a single man, Cesare Lombroso" (vi).

Although the specific ideas of the Italian-based researcher were new, his methods were not. Lombroso drew heavily on existing nineteenth-century practices of phrenology, craniometry, and anthropometry in his study of criminals. These fields were based on the belief "that physical traits constituted visible signs of interior psychological and moral states" (Gibson and Rafter 9). Over the course of his more than thirty-year career, Lombroso measured and categorized the bodies of thousands of criminals, documenting everything from the size of their ears and the length of their arms to the shape of their feet and the slope of their heads. Through these efforts, Lombroso believed that he had discovered a "criminal type" or a set of specific anatomical traits that distinguished law-breaking individuals from law-abiding ones. In the mind of the Italian researcher and his followers, "the criminal was knowable, measurable and predictable, largely on the basis of cranial, facial and bodily measurements" (Savitz xi). Indeed, while Lombroso never entirely discounted the influence of social forces like poverty, lack of education, or inebriation on criminal behavior, he also believed that some individuals were what he termed "delinquente nato," or "born criminals." Offenders of this type, Lombroso argued, were "a natural phenomenon, representing a distinct species, *homo delinquens*" (Savitz x).

The physiological traits distinguishing criminals from the rest of the populace were not simply atypical, but—as Lombroso termed it—"anomalous." Thieves, prostitutes, and murderers could be readily visually identified because they possessed "deviant" heads, "abnormal" features, and "aberrant" limbs. In prefatory comments to the first edition of *Criminal Man*, Lombroso asserts that criminals, "compared to 'healthy' individuals, have smaller and more deformed skulls, greater height and weight, and lighter beards. They are more likely to have crooked noses, sloping foreheads, large ears, protruding jaws, and dark skin, eyes, and hair. They also tend to be physically weak and insensitive to pain" (9).

For Lombroso, the identification of these traits had important sociological implications; as he repeatedly pointed out, they gave everyone from police officers and judges to employers and pedestrians the ability to readily identify troublemakers. Men and women would know murderers, thieves, and rapists because they "looked like" criminal types. Lombroso was so confident in his ability to distinguish law-abiding citizens from lawbreakers that he claimed that he could do so merely by examining photographs of them. As Stephen Jay Gould recounts, at several points during his career, Lombroso testified for both the defense and the prosecution at trial, arguing that a defendant either could or could not have committed the crime based simply on his or her physical appearance (168). Even when the Italian researcher was not personally present, his ideas "became important criteria for judgment in many criminal trials" (Gould 168).

The impact of Lombroso's work extended beyond the realms of applied sociology or empirical criminal justice. The popularity of Darwinian viewpoints during this era led to the characteristics that the Italian researcher attributed to criminal types being seen as further proof of race hierarchy. In the eyes of both Lombroso and the general public, the physical and psychological traits that felons possessed were not merely abnormal; they were atavistic. Since offenders were seen as less "civilized" and more "barbaric" than law-abiding men and women, they were also seen as less "evolved" and more "primitive." In the words of Gibson and Rafter, Lombroso argued that the physical anomalies embodied in criminal men and women "resembled the traits of primitive peoples, animals and even plants, 'proving' that the most dangerous criminals were atavistic throwbacks on the evolutionary scale" (1).

Starting with the very first edition of *Criminal Man*, the Italian researcher made a case for "the many characteristics shared by savages, colored races, some of the higher animals, and born criminals" (Savitz xiv). While Lombroso would recalculate the precise percentage of "born criminals" among the populace of civic offenders—declaring "40 percent of all offenders" to be "born criminals in the third edition of *Criminal Man*" and then reducing "his estimate to 35 percent in the fifth edition" (Gibson and Rafter 10)—he would never waver in his belief about the atavistic nature of these men and women. As Gibson and Rafter have demonstrated, this argument was the signature facet of his work and the one that would form a cornerstone for the growing field of criminal anthropology.

The impact of Lombroso's work extended far beyond scientific circles; his belief in what Stephen Jay Gould has called "the born criminal with his apish stigmata" (172) also influenced the perception of criminals in the popular imagination. As Gibson and Rafter point out, "With the publication of the first edition of *Criminal Man*, Lombroso's image of the atavistic offender—with his small skull, low forehead, protruding jaw, and jutting ears—fired the imagination of not only jurists and doctors but also writers, journalists, and artists" (28–29). They go on to note the presence of Lombrosian ideas in the work of figures ranging from Sir Arthur Conan Doyle to Franz Kafka.

In what follows, I make the case that Edgar Rice Burroughs and *Tarzan of the Apes* was among them. As Savitz has documented, while the work of the Italian researcher was popular in Europe, he "had his greatest impact in the United States" (xix). Lombroso himself would remark in an article that was published posthumously in *Putnam's Magazine* in April 1910 that his theories became the object of "almost fanatical adherence" in America (793). The following year, in fact, not one but two separate compendiums of his research appeared in the United States: *Crime: Its Causes and Remedies*, and *Criminal Man, According to the Classification of Cesare Lombroso*. The latter, which was begun collaboratively with his daughter, Gina Lombroso-Ferrero, before his death, featured a new introduction by Lombroso.

As Marianna Torgovnick postulates, "It is possible that Burroughs read anthropology" (45). Both John Kasson and Porges note that the author's library contained a copy of Darwin's *The Descent of Man*, a book that heavily influenced Lombroso and the field of criminal anthropology (Kasson 205; Porges 75). Even if Burroughs did not encounter *Criminal Man* firsthand, it is likely that he absorbed the ideas in it "by osmosis and hearsay, especially given the popularization of anthropological studies in his lifetime" (Torgovnick 45). Burroughs began penning *Tarzan of the Apes* in December 1911, after both *Crime: Its Causes and Remedies* and *Criminal Man, According to the Classification of Cesare Lombroso* had been published. Moreover, the previous year, the first National Conference of Criminal Law and Criminology was held on the campus of Northwestern University and received widespread media attention. The *Chicago Tribune*, for example, ran a series of bulletins about the conference, discussing everything from its focus and participants to events and significance. The first article, published on 26 April 1909, carried the proud headline "Chicago Leader in Criminology."

Edgar Rice Burroughs was not only born in Chicago but was residing in the Windy City when the National Conference of Criminal Law and Criminology took place. An avid reader of daily newspapers, the author likely encountered coverage of the landmark meeting. Moreover, one of the resolutions passed by attendees at the conference was the pledge "that important treatises on criminology in foreign languages be made readily accessible in the English language" (v). At the top of this list was the work of Cesare Lombroso (general introduction v).

Elements of Lombroso's theory that criminals possess heavily racialized and atavistic qualities permeates Burroughs's novel. Throughout *Tarzan of the Apes*, characters who commit murder—be they English sailors, anthropoid apes, or indigenous Africans—are routinely described in Lombrosian ways. From their sloping foreheads, small skulls, and animalistic features to their sadistic cruelty, lack of empathy, and compulsion for violence, their similarities to the Italian researcher's portrait of the "born criminal" are too numerous to be merely coincidental.

In the first edition of *Criminal Man* and in many subsequent versions of the text, Lombroso articulated the signature physical features of habitual criminals. Thieves, he noted, are characterized by their "expressive faces and manual dexterity, small wandering eyes that are often oblique in form, thick and close eyebrows, distorted or squashed noses, thin beards and hair, and sloping foreheads" (51). Meanwhile, he continued, "habitual murderers have a cold, glassy stare and eyes that are sometimes bloodshot and filmy; the nose is often hawklike and always large; the jaw is strong, the cheekbones broad; and their hair is dark, abundant, and crisply textured. Their beards are scanty, their canine teeth very developed, and their lips thin. Often their faces contract, exposing the teeth" (51). Although some of these characteristics were associated with certain types of criminals, all deviants shared an array of specific physical qualities. Chief among these, Lombroso argued, were "prognathism or an ape like forward thrust of the lower face," "a receding forehead," and microcephaly, or a "small cranial capacity" (48–49). The Italian researcher makes the atavistic implications of these traits explicit: "I cannot avoid pointing out how closely they correspond to characteristics observed in normal skulls of the colored and inferior races" (48). More specifically, Lombroso claims, "these features recall the black American and Mongol races and, above all, prehistoric man much more than the white races" (9).

From the opening pages of *Tarzan of the Apes*, villainous figures are associated with the atavistic traits outlined in the work of Cesare Lombroso. These men and women resemble criminal types via their possession of the heavily racialized and routinely animalistic qualities associated with "lesser" species and "lower" races. One of the mutineers aboard the *Fulwalda*, for example, is characterized as "a huge bear of a man, with fierce black mustachios, and a great bull neck set between massive shoulders" (5). Moreover, the leader of the group is known by the racially charged name "Black Michael."

The men who overthrow the captain of the *Arrow*—the vessel that delivers love interest Jane Porter and her companions later in the novel—possess similar qualities. These individuals are introduced as "swarthy, sun-tanned, villainous looking fellows" (112). The physical appearance of the group of them who comes ashore is seen as an accurate indicator of their innate criminal natures: "Some twenty souls in all there were, if the fifteen rough and villainous appearing seamen could have been said to possess that immortal spark, since they were, forsooth, a most filthy and blood-thirsty looking aggregation" (114). Although Tarzan is unable to understand the language that they are speaking, he is able to recognize—as Lombroso himself often claimed—their wickedness based on their appearance and behavior: "He knew by their threatening gestures and by the expressions upon their evil faces that they were enemies of the other party" (123). Indeed, the King of the Apes repeatedly calls the first leader of the group a "mean-faced" little man (112). His successor is cast in even more Lombrosian terms, as "rat-faced" (112).

The connections between Lombroso's views on born criminals and the villainous characters in Burroughs's novel are not reflected merely in physical traits; they are mirrored in various psychological ones as well. One of the most prominent, as well as most alarming, qualities that Lombroso identified among habitual thieves and murderers was an acute lack of empathy. In the first edition of *Criminal Man*, he assert that "complete indifference to their victims and to the bloody traces of their crimes is a constant characteristic of all true criminals, one that distinguishes them from normal men" (63). Expanding on this idea, he states that

> more generally, criminals exhibit a certain moral insensitivity. It is not so much that they lack all feelings, as bad novelists have led us to believe. But certainly the emotions that are most intense in ordinary men's hearts seem in the criminal man to be almost silent, especially after puberty. The first feeling to disappear is sympathy for the misfortune of others, an emotion that is, according to some psychologists, profoundly rooted in human nature. (63)

Not surprisingly, Lombroso posits a causal connection between individuals' inability to feel empathy and their criminal behavior.

These elements are powerfully present in *Tarzan of the Apes*. Characters who engage in criminal activities demonstrate a profound lack of compassion and an alarming dearth of remorse. In the opening chapter of the novel, for instance, the narrator describes the cold, unfeeling way that the mutinous sailors aboard the *Fulwalda* treat the casualties from their revolt: "The men had by this time surrounded the dead and wounded officers, and without either partiality or compassion proceeded to throw both living and dead over the sides of the vessel" (13). While such conduct toward the enemy might be understandable, the narrator goes on to reveal how "with equal heartlessness they disposed of their own wounded" (13).

When the sailors see John and Alice Clayton—who are mere passengers aboard the ship and thus neutral parties in the skirmish—they display even more heartlessness. As the narrator relays, one of the seamen shouts, "Here's two more for the fishes," as he rushes toward them "with uplifted axe" (14). Ironically, it is Black Michael's equally callous disregard for human life that saves them. Instead of trying to reason with his murderous shipmate by logically convincing him that the Claytons do not deserve to die or appealing to the seaman's emotions by making a case for sparing the lives of an innocent young couple, the leader simply kills him: "But Black Michael was even quicker, so that the fellow went down with a bullet in his back before he had taken a half dozen steps" (14).

The mutinous crew aboard the *Arrow* is no different. After Tarrant impulsively murders Snipes by gruesomely sinking a pick axe into his shipmate's brain, the other men respond quite pitilessly: "'Served the skunk jolly well right.' . . . There was no further comment on the killing, but the men worked in a better frame of mind than they had since Snipes had assumed command" (154). Tarzan witnesses this and other acts of brutal violence and thus he associates the seamen not simply with animalistic but simian qualities, musing that these individuals are "no more civilized than the apes" (112).

Given that whites who engage in criminal activity in *Tarzan of the Apes* are associated with atavistic qualities, it is not surprising that individuals who are already seen as members of a racially "inferior" group—namely, the black tribal Africans—fare even worse. Burroughs's subscription to Progressive-era beliefs in race hierarchy has been well documented by critics and biographers. As a teenager, for example, the future author attended the Columbian World Exposition where, among other attractions, he undoubtedly visited the Midway Plaisance. John Taliaferro has described this exhibit as

> a riot of racial and ethnic exhibitionism, a cosmic bazaar the likes of which the world had never witnessed. Lined up cheek by jowls were Africans, Indians, Bedouins, Laplanders, and South Sea Islanders, living in their respective huts, tents, and temples, wrapped in their respective robes, capes, kilts, and loin cloths. (35–36)

Far from a haphazard collection of various cultural groups, these individuals were arranged in a specific order for a particular purpose. A journalist for the *Chicago Tribune* explained the rationale: "What an opportunity was here afforded to the scientific mind to descend the spiral of evolution, . . . tracing humanity [from] its highest phases down to almost its animalistic origins" (qtd. in Taliaferro 36). Indeed, as Robert G. Spinney notes, "for many visitors to the fair, the Midway offered a kind of evolutionary yardstick against which the triumphs of modern man could be measured" (118). As he goes on to explain,

> The implicit message regarding the "progress" of the races was unmistakable. "From the Bedoiuns of the desert and the South Sea Islanders," wrote Marian Shaw, a journalist who toured the Midway, "one can here trace, from living models, the progress of the human race from savagery and barbarism through all the intermediate stages to a condition still many degrees removed from the advanced civilization of the nineteenth century." (118)

Exposed to such attitudes during his adolescence, Edgar Rice Burroughs—like many of his contemporaries—subscribed to them throughout his adulthood.

While evidence of the author's belief in race hierarchy permeates many of his fantasy and science fiction novels, they are perhaps most powerfully expressed in *Tarzan of the Apes*—a text that is not only set in the "dark continent" of Africa but also features indigenous black peoples. The first time that readers encounter members of the African tribe who populate the jungle region inhabited by Tarzan, in fact, these black men and women are described in a manner that could have appeared in either Stanley's *In Darkest Africa* or Lombroso's *Criminal Man*: "Their great protruding lips added still further to the low and bestial brutishness of their appearance" (71). Later, these individuals are also associated with animalistic physical qualities. The narrator repeatedly describes the hands of the men and women in the village as "claw-like" (198), echoing Lombroso's description of the stalled or stunted physical development of criminal types along with the "lower" races.

The indigenous Africans possess many additional and even more alarming Lombrosian characteristics, including their interest in orgiastic frenzies, their sadistic cruelty, and their cannibalistic appetites. In the introduction that Lombroso wrote for the compendium *Criminal Man, According to the Classification of Cesare Lombroso* (1911), he argues that born criminals are united by their "love of orgies, and the irresistible craving for evil for its own sake, the desire not only to extinguish life in the victim, but to mutilate the corpse, tear its flesh, and drink its blood" (xxv). This scene is re-created almost exactly in *Tarzan of the Apes*. As I have noted, Burroughs presents the tribal men and women feasting on human flesh. After capturing a French naval officer, they tie him to a stake and commence eating him alive: "They fell upon D'Arnot tooth and nail, beating him with sticks and stones and tearing at him" (198).

The anthropoid apes likewise possess many Lombrosian qualities. As Rose Lovell-Smith has remarked, apes were a "key symbol of evolutionary debate" during this era (386). Accordingly, Burroughs describes these creatures as "the most fearsome of those awe-inspiring progenitors of man" (31). From the moment that John and Alice Clayton catch a glimpse of these animals, they take their physical appearance to be a clear indicator of their violent natures: "And behind them, over the edge of a low ridge, other eyes watched—close set, wicked eyes, gleaming beneath shaggy brows" (18). As the creatures come closer, their ominous traits only become more obvious to the couple: "The ape was a great bull, weighing probably three hundred pounds. His nasty, close-set eyes gleamed hatred from beneath his shaggy brows, while his great canine fangs were bared in a horrid snarl as he paused a moment before his prey" (25).

Later, Tarzan's vicious foster father is described in a similar manner: "Tublat's little, close-set, blood-shot, pig eyes shot wicked gleams of hate" (61).

The brutal leader of the apes, Kerchak, possesses the most Lombrosian characteristics: "His forehead was extremely low and receding, his eyes bloodshot, small and close set to his coarse, flat nose; his ears large and thin, but smaller than most of his kind" (30). He is described as suffering from the microcephaly routinely associated with human criminals: "The back of his short neck was a single lump of iron sinew which bulged beyond the base of his skull, *so that his head seemed like a small ball* protruding from a huge mountain of flesh" (142; my emphasis). Not surprising, given the hereditary nature of such traits, Kerchak's son Terkoz possesses similar qualities. As the narrator notes, the fierce ape had a large "bull neck" and disproportionately small "bullet head" (105).

The various Lombrosian physical traits that the apes embody are matched by assorted psychological ones. According to Lombroso, "Once criminals have experienced the terrible pleasure of blood, violence becomes an uncontrollable addiction. Strangely, criminals are not ashamed of their bloodlust, but treat it with a sort of pride" (66). Akin to the mutinous British sailors and cannibalistic Africans, many of the anthropoid apes lack compassion for others and have a seemingly insatiable appetite for cruel, senseless violence. From the moment these creatures see John and Alice Clayton, for instance, they are intent on killing them. During the couple's first few days living on the beach, one of the apes bursts into the cabin and—without provocation—beats John and knocks Alice unconscious. Over the course of the coming months, "Clayton was several times attacked by the great apes which now seemed to continually infest the vicinity of the cabin" (27). By the end of the year, both he and his wife are killed at their hands.

The apes do not reserve their murderous violence for strangers; they also direct it at each other. One of the early scenes of the novel describes the senseless, murderous rampage of Tarzan's ape foster father against members of his own pack:

> And then Tublat went mad.
> With horrifying screams and roars he rushed to the ground, among the females and young, sinking his great fangs into a dozen tiny necks and tearing great pieces from the backs and breasts of the females who fell into his clutches. (62)

Recalling Lombroso's research once again, many of these outbursts conclude with an orgiastic frenzy. After killing a large gorilla who had been a longtime enemy, the apes "laid their burden before the earthen drum and then squatted there beside it as guards, while the other members of the community curled themselves in grassy nooks to sleep until the rising moon should give the signal for the commencement of their savage orgy" (58). This event culminates in a cannibalistic feast: "Their leaps and bounds increased, their bared fangs dripped saliva, and their lips and breasts were flecked with foam" (60). Burroughs here makes a tacit connection between the anthropoid apes and the black Africans who engage in similar orgiastic acts of cannibalism. Although the simian creatures are ostensibly the evolutionary intermediary between the "higher" animals and "lesser" humans, the Lombrosian traits that they share with the black Africans closes the gap, reframing them as equals.

Tarzan of the Apes was not the only work in which Edgar Rice Burroughs presented Lombrosian ideas about criminals and criminal behavior. Such attitudes also appeared in his pulp novel *The Mucker*, a narrative that Burroughs began writing six months after *Tarzan* made its serial debut. Although the novel's protagonist, a working-class hoodlum named Billy Byrne, and his life in the Chicago slum may not seem to have anything in common with the aristocratic Tarzan and his world of the African jungle, they are united through Burroughs's belief in social Darwinism and the biological inferiority of criminal types. As Taliaferro notes, "In Billy Bryne's Chicago . . . the fundamental law was survival of the fiercest" (105). Indeed, Burroughs's narrator notes at the outset that during fights between rival gangs, "there was nothing fair, nor decent, nor scientific about their methods. They gouged and bit and tore" (6). Reflecting Cesare Lombroso's ideas about criminals, these crooks and thugs are associated with animalistic and even atavistic elements. Readers learn, for instance, that these individuals "are equipped by Nature with mitts and dukes. A few have paws and flippers" (8). Lest such suggestions about the biological basis for their criminal behavior go unnoticed, the author says openly of his protagonist that "from a long line of burly ancestors he had inherited the physique of a prize bull" (11).

Burroughs's most powerful statements concerning criminality appear in his nonfiction writing: appropriately, in the columns that the author wrote about the murder trial of William Edward Hickman. As Bill Hillman has commented about the author's ten articles covering the case, "From the start Ed emphasized his belief that heredity determined criminal tendencies. His important point was that the hanging of Hickman would be a protective measure for the safety of future generations" (par. 10). Indeed, Burroughs flatly asserts that "moral imbeciles breed moral imbeciles, criminals breed criminals, murderers breed murderers just as truly as St. Bernards breed St. Bernards and thoroughbreds breed thoroughbreds" (qtd. in Hillman par. 10). Burroughs's missive of 28 January 1928 takes such observations one step further. In language that recalls that of Lombroso, the author characterizes Hickman as an "instinctive criminal" and offers suggestions for ways that society might manage "this new and terrible species of beast" (qtd. in Hillman par. 10).

In what has become an oft-quoted remark, Burroughs famously quipped that he wrote *Tarzan of the Apes* "with the aid of only Henry Stanley's *In Darkest Africa* (1890) and a fifty-cent Sears dictionary" (qtd. in Kasson 184). Given the numerous Lombrosian elements in his text, it seems equally likely that he had—either consciously or unconsciously—*Criminal Man* in mind as well. Of course, Stanley's *In Darkest Africa* and Lombroso's *Criminal Man* were not entirely unrelated texts; the era's ideas about race fueled the content of both of them. As Alex Vernon has observed about the period in which *Tarzan of the Apes* was written and released, "Africa and the primitive were in the air; they were the environment that nurtured Burroughs's and his audience's imagination" (61). I contend that so too was the work of Cesare Lombroso. While British imperialism has received the most attention in both past and present analysis, criminal anthropology is an equally palpable and just as powerful presence in Burroughs's novel. This detail adds a new ideological element to *Tarzan of the Apes*. But, given the way in which Lombroso's ideas were fueled by turn-of-the-century beliefs in "inferior" people and "lesser" cultures, it simultaneously expands on the presence of race, class, and colonialism in the text.

"A Perfect Type, . . . Unmarred by Dissipation, or Brutal and Degrading Passions": Burroughs's Ape-Man as the Anti-Lombrosian Man

While nearly all of the animal and human characters in *Tarzan of the Apes* engage in acts of criminality, not all of them are associated with Lombrosian traits. Tarzan's foster mother, for example, is noticeably devoid of these elements. When readers first meet her, she is described as "a splendid, clean-limbed animal, with a round, high forehead" (30–31). Echoing the Lombrosian belief that such outward physical traits provide an accurate indicator of inner mental qualities, the narrator explicitly comments that these features "denoted more intelligence than most of her kind possessed" (31). Indeed, unlike many of her fellow apes who lack empathy, "she had a greater capacity for mother love and mother sorrow" (31). Lest we forget Kala's distinct physiology and the positive qualities associated with it, the narrator reminds us a few pages later that "Kala was a fine clean-limbed young female" (38).

Of course, Tarzan is not biologically related to his ape foster mother, but he does share these features. In a comment that directly links Burroughs's title character to Kala, the French naval officer D'Arnot describes Tarzan as "a clean limbed young giant" (201). Although the eponymous figure commits repeated acts of murderous violence, he lacks any trace of atavism. Indeed, not only is the King of the Apes devoid of any Lombrosian elements, but he is often cast as the antithesis of this type. Burroughs calls repeated attention to Tarzan's finely formed features, well-proportioned face, and good-looking appearance, details that are framed as outward manifestations of his inner goodness. When the title character is still a young boy, for example, the narrator highlights "his well shaped head and bright, intelligent eyes" (53). Likewise, later, Jane and others repeatedly comment on Tarzan's "handsome face" (137). D'Arnot reflects that "he was very handsome—the handsomest . . . that he had ever seen" (214). Even when Tarzan is engaged in acts of bloody violence, he remains a flawless example of the ideal man. Jane muses about him, noting

> the graceful majesty of his carriage, the perfect symmetry of his magnificent figure and the poise of his well shaped head upon his broad shoulders.
>
> What a perfect creature! There could be naught of cruelty of baseness beneath that godlike exterior. Never, she thought had such a man stroke the earth since God created the first in his own image. (184)

Burroughs goes to great lengths to make clear that his title character's skill for and even pleasure in violence do not arise from a Lombrosian taint. As the narrator states explicitly, "That he joyed in killing, and that he killed with a joyous laugh upon his handsome lips *betokened no innate cruelty*" (82; my emphasis). Later, after Tarzan rescues Jane from the brutal Terkoz, the "purity" of his inclination for killing is reiterated: he is "a perfect type of the strongly masculine, *unmarred by dissipation,* or brutal and degrading passions" (182; my emphasis). These qualities, in fact, are what let Jane know that she can trust him: "No, he could never harm her; of that she was convinced *when she translated the fine features and the frank, brave eyes* above her into the chivalry which they proclaimed" (183; my emphasis).

Readers and critics have been commenting on the title character's status as not merely a superior man but a superior *white* man ever since the novel was first published. Indeed, even before Tarzan is born, Burroughs establishes his exceptional race pedigree. The central character's father, John Clayton, Lord Greystoke, is a member of the British aristocracy and thus a product of fine breeding. Describing Lord Greystoke as "a strong, virile man—mentally, morally, and physically," the narrator goes on to assert how "in stature he was above average height; his eyes were gray, his features regular and strong; his carriage that of perfect, robust health influenced by his years of army training" (2). At repeated points throughout the novel, Burroughs calls attention to the fact that Tarzan has inherited these traits. When the King of the Jungle is teaching himself to read, for instance, the narrator accounts for this astounding feat by referring to "the active intelligence of a healthy mind *endowed by inheritance* with more than ordinary reasoning powers" (56; my emphasis). Likewise, in a subsequent chapter, the narrator explains that the title character's jungle prowess results not simply from his well-conditioned muscularity but also from "the intelligence that was his by right of birth" (173). This description of Tarzan is reiterated when he meets Jane. The apeman treats the young woman in a chivalrous manner, and his behavior is framed as "the hall-mark of his aristocratic birth, the natural outcropping of many generations of fine breeding, an hereditary instinct of graciousness which a lifetime of uncouth and savage training and environment could not eradicate" (189). Finally, near the end of the novel, when Tarzan is pondering the possible identity of his biological mother and father with D'Arnot, the naval officer assures him that he is "a pure man, and, I should say, the offspring *of highly bred and intelligent parents*" (238; my emphasis).

An awareness of the influence of Cesare Lombroso's criminal anthropology on *Tarzan of the Apes* reveals that the central character's status as a physically, mentally, and intellectually superior man is not predicated simply on his whiteness. After all, it was Caucasian men and women who committed crimes like murder, arson, and theft that Lombroso associated with animalistic and even atavistic qualities. Their engagement in such behavior, in fact, was prima facie evidence of their status as evolutionary throwbacks. As the "clean-limbed," compassionate and intelligent ape Kala, and the "swarthy, sun-tanned, villainous looking" white British seamen in Burroughs's novel reveal, an individual's racial status alone did not determine their position along the Darwinian evolutionary scale. Instead, a more complicated conception that draws on the interplay of biological determinism and social hierarchy is at play in *Tarzan of the Apes*.

Everything Old Is New Again: The Periodic Return of Tarzan and the Public Revival of Biocriminology

Significantly, every time that *Tarzan of the Apes* has enjoyed increased popularity in the United States, it has coincided with a rejuvenation in the belief that there is a biological basis for criminal behavior. After Burroughs's novel had fallen out of print and even out of the public consciousness for several decades, it experienced a renaissance in the 1960s. As Marianna Torgovnick notes, in 1963 "one out of every thirty paperbacks sold was a Tarzan novel" (42). Alex Vernon has discussed the tremendous popularity of Burroughs's title character during this era, especially among children: "A 1963 *Life* magazine article reported that 'one day during the time of Tarzan's greatest success'—presumably sometimes between the world wars—'there were 15 children in Kansas City hospitals who had hurt themselves falling out of trees while playing Ape Man'" (14). Tarzan was not just appealing to juvenile readers. Adults likewise both enjoyed the novel and were interested in the life and career of its creator. As Torgovnick notes, the 1960s and 1970s saw the appearance of "several popular biographies of Burroughs" (44).

This revival of Tarzan coincided with the revival of biocriminality. Beginning in the mid-1960s, scientists in the United States posited a new genetic basis for criminal behavior: the XYY genotype. The Y chromosome causes humans to develop into males, and most males have only one. However, geneticists discovered that approximately one male in every one thousand live births possess an extra Y chromosome, giving them a genotype of XYY ("XYY trisomy"). Given that the Y chromosome was responsible for engendering sexual maleness in humans—and that males were known for being more aggressive than females—biologists, psychologists, and sociologists posited a possible causal connection between XYY males and antisocial and even criminal behavior. Initial examinations of male prisoners seemed to affirm this viewpoint. Various studies, such as the one conducted by W. H. Price and P. B. Whatmore at a maximum security prison hospital in Scotland in 1967, for example, reported a far greater proportion of XYY males than in the general population: 3 percent, compared to 0.1 percent (533). Although the findings of subsequent research were far less clear—setting off what Stephen Jay Gould aptly characterized as "the great XYY debate" (24)—the link had been made. In everything from scientific textbooks to the popular imagination, the XYY genotype was seen as a catalyst for aggressive behavior. Indeed, indicating the credence given to this belief, in 1968, attorneys at murder trials in France and Australia used their client's possession of the XYY genotype as a defense strategy. The cases made headlines around the world (see Moore 1093n6).

A similar phenomenon occurred during the final decade of the twentieth century. Once again, Tarzan experienced a literary and cultural rejuvenation during this era. In 1990 alone, for example, Penguin, Ballantine, and the New American Library all released new editions of Burroughs's original novel. This new popular interest in Tarzan would reach its apogee in 1999, when the Walt Disney Company released a feature-length animated film based on the King of the Apes. Disney's *Tarzan* was the top-grossing film during its opening weekend, earning more than $34 million at the box office. Moreover, it received overwhelmingly positive reviews, with more than 70 percent of critics giving it a rating in either the A or B range (*"Tarzan"*).

This increased interest in *Tarzan of the Apes* emerged against the backdrop of a new book that revived biological-based arguments about human behavior, *The Bell Curve* (1994). Co-authored by Richard J. Hernstein and Charles Murray, the volume argues that "cognitive ability is substantially heritable" (23). The duo devotes an entire chapter to the relationship between what they regard as the heavily biologically determined category of intelligence and criminal conduct. In a matter-of-fact tone, they preface their discussion with the pronouncement that

> among the most firmly established facts about criminal offenders is that their distribution of IQ scores differs from that of the population at large. Taking the scientific literature as a whole, criminal offenders have average IQs of about 92, eight points lower than the mean. More serious or chronic offenders generally have lower scores than casual offenders. (235)

Although Hernstein and Murray never use the phrase "born criminal," comments that they make later in *The Bell Curve* are evocative of this Lombrosian idea. Discussing one longitudinal study, for instance, they assert that "the eventual relationship between IQ and repeat offending is already presaged in

IQ scores taken when the children are 4 years old" (242–43). In light of such evidence, the authors conclude that "the idea is that criminals are distinctive in psychological (perhaps even biological) ways," a viewpoint that they assert has "lately regained acceptance among experts" (238).

They were not wrong. Theories about the possible biological origins for criminal behavior appeared in numerous sources during the final decade of the twentieth century and opening years of the new millennium. According to Gibson and Rafter, "Today, criminologists are again considering the possibility that crime may be rooted (at least partially and occasionally) in biological factors" (30). While they are careful to point out that major differences exist between the viewpoints of early criminal anthropologists like Lombroso and those working today—whose perspectives are informed by the post-Lombrosian discovery of genes, an awareness of antisocial risk factors, and a recognition of causational factors—they also call attention to significant areas of overlap. In everything from the ongoing importance of the nature-nurture debate to the emergence of the new field of evolutionary psychology, "Lombroso," Gibson and Rafter conclude, "foreshadowed one of the major currents in biocriminology today" (31).

Tarzan of the Apes can be connected with this phenomenon. The narrative was initially influenced by Progressive-era theories about the biological basis for criminal behavior, and its plot, characters, and themes are relevant to more recent work in biocriminology. Matt Cohen has argued that "Tarzan, if not Burroughs himself, has emerged at the center of recent debates among cultural studies scholars and theorists interested in the development of mass media, imperialism, and gender and sexuality" (3). Criminology should be added to this list. Placing violent crime and habitual offenders at the center of our examination of Burroughs's text provides a more complete portrait of his protagonist and antagonists alike. At the same time, doing so adds a new dimension to the interplay among biological determinism, social Darwinism, eugenics, masculinity, and race hierarchy throughout the text. *Tarzan of the Apes* is commonly classified as a "boys' book" or an adventure novel, but we could also describe it as "crime fiction." Although far from a traditional murder mystery, the narrative is interested in the two quintessential questions of such literature: whodunit and why.

CHAPTER FOUR

"A Sixth Sense Seemed to Tell Her That She Had Encountered Something Unusual"

Psychic Sleuthing in the Nancy Drew Mystery Stories

> There simply must be a corpse in a detective novel, and the deader the corpse the better.
>
> S. S. VAN DINE, "Twenty Rules for Writing Detective Stories" (1928)

Of all the myriad forms of print material that discuss murder, perhaps none is more popular than mystery novels. Detective fiction "is possibly the most widely read kind of literature" (Mansfield-Kelley and Marchino 2), and statistical surveys taken during the 1990s indicated "that 20 to 22 percent of all books sold in the United States" were "some form of mystery or detective fiction" (Klein 2). In fact, since the 1980s, it has not been "unusual for at least three or four of the ten novels on the *New York Times* best-seller list to be detective fiction" (Mansfield-Kelley and Marchino 1). Analogous figures typify the twenty-first century.

Detective fiction is likewise a popular genre in children's literature. While narratives for young readers are commonly divided into categories like picture books, YA novels, and historical fiction, mystery tales form an equally powerful subgenre and have been published for young readers for generations. Moreover, these books contain some of the most beloved characters in children's literature, from Tom Swift, the Bobbsey Twins, and Trixie Belden to the Hardy Boys, Judy Bolton, and the Boxcar Children. Taken collectively, they demonstrate, in the apt words of Dean Mansfield-Kelley and Lois A. Marchino, that "the audience for detective fiction obviously begins at an early age" (7).

Of all the mystery narratives written for young people, arguably none are more well known than the Nancy Drew stories. Conceived by publishing mogul Edward Stratemeyer and penned by various ghost writers publishing under the pseudonym Carolyn Keene, the novels appeared during the golden age of both children's literature and mystery fiction. From the release of the inaugural title, *The Secret of the Old Clock*, in 1930, Nancy Drew was an immediate commercial success. Deborah L. Siegel has documented that "by Christmas of 1934 . . . the Nancy Drew Mystery Stories were outselling every other juvenile title on the shelves" (166). In the decades since, the girl sleuth has become not simply a literary legend but a cultural icon. As Michael G. Cornelius has observed, "Few other figures have so dominated their genre as effectively as Nancy Drew" (5). By 2004, the narratives had sold collectively more than two hundred million copies (O'Rourke, par. 4). In addition, they "have been translated into more than twenty-five languages" (Cornelius 7).

Unlike the majority of detective novels written for adults, the mysteries that Nancy solves are not cases of murder. Instead, as Sally E. Parry notes, the girl sleuth spends her time "helping insecure and frightened people find security, sometimes in the form of financial stability through inheritances, legacies, or missing valuables, and sometimes through returning children to a safe family environment" (146). That said, the plots always involve various forms of physical peril, as the central character is caught in a sudden storm, stranded by a stalled engine, or injured by a tumble down a steep staircase. Moreover, each book contains at least one direct threat to Nancy's life. As Patricia Craig and Mary Cadogan have aptly noted, "In every story there's a thrilling moment when she is dragged off by a person of evil appearance, soon to be threatened with the prospect of never seeing daylight again" (152).*

---

* This plot element appears in the very first novel of the series, *The Secret of the Old Clock*. Near the middle of the book, a robber catches Nancy attempting to foil his scheme and locks her in the closet, leaving her there to starve (133). This scenario is repeated with seemingly endless variation in nearly every subsequent novel. In *The Secret of Red Gate Farm* (1931, #6), when Nancy is captured by a group of counterfeiters, one of them proposes the following murderous means to silence her: "How about the shack at the river? It's in such a desolate spot no one would think of looking there until after—" (184). Likewise, in *The Mystery at Lilac Inn* (1930, #4), the girl sleuth is apprehended by a team of jewel thieves who plot her demise: "'Leave her here and let her starve,' Mary suggested cruelly. 'It

Nancy's life is not the only one that is regularly imperiled in the series. Most books feature the attempted murder of various other major or minor characters. In *The Hidden Staircase* (1930, #2), the girl sleuth's father, Carson Drew, is abducted and—in typical Nancy Drew fashion—nearly starved to death by the book's villain. When Nancy finally discovers her father several days later, he is very weak. "'I'll be all right,' Carson Drew forced a wan smile. 'Couldn't have stood it much longer, though. If you hadn't come just when you did—'" (195). Similarly, in *The Secret at Shadow Ranch* (1931, #5), the father of one of Nancy's friends is nearly killed when he attempts to stop a bank robber. As the criminal confesses after being apprehended by the girl sleuth, "He was struck squarely on the head and he fell without a word. We dragged him into the house, but we couldn't bring him to. He was as white as a ghost and his heart didn't seem to beat. We worked over him for fifteen minutes and finally gave up. Zany thought he had killed him" (189). These elements confirm S. S. Van Dine's maxim: "There simply must be a corpse in a detective novel, and the deader the corpse the better" (par. 8).

To foil these attempted murders—as well as solve the mysteries with which they are connected—Nancy Drew relies on some of the signature facets of the mystery genre: deductive reasoning and forensic evidence. As the girl sleuth coolly comments during a key moment in *The Secret of the Old Clock*, "I must try to think logically. If I don't, I'm lost" (135). Nancy's sharp intellect and impressive ability to detect clues is often the subject of praise by her friends and foes alike. As a character in *The Sign of the Twisted Candles* (1933, #9) attests, the girl sleuth has "the best ordered mind and keenest ability to put two and two together of any person I ever met" (160). In a powerful indication of the centrality of Nancy's forensic investigatory practices, the original hardcover books feature a silhouette of the central character peering through a magnifying glass—an image that has become iconic.

This chapter explores another tool Nancy Drew draws on in her detective work: extrasensory perception (ESP). A central but commonly overlooked feature of the title character's crime-fighting prowess is her psychic ability. In narratives throughout the series, Nancy's famous hunches, her powerful sense of intuition, and her unfailingly accurate gut feelings play as vital a role in her ability to solve cases as her use of reason, logic, and material evidence. Indeed,

---

would serve her right for meddling'" (157). Worried that Nancy will either escape or be discovered before she dies, they decide instead to bind, gag, and drown her. "The boat will sink before anyone can get to her," one of the goons says sinisterly (172).

as the narrator says about the girl sleuth in the very first book of the series, "a sixth sense seemed to tell her that she had encountered something unusual" (32). Far from a trait with which Nancy is associated only in this inaugural novel, a sixth sense is attributed to her throughout the stories. Frequently, the central character is able to solve the case not because she has discovered a previously overlooked physical clue—a footprint, a stray hair, a clothing fiber —but because she has had a hunch that pointed her in the correct direction.

The pages that follow explore what happens when Nancy Drew's psychic sleuthing is moved from the background to the forefront of her detective work. I examine an array of narratives from the original series that was first published between 1930 and 1957. These novels feature the original girl sleuth and, thus, were responsible for her initial public popularity. Spotlighting classic texts like *The Secret of the Old Clock* and *The Bungalow Mystery* (1930, #3) but paying special attention to *The Mystery of the Ivory Charm* (1936, #13), this chapter uncovers the heretofore undetected presence of parapsychology that permeates the novels. Not only does this psychic ability constitute a key component of Nancy's sleuthing skills but its appearance in the mystery series represents a radical break from the traditional, forensic-based mystery formula. The girl sleuth's sixth sense thus introduces a subversive component to a book series that has commonly been seen as conventional, conformist, and even conservative. Nancy's psychic ability enables her to save people from being killed and keeps murder at the periphery of the novels, thereby allowing the books to remain more "child appropriate," at least in terms of what was considered appropriate for children to read during the 1930s.

The role that psychic sleuthing plays in the Nancy Drew Mystery Stories series has significance that extends far beyond its contribution to genre theory. The famous girl sleuth does not just engage in the broad practice of parapsychology but also may have been modeled after a specific real-life practitioner: Eugenie Dennis. Making national headlines throughout the 1920s and 1930s for her psychic detective abilities, Dennis's life and work is uncannily similar to that of Nancy Drew in a number of ways. Like Stratemeyer's fictional creation, Dennis hailed from the Midwest, solved her first big mystery when she was sixteen, and specialized in cases of stolen jewels, missing wills, and kidnapped children. Accordingly, this chapter takes its cue—or, rather, *clue*—from the Nancy Drew mystery series itself and examines the case of the hidden psychic sleuth.

"The Blue Sense": Psychic Criminology

While advances in criminology are most commonly associated with break-throughs in forensic science—such as the discovery of fingerprint technology in the nineteenth century, the advent of DNA matching during the twentieth century, and the implementation of spectrophotometry in the new millennium—police have also relied on a second, less often-discussed form of criminal detection over the years: ESP. A broad term that refers to paranormal powers, ESP encompasses both well-known phenomena like telepathy and clairvoyance to lesser-known processes like psychometry through which "touching an object" allows an individual to allegedly "'see' something about its owner" (Wilcox 12) and dowsing, "a form of ESP in which underground water, minerals, objects (e.g., bodies, artifacts, lost articles) are located by sensitive individuals, usually with the aid of a dowsing rod or pendulum" (Hibbard, Worring, and Brennan 25). Since the birth of modern parapsychology during the antebellum era, these forms of psychic detection have been a consistent and even valuable, if controversial and usually less publicly visible, tool for the investigation of crime.

While the use of paranormal powers to capture criminals may seem like a contemporary phenomenon—the product of a postmodern, new-age sensibility—Whitney Hibbard, Raymond Worring, and Richard Brennan remind us that "throughout the ages, humans have sought to divine the answers and solutions to many questions and problems, including the determination of sources of ill fortune and ill will, the whereabouts of lost objects and people, and the perpetrators of crime" (10). In examples ranging from the Oracle at Delphi and Nostradamus to newspaper horoscopes and even fortune cookies, "men and women of all races and nationalities have consulted various oracles to look into the future, examined the stars and planets to determine the forces that influence their lives, and visited seers, shamans, witch doctors, and practitioners of the occult arts for information and advice" (10).

While a belief in various forms of ESP has been a constant in human civilization, the advent of modern psychic detection is commonly traced to the 1840s with the birth of the Spiritualism movement. In what has become an oft-recounted story, in 1847, "the Fox sisters of Hydesville, New York, said they heard spirit rappings in their home. Kate and Margaret Fox sat at a table and asked questions of their visiting spirit, a being called Mr. Splitfoot. As scary as his name sounded, the spirit was helpful. He answered their questions by rapping once for *no*, twice for *yes*, and three times if the question couldn't be answered" (Larsen 78). As news of this event spread, the rappings ignited public curiosity and, over time, a nation-wide movement. Howard Kerr and Charles L. Crow have written that, as evidenced in phenomena ranging from spirit photography, séances, and mesmerism to trance writing, Ouija boards, and ghosts, the Spiritualist movement "claimed the curiosity of millions and the belief of not a few Americans with its demonstrations of intelligible communication from the dead" (2).

The Fox sisters were not only the first modern Spiritualists but, as Anita Larsen notes, they "were also the first modern psychic detectives" (78): "In 1848, the spirit rapped out information about himself in code. He was a thirty-one-year-old peddler who had unfortunately called at the Hydesville house in which the Fox sisters now lived. He'd been murdered for his money by some-one whose initial were C. R., who then buried him in the cellar" (78). Before long, curiosity concerning the veracity of this claim grew so great that "the cellar was dug up," whereupon "human hair, some bones, and part of a skull were found. The immediate suspect was a man named Charles B. Rosana, a previous tenant who had moved to Lyons, New York" (Larsen 78–79).* When confronted with this evidence, Rosana protested his innocence, going "so far as to acquire signatures, on a petition, of forty-four people who swore to his good character" (Larsen 78–79). The public was seemingly satisfied with such assurances, and the matter was dropped. However, in 1904, when the excavation of a wall on the former Fox home in Hydesville "uncovered most of the rest of the skeleton's bones, as well as a tin peddler's box" (Larsen 79), the spirit's assertions were seemingly confirmed.

As the nineteenth century progressed, many other men and women fol-lowed in the Fox sisters' footsteps. As Joe Nickell has documented, "during the heyday of Spiritualism, some séance mediums claimed to solve crimes through contact with the spirit world" (12). Both in the United States and throughout Great Britain, an array of crime-solving fortune-tellers, clairvoy-ants, and hypnotists attained great fame and even fortune. In a telling indica-tion of the credence given to extrasensory perception during the Victorian era,

---

*It should be noted that different historians offer different spellings of this surname. Some scholars, such as Todd Jay Leonard in *Talking to the Other Side: A History of Modern Spiritualism and Mediumship*, list it as "Rosna" (61). Meanwhile, others, like Kenneth Boa in *Cults, World Religions and the Occult*, spell the name "Rosma" (166). Finally, Rosemary Ellen Guiley in *The Encyclopedia of Ghosts and Spirits* records the name as "Rosa" (161). For more on the past as well as present search for the official surname and thus true identity of this figure, see Nickell.

a psychic detective was used in the era's most infamous murder case: Jack the Ripper. Although the exact role that London medium Robert James Lees played in the case remains the subject of much debate, his involvement is a point of fact: "The first reference tying Lees to the case came from the criminal himself, whoever he was. In a July 25, 1889, letter to Scotland Yard, the FBI of Great Britain, someone signing himself 'Jack the Ripper' wrote 'Dear Boss, You have not caught me yet you see, with all your cunning, with all your "Lees," with all your blue bottles,'" referring "to the pesky, flylike, blue-coated police" (Larsen 80).

Although the Spiritualist movement faded by the late nineteenth century, psychic detection endured. The Society for Psychical Research was founded in London in 1882 ("History of the Society for Psychical Research"). Meanwhile, its U.S. counterpart, the American Society for Psychical Research, appeared three years later in 1885 ("About the Society"). Parapsychology also remained popular outside of academia. As Colin Wilson has written, "In 1893, a book called *The Law of Psychic Phenomena* caused widespread discussion all over America" (36). Written by Thomas Jay Hudson, "a Detroit newspaper editor and official at the U.S. Patent Office," the book claimed to provide scientific evidence for paranormal activities like telepathy and clairvoyance (36). Significantly, many of the examples that Hudson features are cases in which figures used their psychic powers to solve crimes (see Wilson 37). By the early 1900s, parapsychology had captured the attention of noted psychologist William James. After observing a series of séances, he concluded, "There seems fair evidence for the reality of psychometry" (qtd. in Wilson 62).

Such comments fueled further popular and professional interest. Paul Tabori, in *Crime and the Occult: How ESP and Parapsychology Help Detection*, discusses a variety of well-publicized psychic sleuths operating in both the United States and Europe throughout the first half of the twentieth century. As a result of their success in solving murders, locating missing people, and finding stolen property, psychic detectives like Dutch national Peter Hurkos became a household name. Using his powers of psychometry, Hurkos helped police apprehend the Boston Strangler, Albert DeSalvo, in 1943—though law enforcement officials later minimized and even discredited his role (Larsen 90–94). In later years, Hurkos would assist detectives on many other high-profile cases, including the kidnapping of Patty Hearst (Wilcox 18–21). As Tamara Wilcox has said of Hurkos, "He is one of a small group of psychics whom the police departments of every country call in when their own detectives are completely baffled about some crime" (7).

In the wake of these events, ESP grew in both public popularity and scientific legitimacy. In 1952, the CIA revealed that it "had been studying psi . . . and its potential applications in the Cold War" (Hibbard, Worring, and Brennan 32).* As Hibbard, Worring, and Brennan have documented, "Revelations from behind the Iron Curtain indicated that the Soviets were not only heavily financing experiments in various psychic phenomena, but that they were having considerable success with their research program" (32). As a result, the United States decided to launch its own investigation into this area. "For instance, the CIA wanted to find out if a psychic could see a remote location and accurately describe the specific military installations there" (33). Over the years, the U.S. government would use remote viewers for a variety of military and civilian purposes, "including locating American hostages, finding and describing secret Soviet military installations, and pinpointing North Korean biological and nuclear weapons" (Olshaker 22). Chief among these remote viewers were Joseph McMoneagle, Leonard "Lyn" Buchanan, and Paul H. Smith, who were highly regarded. McMoneagle, for example, "was awarded the Legion of Merit, one of the Army's highest peacetime awards for 'producing crucial and vital intelligence unavailable from any other source' for such agencies as the Defense Intelligence Agency, CIA, DEA, the Secret Service, and even the Joint Chiefs of Staff" (Hibbard, Worring, and Brennan 16).

The federal government's psi program operated clandestinely until the mid-1970s, when "a number of scandals involving the CIA forced it to divest itself of any sort of controversial activities in which it was engaged at that time" (Hibbard, Worring, and Brennan 33). That said, the government's psychic detection program was not dismantled, just reassigned. Under the auspices of various federal intelligence agencies and code names, research into psychic detection continued through the mid-1990s when, in the waning years of the Cold War, it was finally declassified (see Hibbard, Worring, and Brennan 15–16). Far from delegitimizing psychic detection, declassification

* The United States was neither the first nor the only nation to explore the investigative possibilities of parapsychology. As Heather Wolffram, who provides an overview Germany's various programs about and experiments with parapsychology from 1918 through the end of World War II, explains, "During the Weimar years, German's police experimented with a wide range of new technologies and forensic techniques. Among the more unusual of these was so-called criminal telepathy (*Kriminal-telepathie*): the practice of using a telepath or clairvoyant to shed light on unsolved crimes" (581).

actually enhanced it. "With the decommissioning of the government's program in 1995, the highly trained remote viewers were free to become involved in the private sector" (Hibbard, Worring, and Brennan 16). In the years since entering the civilian ranks, McMoneagle, for instance, "also has worked as a remote viewer for numerous police departments, a number of State's Attorneys General Offices, the FBI, U.S. Customs, Department of Defense, and the National Security Council" (Hibbard, Worring, and Brennan 16).

The U.S. government continues to explore the potential military use of ESP. In the wake of the attacks on 11 September 2001, for example, the federal government employed a group of remote viewers in the war on terror. "The *London Sunday Times* reported on November 11, 2001, that 'Prudence Calabrese, whose Transdimensional Systems employs 14 remote viewers, confirmed that the FBI asked the company to predict likely targets of future terrorist attacks'" (Olshaker 22–23). This story was confirmed a few months later. In the 21 January 2002 edition of *New York* magazine, reporter Geoff Gray quotes a former Justice Department attorney on the department's past and current use of remote viewers: "The FBI does not use psychics as its official sources, the lawyer says; it happens 'under the table.' After September 11, 'the attorney general told us to think outside the box,' says this person, who still works closely with federal law-enforcement officials. 'This is definitely thinking outside the box'" (Olshaker 23).

These events occurred against a backdrop of heightened public interest in ESP and increased professional respect for the field of parapsychology. The final decade of the twentieth century and opening years of the new millennium was something of a heyday for psychic detection in the United States, with the practice being openly employed by law enforcement officials, widely discussed in newspaper articles, and repeatedly featured on television programs. New Jersey native Dorothy Allison, for instance, attained national prominence for her involvement in several high profile cases, including the Atlanta child murders and the serial killings by John Wayne Gacy. According to Douglas Martin in his obituary for her for the *New York Times*, "In interviews over the years, Ms. Allison said she had worked on more than 5,000 cases, so many that she had trouble recalling the names of victims. She said she had led detectives to 250 bodies and had solved hundreds of murders. Among the police departments that consulted her was New York City's" (par. 13). Similarly, Illinois astrologer Irene Hughes and Newark-based psychic Nancy Czetli both secured national reputations, the former having worked with "the

Chicago area police for over ten years" (Wilcox 30) and the latter involved with "more than 200 homicide cases" (Larsen 21). Perhaps the most famous modern-day psychic is Florida native Noreen Renier. As she recounted in her 2008 memoir: "I have worked on more than four hundred unsolved homicides, missing persons, and rape cases with city, county, and state law enforcement agencies in thirty-eight states and six foreign countries. My work has been featured in the newspapers, on television, and even in a textbook for homicide detectives" (xiv). Renier has been profiled on the true-crime programs *48 Hours*, *Unsolved Mysteries*, and *America's Most Wanted*. In a groundbreaking event in 1981, Renier became the first psychic detective to lecture at the FBI Academy in Quantico, Virginia. Even more impressively, in 1986, when Renier brought a libel suit against journalist John Merrell who had published an article accusing her of being a fraud, the FBI testified on her behalf. Special Agent Robert Ressler, the then-head of the Behavior Science Unit and the individual who had invited her to lecture at Quantico, took the stand and termed her predictions "'uncanny in their accuracy.' Apparently convinced by the testimony, the jury awarded Renier $25,000 from Merrell" (Lyons and Truzzi 7). Most recently, Renier was a consultant on the Laci Peterson murder case (Renier 237–44).

In response to both the growing number of psychic sleuths and their importance in criminal detection, Beverly Jaegers founded the U.S. Psi Squad. Initially termed the "Psychic Rescue Squad" and intended as a study and discussion group, the organization evolved into a crime-fighting body in the early 1970s (Wilcox 41). As Hibbard, Worring, and Brennan explain, the U.S. Psi Squad is "a group of trained and experienced" remote viewers who "work on cases throughout the country" (13). The organization serves as a standing resource for law enforcement officials in the United States and nations around the world (Wilcox 39).

In the wake of its increasing visibility, psychic criminology began "coming out of the law enforcement closet," to borrow a comment made by Pomona police lieutenant Kurt Longfellow on the subject (qtd. in Larsen 64). In the late 1970s, Longfellow's department made history when it drafted the first-ever "official policy for the use of psychic sleuths" (Larsen 64). In an equally ground-breaking acknowledgment, "a 1979 survey conducted by the California Department of Justice concluded that 'a talented psychic can assist you by helping to locate a geographic area of a missing person, narrow the number of leads to be concentrated upon, highlight information that has been overlooked, or provide information previously unknown to the investigator'" (Larsen 63–64).

Such sentiments have spread to law enforcement departments throughout the United States. According to the *Encyclopedia of Forensic Science*, "Approximately 35 percent of city police departments have used a psychic at least once in an attempt to solve a crime or find a missing body or article" ("Psychic Detectives" 229). Moreover, as psychologist Dr. Louise Ludwig has noted, "In every police department, there is at least one cop who is in contact with a psychic" (qtd. in Lyons and Truzzi 5). In an assertion that would have seemed impossible only a few generations ago, Karen Henrikson and Joseph Kozenczak, the chief investigator on the John Wayne Gacy case, argue in their article "Still Beyond Belief: The Use of Psychics in Homicide Investigations" that "the world of parapsychology has a great deal to offer. . . . Having once experienced the positive attributes a psychic can lend to a case, parapsychology seems to be a natural companion to the world of criminology" (qtd. in Hibbard, Worring, and Brennan 9). Echoing these sentiments, discussions about the application and value of psychic detection have appeared in numerous prestigious law enforcement publications, including *Policing, Police Chief, National Law Review, Practical Homicide Investigation,* and *Journal of Police Science and Administration* (Hibbard, Worring, and Brennan 20). In 2002, a full-length volume titled *Psychic Criminology: A Guide for Using Psychics in Investigations* was released. As its subtitle suggests, the book is dedicated to the subject of how law enforcement can use ESP in its work. *Psychic Criminology* has since gone into a second edition.

One final salient detail about criminal parapsychology is that many law enforcement squads do more than simply bring in psychics from the outside; they often have one or two detectives on their own staff who possess an uncanny sixth sense. As Hibbard, Worring, and Brennan have commented, "Most departments have one particular officer whose intuition, hunches, and gut feelings seem to be uncannily accurate, whether it's the patrol officer who always seems to be in the right place at the right time or the detective whose hunches prove consistently accurate" (5). Echoing these remarks, Anita Larsen notes that "the hunch that motivated the officer's behavior may be connected with her rational knowledge of a rash of burglaries in the neighborhood or in shops similar to those reached via the alley. But why *that* car? *That* alleyway? *That* night?" (60; italics in original). Arthur Lyons and Marcello Truzzi describe this ability as "that unknown quantity in the policeman's decision-making process, the heightened sense of intuition that that goes beyond what he can see and hear and smell" (12).

During the 1990s, this phenomenon acquired the name "the blue sense" after the common color of police uniforms (Lyons and Truzzi 12). As Lyons and Truzzi explain, "The 'blue sense' . . . is that hunch that sends a cop back to that gas station or down an alley; that feeling of impending danger that tells him to draw his gun" (12). "Because," they add, "the blue sense specifically relates to the practical application of this unknown faculty to law enforcement, we have chosen to extend the term to all those persons—police or non-police—who use psychic powers to solve crimes" (12).

The Drew Sense: Nancy Drew and ESP

For generations, Nancy Drew has been firmly associated with combating elements of the supernatural, paranormal, and occult. As Patricia Craig and Mary Cadogan observe, the plotlines to many of the novels showcase her "exposing the trickery behind an apparent haunting" (151): "This, in fact, is the most persistent theme in the Nancy Drew saga; the girl sleuth's world is populated to a remarkable extent by crooks who specialize in faking ghostly phenomena for the purpose of furthering a wicked objective" (151). From the "apparition" who terrorizes the two elderly women in *The Hidden Staircase* to the clandestine "cult" whose bizarre behavior frightens a small community in *The Secret at Red Gate Farm*, seemingly supernatural elements abound. However, as Craig and Cadogan sagely remark about the girl sleuth, "Like every heroine of the era gifted with common sense, she knows that anything mysterious must have a rational cause" (152).

While the central plot of many novels features Nancy Drew debunking an element of the occult, she ironically does so via the use of various psychic detective techniques. The girl sleuth is never directly associated with "the blue sense," but she does possess what could be termed "the Drew sense." Nancy does examine various material clues—an old clock, an abandoned bungalow, a beautiful jewelry box—but she is typically able to crack a case because of her famous hunches. In typical Nancy Drew fashion, the girl sleuth makes a breakthrough on a mystery because her "sixth sense" tells her to turn down an alley, reinspect an old antique, or take a drive back out to a country house.

Even a cursory examination of the Nancy Drew series reveals the centrality of the girl sleuth's unfailingly accurate hunches. In the opening sentence of

The Hidden Staircase, for example, Nancy announces, "I declare, I don't know what makes me so nervous this afternoon! I have the strangest feeling—just as though something were about to happen" (1). Of course, she is correct. As Nancy works to solve the resulting mystery, her intuition proves invaluable: "For a reason she could not explain, she felt that someone was watching her" (61). Later, she is "reluctant to leave, for although she had unearthed nothing, she could not help but feel she had overlooked something of vital importance" (74). Nancy lingers, and her hunch proves correct, as she discovers a crucial clue.

Similar events occur in nearly every Nancy Drew novel. As the narrator remarks about the girl sleuth in *The Bungalow Mystery*, "She knew only that she was playing a 'hunch' and that frequently her swift impressions were correct" (93). Likewise, as gal pal George Fayne says of the girl sleuth in *The Secret at Shadow Ranch*, "I'm willing to trust your intuition. . . . It hasn't failed in times past" (124). Nor does it fail in any subsequent novels. For instance, Nancy makes a breakthrough in *The Message in the Hollow Oak* (1935, #12) by relying on one of her unfailing gut feelings. Midway through the book, the narrator notes that she was "impelled by an impulse which she could not explain" (106) and proceeds to peer through a crack in the wall, with the result that she catches a glimpse of the book's scoundrel and foils his plans. Similarly, in *The Clue in Jewel Box* (1943, #20), Nancy muses, "We may not be too late to nab the pickpocket, if a hunch of mine is correct" (129). Of course, it is, and the thief is apprehended.

Of the more than thirty novels that constitute the original series, no book is more infused with the paranormal than *The Mystery of the Ivory Charm*. This story about a young Asian Indian prince who was abducted as an infant so that another figure could be installed as the maharajah has many classic features of a Nancy Drew mystery: a kidnapped heir, stolen documents, a lost fortune, and an abandoned cabin containing a secret underground tunnel. As Nancy encounters each of these elements and works to solve the mystery with which they are connected, her life as well as the lives of her companions are repeatedly put in danger. At various points, the girl sleuth or her pals endure one or more of the following: near suffocation by a killer snake, near strangulation in trapeze ropes, physical assault by robbers, trampling by a herd of stampeding elephants, infliction of a serious head wound by a band of intruders, drugging and abduction by kidnappers, and, in a quintessential Nancy Drew element, imprisonment in a cavern.

What separates *The Mystery of Ivory Charm* from other novels is that it is the only one in the original series that contains a murder: near the end of the narrative, one of the kidnappers, a circus performer named Rai, kills the missing prince, Coya. Both before and after this dramatic event, paranormal events abound, from Nancy's firm reliance on her signature sixth sense to trances, mysticism, precognition, fortune-telling, magic charms, and—in the closing pages—a bona fide resurrection. In so doing, *The Mystery of the Ivory Charm* stands out as both the most murderous and the most mystical Nancy Drew novel. Demonstrating the centrality that ESP occupies in the series, the 1936 narrative does not feature a battle between competing intellects but rather between competing types of paranormal power.

The Mystery of the Ivory Charm wastes no time establishing the centrality that the occult will play in the narrative. The first chapter is appropriately titled "Fortune Telling." The opening scene finds Nancy Drew and her two closest friends—cousins Bess Marvin and George Fayne—waiting in a railroad station on their way back to River Heights after spending the summer at a mountain camp. The girls are disappointed to learn that the train is delayed, but their spirits are lifted when railcars for a traveling circus pull into the station. In true Nancy Drew fashion, the first two figures that the group sees prove to be the source of their next mystery adventure: twelve-year-old Coya and the villain Rai, who is working as for the circus troupe and fraudulently posing as the boy's father. When Rai begins brutally whipping Coya for what he perceives to be the boy's incompetence in unloading the elephants, Rai attempts to distract the girls from their shock and even outrage by suggesting that "the young ladies" might "be amused to have their fortunes told" (6). The girl sleuth's skeptical response to this offer is perhaps intended to indicate that there is a difference between authentic psychic powers and fraudulent ones. "Nancy was about to refuse the offer, but Bess forestalled her by saying eagerly: 'Shall we girls? It might be fun'" (6). The trio consents, but Rai's subsequent remark only makes Nancy even more skeptical of his parapsychic abilities: "'First,' said Rai significantly, 'my hand must be crossed with silver'" (6). Bess takes a coin from her purse and, in yet another sign of his poor character, Rai frowns "slightly as if it were not large enough" (7). Nonetheless, he proceeds to tell the young woman's fortune, and his reading is anything but satisfying. Echoing another common criticism of pseudo-psychics, Rai's predictions for Bess are bland and general: "He told her a very acceptable fortune which included a year of good luck, an important letter to arrive soon, and a pleasant journey to be made in the immediate future" (7). As Nancy Drew aptly points out, "Since we're all waiting for a train now, the journey is fairly well assured" (7).

The circus performer's reading for George is equally nonspecific: "It too was a routine fortune, and for that reason disappointing" (7). As a consequence, the girl sleuth does not desire to hear her fortune: "'Never mind telling mine,' Nancy remarked indifferently" (7). However, her friends urge her to be a good sport, and so she relents: "To satisfy her companions, Nancy obediently submitted herself to Rai's strange scrutiny" (8). She then gets a glimpse of the paranormal: "As he fixed his piercing dark eyes upon her face she experienced an uncomfortable sensation which she was at a loss to explain" (8). When the circus performer finally delivers his prophesy, it is not what Nancy expects. In comments that wed the occult and murder, Rai tells her that he "can see no good fortune ahead. Alas, my daughter, it is written that you shall have great trouble. Ay! There will be dangers—one of which may claim your life—!" (8). Adding to the drama of the scene, "the monotonous voice of the man from India ended in a choked gasp, while Bess and George suddenly uttered a terrified scream" (8).

Rai's prediction proves immediately accurate. The very next sentence—which also forms the cliff-hanger to the opening chapter—reports that "from the lower branches of the tree a huge jungle snake had dropped directly upon the unsuspecting Nancy, wrapping its powerful coils about her in a venomous grip of death!" (8). While Bess and George shriek at the sight of the killer reptile, Rai has a more unusual reaction. Reflecting the occult's long-standing association in the West with racial, ethnic, and cultural otherness—coupled with the oft-discussed negative portrayal of nonwhite minority groups in the Nancy Drew series—the narrator notes that "the Indian's eyes bulged with superstitious fear. Instead of hurrying to Nancy's assistance he dropped down upon his knees in a state of half-trance, and in a sing-song voice began an incantation in his native tongue" (9).* Even after the danger has passed, Rai remains in this mesmeric state: "He continued to mutter and chant and make strange motions with his arms" (11). When Nancy and her companions are finally able to rouse him, he makes an unnerving remark, muttering to the girls that "a reptile will kill with the look of the eye. . . . So it has been written and so it is" (11).

---

* For more on the unflattering portrayal of minorities both in the original Nancy Drew series and in more recent narratives featuring the girl sleuth, see Fisher.

Nancy is saved from the snake's grip through the aid of young Coya and circus owner Harold Blunt. However, Rai posits a different reason for her rescue: "'You have supernatural powers,' he said in a hoarse whisper. 'It was that power which saved you from the reptile'" (11). In acknowledgment of Nancy's abilities and also in an effort to help her hone them, Rai gives her a gift: an ivory charm carved in the shape of an elephant. "It was a very old piece, an odd charm which hinted of a mysterious past" (12). Rai's response to the girl sleuth's inquiries about its history only adds to the item's occult intrigue:

> The man smiled mysteriously.
>
> "It has a story which fades far back into the past—a strange tale of a little known mystic province of India. This charm was once a prized possession of a great ruler—a Maharajah who is said to have been endowed with supernatural powers." (14)

Nancy is skeptical; she asks in a somewhat mocking tone, "And if I wear the charm, these powers will pass to me?" (14). Rai, however, is deadly serious: "The strange man replied soberly. 'The charm will so endow you. And since I have bestowed the gift on you, my own fortune should change for the better'" (14).

Once Nancy, Bess, and George have boarded their train and left the station, they discuss the bizarre encounter. Nancy reiterates her disbelief in the charm's occult powers:

> "Of course I don't believe all that nonsense Rai was telling us."
>
> "Not even about the mystical ruler?" Bess inquired.
>
> "That part may be true. I haven't any faith that this charm will endow me with supernatural powers." (16)

In a comment that calls attention to Nancy's well-established psychic powers, George replies, "I hope not. . . . You're efficient enough now!" (16). These scenes foreshadow happenings throughout the remainder of the novel. Para-normal events, psychic visions, and occult superstitions play a recurring and important role in nearly every scene in *The Mystery of the Ivory Charm*. More-over, these paranormal phenomena are inextricably linked to questions of murder, whether merely attempted or successful. In the very next chapter, for example, the Drew household is visited by a figure named Anita Allison. The middle-aged woman wishes to consult with Nancy's lawyer-father about a possible real estate deal. Miss Allison explains to the girl sleuth that a group of promoters has recently offered an excellent price for a piece of land that she inherited. However, an unusual event is preventing her from accepting the generous deal: a prophesying dream. In a comment that suggests the troubled woman is drawn to the Drew household more for Nancy's long-standing association with a sixth sense than for her father's reputation for handling legal matters, she asks the girl sleuth,

> "Do you believe in dreams?"
>
> "Well, in a way yes, and in a way no," Nancy returned, purposefully vague.
>
> "I am dreadfully upset over one which I had a few nights ago. That's why I've come to consult with your father." (27)

When Nancy points out to the visitor that her father "isn't a specialist on dreams" (27), Miss Allison is not deterred, explaining, "You see I had this dream. A strange man appeared to me and forbade me to go ahead with the deal. It upset me so much that I decided to talk the matter over with Mr. Drew" (27).

Before the pair can discuss the matter further, Miss Allison sees the ivory charm that Nancy is wearing and has a bizarre reaction: "She rose from her chair, taking a step toward Nancy. Her thin hand reached out as if to snatch the trinket, then fell to her side again. The color drained from her face. Before Nancy could move forward to assist her, Miss Allison sagged back into her chair in a faint" (28). While the woman's chauffeur attributes her wooziness to an ongoing medical condition, the girl sleuth has another theory: "She felt convinced that the woman's fainting spell had been brought on by a glimpse of the carved ivory charm" (30). This suspicion, of course, only enhances the object's allure: "Taking the trinket from the velvet cord about her neck she studied it intently. Surely it guarded some secret. Yet about its mysterious nature she could not even hazard a guess" (30–31). Indicating the veracity of these sentiments—and the importance that they will play as the novel progresses—Nancy says to her father, "The charm must have some strange significance. I feel certain there's a mystery connected with it" (32).

In typical Nancy Drew style, this suspicion proves correct. The occult nature of the charm is noted repeatedly, and its supernatural powers further enhance the girl sleuth's detective abilities. Coya remarks several times, for instance, that as long as Nancy is wearing the amulet, no harm can befall her. When the teenage girl is missing in the underground tunnel beneath an abandoned house on Anita Allison's property, Coya tells Bess and George not to worry. In a passage that typifies his speech patterns throughout the novel—and that contribute greatly to the racial stereotyping at work within the narrative—the young boy informs the girls that "if she meet bad trouble charm's mystic power will save her" (51).* He reiterates this sentiment a short time later: "Ivory charm will never fail" (52). Bess and George are not convinced, however, and contemplate venturing into the underground cavern to search for Nancy. "'No need,' Coya interposed earnestly. 'Wonderful ivory charm save her'" (53).

Professor Lowell Stackpole, an expert in the language, culture, and history of India whom the Drews hire to tutor Coya after he runs away from Rai and comes to live with them, expounds further on the amulet's occult nature. Examining the trinket, he confirms that the item most likely "belonged to a ruler of a mystic Indian province" (78). Stackpole remarks that "the ancient ones are especially interesting. Some of them are said to have contained precious jewels; others held a poison to be used against enemies, and a very few, a unique life-saving balm. . . . The poison was dark in color, the life-giving balm of light hue" (79).

The full paranormal powers of the ivory charm are revealed in the final pages of the novel when Rai kidnaps Coya from Professor Stackpole's house. Nancy and her chums track the missing boy to Miss Allison's abandoned abode, but they arrive just in time to witness his murder. Rai tells the girl sleuth that "it is decreed that Coya must die by my hand. He shall die slowly and in a manner befitting a rajah" (207). Of course, Rai does not kill the long-lost royal prince via a conventional method but an occult one: "Overhead Nancy and George could hear Rai muttering in a sing-song voice, apparently saying a weird incantation over Coya. They could distinguish moans from the boy, and knew that he must be suffering intensely. Then all became quiet" (209). By the time the police arrive to arrest Rai, his maniacal work has been done: "A group of dejected detectives standing in a semi-circle about Coya,

* This trait is even more puzzling given that English was the official language of British-controlled India during this era and Coya was born and spent the bulk of his life living in this locale. Given that the young boy is a member of the aristocracy—and, thus, presumably, the recipient of a top-quality education—he should be a fluent speaker of English, not one whose written and verbal communication is riddled with grammatical errors. Furthermore, Coya speaks here and throughout the remainder of the novel using not merely broken speech patterns but ones that are highly reminiscent of the plantation dialect stereotypically ascribed to blacks in the American South, especially during the time of slavery.

who lay stretched out on a blanket. The lad's face was colorless and he did not appear to be breathing. . . . 'I am afraid we have arrived too late. The boy is dead'" (211, 212). Nancy however, knows better and explains to George that if they could tap into the full power of the charm, it "would bring him back to consciousness. . . . For a long time I have suspected the truth—now I am certain of it. The Ivory Charm guards the secret of life and death!" (210). Of course, her belief subsequently proves correct: "While the detectives watched in amazement, Nancy twisted off one of the elephant tusks. . . . In the cavity of the elephant's body lay a tiny vial of fluid, light amber in color. Opening it, Nancy forced some of the liquid between Coya's lips. . . . Minutes passed, and the color began to return to the boy's face" (212). While the girl sleuth has saved the lives of many of her companions before—rescuing Bess from a flash flood in *The Secret at Shadow Ranch* and liberating Mr. Aborn from sure starvation in *The Bungalow Mystery*—she has never brought a person back from the dead. However, when her fail-safe hunches are combined with the mystical powers of the ancient charm, the girl sleuth is not simply able to solve a mystery but to defy the very laws of nature, allowing her to keep murder from actually occurring in the narrative—or, perhaps more accurately, to reverse its lethal effect.

Elements of the occult in *The Mystery of the Ivory Charm* are not limited to the object showcased in the book's title. Drawing on some historical facts but mainly on prevailing cultural stereotypes about India, Professor Stackpole discusses the region's religious traditions. First, in another detail that adds to the negative portrayal of non-Western peoples and cultures in the book, he links one of the central tenets of Hinduism with the occult, telling the girl sleuth that "some groups believe in reincarnation—that they are to be twice-born" (76). Nancy is intrigued and engages the professor in further conversation on the subject. During this discussion, faiths that fall outside of the Judeo-Christian tradition are further likened to mere superstition: "'I suppose certain natives place great faith in charms and omens,' Nancy commented. 'Indeed they do. You might say that many of them are very superstitious. They believe in all sorts of miracles and sacrifices. . . . Many wear amulets and charms to ward off disease, preferring such protection to the services of a doctor'" (77). The professor's closing observations raise the specter of voodoo, telling Nancy matter-of-factly that "there are natives who claim to have ability in Black Magic. They make clay images of those whom they wish to injure, thrusting spikes into them to cause illness" (77).

Coya seems to affirm these claims when suddenly, in the middle of reciting his lessons, he slips into a trancelike state: "Then gradually the tone of his voice changed, and in a dreamy, sing-song chant, the lad began a strange, senseless jargon" (81). Subsequently, the young boy becomes a psychic himself. "Coya have sudden premonition!," he unexpectedly announces to Nancy Drew one afternoon (96). As he goes on to explain, "I have strange premonition. . . . Strange vision. Coya see himself on way to India to rule as great Rajah! Great honor come to me through help of Nancy!" (96). By the close of the novel, of course, this psychic vision comes true: the girl sleuth discovers that the Indian boy is in fact a kidnapped prince who is the rightful ruler of his home province in India.

Likewise, Anita Allison acts on a sixth sense. When John Bruce, who represents the land developers, offers to buy the property that she has inherited, she rebuffs him. Rather than citing a financial, familial, or even personal reason for her refusal, she offers a mystical one: "The signs are not favorable for a transaction as this time" (83). Confused, Mr. Bruce inquires "The signs? . . . What signs do you mean?" He receives another mystical answer from the middle-aged woman: "I must have an omen. A favorable omen" (83). Mr. Bruce explains that if Miss Allison has any questions about the terms of the deal, she should consult local lawyer Carson Drew, who "is well versed in the value of real estate" (84). Miss Allison, however, has another method for evaluating business transactions and tells him that she would prefer to "consult the stars" (84).

Miss Allison's comments are far from empty rhetoric. As Nancy, Bess, and George witness firsthand, the strange single woman routinely slips into a trancelike state. Not coincidentally, the first one is precipitated by seeing the ivory charm: Nancy "became aware that Miss Allison no longer was gazing at her. The misty brown eyes were fastened upon a faraway hillside, and a strange expression came over the woman's face. As if in a trance she began to murmur: 'The elephant—the sacred elephant. Yes, yes, we were speaking of it—Rai and I—the sacred elephant'" (85). Then Miss Allison removes a book "from a handsome white beaded bag. . . . The girls were further bewildered when Miss Allison began to read in a musical voice from the tiny book" (85). While Bess fears that the woman has lost her mind, George offers the alternative and more accurate explanation: "She has some sort of psychic obsession" (85).

Nancy is fascinated by Miss Allison's behavior: "Nancy was not bored. She listened, absorbed, for the excerpts, which seemed to have been taken from an ancient Hindu legend, related the tale of an Indian prince who had been spirited away from his parents" (86). Miss Drew, who already suspected that Coya hailed from royalty, immediately realizes that this story is about him. "It occurred to her now that the Indian lad might be a person of regal birth, who, through the machinations of Rai and Allison, had been stolen from his own country as a royal babe so that another might rule in his stead" (87). The novel may assert that "with her usual ability to make shrewd deductions, Nancy had gone directly to the heart of the situation" (86), but the real breakthrough in the case arises via the paranormal, not logic or reason. Nancy asks Miss Allison to elaborate on this legend: "'Iama Togara,' Miss Allison murmured dreamily. 'He will rule with far more wisdom than will the boy Coya'" (87). Before the sleuth can question the woman any further, Jasper Batt, the man Miss Allison employs to watch her property, approaches and the trance is broken: "Observing the man, Miss Allison seemed to recover from her trancelike state. She closed the gold-covered book and hastily replaced it in her purse" (87). When the girl sleuth attempts to speak with Miss Allison about her chantings a few moments later, the woman mysteriously has no recollection of them: "I'm sure I don't know what you're talking about, Miss Drew" (88).

Miss Allison enters into a second mesmeric state when a suspicious fire destroys the old house on her property. Nancy and her friends drive out to investigate the blaze, and they find her digging through the ruins, trying to make her way into the secret tunnel beneath the structure to salvage some valuables. After enduring choking smoke, smoldering coals, and a near-fatal cave-in, Nancy, Ned and her father are able to retrieve the boxes that contain priceless jewels. Although the woman had previously been fixated on finding the items, she suddenly loses all interest in them: "'Ned and I will take the boxes to a bank vault for you if you wish,' Mr. Drew added. Miss Allison did not appear to comprehend. A dazed far-away look came into her eyes and she muttered incoherently" (110). When Mr. Drew repeats his question, he receives the following curt response: "'Please don't trouble me now,' Miss Allison murmured indifferently. 'I am meditating'" (111).

While Mr. Drew and Ned take the valuables to Riverside for safekeeping, the narrator relays what happens back at the ruins of the abandoned house:

> Left alone with Miss Allison, Nancy and her chums tried to arouse the woman from her state of stupor. She paid no attention to anything they did or said until Nancy, hopeful of gaining information, deliberately mentioned Coya's name.

The word seemed to arouse a strange train of mental pictures in the woman's mind, for she began to mutter again. (111–12)

Eventually, they realize that Miss Allison is discussing the Indian belief in reincarnation. Then, she spots Nancy's ivory charm again and her mood changes: "The woman lapsed into another silence. . . . Miss Allison made no immediate response. Her eyes had focused upon the elephant charm which hung from its velvet cord about Nancy's throat. With trembling fingers the woman reached out and touched it reverently" (112). After a few moments, she affirms the item's paranormal powers, telling Nancy that "the Ivory Charm will bring you good luck. . . . Both in this world and the next" (112).

As suddenly as Miss Allison's trance commenced, it ends. And once again, she has no recollection of it whatsoever: "'Dear me, have I been sleeping?' she inquired, looking about in bewilderment. 'Where am I?'" (113). While the episode prompts Bess to declare that the older woman is not "normal" (113), it compels the formerly skeptical Carson Drew to affirm "Miss Allison's psychic powers" (116).

This character's third and final trance state occurs when Miss Allison is invited to Professor Stackpole's house ostensibly to discuss Indian mysticism but really to be questioned about Coya and his background. The narrator describes the woman's otherworldly demeanor upon her arrival: "Miss Allison, wearing a long flowing white costume and turban, with a jewel-bound book in her hand, entered the room as one walking in a trance" (172). When Professor Stackpole offers her a seat, she stares at him "with a glazed expression in her eyes" (172). With only minimal effort, the professor gets her to discuss Maharaja Iama Togara. Negating any need for Nancy to engage in deductive reasoning or forensic investigation, Miss Allison freely admits to her involvement in the kidnapping and coup. "'The real story of how Iama Togara became a great ruler has never been told,' Miss Allison boasted. 'You would not believe me were I to say that I aided in placing him on the throne'" (173). In the exchange that follows, though, she explains how "through various political and psychic connections" she was able to achieve this goal (174).

When Miss Allison refuses to admit either to working with Rai on this plot or to receiving the jewels as a reward, Nancy emerges from her hiding place and attempts to extract this information from the woman herself. Rather than grilling Miss Allison with a series of tough, logic-based questions or confronting her with a barrage of hard physical evidence, Nancy invokes her sixth sense. Professor Stackpole explains to the girl sleuth that he has been discussing the subject of mysticism with Miss Allison. "'How interesting!' Nancy exclaimed. 'I have always been deeply intrigued by that subject myself. In fact, some of my friends believe that I have psychic powers'" (175). Miss Allison, however, dismisses this claim, informing Nancy in a haughty tone that "psychic powers are far more rare than you think" (176).

Nancy offers to demonstrate her paranormal powers, and the still-skeptical Miss Allison is only too happy to oblige her. The scenario that transpires reveals the girl detective's conversance with stereotypes about psychics, clairvoyants, and mystics. First, to create a spooky atmosphere, Nancy commands Professor Stackpole to "lower the blinds" (176). Then, after the room "was shrouded in semi-darkness," she changes her attire, turning to Miss Allison and saying, "I must have your turban" (176). Having transformed her physical appearance and created the proper ambiance in the room, she commences playing the part:

> Placing herself in front of a dark velvet drapery, Nancy closed her eyes. She began to rock slowly back and forth, chanting in low, musical tones. At first her words were unintelligible. Then she began quoting passages from the documents which she had taken from Peter Putnam. (176)

The documents outline Miss Allison's and Rai's role in Coya's abduction, and Nancy can see that her guest is becoming increasingly unnerved by the uncannily accurate recount of events. And so the girl sleuth brings her performance to its dramatic conclusion: "'YOU are the guilty person!' she proclaimed. 'You are the person who deprived Coya of his right to the throne and brought him to this country. Confess! Confess!'" (177). This tactic proves successful, and Miss Allison tearfully discloses: "Yes, yes! I did it! I employed Rai to kidnap the boy that Iama Togara might be put upon the throne!" (177).

Of all the myriad styles of literature, perhaps none is more strictly regimented than detective fiction. As Kathleen Gregory Klein has commented, "The parameters of the genre are well known, widely accepted, easily accessible" (1). From edicts like "The culprit must turn out to be a person who has played a more or less prominent part in the story" in S. S. Van Dine's classic "Twenty Rules for Writing Detective Stories" (1928) to maxims such as the writer may "never conceal a vital clue from the reader" as articulated in the oath to Dorothy Sayer's famed Detection Club, these rules are as widely known as they are inviolable.

One central imperative of mystery fiction is the prohibition against the supernatural. Given the genre's firm foundation in the realms of logic, order, and reason, writers are expected to rebuff elements of the occult. As S. S. Van Dine asserts,

> The problem of the crime must be solved by strictly naturalistic means. Such methods for learning the truth as slate-writing, ouija-boards, mind-reading, spiritualistic se'ances, crystal-gazing, and the like, are taboo. A reader has a chance when matching his wits with a rationalistic detective, but if he must compete with the world of spirits and go chasing about the fourth dimension of metaphysics, he is defeated *ab initio.* (par. 9)

The Detection Club likewise imposes a prohibition on the paranormal: "Do you promise that your detectives shall well and truly detect the crimes presented to them, using those wits which it may please you to bestow upon them and not placing reliance on nor making use of Divine Revelation, Feminine Intuition, Mumbo-Jumbo, Jiggery-Pokery, Coincidence or the Act of God?" ("Oath" par. 6).

The Nancy Drew series has always been seen as adhering to the classic mystery formula. To be sure, the books share many features with Agatha Christie's *Murder on the Orient Express* (1934) and Dorothy Sayers's *Murder Must Advertise* (1933); they concern largely upper-class characters, take place in genteel settings, contain one central crime scene, feature villains who have clear motives, and spotlight an amateur sleuth who is unpaid for her detective work.

But the paranormal phenomena in Nancy Drew novels like *The Mystery of the Ivory Charm* introduce an element of resistance, revolt, and rebellion that is commonly seen as being absent from classic drawing-room mysteries. The seemingly conservative and even conformist girl sleuth contains qualities that are unexpected and even unconventional: she combines the intuitive with the intellectual, the mental with the material, and the paranormal with the physical.

Searching for the Girl behind the Girl Sleuth: Eugenie Dennis and Nancy Drew

Arthur Prager, in *Rascals at Large; or, The Clue in the Old Nostalgia* (1971), has written about the ahistorical quality of the original Nancy Drew novels.

From the very first volume through the dozens of subsequent narratives that comprise the series, he argues, "the books have an odd, timeless quality. . . . Like the land of Oz, Nancy Drew Country is in another time dimension, untouched by the outside world" (76). Prager elaborates: "The Depression came and went, followed by three wars, but they were passed unnoticed in Midwestern, suburban River Heights" (76). Deborah L. Siegel echoes this observation. Commenting on the tremendous popularity of the mystery stories both in the 1930s when they were initially published and on the eve of the new millennium when she was writing, Siegel asserts that "the appeal and the allure of Drewness thus lay in its extreme ahistoricity" (164).

The paranormal elements permeating *The Mystery of the Ivory Charm* call this belief into question. Far from existing outside of history, the books are heavily influenced by at least one phenomenon permeating their era: popular interest in the supernatural. While the Nancy Drew series is commonly seen as being written during the heyday of mystery fiction in the United States, it was also conceived during a time of tremendous public fascination with ESP. In 1930, the same year that the first novel about the girl sleuth debuted, the psychology department at Duke University made history by becoming the first academic institution to begin researching paranormal activity. Four years later, Duke psychologist J. B. Rhine—who is regarded as "the founder of modern parapsychology" (Renier 28)—published *Extra-Sensory Perception*. The volume provided a detailed discussion of Rhine's research methodology, experiments, and findings.

Based on the strength of the initial work by Rhine and his colleagues, in 1935, Duke University formalized its commitment to the paranormal when it founded the Parapsychology Laboratory. Within two years, C. E. Stuart and J. G. Pratt had released *A Handbook for Testing Extra-Sensory Perception* (1937). As Rhine remarks in the foreword to the text: "Few books have been written, I believe, in response to a more definite demand than lies behind this one. For the last few years there has been a mounting interest in the subject of ESP" (7). As he goes on to explain, this fascination emanated not simply from the professional sector but the popular one:

> Our mail [at the Parapsychology Laboratory] has been larger and larger every year, and in response to the thousands of requests for further information and suggestions we have mailed out a great many packs of test cards, record sheets, and sets of mimeographed instructions on how to test for ESP. But this demand

has continued to increase to the point where a university laboratory . . . can no longer cope with it. (7)

A Handbook for Testing Extra-Sensory Perception, he explains, serves this purpose by making public the research methods used at Duke.

For some individuals, testing paranormal powers was moot, for they were already assured that such abilities existed. Sir Arthur Conan Doyle, author of the wildly successful (and supremely rationalistic) Sherlock Holmes stories and an avid enthusiast of the occult, predicted in 1925 "that the detectives of the future would be, or at least employ, clairvoyants and mediums" (Hibbard, Worring, and Brennan 21). He was not wrong. Throughout the 1920s and 1930s, newspapers in the United States frequently reported that psychics had helped to solve baffling crimes both at home and in locations around the globe. "In 1926, when mystery novelist Agatha Christie suddenly disappeared, setting off a national manhunt, Conan Doyle called in psychic help to try to solve the mystery" (Lyons and Truzzi 24). Likewise, in 1928, Vienna-born mentalist Maximillian Langsner attained international renown when he assisted Canadian police "who had reached an impasse in [their] attempt to solve a quadruple murder" (Lyons and Truzzi 30). As Lyons and Truzzi have documented, "A remarkably similar Canadian case took place in Saskatchewan" in 1932 when a man who called himself "the phenomenal mind reader" gave a Royal Canadian police officer an accurate precognition of the site, the circumstances, and the perpetrator of a brutal local murder (30). After leading officials to the body, the seer confronted the suspect, who was "so shocked . . . with his knowledge of the murder's details that [detectives] were able to obtain a confession from him" (30–31). Back in the United States, psychics were being used to solve crimes both big and small. On 9 July 1936, for instance, the *Milwaukee Journal* "contained a half-page article by A. B. Macdonald reporting an Ozark 'Mystery Woman' . . . who was able to counsel her neighbors and the sheriff on where to look for missing objects" (Lyons and Truzzi 29).

Of the various psychics making headlines for their detective work during this era, one of the most accomplished was Eugenie "Gene" Dennis. Lyons and Truzzi have written of this once widely known but now nearly forgotten figure: "Born in Atchison, Kansas, Eugenie Dennis' fame started in high school when she achieved some remarkable results locating lost articles" (32). David P. Abbott, a figure who was "well-known among magicians as an exposer of fraudulent mediums" (Lyons and Truzzi 32) tested the then-fourteen-year-old girl's psychic detective skills and confirmed them. Abbott was so convinced of Dennis's paranormal powers, in fact, that he "became Dennis's manager and set up a tour for her through the western states" (Lyons and Truzzi 32). This circuit of public appearances was a phenomenal success and catapulted Dennis into the national spotlight. As Lyons and Truzzi explain, "During her travels, she reportedly helped police in several states with minor cases" (32). While in New York City in 1922, for instance, the female sleuth amazed local detectives when she "found stolen jewels valued at several hundred thousand dollars" (Larsen 87). A few months later, after Dennis had assisted law enforcement on several additional occasions, *The New York Times* published an editorial about the case saying that the whole episode demonstrated the city's credulity" (Lyons and Truzzi 33).

Throughout the 1920s and 1930s, Dennis routinely made headlines in newspapers around the United States. The teenage psychic continued to tour and "offered her services to police departments in many cities" (Larsen 86). Just two years before the publication of *The Mystery of the Ivory Charm*, "one of [Dennis's] most publicized [events] took place during her 1934 tour of England" (34). There Dennis became involved in a homicide case that would become known as the "Brighton trunk crime" (Lyons and Truzzi 34) that bears similarities to the rare murder that occurs in *The Mystery of the Ivory Charm*. The details of the case were far grislier than those in the Nancy Drew novel: "On June 17, a luggage clerk at the Brighton railway station discovered a trunk containing a human torso. The trunk had been left in the cloakroom eleven days earlier" (Larsen 87). While the crime was never solved, Dennis "gave an estimate of the age and height of the victim and said she was pregnant"—details that were all confirmed by the medical examiner's autopsy (Lyons and Truzzi 35). In addition, echoing Nancy's Drew's famous sense of intuition, Dennis "also predicted that another, similar crime would come to light" (Larsen 35). Of course, this premonition proved accurate: "A few weeks later, after a house-to-house search, a second trunk containing another corpse was found" (Lyons and Truzzi 35). Moreover, the location of this item could have been taken directly out of a Nancy Drew novel. The trunk containing the second body was discovered "in a locked and empty lodging house" (Larsen 87).

Eugenie Dennis died in Seattle, Washington, in 1948 at the age of forty-one. During the final decade of her life, she remained in the media spotlight. The psychic detective made countless public appearances and was the subject of numerous essays, articles, and editorials. In a telling indication of the esteem in which Dennis was held, Lyons and Truzzi relay that by the time she died, she had "reportedly acquired many well-known film stars and celebrities as private clients" (35). Indeed, Walter Rowe identifies Dennis as one of the "two most celebrated American psychic detectives of the early twentieth century" (585).

It was within this sociocultural environment that Edward Stratemeyer conceived of the figure of Nancy Drew. As various critics and biographers have written, the publishing mogul was a keen observer of current fads, if for no other reason than the potential for profitability that they represented (107). Indeed, as Melanie Rehak notes, Stratemeyer would wait until a popular trend—such as the mystery craze—trickled down to young people to start a new series, "and he had an eye for exploiting it when it did" (107). One can certainly see this technique at work in connection with the Nancy Drew mystery stories. As Patricia Craig and Mary Cadogan have written, Stratemeyer's series about the girl sleuth was "a product of commercial expediency, planned to exert the maximum appeal for the greatest number of readers" (150).

Given the extensive publicity that Eugenie Dennis received throughout the 1920s and early 1930s, it seems probable that the astute publisher was cognizant of her life and accomplishments. To be sure, Stratemeyer's fictional girl sleuth bears many uncanny similarities to this factual psychic detective. As in the case of Nancy Drew, Eugenie Dennis "frequently got full public credit from the police" for her help solving crimes (Lyons and Truzzi 32). Likewise, as with the girl sleuth, Dennis came to national prominence when she was sixteen years old, at which point she embarked on her first national tour (Lyons and Truzzi 32). Moreover, mirroring Nancy Drew's penchant for retrieving missing valuables, Dennis began her psychic detective career solving property crimes. As Anita Larsen documents, "She found fifteen stolen bicycles in Joplin, Missouri . . . and twenty-three missing diamonds in Omaha, Nebraska" (86).

In spite of these areas of personal and professional overlap, various differences remain. For instance, while Nancy Drew largely relies on her famous hunches to solve crimes, Dennis used a method of ESP now known as remote viewing: she was able to "see" a crime scene that she had never actually visited. As the caption on one of her publicity photographs explains, "She just thinks for a moment or two, and then tells where the missing article can be found" ("Girl Psychic Wonder"). Likewise, Dennis showcased her psychic skills by making paid public appearances and doing profitable national tours, endeavors that the ardently not-for-profit Nancy Drew would scorn.

Such issues aside, the similarities between the two figures seem too great to be merely coincidental. While Eugenie Dennis is not the exclusive model for Nancy Drew, it seems plausible that her life and career was a source of inspiration for this character. Moving psychic sleuthing from the background to the forefront of Stratemeyer's beloved mystery series reveals that his idealized girl sleuth is not so imaginary after all. Nancy Drew, who is commonly seen as being larger than life, may have her roots or origins in real life after all.

An oft-mentioned facet of the publication history of the Nancy Drew series is how the original narratives were revised and reissued beginning in 1959. Seeking to keep the novels fresh and also wanting to enhance their appeal to a new generation of juvenile readers, Harriet Stratemeyer employed a bevy of editors to overhaul the series. As Carolyn G. Heilbrun, Carolyn Stewart Dyer, and Nancy Tillman Romalov have documented, Stratemeyer gave these men and women explicit instructions for revision: simplify the plots by eliminating extraneous characters and tangential storylines, shorten the texts by condensing them from twenty-five to twenty chapters, change the main character's age from sixteen to eighteen to reflect the new national standard for obtaining a driver's license, and delete the more overt instances of racism (see Heilbrun 11; Dyer and Romalov 92–93).

An additional but overlooked aspect of these editorial guidelines is that the new editions of Nancy Drew also greatly reduced the paranormal elements. The revised version of *The Mystery of the Ivory Charm*, released in 1964, contains many changes: Coya is renamed Rishi; Nancy is spared being nearly strangled by the circus snake; Rai does not give the girl sleuth the ivory charm but rather Rishi does after stealing it from his cruel guardian; a young boy named Tommy is added and plays a significant role in the first few chapters; Rishi's maharajah father is not only alive and well but living in River Heights.

Of the various alterations to the text, the most significant appear in the book's ending. Rai does not actually kill Rishi; instead, he merely knocks him unconscious. While the ivory charm is still used to revive him, it is Rishi's father—a man named Vivek Tilak—who administers the curative, not Nancy. "Mr. Tilak deftly broke off one of the elephant's feet and poured the fluid it contained under Rishi's tongue" (176). Even more significantly, though, the liquid works not because of some mysterious occult properties, but because of forensic science. Nancy asks Tilek whether the charm possesses "magical power," but he says it doesn't, pointing out that "it contains a special antidote against various harmful drugs" (176). In this way, the former centrality that the supernatural occupied in the narrative is eliminated. Instead, in a conclusion that is far more conventional as well as firmly rooted in the realm of logic and reason, advances in modern medicine and especially the chemical sciences save the day.

In a memorable quote from Vladimir Nabokov's *Lolita* (1955), Humbert Humbert offers the following apt observation about the ascendency of forensic technology in the postwar period: "Nowadays you have to be a scientist if you want to be a killer" (87). The current version of the Nancy Drew mystery series affirms this assertion. But, the girl sleuth's signature magnifying glass notwithstanding, this is not how the narratives were originally written, nor culturally intended.

CHAPTER FIVE

"How'd You Like That Haircut to Begin Just Below the Chin?"

Juvenile Delinquency, Teenage Killers, and a Pulp Aesthetic in The Outsiders

> They wanted to jump me, but I had a knife in my belt.
> "Don't worry," I said. "I'll come back with my gang, and we'll really go at it."
> BENJAMIN FINE, *1,000,000 Delinquents* (1955)

Since its appearance in 1967, *The Outsiders*, S. E. Hinton's novel about a group of working-class boys struggling to survive in an environment riddled with gang violence, has been heralded as a landmark in the history of literature for young readers. For more than four decades, Hinton's novel has been "a yearly best-seller" (Hipple par. 2). Frequently taught in schools, commonly found in libraries, and often included on summer reading lists, *The Oustiders* has earned the status as "a classic that gets passed down from generation to generation" (A. Wilson 10).

The critical success and commercial popularity of Hinton's book is commonly attributed to its innovative nature. Kenneth L. Donelson and Alleen Pace Nilsen have noted that the year 1967 when *The Outsiders* made its debut was "a milestone [one], when writers and publishers turned in a new direction" (14). Prior to this period, narratives aimed at an adolescent audience were typified by titles like Maureen Daly's *Seventeenth Summer* (1942). In the words of Michael Cart, "These books were set in a *Saturday Evening Post* world of white faces and white picket fences surrounding small-town, middle-class lives where the worst thing that could happen would be a misunderstanding that threatened to leave someone dateless for the junior prom" (20).

Hinton's novel was markedly different. As Jay Daly explains, "Into this sterile chiffon-and-orchids environment then came *The Outsiders*. Nobody worries about the prom in *The Outsiders*; they're more concerned with just staying alive till June" (i). Indeed, the narrator and central character Ponyboy Curtis is not simply assaulted by members of a rival gang at the outset of the text but his very life is threatened. While holding a knife to the fourteen-year-old's throat, one of his assailants snarls, "How'd you like that haircut to begin right below the chin?" (5). Interpersonal violence is a recurring feature throughout the book, as the teenage characters square off against each other armed with everything from fists and broken bottles to switchblades and guns. Far from mere macho posturing, these encounters routinely turn lethal. Indicating the way in which the origins of YA genre is intimately connected with homicide, no fewer than three teenage characters are killed by the end of the story: one is stabbed during a fight, another is fatally injured during a fire in the book's climax, and a third is shot by police during a failed robbery.

The subject matter of Hinton's text was groundbreaking; "no one had seen anything quite like *The Outsiders* before" (A. Wilson 14). Antoine Wilson has argued that Hinton "started a completely new trend in young adult literature" (9). Similarly, Cart has written that the 1967 novel precipitated a "sea change" in narratives for adolescents (43). Meanwhile, Patty Campbell goes one step further, claiming that "Hinton founded young adult literature with the publication of *The Outsiders*" ("Outsiders" 177). The narrative's gritty plot, combined with its stark language, led critics to credit Hinton with inaugurating a literary style, known as the "new realism" (Cart 39; J. Daly 15). Whereas previous books for young readers had been characterized by romantic sentimentality, *The Outsiders* took its cue from sociological verisimilitude. In what has become an oft-quoted remark by the author about her motivation for writing the text, she said, "There was no realistic fiction being written about teenagers when I was in high school—everything was 'Mary-Jane Goes to The Prom'" ("Speaking With S. E. Hinton" 185). Hinton wanted to document the lives of young people not as adults nostalgically remembered them or naively idealized them but as they actually were, and she succeeded. Introducing "new kinds of 'real' characters" to young adult fiction (Cart 47), *The Outsiders* is, according to critics, nothing less than a "mold-breaking novel" (Hipple par. 2).

In this chapter, I argue that while *The Outsiders* may have been a "mold-breaking" novel for young readers in many ways, its tone, characters, and content were not entirely innovative. Far from inventing a completely new style of writing, Hinton's book can be seen as incorporating elements from an already popular one: the growing legions of paperback books about juvenile delinquency. Making their debut in the United States during the late 1930s and reaching their commercial peak during the 1950s and 1960s, these cheaply printed, inexpensively priced, and mass-marketed books became one of the biggest cultural forces in midcentury America. As Kenneth C. Davis notes, these pocket-sized texts "would completely change the face of the publishing industry in the postwar period" (68). I make a case that they also played a role in shaping Hinton's novel. *The Outsiders* is an amalgamation of some of the most important features and signature qualities of paperback books about juvenile delinquency. In everything from the novel's physical description of its characters, its explanation for the causes of delinquent behavior, and its portrayal of gang violence to its fast pace, shocking subject matter, and cinematic quality, *The Outsiders* reflects gang-themed postwar paperbacks from an aesthetic, material, and literary standpoint.

Anita Silvey, in an article commenting on innovations in literature for young readers, remarks that "when I look at the last fifty years of children's book history, inevitably, almost always, the books that changed the industry were published contrary to all trends. By going against the current wisdom, creators and publishers set new standards and directions and gave children and young adults some of their finest books" (par. 2). While children's literature is commonly cast as a conservative genre—one whose primary aim is to acculturate boys and girls in the conventional manners and mores of society—she detects a contrary strain. "The ultimate irony about children's books," Silvey asserts, "is that, over time, the greatest successes come from those who defy the trends" (par. 8).

In the case of *The Outsiders*, this observation is simultaneously accurate and inaccurate. While the 1967 novel rejects the formula commonly found in young adult fiction from its era, it ironically does so by embracing the literary ingredients from another and arguably even more powerful genre. The presence of a pulp aesthetic throughout *The Outsiders* offers another source of literary and cultural influence that has been overlooked. At the same time, and in a perhaps even more important implication given the status of *The Outsiders* as a landmark text, it demonstrates that the YA genre owes at least as much to the lowbrow world of paperback sensationalism as to the more commonly identified highbrow realm of literary realism.

Judging a Book by Its Cover:
The Postwar Paperback Revolution

Although cheaply printed, inexpensively priced, softbound books have existed in the United States since the advent of pulpwood paper and the invention of the steam-powered cylinder press in the mid-nineteenth century, they attained a new cultural influence during the early decades of the twentieth century.* As Davis, Kurt Enoch, and Frank Schick have all pointed out, the year 1939 inaugurated what would become known as the "paperback revolution" in the United States. In June of that year, the first "mass-market paperback" was released by a fledgling company called Pocket Books (Davis 15). While this book form is commonplace today, mass-market paperbacks were materially, economically, and aesthetically alien to prewar Americans. In addition to having soft backings, they also were bound via a method called "'perfect binding,' an incongruously named gluing process that is vastly cheaper than the regular stitched binding of hardcover books" (Davis 39). In part because of this cost-saving technique, paperback books sold for a fraction of the price of their hardcover counterparts. Throughout the 1930s and into the 1940s, they were "universally priced at 25 cents" during a time when the average selling price for a hardcover book was a dollar or more (Davis xii).

It was fitting in many ways that mass-market paperbacks cost a fraction of the price, for they were also a fraction of the physical size. Measuring just 4¼ by 6½ inches, these texts were slim enough, as the name "Pocket Books" implied, to fit in the pocket of a jacket or blazer.† This portability allowed paperbacks to be carried in more than one sense to new locales. While their hardbacked counterparts were only available in bookstores, softbacks could be found in an array of unexpected retail venues: newsstands, airport termi-

---

*As Kurt Enoch has discussed, "Paper-bound books have substantially as long a history in the United States as they have in Europe" (212). The first softbacked book dates back to 1829; it was published by the Boston Society for Diffusion of Knowledge, which had assigned itself the mission of issuing "a cheap form of a series of works, partly original and partly selected in all the most important branches of learning" (212). Advances in printing technology, improvements in mass transportation, and increases in the national literacy rate sparked a rapid expansion of the industry in the 1870s and 1880s (212). As Enoch notes, "The enormous significance of inexpensive paper-bound publishing in that era is clearly illustrated by the fact that in 1885, out of a total of 4,500 titles published, almost 1,500 were paper-bound" (213). The combination of increasing competition, rising production costs, and the passage of the Copyright Act of 1891—which ended the supply of royalty-free foreign source material—signaled the death knell for the industry. "From then until the mid-1930s," Enoch points out, "no important activity took place" (213).

†Mass market paperbacks today are slightly larger: they measure 4¼ by 7 inches (Davis 13).

nals, cigar shops, drugstores, bus stations, grocery stores, train depots, five-and-dimes, stationers, hotel lobbies, and "just about anywhere else one of the [display] racks could be squeezed in" (Davis 47). By placing their books in such venues, publishers were able to reach a new demographic of customer: ones who did not frequent bookstores. As Rona Jaffe quipped about the nation's literary climate at midcentury, "Do you realize that there are towns in America where there are no libraries at all? Not even a bookstore! The only place the people in those small towns can get a book is at the drugstore. And what do they read? Our books" (28).

And read paperbacks they did. "Before these inexpensive, widely distributed books came along, only the rarest of books sold more than a hundred thousand copies; a million-seller was a real phenomenon" (Davis xii). However, as Davis notes, "Overnight, the paperback changed that. Suddenly, a book could reach not hundreds or thousands of readers but millions, many of whom had never owned a book before" (xii). The instant success of the first ten titles released by Pocket Books "was unprecedented in American publishing history" (Davis 13). An article in the trade magazine *Publisher's Weekly* stated that "so far since publication in June, Pocket Books have sold 325,000 books with reorders now averaging 12,000 to 15,000 copies a day" (qtd. in Davis 15). By spring 1941, this figure had climbed to an astounding "8.5 million copies" (Davis 43). In the wake of the massive success of Pocket Books, many additional paperback publishers emerged. As Enoch has documented, "Avon Books followed soon thereafter, and Penguin Books, previously imported from England, organized an American branch" (213).

While one might have expected World War II—with its paper rations, labor shortages, and transportation disruptions—to have stemmed this tide, it had the opposite effect. "The war, with its captive market, would take the production and consumption of cheap paperbacks into a higher gear, forcing publishers to cultivate, and respond to, a mass readership" (Haut 4). The enlistment of millions of men into the armed services did not lead to a massive loss of potential book buyers but an increase in them. "In a stroke of good luck, a single Penguin Book fit exactly into a pocket of a soldier's uniform that had been designed to carry an entrenching tool. This serendipitous bit of tailoring made Penguin many lifelong friends among soldiers who carried their books to the front" (Davis 56). In April 1941, a full nine months before the United States even entered the war, "Fort Dix in New Jersey ordered one thousand assorted titles and in a few days reordered a thousand more, specifying that they wanted mostly mysteries" (Davis 57). After the attack on Pearl Harbor, such requests increased exponentially. "By the middle of 1942, sales of Pocket Books to the services had reached the level of 250,000 copies per month" (Davis 63). In the words of Davis, "The American fighting man had shown that he wanted to read, and paperbacks could play an important role in informing and entertaining the troops" (68).

This period of paperback prosperity continued in the postwar period. According to Enoch, "The census figure for the year 1945 . . . shows four firms printing 83 million copies of 112 titles" (213), and the data for 1953 indicates "a production of 292 million copies of 1,061 titles by sixteen firms" (213). With titles ranging from Dr. Spock's instruction manual on child rearing to the emerging genre of science fiction—which, coincidentally, also featured a famous Spock—pulp novels democratized reading in the United States. As Davis puts it, "Paperback books and the baby boomers were made for each other, a mass medium for a mass generation" (1). Marketed like magazines and adorned with colorful, eye-catching covers that featured original art, these paperbacks found a diverse and devoted audience. In the words of Schick, "Never before had so many books at such a low price found such a large number of readers" (72).

When paperback books made their debut during the late 1930s, their content varied little from their hardbacked counterparts. As Enoch reports, "The majority of American inexpensive paper-bound books [were] complete and unabridged editions of copyrighted books originally published in hard covers" (214). "To remove the doubts of skeptical readers who might be wary of the small books and their twenty-five cent price, each cover carried the guarantee 'Complete and Unabridged'" (Davis 13).

After the success of the first offering of paperbacks, editors added more titles. By the end of World War II, "works of virtually every prominent writer and many of the more popular classics [were] available. Winners of Nobel prizes, Pulitzer prizes, National Book awards, and other literary accolades, and talented novelists from many countries in the world, appear[ed] side by side on drugstore racks" (Enoch 214). As Davis documents, "The first list of titles, designated the 'A' list and delivered to the army in September 1943" included such classics as *Oliver Twist* by Charles Dickens, *Tortilla Flat* by John Steinbeck, *Typee* by Herman Melville, and *Lord Jim* by Joseph Conrad (73). Subsequent orders included *The Grapes of Wrath*, *Selected Stories* by Edgar Allan Poe, and Carl Sandburg's *Selected Poems* (Davis 75).

As both the number of paperback publishers and the sales of softcover books increased, so did the competition among companies. Publishers searched for ways to set their books apart from those by their rivals. Some presses, such as Penguin, began releasing original titles. *What's That Plane?* (1942), a nonfiction work by Walter Pitkin explaining how to identify American and Japanese aircraft from the ground, was an early best seller for the company (Davis 60). Other firms, most notably Bantam, took a different tack. Instead of introducing new content, they added flashy style. Bantam began featuring more original cover art designed to catch the customer's eye. In contrast to the covers on many other softbound books that generally featured minimalist images and often muted colors, theirs were both busy and in vivid Technicolor. Bantam's cover for Kenneth Perkins's western-themed novel *Relentless*, for instance, featured a portrait of an outlaw dramatically shooting a sheriff.

Finally, and most detrimentally to the industry, the increased competition among publishers caused many to begin repackaging even canonical classics to make them more shocking, sexy, and sensational. The Popular Library became infamous for its cover image to the 1948 edition of John Erskine's *The Private Life of Helen of Troy*. The jacket presents an alluring portrait of the book's title character, and her nipples are clearly visible beneath the sheer dress that she is wearing (Davis 140). The new edition of Pocket Book's *The Maltese Falcon* caused a similar buzz. The cover to the company's original 1944 copy simply showed three male hands reaching for the falcon statue. Above them appeared the matter-of-fact tagline: "Sam Spade and the Black Bird." Their new edition, which was released in 1947, had a markedly different image and teaser. This version showcased a topless girl in the foreground— her back turned to the reader—and a pair of male hands extending behind a gauzy sheet holding a high-heeled shoe; meanwhile, a pair of panties lay on a chair beside him. The tagline read, "Sam Spade searched each article of the girl's clothing" (see Davis 136–37).

Such sleazy marketing campaigns not only angered many authors—J. D. Salinger was so incensed by the way *The Catcher in the Rye* (1951) was packaged that he famously severed ties with its original paperback publisher (Davis 141)—but it also compromised the status of these texts. As Davis notes, "Sadly, at the moment that the paperback book was beginning to win praise for its contribution in improving literacy and spreading the market for writers, the trend toward exploitation blackened the industry's image" (141).

Many readers had always been skeptical of the literary merit of these cheaply made books, and these new advertising techniques only provided concrete proof that their suspicions were justified. "Critics who called them junk or trash had legitimate reason" (Davis 141).

As the 1950s progressed, this trend continued. Paperbacks became increasingly shocking in content, salacious in character, and sex-crazed in focus. From books like N. R. de Mexico's *Marijuana Girl* (1951) about drug use, Tereska Torres's *Women's Barracks* (1950) concerning female homosexuality, and E. S. Seeley's *Street Walker* (1959), which showcased the seedy world of prostitution, paperbacks quickly earned a reputation in postwar America as "little more than second-rate trash. Literary flotsam. Schlock turned out to appease a gluttonous mass appetite for sex and sensationalism" (qtd. in Smith 25).

In spite of the low literary esteem in which paperback books came to be held by the 1950s and 1960s, they had an irrefutable cultural impact. According to Enoch, "They . . . altered the literary landscape of the United States" (214). These seemingly inconsequential, even disposable, texts forever changed the nation's publishing industry, the marketing strategies used for print media, and the reading habits of the general public. In the words of Davis, "For better or worse, the paperback stood at the entrance to a new realm—of power, profits, and influence unlike anything seen before in American publishing history" (82).

"I am a Greaser. . . . I am a JD and a Hood": *The Outsiders* and the Paperback Presentation of Juvenile Delinquency

Although the most common fodder for postwar paperbacks were fictional tales about courageous cowboys, strange space aliens, or gruff gumshoes, factual events were also popular. Not only did real-world happenings come with a ready-made story but they also had a built-in audience. As Thomas Doherty notes, books based on topical issues "drew on the public curiosity and free publicity surrounding a popular current event" (7).

The social, economic, and familial disruptions precipitated by World War II provided paperback editors with an engrossing new subject to feature in their pages: juvenile delinquency. With large numbers of married women working in factory positions outside the home and large numbers of men fighting overseas, many adolescents were left without adult supervision. Especially in urban areas, these youths roamed the streets either individually or in "gangs" and engaged in an array of illicit and sometimes illegal activities, from smoking and drinking to fighting and vandalism. As a result, delinquency rates skyrocketed during the war. Paul W. Tappan, in his landmark book on the issue, noted that arrests of individuals under eighteen years old increased 33 percent from 1942 to 1943 (45). As one commentator reported about wartime conditions, "Almost every week our newspapers are filled with stories about the offenses and violations of teenagers. Today, delinquents account for 50 percent of the burglaries and over half the car thefts. About 17 per cent of our drug addicts are juveniles" (Mayer 7).

The end of the World War II did not solve the problem. On the contrary, both the numbers of wayward youth and the seriousness of their antisocial behaviors only increased. In 1947, J. Edgar Hoover, director of the Federal Bureau of Investigation, announced in a radio broadcast "that in the first nine months of 1947, arrests of youth 18 to 20 years of age were 27 per cent higher than the 1946 total" (Tappan 31). Moreover, far from engaging in "harmless" adolescent pranks like skipping school and smoking cigarettes, young people were increasingly partaking in more serious criminal activities. As Benjamin Fine reported in 1957, "From 1948 on, for example, more children under eighteen have been involved in such offenses as burglaries, robberies, and automobile thefts. The FBI found that 50 percent of those arrested in 1953 for burglary were under eighteen years of age. One out of three was not yet sixteen" (20). These figures represented a sharp increase in the crime rate among young people compared to the population as a whole. "An FBI survey of two hundred cities showed a rise in the crime rate of adults in 1953 of 1.9 per cent as compared with an increase of 7.9 per cent in the crime rate of boys and girls under eighteen" (Fine 18).

Such statistics prompted President Dwight D. Eisenhower to ask Congress in 1954 for $3 million "with which to attack the problem of juvenile delinquency" (Fine v). The following year, the Senate convened a special subcommittee to explore the social causes of, as well as possible solutions to, what it termed this "major American problem" (Fine v). Thomas Doherty has documented that in the minds of many politicians, juvenile delinquency was as serious an internal threat to the integrity of the United States as the external one of communism (40). Moreover, it was a crisis for which there was no end in sight. As journalist Virginia Held wrote at the time, "Juvenile delinquency, particularly in the United States, has come to be considered one of the most urgent social problems of the day, and the epidemic . . . seems to be spreading so fast that it obliterates the best efforts society can make to control it—or even to understand it" (qtd. in Fyvel 255). Benjamin Fine, the former education editor for the *New York Times*, offered an alarming prediction. He asserted that if current trends went unchecked, then, by 1965, the United States might "have over 2,500,000 delinquents and some experts believe that this figure is conservative" (qtd. in Mayer 7). For this reason, Frederick Mayer lamented that "delinquency has assumed truly frightening proportions" (7). Even if this statement was hyperbolic, the problem had become so ubiquitous that juvenile delinquency came to be referred to by both child care professionals and the general public simply by the initials "JD."

Juvenile delinquency was a seemingly tailor-made subject for paperbacks. Publishers did not need to artificially generate sensationalism in narratives about it. With juvenile delinquents engaged in robberies, car chases, and knife fights, stories about them were already infused with an abundance of drama. As a result, from the end of World War II through the 1950s, books about juvenile delinquency were released by many paperback presses. Irving Shulman's novel *The Amboy Dukes*, which was initially published in hardback in 1946 and released in paperback two years later, was among the first. An array of both fiction and nonfiction titles followed. From Willard Motley's *Knock on Any Door* (New American Library, 1950), Miriam Colwell's *Young* (Ballantine Books, 1955), Benjamin Fine's *1,000,000 Delinquents* (Signet, 1957), Harrison E. Salisbury's *The Shook-Up Generation* (Fawcett, 1958), and Frederick Mayer's *Our Troubled Youth* (Bantam Books, 1960) to William P. McGivern's *Savage Streets* (Pocket Books, 1961), David Wilkerson's *The Cross and the Switchblade* (Pyramid, 1963), and Lewis Yablonsky's *The Violent Gang* (Pelican, 1966), these books were a mainstay of the paperback industry. In addition, they were among the era's most popular titles. "Appearing on the newsstands in August 1950, *Knock on Any Door* sold out its first printing of 250,000 copies in two weeks" (Davis 151). Some authors took advantage of the success of delinquency-themed narratives and made entire careers writing about JDs. Hal Ellson, for example, penned what has become known as the "Raw Rumbles" trilogy: *Duke* (1949), *Tomboy* (1950), and *The Knife* (1961). Evan Hunter experienced even greater success, authoring some of the era's best-selling books about juvenile delinquency: *The Blackboard Jungle* (1954) and *The Jungle Kids* (1956).

Susan Eloise Hinton—who published under the name "S. E. Hinton"—was born in 1950 and came of age during the golden era of postwar paperbacks in general and juvenile delinquency-themed narratives in particular. While the author has never explicitly mentioned reading a work of pulp fiction—on the contrary, she frequently cites canonical writers like Shirley Jackson, Jane Austen, and F. Scott Fitzgerald as her favorites (see "FAQ"; Peck par. 3)—the public popularity that these books enjoyed suggest the likelihood that she knew about them. Indeed, in numerous essays, articles, and interviews, Hinton has mentioned her enthusiasm for all styles of writing. In the question-and-answer section that appears in the back of the Penguin edition of *The Outsiders*, for instance, she remarks, "When I was young I read everything, including cereal boxes and labels. Reading taught me sentence structure, paragraphing, how to build a chapter" ("Speaking" 184). *The Outsiders* confirms this claim, filled as it is with references to other well-known books and popular authors. In one of the early chapters, Ponyboy likens himself and the working-class members of his gang to characters from a Dickens novel: "I had read *Great Expectations* for English, and that kid Pip, he reminded me of us—the way he felt marked lousy because he wasn't a gentleman or anything, and the way that girl kept looking down on him" (15). Later, the fourteen-year-old narrator and Johnny pass the time while they are hiding out in an abandoned church by reading aloud from *Gone with the Wind*: "Johnny sure did like that book, although he didn't know anything about the Civil War and even less about plantations" (75). Then, just as the big rumble with their rival gang commences, Ponyboy makes a comparison between it and scenes from naturalistic novels like *The Call of the Wild*: "I was reminded of Jack London's books—you know, where the wolf pack waits in silence for one of two members to go down in a fight" (143). Finally, as Ponyboy recovers at home, he reads Harold Robbins's best-selling novel *The Carpetbaggers* (1961), "though [Darry] told me I wasn't old enough to read it. I thought so too after I finished it" (177).

These overt literary references are coupled with more subtle ones. Echoing the observation of many other critics, Dale Peck notes a conscious or unconscious allusion to J. D. Salinger's *The Catcher in the Rye* in "Hinton's literalization of Holden's 'If a body catch a body coming through the rye' into the rescue of a group of children from a burning church" (par. 3). Likewise, he finds traces of the work of Shirley Jackson. Peck argues that Ponyboy's comment that "I have light-brown, almost-red hair and greenish-gray eyes. I wish they were more gray, because I hate most guys that have green eyes, but I have to be content with what I have" recalls a passage from Jackson's narrative "We Have

Always Lived in the Castle" (1962). The short story contains the line "I have often thought that with any luck at all I could have been a werewolf, because the two middle fingers on both my hands are the same length, but I have to be content with what I had" (par. 3).* Given both the number and the variety of literary references, Peck muses on the fortieth anniversary of Hinton's text that "what struck me most as an adult reader (and sometime Y.A. novelist) is the degree to which 'The Outsiders' is derivative of the popular literature of its time" (par. 3).

I want to expand on this observation by demonstrating the presence of another genre. *The Outsiders* reflects the popular and pervasive realm of postwar paperbacks about juvenile delinquency. Presenting a story about teenagers from troubled homes who get into "rumbles" and wield what Thomas Doherty has called "the obligatory switchblade" (58), the novel embeds many of the signature traits in the pulp presentation of juvenile delinquents. Although Hinton's 1967 text may have appeared after the chronological apex of delinquency-themed paperbacks in the United States, it carried on this tradition in a different literary arena and for a different target audience.

The affiliation between Hinton's *The Outsiders* and postwar pulps begins even before readers encounter the first sentence. The moniker that Hinton selected for her text is evocative of many of the era's paperback narratives about juvenile delinquency, such as *The Violent Gang, Our Troubled Youth, The Cross and the Switchblade*, and *The Shook-Up Generation*. Moreover, the taglines used by a number of these books could just as easily be applied to *The Outsiders*. The teaser "A Novel of Restless Teen-agers Who Will Go Anywhere but Home," from Miriam Colwell's fictional narrative *Young* (1955), for example, aptly summarizes the familial situations of Hinton's characters Johnny Cade and Dallas Winston. As Dally remarks at one point, "Shoot, my old man don't give a hand whether I'm in jail or dead in a car wreck or drunk in the gutter" (88). And a tagline such as "The Gray Flannel Crowd Meets a Rough Teen-age Gang Head-on," from William P. McGivern's novel *Savage Streets* (1961), could just as easily describe the clash between the middle-class gang, the Socials, and the working-class one, the Greasers, in Hinton's text. As

---

* As Peck goes on to discuss, *The Outsiders* does not merely contain references to popular novels but to films as well. "Ponyboy's older brother, Sodapop, is characterized as '16-going-on-17.' A quotation from 'The Sound of Music' would seem out of place in a novel rife with 'blades' and 'heaters' and teenage pregnancy, but it's hard to deny after Ponyboy's immediate assertion that 'nobody in our gang digs movies and books the way I do'" (par. 6).

Ponyboy comments about his neighborhood, "The warfare is between the social classes" (11).

The cover design selected for Hinton's original 1967 edition of *The Outsiders* furthers the connection between it and pulp. Featuring the book's title and author's name on top and a black drawing of sticklike figures on the bottom all set against a bright red backdrop, the design is highly reminiscent of Davis Wilkerson's *The Cross and the Switchblade* (1963). The links between it and the paperback genre were even more explicit in the softback edition released later that year by Dell. Hinton's novel was not simply republished for this market but repackaged for it. The book's new cover image—a black-and-white photograph of a group of young men against a solid red background with the book's title in bold white lettering—resembled what had become in many ways the quintessential "look" of other paperbacks about juvenile delinquency. Indeed, the covers to Harrison E. Salisbury's *The Shook-Up Generation* (1958), Frederick Mayer's *Our Troubled Youth* (1960), and Benjamin Fine's *1,000,000 Delinquents* (1955) all had similar designs.

The connections between delinquency-themed paperbacks and *The Outsiders* do not stop at the cover. Both the novel's plot and its characters reflect many of the most well-known aspects of these postwar "hoodlums." In *The Shook-Up Generation*, for instance, Harrison E. Salisbury offers the following concise description of JDs: "These are the youngsters who hold up highway filling stations 'for kicks'" (46). At the beginning of *The Outsiders*, Ponyboy offers an almost analogous description of himself and his fellow Greasers: "We steal things and drive old souped-up cars and hold up gas stations" (3). While juvenile delinquents could be either male or female, this identity was overwhelmingly associated with adolescent boys. As Ruth Shonle Cavan notes, "It is generally true that for every one girl brought to the attention of the juvenile courts, there are four or five times as many boys" (6). This observation holds true in the world of *The Outsiders* as well. Although female characters do make occasional appearances in the course of the novel—most notably with the figure of love interest Cherry Valance—the book is overwhelmingly focused on young men, from the smart, sensitive narrator Ponyboy Curtis and his two brothers, athletic Darry and good-looking Sodapop, to their friends and fellow Greasers, tough-guy Dally Winston, timid Johnny Cade, and comedian Steve "Two-Bit" Mathews.

The Outsiders is set in the author's hometown of Tulsa, Oklahoma, reflecting T. R. Fyvel's observation in his nonfiction book *Troublemakers* (1961) that "the lawlessness has been spreading from the big cities into the small towns and suburbia" (32). While juvenile delinquency could be found in nearly every region of the United States by the time *The Outsiders* was published, it remained predominantly associated with major metropolitan areas, especially New York City. In a comment that is reiterated in countless other paperbacks about juvenile delinquency, Harrison E. Salisbury asserts in *The Shook-Up Generation* that "the institution of the rumble has reached its most complex development in New York" (45). Accordingly, the majority of both fiction and nonfiction books about the subject were set in Manhattan, Brooklyn, or the Bronx, from novels like Irving Shulman's *The Amboy Dukes* and Evan Hunter's *The Blackboard Jungle* to memoirs such as David Wilkerson's *The Cross and the Switchblade* and sociological analyses like Benjamin Fine's *1,000,000 Delinquents*.

Hinton's novel reflects this link. The most hardened member of the Greasers, Dallas Winston, is a transplant from the Big Apple: "Dally had spent three years on the wild side of New York and had been arrested at the age of ten. He was tougher than the rest of us—tougher, colder, meaner" (10). In fact, as Ponyboy says of Dallas, "He had quite a reputation. They have a file on him down at the police station. He had been arrested, he got drunk, he rode in rodeos, lied, cheated, stole, rolled drunks, jumped small kids—he did everything" (11).

From wherever juvenile delinquents hailed, they had one trait in common. As Lewis Yablonsky remarks in his nonfiction paperback about JDs, "illegal behavior" was "viewed as a badge of merit" (3). When Dallas, Ponyboy, and Johnny go out for a snack in one of the opening scenes of Hinton's novel, they demonstrate how committed they are to behaving badly: "We bought Cokes and blew the straws at the waitress, and walked around eying things that were lying out in the open until the manager got wise to us and suggested we leave. He was too late, though; Dally walked out with two packages of Kools under his jacket" (19). Soon after, the young men flaunt the law again, this time by sneaking into a drive-in: "We all had the money to get in—it only costs a quarter if you're not in a car—but Dally hated to do things the legal way. He liked to show that he didn't care whether there was a law or not. We went around *trying* to break laws" (20).

One law that postwar JDs commonly violated was the one about underage drinking. From cheap beer to hard liquor, juvenile delinquents were infamous for their tendency to imbibe. As Salisbury asserts in *The Shook-Up Generation*,

"Drink is the curse of the shook-up kids. With few exceptions boys and girls drink from the age of eleven or twelve" (33). Discussing a boy named Chico who is a member of a gang, he points out that "he drinks every day" (35). Similarly, discussing a young man named Charley who belonged to a rival organization, Salisbury laments again that "he drinks every day" (35). For this reason, as Frederick Mayer observed in *Our Troubled Youth*, "Alcoholism today is a problem which is faced not only by the middle-aged population, but by thousands of teen-agers" (11).

Alcohol abuse is common in *The Outsiders*. Ponyboy confesses that "in our neighborhood it's rare to find a kid who doesn't drink once in a while" (8). To be sure, all of the Greasers partake of some form of alcohol. When the group convenes one afternoon, for instance, "Dally was sleeping off a hangover" (66). And then later, before the big rumble with the Socs in the final chapters, "Two-Bit was the only one wearing a jacket; he had a couple of beer cans stuffed in it. He always gets high before a rumble. Before anything else, too, come to think of it" (136–37).

Second only to juvenile delinquents' taste for alcohol was their predilection for the new musical genre of rock 'n' roll and especially the songs of Elvis Presley. As Frederick Mayer flatly states about JDs in *Our Troubled Youth*, "They love the sound of rock-and-roll music" (29). To illustrate this point, he offered the following chilling anecdote about one girl gang member:

> I shall never forget the ecstatic look on her face when she listened to rock-and-roll music and to Elvis Presley and how she disliked authority and how she looked down on her parents and teachers, who were to her "squares." Here was the semibarbarian who had no sensitivity and who lived on an impulsive basis. (10)

Far from an isolated opinion, the idea that there was a link between rock 'n' roll and teenage misbehavior is voiced in numerous texts. Most sociologists, educators, and psychologists at the time made a "simple equation between a taste for Elvis Presley and a taste for switchblades. This goes for children of all races, creeds, colors, sizes, shapes, and varieties" (Salisbury 108). Such predilections are likewise apparent in *The Outsiders*. As Ponyboy reveals about the Greaser's musical tastes: "we thought the Beatles were rank and that Elvis was tuff" (37).

While the pernicious influence of rock 'n' roll was commonly identified as a cause of juvenile delinquency, it was not the only one mentioned. The more commonly cited reason was a dysfunctional family life. As Salisbury discusses in *The Shook-Up Generation*, "Home is the root of 95 per cent of the gang conduct and behavior problems" (166). This view is mirrored in numerous other JD-themed paperbacks. In *The Cross and the Switchblade*, David Wilkerson remarks about the gang members that he encounters in New York that "virtually without exception they had no real home" (122). Likewise, Benjamin Fine asks in *1,000,000 Delinquents*, "Why blame these children for meeting in cellars, on the streets, in poolrooms? Their families were not units; they were singularly lacking in cohesiveness" (57). Finally, Frederick Mayer offers the following simple explanation in *Our Troubled Youth*: "Why had they become delinquents? . . . The reasons were manifold, but the main cause was that actually few cared about them. At home they usually received beatings" (3).

All of the characters in *The Outsiders* come from strained family circumstances. Johnny Cade's home life is marked by neglect, alcoholism, and domestic violence. As Ponyboy says about the sixteen-year-old's daily experiences, "His father was always beating him up, and his mother ignored him, except when she was hacked off at something, and then you could hear her yelling at him clear down at our house" (12). Years of such chronic mistreatment had emotionally hardened the otherwise tender young man: "I had seen Johnny take a whipping with a two-by-four from his old man and never let out a whimper" (33).

While Ponyboy does not face such horrific abuse, his home life is equally difficult: the fourteen-year-old and his two older brothers were orphaned earlier that year after their parents were killed in a car crash. Ponyboy recounts his emotional state in the wake of this event: "I had nightmares the night of Mom and Dad's funeral. . . . I woke up screaming bloody murder" (110). The death of Mr. and Mrs. Curtis has been especially difficult for Ponyboy's brothers, who have dropped out of school to work full-time so that the family can remain together. His oldest sibling, Darry, assumes the bulk of this responsibility. As Ponyboy says of him, "Darry's gone through a lot in his twenty years, grown up too fast" (2). "He's just got more worries than somebody his age ought to" (17). At one point, Hinton's characters reveal their awareness of the various environmental reasons for their delinquent behavior. As the group engages in revelries before the big fight with the Socs, one member of the gang shouts: "Greaser . . . greaser . . . greaser. . . . O victim of environment, underprivileged" (136).

Denied love, affection, and belonging at home, juvenile delinquents find these elements among the fellow members of their gang. As David Wilkerson relays about one of the boys he met on the streets of New York: "Angelo said that the feeling came because nobody loved you, and that all of his friends in the gangs were basically very lonely boys" (49). Salisbury offers a similar explanation for why JDs form gangs: "If a kid doesn't get it at home he goes to the street and gets it from the boys he finds there" (166). As a result, the bonds among gang members are typically very strong, taking the place of the affection normally received from mothers, fathers, sisters, and brothers. As one JD told Salisbury, "'I love every one of them!' he said of the gang. . . . 'I would do anything for those boys'" (51).

Comparable sentiments permeate *The Outsiders*. As Ponyboy reflects, "If it hadn't been for the gang, Johnny would never have known what love and affection are" (12). Moreover, both he and his fellow Greasers are very affectionate with one another, verbally as well as physically. In one scene, for example, the fourteen-year-old narrator says about Johnny, "He was crying. I held him like Soda had held him the day we found him lying in the lot" (74). Even seemingly hardened hoodlum Dally Winston reveals his softer side. "'Johnny,' Dally said in a pleading, high voice, using a tone I had never heard from him before, 'Johnny, I ain't mad at you. I just don't want you to get hurt. You don't know what a few months in jail can do to you. Oh, blast it, Johnny, . . . you get hardened in jail. I don't want that to happen to you. Like it happened to me.'" (90). Later, Ponyboy realizes that "Johnny was the only thing Dally loved" (152). Such passages prompted Michael Mallone to assert that "these characters do sometimes have girlfriends, but their erotic relationships come nowhere near the power of male camaraderie" (278).

More than simply possessing the behavioral and psychological traits of stereotypical postwar JDs, the characters in Hinton's novel also possess the physical attributes. Frederick Mayer describes the appearance of a typical member of a teenage gang: "He wore a leather jacket and dungarees; he looked like a junior version of Marlon Brando in *The Wild One*" (30). In *Savage Streets*, William McGivern adds more detail to this image: "He wore only a white T shirt which was tucked into the belt of his tightly pegged blue jeans" (42). Irving Shulman in *The Amboy Dukes* completes the portrait: "Their slick vaselined hair shone in the reflections of light" (2).

In *The Outsiders*, Ponyboy offers the following description of himself and his fellow Greasers: "We wear our hair long and dress in blue jeans and

T-shirts, or leave out shirttails out and wear leather jackets" (3). Far from ignoring the similarities between her characters and popular images of juvenile delinquents, Hinton acknowledges her awareness of it. As Ponyboy comments about Tim Shepard, a leader of a rival greaser gang who comes to help in the rumble with the Socs, he "was a lean, catlike, eighteen-year-old who looked *like the model JD you see in movies and magazines*" (138; my emphasis). Just before the big rumble with the Socs, Ponyboy again likens the scene to a Hollywood film: "For a minute, everything looked unreal, like a scene out of a JD movie or something" (142). An outburst by Randy Anderson about slain friend Bob Sheldon—"If his old man had just belted him—just once, he might still be alive"—is reminiscent of a remark made by one of the most famous cinematic juvenile delinquents of all time: Jim Stark from *Rebel Without a Cause* (1955). In a dramatic scene near the end of the movie, James Dean's character says of his emasculated father that "if he had the guts to knock Mom cold once, then maybe she'd be happy."*

The Outsiders echoes other passages from various fictional and nonfiction narratives about juvenile delinquency. Ponyboy frequently laments the class-bias inherent in both cultural and legal constructions of JDs. While talking with a member of the wealthy Socs, the fourteen-year-old reflects, "Besides, what did he have to lose? His old man was rich, he could pay whatever fine there was for being drunk and picking a fight" (165). An almost analogous remark appears in Benjamin Fine's *1,000,000 Delinquents*: "A report on juvenile delinquency in the schools, prepared in 1951 by the New York City Board of Education, made this point: 'The child who steals and is apprehended is legally a delinquent. . . . The boy who breaks a store window and whose parents refuse, or are unable, to pay for it is a delinquent; the one whose parents pay for it is not'" (200).

Several other textual details also resonate with various postwar paperbacks. Harrison E. Salisbury, for example, discusses gang members in *The Shook-Up Generation* with names "Seven-Up" and "Coke" (52, 54), which

---

* As both Michael Mallone and Dale Peck have observed, the similarities between *The Outsiders* and *Rebel Without a Cause* do not end here. Hinton's character Johnny is highly evocative of the equally shy, emotionally damaged, and darkly handsome Plato from Nicholas Ray's film. Both young men are the "pet" of their respective social groups and also, as Mallone points out, both are "clearly pegged for sacrifice" (278). Although Plato does not meet his fate while rescuing a group of children from a burning church, he is killed in a shootout with the police that can be seen as a suicide, just as Dally Winston's botched robbery in the finale to Hinton's novel is commonly seen as arising from his own wish to die.

recalls the unusual legal name of Ponyboy's older brother—Sodapop. Salisbury also mentions one youngster who has adopted the moniker "Sosh" (139), which mirrors the pronunciation of the nickname that Hinton chose for the rival gang of middle-class kids in *The Outsiders*.

Erin A. Smith, in the introduction to her book *Hard-Boiled: Working-Class Readers and Pulp Magazines* (2000), opens with the remark "What's a nice girl like you doing in a genre like this?" (1). Smith reveals that given the gritty, gruff and male-dominated realm of midcentury American pulp fiction, she has been asked "some version of this question more times than I can count" (1). A similar remark could be made about S. E. Hinton with regard to *The Outsiders*. While the critically acclaimed text may seem ostensibly far removed from the seedy world of postwar paperbacks, it possesses an array of artistic, literary, and material links to them that have gone unnoticed for far too long.

"Bloody Ambushes, Night Assaults, Pitched Battles with Gun, Broken Bottle and Knife": The Centrality of Killing or Being Killed for Postwar JDs

Juvenile delinquents were most infamous for getting into fights or "rumbles" with rival gangs. As Salisbury explains in *The Shook-Up Generation*, the typical juvenile delinquent "is ready to run for his life at any moment. The reason is simple. The route from subway to project is controlled by [another] gang" (12). As a result, according to Wilkerson in *The Cross and the Switchblade*, JDs "carried weapons against unknown dangers, ready at a moment's notice to run or to fight for their lives" (122). Their fears were not unfounded; as Salisbury explains, streets in the neighborhoods of teenage gangs were "the scene of bloody ambushes, night assaults, pitched battles with gun, broken bottle and knife" (12–13). The possibility of either committing murder or being murdered was an ever-present reality for postwar JDs.

Hinton's novel reflects this condition. When the group of Socs threatens the life of the narrator-protagonist by asking him if he needs a haircut, one boy pulls "a knife out of his back pocket" and flips "the blade open" (5). Realizing that the young men might kill him, Ponyboy explains that he "went wild. I started screaming for Soda, Darry, anyone. Someone put his hand over my mouth and I bit as hard as I could, tasting the blood running through my teeth" (5).

As readers learn, such events are common in Ponyboy's life. Every day, the protagonist and his friends live in constant fear that they may be beaten or even killed. A Greaser merely encountering a Soc—on the street or at a drive-in—is usually sufficient cause for a fight to erupt. A few months earlier, in fact, a group of Socs brutally attacked one of Ponyboy's friends simply for wandering in an empty lot to look for a lost football:

> Johnny's face was cut up and bruised and swollen, and there was a wide gash from his temple to his cheekbone. He would carry that scar all his life. I just stood there, trembling with cold. I thought he might be dead; surely nobody could be beaten like that and live. (32)

Even though Ponyboy asserts that "skin fights"—or skirmishes where only fists are allowed—are the most fair conflicts and also the best way to "blow off steam" (29), both he and his fellow Greasers carry knives and even guns, known respectively as "blades" and "heaters." As Hinton's protagonist recalls, "One time in biology I had to dissect a worm, and the razor wouldn't cut, so I used my switchblade. The minute I flicked it out—I forgot what I was doing or I would never have done it—this girl right beside me kind of gasped, and said, 'They are right. You are a hood'" (15). Likewise, fellow Greaser Keith "Two-Bit" Mathews is known for "shoplifting and his black-handled switchblade (which he couldn't have acquired without his first talent)" (10). Dally Winston, alarmingly, does not limit himself to simply switchblades; he has recently started carrying a gun.

Ponyboy insists that he and his Greaser friends carry weapons "mostly just for looks" (140), but they play a central role in the climactic scene of the novel in which Johnny Cade fatally stabs Bob Anderson. Hinton provides a graphic account of the young man's death: "Bob, the handsome Soc, was lying there in the moonlight, doubled up and still. A dark pool was growing from him, spreading slowly over the blue-white cement. I looked at Johnny's hand. He was clutching his switchblade, and it was dark to the hilt. My stomach gave a violent jump and my blood turned icy" (56). Haunted by the memory of this event, Johnny reflects later, "There sure is a lot of blood in people" (74). Hinton's novel highlights the physical brutality and psychological horror of murder and thus can be read as a cautionary tale that urges its young adult readers to resist engaging in such acts themselves. Far from glorifying or romanticizing gang violence, *The Outsiders* is a didactic and even moralistic novel that condemns it. At repeated points throughout the narrative, the author calls attention to the senselessness of "rumbles." As Ponyboy and Johnny become acutely aware, murderous violence does not solve difficulties; rather, it exacerbates them.

Although Johnny acted in self-defense, the boys are convinced that he has committed murder. "'Johnny!' I nearly screamed. 'What are we gonna do? They put you in the electric chair for killing people!'" (57). The two boys turn to one of the more experienced members of the gang, Dally Winston, for advice, but he only confirms their fears: "Man, I thought New York was the only place I could get mixed up in a murder rap" (61). Johnny and Ponyboy decide to flee town; they hop a train to rural Windrixville and hide out in an abandoned church. While there, Johnny is wracked with guilt: "'Stop it!' Johnny gasped from between clenched teeth. 'Shut up about last night! I killed a kid last night. He couldn't of been over seventeen or eighteen, and I killed him. How'd you like to live with that?' He was crying" (74).

This sequence of events mirrors the climax from one of the first and most famous JD-themed novels: Shulman's *The Amboy Dukes*. The central character—who is also fourteen years old—and one of his gang friends accidentally kill a teacher during a fight after school. "Benny screamed with pain [as the teacher twisted his arm] and involuntarily pulled the trigger. There was a muffled crack, and Mr. Bannon wavered, looked at them unbelievingly, then staggered forward to the desk, grasped the edge, collapsed, and died" (65). The description of the blood and gore presages the scene in *The Outsiders*: "Benny shook his head dumbly and continued to stare at the gun and the body. Blood soaking from the chest wound had discolored Mr. Bannon's shirt and jacket, and the stain grew larger and bright red" (65). Like Ponyboy and Johnny, in the aftermath of the murder, the two boys contemplate leaving town: "What're we gonna do now? . . . We'll have to blow" (66). Although Shulman's characters are more hardened than those in Hinton's novel, they express comparable feelings of remorse: "He [Frank] would have done anything to bring Mr. Bannon back, but he was dead, and they had killed him and they were murderers" (67). Finally, just as Ponyboy is aware that even though he didn't personally stab Bob Sheldon, he nonetheless played a punishable role in the killing, the main character in *The Amboy Dukes* recognizes that though he was not the shooter, he is an equally indictable accomplice: "But he [Frank] was there and as long as he was there he was an accessory" (69).

Although *The Outsiders* is similar in many ways to paperback books about juvenile delinquents, it of course is not identical to them. Unlike in what

Thomas Doherty has deemed more "hard-nosed" works about juvenile delinquency (100), Hinton's book lacks true profanity. A passage from Motley's bestseller *Knock on Any Door* typifies the language of his characters: "You're the only right guy on this whole goddamn street! That's no crap, Nick!" (322). By contrast, Hinton's novel, as Michael Mallone has commented, is "as free of profanity as *Heidi*. We are told people 'talk awful dirty,' but the only curses we hear are almost comically mild: 'Glory!,' 'Shoot!' 'Oh blast it!'" (278).

The Outsiders is likewise devoid of another staple in many pulp works about juvenile delinquency: illegal drug use, especially marijuana. As one gang member explains to a new initiate in the opening chapter of *The Amboy Dukes*, "They're reefers. If you're gonna smoke y'might's well get a kick outta it" (3). By contrast, while nearly all of the Greasers in *The Outsiders* smoke cigarettes, none of them—not even the more hardened Dally Winston—use cannabis. The boys often offer each other a "weed," but this is just a Lucky Strike, a Winston, or a Kool.

Finally, *The Outsiders* lacks another powerful hallmark of the JD paperback genre: explicit sex acts. A passage from Shulman's *The Amboy Dukes* once again provides a representative example. "We've got a hoo[k]er in the back. . . . And all she's asking is a buck apiece" (30). Over the course of the evening, eleven members of the gang have sex with her. Then, near the end of the book, one of the members of the Amboy Dukes rapes a twelve-year-old girl who had jilted him for another boy. Shulman provides a graphic description of the aftermath of this act of sexual violence:

> The three girls stood transfixed when they saw Fanny stumble dully into the kitchen, her eyes puffed from crying and her lips swollen from the slaps across the mouth. . . . Her stockings were in shreds, and the bodice of her dress was ripped to the waist. . . .
>
> "I never done it before!" The words came out singly from her bruised lips. "I never done it before! I begged him to let me go! Never done it before. Never done it before. Never done it—" (172–73)

The Outsiders contains nothing that even approximates this scene. Although Sodapop's girlfriend is forced to leave town after becoming pregnant, Hinton makes it clear that the protagonist's brother is not the father: "It wasn't Soda, Ponyboy. He told me he loved her, but I guess she didn't love him like he thought she did, because it wasn't him" (174). Even though the young woman had been impregnated by another man, Soda demonstrates his devotion—along with his upstanding moral character—by offering to do "the right thing": "He wanted to marry her anyway, but she just left" (174).

These exceptions aside, *The Outsiders* contains sufficient areas of overlap with postwar pulp paperbacks to challenge long-standing critical assertions about Hinton's "rejection of the established literature" (Cart 48). While the author may have rebuffed the heavily sentimental and largely romantic narratives written for adolescents at the time, she embraced numerous facets from an equally hegemonic narrative formula intended for adults.

Pocket Books promoted the release of its first paperback novel in June 1930 with a large, attention-grabbing advertisement in the *New York Times*: "Out Today—The New Pocketbook that May Revolutionize America's Reading Habits" (qtd. in Haut 4; see also Davis 12). Time would reveal that what seemed like an aggrandized promotional pronouncement was actually far too modest. More than simply forever altering the reading practices of adults, paperback books would also have a profound impact on those of juvenile readers. The pulp elements that permeate *The Outsiders* confirm one critic's observation about postwar paperbacks: "The pulps are already dead. The pulps will never die" (Locke 13).

The Literary Outsider Becomes the Canonical Insider: Postwar Paperbacks and the Birth of Young Adult Literature

Owing to the landmark nature of *The Outsiders* and its role in founding a new genre for adolescent readers, many of the elements that have come to be seen as defining traits of YA literature were also those of pulp fiction. Young adult novels mirror an array of the material, aesthetic, and literary qualities of postwar paperbacks constituting an unexpected and as-yet overlooked source of influence on the genre.

Roger Sutton has observed about YA literature as a whole that "teens . . . don't even read these books so much as they gobble them like peanuts, picking them up by the handful, one right after another" ("Critical" 33). Their recipe for success, he notes, is that they "offer a fast, entertaining read, suspense, and a satisfying conclusion" ("Critical" 33). Maia Pank Mertz and David E. England echo these comments, remarking that "generally, the novels are simple and direct" as well as brief and that "most can be read in a single sitting" (120, 121).

Similar comments have been made about postwar pulp narratives. One of the most beloved qualities of this new genre was the speed with which the books could be read. Most softbacked books were less than two hundred pages in length, and many were scarcely over a hundred. As both Davis and Schick have discussed, the narratives were meant to be quick, easy reads for individuals while they commuted to work, waited in an airport terminal, or relaxed in the evening (Davis xiv–xv; Schick 69–77).

One reason why pulp fiction was able to be read so swiftly was its action-packed, event-driven plot. As Erin A. Smith points out, whether a fiction title or nonfiction one, these books "move at a fantastic rate" (83), with one exciting scene following closely on the heels of another. A case in point is this moment from Salisbury's *The Shook-Up Generation*: "Suddenly came a ragged fusillade of shots and the roar of motors. The rumble was on. The cars raced to the end of Beaver Street, spun on whining tires and whirled back for a second pass at the stunned Rovers" (37).

Young adult literature likewise operates according to this principle. Donelson and Nilsen in *Literature for Today's Young Adults* note that a hallmark of this genre is that it is fast-paced (30). Events in these books unfold quickly, their plots progress rapidly, and page-turning scenes follow closely upon one another.

Postwar pulp fiction was as equally well known for its topical nature and shocking subject matter. As Michael Bronski remarks, "Often these books traded on current social obsessions and 'headline news'—juvenile delinquency, motorcycle gangs, wife-swapping, teen drug use, college scandals, mob racketeering, suburban malaise, and the erotic dangers of psychoanalysis" (3). Indeed, many pulp books likened themselves to works of social realism or even exposé journalism, vowing that they were "ready 'to reveal the sordid truth in a way you have never read before'" (3). The synopsis on the cover of Mayer's *Our Troubled Youth*, for instance, promises to expose "the whole shocking truth of what's wrong with American kids." This strategy gave voice and visibility to issues that were not being addressed in more "polite" publications, but it also made these books a lightning rod for public criticism. As early as "May 1952, the House of Representatives authorized a probe of the paperback, magazine, and comic business to determine the extent of 'immoral, obscene or otherwise offensive matter' or 'improper emphasis on crime, violence and corruption'" (Davis 219). The select committee was chaired by Kansas Democrat E. C. Gathings, and its final report offered the following less-than-flattering pronouncement about the paperback revolution: "The so-called pocket-sized books, which originally started out as cheap reprints of standard works, have largely degenerated into media for the dissemination of artful appeals to sensuality, immorality, filth, perversion and degeneracy" (qtd. in Davis 235). The National Organization for Decent Literature (NODL) testified during the Gathings committee's investigation, submitting a dossier of 275 books that it deemed especially heinous—and believed should be removed from shelves.

Young adult fiction is likewise associated with breaking boundaries and defying taboos. As Mertz and England have documented, books released in this genre routinely engage "with sensationalized topics" (119). They go on to assert that "many of the novels deal with formerly taboo topics—teenage pregnancy, drugs, homosexuality, death, and divorce," a list that could also be used to describe the subject matter addressed in postwar paperbacks (122). And not surprisingly, just as pulp fiction was often challenged and even banned, "concerned parents or the larger public find it necessary to censor [YA] books" (122). The American Library Association's list of the top ten most frequently challenged children's books in 2010 was comprised almost exclusively of titles intended for, or commonly read by, young adults: Sherman Alexie's *The Absolutely True Story of a Part-Time Indian*, Aldous Huxley's *Brave New World*, Ellen Hopkins's *Crank*, Suzanne Collins's *The Hunger Games*, Natasha Friend's *Lush*, Sonya Sones's *What My Mother Doesn't Know*, Amy Sonnie's *Revolutionary Voices: A Multicultural Queer Youth Anthology*, and Stephanie Meyer's *Twilight* ("Top Ten").

In an article that appeared in the *New York Times*, Michael Mallone comments on the difficulty that librarians, teachers, and critics have had defining young adult literature. What age ranges does it encompass? What subject matters does it address? What writers constitute its core? Given the lack of consensus concerning the answers to these questions, the genre often appears to be an amalgamation, comprised of whatever books, authors, and developmental stages a particular scholar is interested in at the time. As Mallone mused after witnessing the seemingly random collection of books in the YA section of the Philadelphia Public Library, "I could come to no clear sense of what constitutes Young Adult fiction" (280).

Such remarks have been echoed by numerous other figures. Cart dedicates many pages in the opening chapter of his now-classic study *From Romance to Realism* to "the very ambiguity of the phrase 'young adult'" (3). Donelson and Nilsen similarly struggle with this issue in the introduction to their *Literature for Today's Young Adults*. In a section aptly titled "A Brief Unsettled Heritage," they discuss the various terms that have historically been used to characterize this genre: "juvenile literature," "junior novel," "teen fiction," "teenage books," and even "juvie" (2). Isabelle Holland provides one of the most comprehensive accounts of this struggle in her article "What Is Adolescent Literature?" After providing a lengthy overview of various opinions, she confesses in exasperation that "I am coming more and more to the conclusion that adolescent literature is whatever any adolescent happens to be reading at any given time" (61). I would add one more element to the already lengthy list of possible components to the genre: whatever YA literature is, postwar pulp fiction is a part of it.

For generations in the United States, artistic creations were viewed according to a clear aesthetic hierarchy. As Lawrence Levine has documented, beginning in the mid-nineteenth century, arbiters of cultural taste began dividing print, visual, and dramatic works into distinct and even mutually exclusive categories: "highbrow," which denoted supposedly aesthetically refined, historically resonant, and intellectually serious works, and, conversely, "lowbrow," which designated creations that were generally lacking in significant intellectual content and thus had a mass appeal.

This previously firm separation began to weaken during the latter half of the twentieth century. As Fredric Jameson has famously charted, the ascendency of postmodernist thought, a growing awareness of the race and especially class biases inherent in judgments about taste, and the increasing recognition of the power wielded by mass culture called such viewpoints into question (*Cultural* 1–20). By the late 1990s and opening decade of the new millennium, these attitudes had all but disappeared: in classrooms around the country, comic books were being studied alongside metaphysical poetry while reality television was getting as much scholarly attention as opera librettos—perhaps more so. Describing this seemingly cultural free-for-all, columnist Rachael Maddux said it best when she quipped "High-Brow, Low-Brow, No-Brow, Schmo-Brow."

The presence of lowbrow pulp elements in S. E. Hinton's highbrow YA novel situates *The Outsiders* on the leading edge of this phenomenon. The 1967 narrative incorporated facets of a literary format deemed inconsequential decades before readers and critics recognized its importance. In this way, *The Outsiders* retains its status as a groundbreaking narrative, but for different reasons than readers and critics have previously cited.

Commenting on the numerous knife fights, gun battles, and homicides in *The Outsiders*, Cart observes that "Hinton had been quite right when she pointed out, in her *New York Times* piece, that 'violence, too, is part of teenagers' lives.' Before her, though, authors had tended to ignore this basic fact of adolescent life" (47). In the same way that the author recognized the centrality of everyday violence at the time, her narrative also recognized the centrality of everyday forms of popular print culture.

CHAPTER SIX

"My Job Is . . . to Make You a Human Being in the Eyes of the Jury"

Confronting the Demonization—and Dramatization— of Murder in Walter Dean Myers's Monster

> To identify the murderer in contemporary culture is *not* the same as to comprehend the evil.
>
> KAREN HALTTUNEN, *Murder Most Foul* (1998)

As the twentieth century drew to a close, the murder rate in the United States revealed a powerful paradox. On one hand, this figure had declined steadily throughout the 1990s. As Peter Vronsky has written, criminal homicides stood at 9.8 per 100,000 citizens in 1991 but, by 2000, had dropped "to a record low of 4.1" (16). As a result, the nation had never been safer or, at least, freer from lethal violence.

These statistics are misleading, however. Although the overall murder rate for the country had decreased, it was experiencing a sharp increase among a specific demographic: young black men. While African Americans had long represented a disproportionate number of homicide victims, the final decade of the twentieth century saw this statistic reach unprecedented new levels.* According to the Bureau of Justice, the national black homicide rate in 1991 was an astounding 51.4 per 100,000. By the end of the decade this figure had dropped, but it was still 25.6—more than six times the national average.

The rising murder rate for blacks was not the result of a nationwide epi-

---

* Roger Lane provides the following statistics: "With the black population of the United States at roughly 12 percent, the number of black homicide victims has hovered close to half: 50 percent in 1974, 51 percent in 1994" (320).

demic of racially motivated hate crimes. On the contrary, the majority of these homicides were the result of intraracial violence. As University of Pennsylvania sociologist Elijah Anderson comments, disheartened by a lack of economic opportunities, disenchanted by a poor education system, and disillusioned with the American criminal justice system, "Many young blacks have become convinced that their lives don't matter and neither do those of the black men around them" (qtd. in Dinges par. 3). Such nihilistic attitudes coupled with dire socioeconomic conditions created a fertile breeding ground for various forms of criminality, from the spread of crack cocaine and the rise in armed robberies to the growth of gangs and the epidemic of drive-by shootings. All of these activities contributed to an uptick in homicide. According to Anderson, "Black males are desperately striving for status and identity. . . . And since so many can no longer assume the roles of breadwinner and reliable husband, they attempt to prove their manhood by waging war against other black men" (qtd. in Dinges par. 40). Whatever the specific cause, the murder of young African American men reached a crisis point during the 1990s. "Louis W. Sullivan, secretary of the U.S. Department of Health and Human Services, has said: 'Not since slavery has so much calamity and ongoing catastrophe been visited on black males'" (Dinges par. 47). As Don Colburn shockingly revealed in the *Washington Post*, "When a young black man dies in this country, the most likely cause is not cancer or cardiac arrest or a car wreck. He is shot to death" (par. 1).

This grim reality placed the black murder rate at the forefront of the American public consciousness and its attendant forms of popular culture. Films such as John Singleton's *Boyz N the Hood* (1991), Mario Van Peebles's *New Jack City* (1991), and Spike Lee's *Clockers* (1995), as well as the music of rap artists like Snoop Dogg, Tupac Shakur, and Public Enemy, addressed the rising rate of gang violence, the growth of black urban drug culture, and the high incidence of murder of African American men.

In 1999, the cultural examination of violent crime by young black men expanded into a new realm when Walter Dean Myers released his young adult novel *Monster*. Set in Harlem and featuring sixteen-year-old Steve Harmon as its narrator-protagonist, the book chronicles the experiences of the young African American man while he stands trial for murder. More specifically, Harmon is accused of having served as the "lookout man" in a drugstore robbery that ended with the fatal shooting of the establishment's proprietor.

Monster is a gripping book in both its form and its content. The narrative opens with Steve's chilling observation about the violence and despair of incarceration: "The best time to cry is at night, when the lights are out and someone is being beaten up and screaming for help" (1). The manner in which Steve tells his story is just as startling: the sixteen-year-old documents his trial in the form of a film script—complete with dialogue prompts, camera angles, and set descriptions. He alights on this approach as a means to help him cope with the anxiety, loneliness, and uncertainty of this period: "Maybe I could make my own movie. I could write it out and play it in my head. I could block out the scene like we did in school. The film will be the story of my life. No, not my life, but of this experience. I'll write it down in the notebook they let me keep" (4–5). Steve supplements his movie script with entries from a journal that he is keeping in jail. The cumulative effect, as reviewer Tammy Currier remarks, renders *Monster* a "fast-paced nail biter [that] will have you on the edge of your seat unable to put it down" (par. 3).

Monster has become one of the most critically acclaimed young adult novels of all time. Patty Campbell, writing in *Horn Book Magazine*, called the book a "once-in-a-decade event, a milestone comparable to *Catcher in the Rye* and S. E. Hinton's *The Outsiders*" (769). In the years since its release, Myers's text has been the recipient of numerous honors and awards. It was selected as one of the American Library Association's Best Book for Young Adults; it was named a *Boston Globe / Horn Book* Honor Book; it was chosen as a National Book Award Finalist; it was a Coretta Scott King Author Honor Book; and it was highlighted as an Editor's Choice selection on *Booklist*. Finally, and perhaps most prestigiously, *Monster* was the recipient of the first Michael L. Printz Award for excellence in young adult literature. This lengthy list of honors bears out Jim Higgins's observation that *Monster* "electrified" the world of juvenile books.

In various articles and interviews, Myers has discussed the role that the rapidly rising rate of violent crime among young black men played in his decision to write the novel: "It's incredible that these kids could go from being in high school now and not much later be faced with a life sentence" ("*Booklist* Interview" 1101). *Monster* is an attempt to examine how this happens. In the words of Myers once again, "When people plan their crimes, they always think that everything will work out perfectly, and it doesn't. That's what scares me. That's what I hope kids reading this book [*Monster*] will do. . . . They'll think more in advance about what they're doing and the outcome" (qtd. in Burshtein 73–4). Critics have largely agreed with this assessment. Mary Ellen

Snodgrass, for example, points out that Myers "recognized a pattern in men who 'were clearly separating their concept of self from their deeds'" (31). As a result, she asserts, the author composed the narrative "as a way to give alienated youth sources of morals and right-thinking about real-life temptations" (161).

In this chapter, I both build on and break from this assessment. I argue that while Myers is tracing the behavioral progression by which formerly law-abiding adolescents become convicted criminals, his book is simultaneously engaged in a second, and equally important, project aimed at challenging the demonization and dehumanization of individuals who commit violent crimes. Myers's protagonist, after contemplating various titles for his movie script about the murder trial, decides that he will "call it what the lady who is the prosecutor called me. **MONSTER**" (5). This moniker reflects common societal attitudes about men and women who engage in violent crime, namely, that in order to have the psychological desire and especially the physical ability to kill another human being, an individual must be deviant, deranged, or even nonhuman.

Although Walter Dean Myers chose the term "monster" as the title for his novel, the narrative does not support this viewpoint. In both its form and its content, the 1999 text works to combat such stereotypes. Steve's film script and especially his journal entries reveal that, far from a psychotic fiend, he is a thoughtful and intelligent individual. Through these techniques, Myers succeeds in the seemingly impossible task of getting his young adult readers to sympathize with—and even develop a fondness for—a narrator-protagonist who may have participated in a murder.

When *Monster*'s sympathetic portrayal of Steve Harmon is combined with its didactic interest in cautioning juvenile readers about the many smaller actions and minor decisions that can lead to serious criminal trouble, the ostensibly topical narrative acquires a new historical component. Although written as a screenplay and released on the eve of the twenty-first century, *Monster* has a kinship with an unexpected literary source: colonial American execution sermons. Delivered by local ministers on the gallows of individuals condemned to death and then later printed and sold, these texts were among the most popular in the sixteenth and seventeenth centuries. In New England alone, "scores of gallows discourses issued from the presses of the region, sometimes two or three to a volume," according to Daniel A. Cohen (4). Bearing titles like *The Penitent Death of a Woefull Sinner* (1641), *A Murderer*

Punished and Pardoned (1668), and *A Mirrour of Mercy and Judgement* (1655), execution sermons "explained how condemned criminals had been led to their fatal wickedness, warned others against the same sort of misconduct, and justified capital punishment" (6). While the didactic message of these orations was, of course, directed at adults, children were seen as an equally appropriate audience. As a readership whose attitudes were still being formed, juveniles, it was thought, would be heavily influenced by the lessons contained in execution sermons. Ministers could not save the condemned prisoner on the gallows, but, as Cohen notes, they "expressed the hope that frightening examples might warn others against wrongdoing" (x).

Monster is in dialogue with this genre. From the narrative's insistence on Steve's humanity and its desire for readers to sympathize and even identify with the protagonist to the focus on the moral rather than legal significance of Steve's action and its emphasis on the numerous lesser decisions that led to the serious transgression, the message of the text mirrors that of this historical genre. The fact that Steve is possibly facing the death penalty for his role in the robbery-homicide only strengthens the connection between these two seemingly disparate genres.

Monster thus does more than simply add to the growing number of artistic forms that have examined the interconnections among adolescent black masculinity, gang culture, and urban violence as the twentieth century drew to a close; it also reveals important information about the social construction of crime and the changing perceptions of criminals in the United States. An awareness of how Myers's ostensibly innovative text is also a literary throwback highlights the different ways that Americans have viewed, interpreted, and responded to murder. Ultimately, *Monster* demonstrates that attitudes about both violence and violent offenders which we commonly consider fixed and universal are actually culturally contingent and historically malleable.

From Familiar to Freak: The Changing Social Construction of Murder and Murderers

For centuries in the United States, men and women who have committed murder have been cast as personal, psychological, and behavioral deviants. Whether old or young, black or white, male or female, any individual who takes another's life is seen as fiendish and even freakish. Even a cursory examination of American popular, material, and literary culture reveals the ubiquity of this viewpoint. Nonfiction books like Peter Vronsky's *Serial Killers: The Method and Madness of Monsters* (2004) and Robert Ressler's *Whoever Fights Monsters: My Twenty Years Hunting Serial Killers for the FBI* (1992) cast habitual killers as beasts. Harold Schechter, in his true crime series, goes even further. The titles that he selects for his texts reveal prevailing societal views of murderers as disturbed, nonhuman, and even demonic. Thus far, Schechter has published the following books: *Deviant*, about the life of serial killer Ed Gein; *Deranged*, spotlighting 1920s child-murderer Albert Fish; *Bestial*, examining sexual thrill killer Earle Leonard Nelson; *Fiend*, concerning fourteen-year-old outlaw Jesse Pomeroy in the 1870s; and *Depraved*, focusing on turn-of-the-century serial killer H. H. Holmes.

Such attitudes are also reflected in cinematic portrayals of homicide. In movies ranging from masterpieces like Alfred Hitchcock's *Psycho* (1960) to more recent releases such as Patty Jenkins's *Monster* (2003), killers are presented as existing outside the realm of established behavioral norms. Classic horror films are especially notorious for this perspective. Movies like *Texas Chainsaw Massacre* (1974), *Halloween* (1978), *The Amityville Horror* (1979), *The Shining* (1980), *Friday the 13th* (1980), and *A Nightmare on Elmstreet* (1984) feature the violent actions of a figure who is depicted as nothing less than a homicidal lunatic.

Far from being a label that is externally imposed, many killers have embraced the identity of "monster" themselves. In a letter that Kansas strangler BTK—now known to be Dennis Rader—wrote to police in the 1970s during the height of his murder spree, he said of his compulsion to kill: "I can't stop it so the monster goes on" (qtd. in Vronsky 20). Likewise, multiple murderer David Berkowitz—better known as the "Son of Sam"—signed his correspondence to authorities "Mr. Monster" (Ressler 79). Not surprisingly, the term "serial killer" appears as an entry in *Monstropedia*, the largest online database about both fictional and factual beasts.

The equation of murderers with monsters is not limited to individuals who kill multiple people; even those who engage in a solitary act of homicide are assigned this label. Discussing a murder that took place in Jacksonville, Florida, in 2008, for example, one community member said about the person who had committed the crime that "it's a monster walking around" (Pinkham par. 19). Such remarks are typical whenever and wherever a killing occurs. Whether described as fiends and beasts or psychos and freaks, men and women who kill are quickly demonized and even dehumanized.

Forming an oft-forgotten detail about the social history of murder in the United States, this association has not always been made. Daniel A. Cohen has shown that in British America, men and women who committed homicide were not cast as sociopathic monsters or amoral freaks. The sermons delivered at the gallows described the criminal as no different from the rest of the populace; they had simply given in to the depravity inherent in all men and women. Informed by biblical viewpoints concerning the origins of mankind, clergymen reminded their congregants that they were all born inherently sinful and, thus, with the capacity for evil. As minster John Rogers explained in an execution sermon from 1701, "Every Child of *Adam* is born . . . with that *Original Sin*, which the hearts of all men are by nature full of, and is a fountain always sending forth its bitter streams" (95; italics in original). Given this postlapsarian state, men and women were more naturally inclined to move toward malfeasance than away from it. As a result, British Americans were acutely aware that "the only difference between the condemned murderer and the rest of humanity was 'the restraining grace of God, to whose Name alone belongs the Praise, that any of us have been with-held from the grossest and most horrid Acts of Wickedness'" (Halttunen 15). Committing murder was not the result of an isolated personality defect but rather a capacity that was present in all humankind. "'The sorrowful Spectacle before us should make us reflect most seriously on *our own* vile Nature; which the Falls of others are but a Comment upon,' Thomas Foxcroft noted in a gallows discourse of 1733, 'and should excite us to humble ourselves under a sense of the Corruption of *our Hearts*, which are naturally as bad as the worst'" (Cohen 84; italics in original).* Far from distancing themselves from killers, colonial Americans identified and even sympathized with them. Sermons delivered at the execution of a convicted killer made "repeated references to 'the sorrowful object before us' and the 'unhappy Malefactor'" (Halttunen 16). In so doing, they "invited hearers and readers to respond to the murderer with a compassionate fellow-feeling bordering on the modern psychological concept of empathy" (Halttunen 16).

Such beliefs in the inherent sinfulness of all humankind challenge theories

---

*I am greatly indebted to the work of both Daniel A. Cohen and Karen Halttunen on early American execution sermons, dying verses, trial reports, and last speeches. Whenever I was able, I located a copy of the seventeenth-, eighteenth- or nineteenth-century murder material that they address in their analyses. But, this was not always logistically or materially possible. Thus, in passages like the one quoted here, I rely on their invaluable archival research.

about the peculiarity of murder and murderers. In a view that is alien to modern culture, "humankind was not divided into rigid categories of normalcy and deviancy, but strung out along a moral continuum, on which all were equally vulnerable to slippage in the direction of major transgressions such as murder" (Halttunen 32). Instead of being viewed as strange or unusual, the murderer was seen as someone who was essentially no different from everyone else in the community. Given that all of humankind possessed original sin and was subject to evil, if British American ministers, lawmakers, or citizens expressed any form of surprise over an act of murder, it was "not that one sinner had committed this crime, but that everyone else in the community had not" (Halttunen 4). Consequently, rather than saying that murderers were not seen as monsters, it may be more accurate to say that *everyone* was viewed as demonic, fiendish, and potentially homicidal.

In one of his many self-styled proverbs, Mark Twain asserts that "if the desire to kill and the opportunity to kill came always together, who would escape hanging?" ("Pudd'nhead" 111). Although Twain was likely being facetious, the remark has historical veracity. Murder was commonly framed in Twain's times and still is today as an "unthinkable" act—something that the majority of men and women would never dare contemplate, let alone actually carry out. However, this has not always been the case. For centuries in the United States, the capacity along with the desire to kill was regarded not as unusual but as universal.

"I Know That in My Heart I Am <u>Not</u> a Bad Person": Steve Harmon and the Humanization of Homicide

Walter Dean Myers seeks to return to this historical view about the construction of crime and perception of criminals. Although he may have titled his 1999 novel *Monster*, he does not subscribe to the belief that people who kill can be accurately characterized by this term. In repeated passages throughout the narrative, the author works to humanize his sixteen-year-old protagonist, presenting him as an individual who has hopes, fears, and—in light of his current circumstances—regrets. Through these revealing and often even tender passages, Myers enables young adult readers to better intellectually comprehend, emotionally sympathize, and—perhaps most astoundingly, given that Steve has been charged with felony murder—even personally identify with his protagonist. As a consequence, they see his character not as a fiendish monster, but as an intelligent, if also imperfect, young man. In so doing, *Monster* conveys a similar message as the execution sermons, representing Steve as a figure who is little different from themselves.

Myers wastes no time debunking societal beliefs that individuals who commit violent crimes are monsters. At the outset, Steve not only explains the inspiration for the title of his script—"I'll call it what the lady who is the prosecutor called me. **MONSTER**" (5)—but also reveals the horror that this label commonly evokes by using a larger font for it, capitalizing it, and bolding it. At numerous points throughout the rest of the novel, this sentiment is reiterated as Steve is deemed inhuman because of his alleged involvement in the robbery-murder. The protagonist relays in a journal entry, for example, that when a fellow inmate saw his script with its attention-grabbing title, "He said when he gets out, he will have it tattooed on his forehead. I feel like I already have it tattooed on mine" (61). Later, at the start of his trial, the sixteen-year-old's lawyer soberly reminds him: "They're accusing you of being a monster" (79).

Although Steve is legally innocent until proven guilty, the strong association of murderers with monsters causes many men and women in the courtroom to view him differently. One day, students from a local school observe Steve's trial as part of a civics lesson. Echoing societal beliefs that criminals are horrifying, the youngsters' recoil from his gaze: "When I looked at the kids in the class, they turned away from me quickly" (97). Amazingly, some members of the jury hold analogous attitudes. As Steve records in his journal, when he accidently locks eyes with one of jurors, "she stops smiling and looks quickly away" (99). Later, another juror shoots Steve an "accusing stare" (199). Views about the inhumanity of violent criminals are so pervasive that they even infect Steve's own family. The young man laments his father's emotional state after a visit to the prison, noting that "it's like a man looking down to see his son and seeing a monster instead" (116).

The chronological age, geographic locale, and racial identity of Myers's protagonist only exacerbates these associations. As Dennis Rome has argued in *Black Demons: The Media's Depiction of The African American Male Criminal Stereotype*, popular portrayals of young black men, especially those living in urban areas, repeatedly associate them with violence and crime. In cultural venues ranging from gangsta rap and blaxploitation films to evening newscasts and reality crime shows like *Cops*, African American males are presented as killers, muggers, rapists, and thieves (Rome 1–4). Such repeated presentations fuel white fears of black men while creating what Rome has called the image of the "black demon."

As John A. Staunton and Francine Gubuan have aptly observed, Myers's novel "confronts the white middle class fear of black youth as public menace and places Steve's story within the troubled history of that image" (792). Steve's lawyer laments that "half of those jurors, no matter what they said when we questioned them when we picked the jury, believed you were guilty the moment they laid eyes on you. You're young, you're Black, and you're on trial. What else do they need to know?" (78–79). Several of the prison guards who escort Steve to the courtroom openly express such opinions. As one asserts when the court stenographer wonders how long the trial will last, "Six days, maybe seven. It's a motion case. They go through the motions; then they lock them up" (14). As such comments indicate, Steve's trial is at least as much about exercising legal due process as it is about combating racial prejudice, challenging personal presumptions, and shattering societal stereotypes. The young man soon realizes "what Miss O'Brien meant when she said part of her job was to make me look human in the eyes of the jury" (62–63).

As quickly as Myers establishes such negative stereotypes about crime and criminals, he refutes them. One of the most frequent strategies by which *Monster* humanizes its incarcerated protagonist is by presenting him realistically and matter-of-factly as a frightened adolescent. Some of the initial directorial notes in the film script call for "CLOSE-UP (CU) of STEVE HARMON. The fear is evident on his face" (15). Indeed, when the young man's lawyer asks him "How are you doing?" as his trial is about to begin, he replies, "I'm scared" (15). Steve repeatedly mentions the terror that he experiences both inside and outside the courtroom. In a comment that makes him sound more like a little boy than a hardened criminal, he confesses, "In the courtroom I am afraid of the judge. The guards terrify me" (96). Not surprisingly, such anxieties increase exponentially the night before Steve is scheduled to testify. As he writes in his journal, "I am so scared. My heart is beating like crazy and I am having trouble breathing" (201–2). The following day, his hands shake noticeably as he takes the stand (222). After he has finished, he attempts to take a drink of water, but he is trembling too much to hold a glass (234).

Such passages present Steve not as a cold-blooded monster but as a fully-feeling and even vulnerable individual. When the narrator-protagonist mentions some of the physical symptoms that have arisen from his constant mental anxiety—waking up in a cold sweat, being unable to sleep, losing his appetite, finding himself unable to use the toilet because of the lack of privacy —it seems likely that even the most hardened reader would feel some sympathy for him.

Myers's description of life in prison also elicits compassion. *Monster* presents the conditions in the Manhattan correctional facility where Steve is incarcerated as brutal and even hellish. The directorial notes describe the scene: "We hear sounds of fists methodically punching someone as the camera goes slowly down the corridor. . . . We see two inmates silhouetted, beating a third. Another inmate is on the lookout" (57). Such cruelty is far from atypical. As Steve relays, "All they talk about in here is hurting people. If you look at somebody, they say, 'What you looking at me for? I'll mess you up!'" (45). The young man goes on to reveal that violent altercations erupt in almost every locale of the prison: the mess hall, the corridors, and even the chapel. Far from simple fist fights, these confrontations are often vicious and brutal. For instance, Steve reports that during a conflict one day before lunch, one prisoner stabbed another in the eye (143–44).

Such graphic, detailed, and horrendous conditions invite young adult readers to imagine themselves in Steve's position and how awful this experience would be. Given the environment that the young narrator-protagonist encounters in prison, it comes as no surprise that he writes in his journal that "I hate this place. I hate this place. I can't write it enough times to make it look the way I feel. I <u>hate</u>, <u>hate</u>, <u>hate</u> this place!!" (46; underlining in original).*

Not all of the scenes in *Monster* that encourage readers to sympathize with the main character are so dramatic. Many are more ordinary—and thus more universal. During one scene told in flashback, for instance, Steve watches cartoons with his younger brother. In an exchange that calls attention to the boys' youth and innocence, the two discuss which superheroes they'd most like to be. When Steve says he'd like to be Superman, his sibling sweetly proposes that he become Batman instead, for this way his younger brother, Jerry, could be his sidekick, Robin. Steve is aware of the humanizing effect of this interaction. As he reflects in his journal, "I like the last scene in the

---

* Ironically, in an attempt to highlight the humanity of his main character, Myers calls attention to the inhumanity of the other prisoners. With their seemingly innate need to engage in violence, the other inmates fit the stereotype of the criminal "monster." In contrast, because Steve dislikes this behavior, we see him as not being a monster. So, while Myers works to combat the dehumanization of criminals in some ways—perhaps with regard to offenders who are still juveniles, like Steve—he reinforces or at least reflects this attitude when it comes to convicts who are adults.

movie, the one between me and Jerry. It makes me seem like a real person" (60). Later, the young man expresses this desire to be seen as a normal person even more directly, stating "I want to look like a good person. I want to feel like I'm a good person because I believe I am" (62).

In many subsequent journal entries, Steve reveals his innermost thoughts, heart-felt emotions, and even strong moral character. Contemplating a re-mark made by his lawyer, Steve writes, "She wanted to know who I was. Who was Steve Harmon? I wanted to open my shirt and tell her to look into my heart to see who I really was, who the real Steve Harmon was" (92). Later, the young man makes his desire to be seen as an individual and not as a stereotype even more explicit, writing pleadingly that "I'm just not a bad person. I know that in my heart I am not a bad person" (93). These comments mirror a remark that Steve made to a fellow prisoner earlier in the novel. When the older inmate asks the young man why he thinks he should be released rather than serve time, Steve gives the following emphatic reply: "Cause I'm a hu-man being. I want a life too! What's wrong with that?" (76). Such remarks challenge *Monster*'s young adult audience to look beyond stock cultural per-ceptions and see a specific individual.

Finally, but not incidentally, Steve's family also greatly adds to his human-ization. Unlike the seemingly solitary nature of a freak or monster, Myers's protagonist has a mother, father, and brother who love, support, and miss him. The first view that readers get of Mrs. Harmon is tender and moving: "CUT TO: STEVE'S MOTHER, on wooden bench in the gallery area, listening in-tently. Her face looks worried" (25). The scene in which Mr. Harmon visits his son in jail is even more touching: "There are tears in his eyes. The pain in his face is very evident as he struggles with his emotions" (111). As the directorial notes relay, when Mr. Harmon's visit ends, "there is the sound of STEVE'S FATHER sobbing" (113). The genuine care, concern, and even anguish that Mr. and Mrs. Harmon experience over their son's incarceration reveals Steve to be an individual who is worthy of love.

Myers's novel closes the gap between his readers and his protagonist and thus between noncriminals and criminals (or, at least, those accused of engag-ing in lethal violence). In case this message is not sufficiently clear, one passage makes it explicit: "CUT TO: STEVE HARMON: Then: CU of the pad in front of him. He is writing the word *Monster* over and over again. A white hand (O'BRIEN'S) takes the pencil from his hand and crosses out all the

Monsters" (24). Of course, Myers hopes that his readers will replicate this action, if not literally then at least metaphorically, by abandoning their association of murderers with monsters.

"The Natural Progress of Sin": The Clear Causes of Crime and the Universal Nature of Evil

Colonial American ministers, together with framing murder as arising from "divine abandonment and the withdrawal of restraining grace" (Cohen 86), offered a second, and more secular, explanation for why some individuals committed murder: what Cohen has labeled "the natural progress of sin" (86). Grave transgressions like homicide did not emerge out of a behavioral void; rather, clergymen explained, they were the culmination of an increasingly serious sequence of misconduct. "'See whither lesser sins will lead you, even unto *greater* till at last you come to the *Great Transgression*,' Joshua Moody warned in 1686" (Cohen 87; italics in original). Increase Mather was even more explicit, naming specific transgressions. In an execution sermon from the 1680s, for example, he "warned against such evils as unjustified anger, cursing, quarreling, and cruelty, suggesting that they all had 'a tendency to, and a degree of Murder in them'" (qtd. in Cohen 87). More than fifty years later, such views were still dominant. In 1738, clergyman Eliphalet Adams told his congregants: "Sinners begin with Lesser Crimes and then they grow worse & worse" (qtd. in Cohen 87). Commonly identified faults included "pride, gluttony, drunkenness, sloth, idleness, irreligion, profanity, evil company, and disobedience to parents and masters" (Cohen 87).

In the minds of British American clergymen, there was a clear causality among and between such transgressions. As Cohen notes, "In explaining how one sin led to another, the minister employed the powerful image of contagion and disease. Wickedness, he suggested, was a deadly inflection that, unchecked, could only spread and destroy its tainted victim" (87). Other ministers offered different analogies—"liken[ing] the progress of sin to a fall down a steep hill, a habit difficult to break, an appetite strengthened by being fed, and a spark that could lead to a conflagration" (Cohen 87)—but their messages were the same. Even the smallest and seemingly most innocuous of transgressions, they asserted, might be the first step on the path to murder. "According to Cotton Mather, even husbands who spoke harshly to their wives were guilty of murder. No one, it appeared, was innocent of the crime" (Halttunen 15). As Karen Halttunen has aptly noted, in light of the vast number of smaller sins that were seen as having a causal link to homicide, "what drunken man, what disobedient servant could be certain that he had not placed his foot on the road to murder?" (15).

Condemned individuals who recognized their wrongdoings and repented were given a status that is unimaginable in modern society: "Most condemned murderers in early New England were represented as models of religious conversion" (Halttunen 18–19). Precisely because they had made a murderous misstep—not in spite of this fact—they were seen as sources of inspiration for the rest of the community. In the words of Halttunen, "The effect of the execution sermon's treatment of criminal causality was to establish a strong moral identification between the assembled congregation and the condemned murderer" (14). These men and women were seen as no different from other members of the community—save for the severity of their sinfulness. As a result, "the printed confessions of condemned murderers were meant to serve as models for the rest of the sinful New England community to emulate" (21). Their lives were object lessons from which the rest of the congregation could learn an important message. "The repentant murderer willingly offered herself as a cautionary example for others to heed: as the Rev. Thomas Foxcroft said of Rebekah Chamblit, 'It appear'd to me one of the best Symptoms upon this poor Criminal, that she seem'd desirous her Example might be a Warning to others'" (Halttunen 21).

"The Trouble I'm in Keeps Getting Bigger and Bigger": Mapping the Behavioral Steps to Murder in *Monster*

Walter Dean Myers may not present his sixteen-year-old narrator-protagonist as a monster, but that does not mean he condones his behavior. On the contrary, the novel is unwavering in its indictment of Steve's conduct. Furthermore, Myers refuses to present Steve's possible involvement in the robbery-homicide as something that emerged from a behavioral vacuum. Instead, the author chronicles in a manner similar to that of colonial execution sermons the numerous smaller personal decisions that led to the situation. In various articles and interviews, in fact, Myers has revealed that documenting this process was one of his primary motivations for writing the novel. He recalls that when he was conducting research for another project, he did a lot of interviews with kids in jail. . . . One of the things that really shook me was that the young men did not understand how they got from the point of innocence to the ability to commit a crime. What got them there, of course, were the small moral decisions they made for which they were not punished. (qtd. in Burshtein 73)

Indeed, as the author notes, "I talked to defense attorneys and prosecutors and they all said the same thing: that no one starts off as a murderer. They all start with small crimes and work their way up" (Myers "*Booklist*" 1101). "Many of these people in jails," Myers states, "think of themselves as basically innocent kids who got caught up. They don't realize the process" (qtd. in Burshtein 73).

Monster is an attempt to chart this progression. "I would like young people to consider what happened to Steve Harmon, as well as why," Myers has explained. "There were decisions that Steve made and some he clearly should have made, but didn't. As the author, I'll be satisfied if the reader forms their own opinions about these decisions and the consequences" ("Questions" 14). Thus almost as prominent as Myers's desire to humanize Steve Harmon is his quest to chart the many small and seemingly inconsequential choices that led to the larger and more serious one. While the secular novel does not frame these steps as a "progress of sin," it does posit their clear causality. Each decision moved the young man further down a path that led to armed robbery, felony murder, and—if he is convicted—the execution chamber.

Myers reveals this objective in the opening pages of *Monster*. In the rolling film credits that serve as the book's prologue, Steve writes:

> This incredible story
> of how one guy's life
> was turned around
> by a few events
> and how he might
> spend the rest of his life
> behind bars. (9)

The sixteen-year-old protagonist then goes on to elaborate on those "few events" that may change his life forever. Far from limiting himself to happenings on the day of the actual robbery-homicide, however, Steve spotlights occurrences in the weeks, months, and even years that preceded it using the cinematic technique of flashback, demonstrating how one decision led to another. The sixteen-year-old begins his account with an event that occurred four years before: "FLASHBACK of 12-year-old Steve walking in a neighborhood park with his friend Tony" (41). The youngsters talk about playing baseball, and Tony complains about their team's coach: "They should let me pitch. I can throw as straight as anything" (42). This seemingly typical and even innocent moment quickly takes a delinquent turn. To illustrate his pitching prowess, Tony picks up a rock and aims for a nearby lamp post. He misses, and so Steve tries. He also fails to hit his target but does strike something else: "We see it sail past the post and hit a YOUNG WOMAN. The TOUGH GUY she is walking with turns and sees the 2 young boys" (42). Steve runs away, but his companion hesitates too long: "TOUGH GUY punches TONY. TONY falls" (42). The young woman breaks up the altercation before it escalates further, but the connections among violence, power, and masculinity have been made. Indeed, in a comment that reflects the epidemic of black gang violence and especially drive-by shootings during the 1990s, the scene ends ominously with Tony vowing: "I'll get an Uzi and blow his brains out" (43).

Although Steve's friend may be the one pledging murderous revenge, Myers's protagonist is clearly captivated by the image of the "tough guy." Another flashback reveals how Steve's strong attraction to this persona leads him further down the path to robbery-murder: "CUT TO: EXTERIOR STOOP ON 141ST STREET . . . JAMES KING and STEVE are sitting on the steps" (49). Two of King's friends join them: a woman named Peaches and another young man named Johnny. Echoing the colonial American belief in the steady progression of sin, this encounter does not begin innocently. As the directorial notes reveal, Johnny "is smoking a blunt" (50). Moreover, the group is discussing plans for a possible robbery. When Peaches suggests that they hold up a bank, Johnny rebuffs the idea: "Naw. Bank money is too serious. The man comes down for bank money" (51). Instead, he proposes a target that resembles the ultimate victim of their robbery-homicide, West Indian immigrant Alguinaldo Nesbitt. "You need to find a getover where nobody don't care— you know what I mean. You cop from somebody with a green card or an illegal and they don't even report" (51). Unfortunately, the young man alights on a sad fact of American culture. As both Barbara Perry and Richard J. Lundman have written, minority-on-minority crime in the United States is both underreported and underprosecuted. The reasons for this phenomenon stem from a complex mix of factors, encompassing everything from "fear [of reprisal and] a lack of confidence in the likely response of law enforcement" (Perry 73) to the fact that whites are the target audience of most news reports and the perception that this group will not be interested in events that do not directly involve members of their community and the relative frequency of such acts causing them to be seen as "common," "routine," or even "normal" and thus "not . . . newsworthy by journalists and their editors" (Lundman 361). Whatever the exact reason, the end result is that American society seems to support minorities hurting other minorities by paying less attention to those crimes than to crimes committed by minorities against whites.* Both Walter Dean Myers and his character James King are aware of this situation. Consequently, King proposes a plan that foreshadows the later plan to rob Mr. Nesbitt's pharmacy: "Restaurant owners got money, too. That's the only things left in our neighborhood—restaurants, liquor stores, and drugstores" (51).

Although Steve does not contribute to this conversation, he is present for it, having made the decision to sit with King and his associates on the stoop. Moreover, he tries to "fit in" with the group, talking tough and acting cool. King complains, for instance, "I need to get paid, man. I ain't got nothing between my butt and the ground but a rag" (50). Steve comes from a middle-class family: his father has a college degree, he attends a high school for gifted students, and his parents hire a good lawyer for him. Nonetheless, he empathizes with King, saying rather preposterously "I hear that" (50). The scene ends with Steve facing another big moral decision. King asks the young man, "What you got, youngblood?"—meaning does he have the nerve to join them in making some quick cash (51). The directorial notes indicate that Steve "Looks up at KING"—not just literally but also clearly figuratively—and offers the noncommittal reply, "I don't know" (51).

Myers thus reveals the way in which popular portrayals of black masculinity do not simply affect whites but blacks as well. As Dennis Rome has written, films, television shows, and news reports routinely equate "young African American males with aggressiveness, lawlessness and violence" (2). As he goes on to note, black audiences "seldom see African Americans, particularly males, as achievers" (2). Instead, in a depiction that "is especially detrimental to African American youth," common media portrayals suggest that "the only way black men can achieve or earn enough is by being involved

---

* For more on both this phenomenon and the attitudes that fuel it, see Lundman.

in the illegal economy" (2). These dynamics are powerfully at work throughout Myers's novel in general and in Steve's understanding of himself in particular. In many ways, King is asking the narrator-protagonist in this scene if he is "like them" despite his class and educational level. At the same time, Steve is affirming beliefs perpetrated by mainstream media that there is a certain "true" black identity, or the idea that the typical black male is urban, poor, not well educated, and involved in criminal activity. As a result, Steve's desire to be included on "the getover" has its root not only in the young man's desire to prove his manliness or toughness, but—given the highly racialized nature of masculinity—his "blackness" as well.

The next flashback spotlights another key moment in Steve's progress toward criminality. In this scene, the narrator-protagonist is sitting on the stoop once again but this time with Osvaldo Cruz, an avowed member of the Diablos gang and a figure who will eventually testify against him in court. Osvaldo's friend, Freddy Alou, who is described as "16 and tough," joins them (80). The directorial notes indicate that Freddy "sits fiddling with a beeper he is trying to repair" (80), an item that even in the late 1990s was still strongly associated with drug dealers. As Calvin Sims wrote in an article that appeared in the *New York Times*, "The staccato tweet of the paging beeper . . . is the latest in high-technology gear for today's enterprising drug dealer" (par. 1). Similarly, James Fleming, the associate superintendent for the Dade County Public Schools in Florida deemed pagers nothing less than "the most dominant symbol of the drug trade" (qtd. in Sims par. 3). Here again, Steve's class and education distances him from the other young black men in his neighborhood, playing a significant role in his decision to act in ways that are contrary to his better judgment in order to fit in. As a result, the question of what it means to be black in America underlies this scene.

In the company of Osvaldo and Freddy, Steve makes the decision to distance himself from his actual identity as a good son, a gifted student, and a respectable citizen and instead to pose as a tough street gangster. When Osvaldo ridicules Steve for attending "that faggot school downtown" where "all they learn . . . is how to be a faggot" (80), the sixteen-year-old responds with a testament of his physical prowess: "I can kick your narrow butt any day in the week" (81). Steve's bravado has seemingly convinced Freddy, who cautions Osvaldo: "You better chill; he hangs with some bad dudes" (81). The Diablo gang member, however, knows better. "He don't hang with nobody. He's just a lame looking for a name" (81). The best retort that Myers's protagonist can muster is the childish "Why don't you shut up?" (81). Osvaldo responds in kind, offering what amounts to a dare: "You ain't got the heart to be nothing but a lame. Everybody knows that. You might be hanging out with some people, but when the deal goes down, you won't be around" (82).

The final flashback brings Steve to the brink of the robbery. Myers's protagonist is sitting with James King once again, this time in Marcus Garvey Park in Harlem. As before, King is smoking a marijuana joint. But, on this occasion, he is not abstractly contemplating a robbery; he is making concrete plans to commit one: "I got a sure getover. You know that drugstore got burned out that time? They got it all fixed up now. Drugstores always keep some money" (150). King explains that he has already put together a "payroll crew," but there's a potential problem: "I talked to Bobo and he's down, but Bobo liable not to show" (149). Consequently, King asks Steve if he wants in: "You don't have to be no Einstein to get paid. All you got to have is the heart. You got the heart?" (150). At Steve's urging, King goes on to provide some more specifics: "All we need is a lookout. You know, check the place out—make sure ain't no badges copping some z's in the back. You down for it?" (150). When Steve does not reply, King asks bluntly "So, what is it?" (151). The flashback ends before the protagonist gives his reply, leaving the reader to consider what it may have been.

Although Steve is initially unaware of the cumulative role that these individual interactions play in his being charged with felony murder, he eventually realizes their importance. In a journal entry after the first flashback with James King, Steve laments about "all the times I had looked at him and wanted to be tough like him" (96). Later, he repeats this regret: "I remembered Miss O'Brien saying that it was her job to make me different in the eyes of the jury, different from Bobo and Osvaldo and King. It was me, I thought as I tried not to throw up, that had wanted to be tough like them" (130). In these moments, Steve becomes aware how these smaller missteps escalated into more serious ones. As he reflects in a journal entry just before the jury's verdict, "The trouble I'm in keeps getting bigger and bigger. I'm overwhelmed by it. It's crushing me" (201–2).* The prosecuting attorney likewise com-

---

* As with Myers's portrayal of Steve's prison inmates, this message is complicated by the presence of other black criminal characters in the book. Steve's smaller missteps are revealed to be not only a matter of his personal decisions but a result of the way he is influenced by social expectations and the black community that he lives in—his desire to be "tough like them" is a desire to fit into the black community. But if Steve is being differentiated from the other black young men, what does that say about how these other figures are presented to us? Are we supposed to see them as true criminals?

ments on the causal connection between his actions. Assuming a role that mirrors that of a colonial minister, she points out to the jury, "Steve Harmon made a moral decision" (270). Later, Steve confesses that this point has been "burned into my brain" (270).

Because Steve recognizes his various mistakes and also because he regrets making them, his life stands as a cautionary tale. The young man writes the screenplay about his trial both as a means to cope with this stressful experience and as a means to prevent other young people from making the same missteps. As he reflects, "Lying on my cot, I think of everything that has happened over the last year. There was nothing extraordinary in my life. No bolt of lightning came out of the sky. I didn't say a magic word and turn into somebody different" (203). In a journal entry near the close of the novel, he explicitly urges other young people to consider their futures and to see how small actions can precipitate a larger chain of events: "I wish Jerry were here. Not in jail, but somehow with me. What would I say to him? Think about all the tomorrows of your life. Yes, that's what I would say. Think about all the tomorrows of your life" (205). As Myers himself has commented, this message has not gone unnoticed by the book's readership. In an interview that is reprinted in the current paperback edition of *Monster*, the author remarks that "the most surprising response has been from inmates, many of whom have expressed the idea that they wished they had read the book prior to their arrests. They empathize with Steve's lack of clarity in his thinking and understand how that got them into trouble" ("Questions" 13).

"Awful Disclosures!": The Rise of Secular—and Sensationalized—Accounts of Killing

Religious-themed narratives that highlighted the humanity of murderers, called attention to the universality of evil, and focused on the progression of sin dominated American crime literature for generations. During the final

---

What if the main character of this novel had not come from a middle-class and educated family? What if he weren't attending a prestigious school? What if he were more like Bobo, Osvaldo, or King? Would it be possible to write a novel that would elicit the reader's sympathy for one of these characters? These questions once again raise the possibility that while the author is countering certain stereotypes, he inadvertently ends up supporting others—that somehow those who have more money and more education are more deserving of our sympathy, are more likely to be seen as victims of society and peer pressure when they do something wrong. At the very least, the way in which figures like Bobo, Osvaldo, and King serve as not simply foils to Steve but also as what might be called moral "straw men" for him is worth noting.

decades of the eighteenth century, however, increased levels of literacy, greater access to printing technology, and a decline in church authority undermined the previously uniform way that murder and murderers had been understood (see Cohen 10–13, 22–24). In the 1770s and 1780s, a growing number of secular publications began to appear about homicide. Cohen has identified five distinct genres: trial reports, dying verses or last speeches, crime ballads, biographies of murderers, and, of course, newspaper articles (viii–ix; 13–16).

No matter the specific form these materials took, they did not possess the same narrative content as execution sermons. In spite of their macabre name, colonial execution sermons were not grisly, graphic, or gruesome. The majority, in fact, "showed relatively little concern for the details of the crime itself'"; they "offered no dramatic reenactment of the crime, and paid limited attention to such matters as time and place or the precise nature of the violence" (Halttunen 8). Others, as Halttunen explains, "never referred directly to the murder" (16). Instead, "primary attention was paid . . . to the course of sinfulness that had preceded it and the religious conversion that followed" (17).

By the 1780s and 1790s, a new body of secular writing began to appear that was not focused on salvation but was rather predominantly interested in sensationalism. As both David Ray Papke and Halttunen have discussed, they provided highly gothicized accounts of crime and killers. *The American Bloody Register*, for example, was a periodical devoted exclusively to the coverage of crime. It first appeared in 1784 and, as its title implies, it focused on the more grisly aspects of murder. Articles in this publication and the many others like it routinely included detailed descriptions about the number of blows or bullets that it took to kill the victim; the amount of blood splattered on the wall, clotted in locks of hair, or pooled on the floor; and aspects of the state of the corpse upon discovery, such as eyeballs forced from their sockets, heads severed from their torsos, and body parts missing or found (see Halttunen 34–36; 49–54). A passage in *A Brief Narrative of the Life and Confession of Barnett Davenport* (1780), which details the murder of Caleb Mallory and his wife, is typical. Using various household items as weapons, Barnett described in this posthumously published narrative how he "mashed [Caleb's] head to pieces" and then beat the wife until her face "was swoll'n to twice its common bigness, disfigured with wounds" and "covered with gore and streaming blood" (9–12). Taken collectively, such elements established what Halttunen has characterized as the "choreography of the crime" (83), a process that is a now-common feature of murder narratives: what the killer did to the victim, with what means or instrument, according to what sequence, and for what duration. *The Confession of Adam Horn* (1843), for example, "detailed how he had killed his wife with two blows of a stick, then chopped off her head and burned it, scattered her teeth in the woods, severed her limbs and buried them under an old bake oven" (qtd. in Halttunen 75).

To accentuate these details, many narratives included illustrations. Trial reports often provided a drawing of the courtroom and thus invited readers to imagine themselves as a witness to the trial (Halttunen 85). Others went one step further, including a map of the crime scene and thereby engaging in the more chilling act of encouraging individuals to place themselves at the site of the murder, if only vicariously (Halttunen 86, 122). Finally, as Papke notes, many newspapers, magazines, and pamphlets employed "artists and photographers [who] elaborately illustrated these works" (xiv). Using information about how the crime was perpetrated, they provided graphic recreations of the violence. The cover image to *The Life and Death of Mrs. Maria Bickford* (1846), for instance, presents the slain woman lying on the floor with a bedpost speared into her back. Meanwhile, the title page to *An Account of the Apprehension, Trial, Conviction, and Condemnation of Manuel Philip Garcia and Jose Demas Garcia Castillano* (1821) shows the two title figures dismembering victim Peter Lagoardette: his amputated arms and legs are piled in a basket, one severed hand protrudes from a bucket, the decapitated head lies near the fireplace, what remains of his torso is heaped on the floor, and his organs and entrails are scattered around the room. As even these few examples reveal, whereas previous accounts of homicide authored by ministers minimized reference to the bloody crime itself, this new genre penned by lawyers, journalists, and sometimes even the killers themselves was heavily concerned with "the construction of murder as a spectacle" (Halttunen 85).*

To justify the inclusion of gory details and graphic images, many accounts often tacked on a pat moral message about controlling one's anger, avoiding strong liquor, or honoring one's spouse. But, as Papke aptly notes, these texts

---

*It should be noted that although this new genre of secular crime literature posed both a commercial threat and a literary challenge to execution sermons, it did not eradicate them. On the contrary, these two modes existed side by side for decades. As Cohen notes, "execution sermons continued to appear in a persistent, if somewhat intermittent, stream well into the nineteenth century" (10). Both Cohen and Halttunen, in fact, cite examples of execution sermons that appeared as late as the postbellum era.

remain "one dash of morality and many more of entertainment" (22). Individuals were drawn to this new style of murder literature not because they were seeking spiritual guidance but because they were seeking personal thrills. Murder literature provided an escape from the dullness, routine, and even ennui of everyday life.

The growing body of secular crime narratives thereby introduced elements to the cultural consideration of murder in the United States that had been absent before: namely, shock, revulsion, and even terror. Titles like *Awful Disclosures!* (1846), *Confessions, Trials, and Biographical Sketches of the Most Cold Blooded Murderers* (1837), and *The Horrible Murder of Mrs. Ellen Lynch and Her Sister, Mrs. Hannah Shaw* (1853) foregrounded the chilling nature of crime and criminals. Meanwhile, characterizations of events as "shocking" or "horrid" provided clear instructions for how readers ought to react to lethal violence: not via identification and empathy but rather recoil and repugnance (Halttunen 83). Such sentiments dovetailed with shifting societal attitudes about death and dying. As Gary Laderman has documented, in the nineteenth century, the way that Americans regarded and reacted to the human corpse underwent a dramatic transformation. Evidenced in everything from the privatization of the deathbed and the professionalization of funerary services to the growth of cosmetic restoration artists and the strict segregation of areas permissible for burial, the dead body went from being a comfortable and customary sight to an unpleasant and even unnerving one.

The new genre of secular crime literature reflected what Laderman calls this growing "disenchantment with the mortal remains" (136). In so doing, these narratives aligned themselves not with documentary reportage but with the emerging literary mode of horror writing: a genre that, as Halttunen has discussed, "employed inflated language and graphic treatment of violence and its aftermath in order to shock the reader into an emotional state that mingled fear with hatred and disgust" (3).* Whatever the literary antecedents of these narratives, they signaled a shift in the way that Americans viewed, interpreted, and responded to murder.

The changing means by which violence was presented in U.S. print culture

---

*Halttunen points out that colonial execution sermons were not entirely devoid of elements of horror. However, when present, these details were employed for a far different literary and cultural purpose. The fire-and-brimstone language that was used by some Calvinist ministers was designed to relay "the murderer's 'horror' in contemplating his own damnation" (30), not to excite, shock, or entertain the reader.

were precipitated, in part, by changing societal beliefs about the causes of crime and the origins of evil. Colonial execution sermons had offered a confident, concrete explanation of why men and women killed: the innate sinfulness of humanity. The Age of Reason, however, rejected such beliefs in universal depravity. Influenced by the writings of John Locke and Jean-Jacques Rousseau, "Enlightenment liberalism understood human nature as essentially good, rational, and capable of self-government" (Halttunen 4). Thus, when a man or woman killed, it was puzzling and even inexplicable. No environmental, psychological, or circumstantial explanation seemed wholly adequate to account for why a rational human being would engage in such irrational violence. Indeed, as various trial reports, criminal biographies, and newspaper accounts relayed, "some men and women murdered despite their good religious and moral upbringings; some murdered without any discernible motive; and some killed coolly and dispassionately" (Halttunen 4). In the face of such facts, murder in the United States went from an act that was understandable to one that was unfathomable.

The authors of secular murder narratives recognized that they could never provide a complete portrait of the crime—too much of the killer's thoughts, feelings, and motives were unknown and even unknowable. As a result, they provided the next best thing: a complete portrait of all of the information that had been gathered about the killing. This way, readers could examine the evidence themselves and come to their own conclusions about the case. Together with a prose narrative detailing the crime, many murder anthologies, criminal biographies, and especially trial reports included "photographs of murder weapons, bloodstains, and other physical evidence, to enable them to explore for themselves 'the shadowy events surrounding the mysterious murder'" (Halttunen 243). The booklet *Awful Disclosures and Startling Developments, in Relation to the Parkman Tragedy* (1849)—concerning the murder of a Harvard University medical professor, Dr. George Parkman, by his colleague, John W. Webster—is an excellent example. Along with a recap of the brutal slaying, the text contains an array of supplemental materials: drawings of all the physical evidence introduced in court; a detailed map of Webster's laboratory and dissecting room where the crime was thought to have been committed; a skeletal diagram indicating which parts of Parker's body were discovered in the vault, the furnace, and a tea chest, as well as those that were never found; and portraits of various witnesses, including Ephraim Littlefield, the university janitor who initially uncovered the remains. While such materials add to the voyeuristic quality and thrilling nature of the crime —allowing readers to experience the blood, gore, and violence vicariously— they also reinforce the murder's inherent mystery and ultimate unknowability. Readers may never fully understand what drove John W. Webster to commit this horrid act, exactly how it was conducted, or what happened to the missing parts of Parker's body. But, at least they can take comfort in knowing that they had access to all of the available information.

It has become commonplace in the United States today to decry our seemingly national obsession with violence. From the mass slaughter depicted in Hollywood movies, the bellicose nature of many video games, and the blood and gore shown on numerous television programs, the saturation of American popular, literary, and visual culture with murderous violence is commonly cast as a contemporary phenomenon, a feature that was absent from previous forms of mass entertainment. In a remark that typifies this viewpoint, the advocacy group Media Awareness Network, which is based in Canada but examines the heavily influential slate of American programming, asserts that "media violence has not just increased in quantity; it has also become much more graphic, much more sexual, and much more sadistic" (par. 7). To illustrate this claim, the organization explains how "explicit pictures of slow-motion bullets exploding from people's chests, and dead bodies surrounded by pools of blood, are now commonplace fare" (par. 8). The millennial popularity of the new horror subgenre known as "torture porn" in films like *Saw* (2004), *Hostel* (2005), and *The Human Centipede* (2009) presents corporeal violence with unprecedented graphic detail.

An awareness of the social construction of murder and the evolution of crime literature in the United States calls such views into question. Far from being a solely contemporaneous phenomenon, the popular presentation of violence, blood, and gore extends back to the late eighteenth century. Indeed, the description of murder victim Joseph Porter from the blandly titled pamphlet *Murder: Narrative of the Trial, Conviction and Execution of Captain William Corran* in 1794 surpasses many of our even most graphic and gruesome narratives today. As the pamphlet relays, the deceased's body had "large gashes about the hips, above a foot long and three or four inches deep, one ear totally cut off, the nose almost cut through, the right eye forced out of the socket and hanging down the cheek suspended by a bloody membrane" (5–6). In this and many other examples like it, the American fascination with gore reveals itself not as a culturally new phenomenon but as a historically rooted one. In what has become an oft-quoted remark, H. Rap Brown once asserted that "violence is as American as apple pie" (qtd. in Mazzocco). Both the extensive print coverage of murderous violence during the Federalist era and the inclusion of numerous grisly details about killers and their victims demonstrate that this observation is truer than many realize—or, perhaps, are comfortable acknowledging.

"It Was Pretty Gruesome": Employing the Dramatic to Enhance the Didactic

Monster may possess a kinship with colonial execution sermons, but it does not completely reject contemporaneous conventions for representing violent crime. On the contrary, Myers demonstrates his awareness of modern methods for presenting murder, and he draws on many of them. For example, in the opening pages of the text, Myers's protagonist reflects the now-prevailing view that murder cases are exciting events. Steve dramatically titles his film script "Monster! The Story of My Miserable Life," instead of matter-of-factly calling it just "Monster" (8). In subsequent passages, the narrator-protagonist reiterates this point of view. Echoing the claims to veracity contained in many nineteenth-century trial accounts and criminal biographies, Steve describes his story as "told as it actually happened!" (9). Likewise, in the scrolling credits, he offers another spine-tingling detail:

> *And Starring*
> 16-year-old Steve Harmon
> as the Boy on Trial for Murder! (10; italics in original)

This flair for the dramatic recurs at various points in the text. At the end of Steve's trial, the judge delivers his instructions to the jury before they begin deliberations: "Mr. Harmon did go into the store with the purpose of . . . (Voice fades out) without regard to who actually pulled the trigger . . . Then you must return a verdict of Guilty of felony murder" (264). This final remark —"Then you must return a verdict of Guilty of felony murder"—is repeated three separate times, as if it had been put on reverb.

Second only to the association of murder cases with excitement is their association with blood and gore. Here, again, *Monster* conforms to such expectations. José Delgado, a clerk at the drug store, testifies about what he saw upon returning to work from his dinner break: "I went around behind the counter and I saw Mr. Nesbitt on the floor—there was blood everywhere" (29). Later, Detective Karyl provides more details: "It was pretty gruesome" (67). Steve's directorial notes elaborate: "CUT TO: CU of photos. We see legs of the slain drugstore owner, NESBITT. CUT TO: BLACK-AND-WHITE SHOTS from various angles of the body in a grotesque position" (68). Later, the photographs are given to defense attorney Kathy O'Brien for inspection, and Steve gets an opportunity to view them directly. He describes the gruesome scene in detail: "Mr. Nesbitt's right foot was turned out. His left arm was lifted and bent at the elbow so that his fingers almost touched the side of his head. His eyes weren't completely closed" (92). The young man is haunted by these images. Steve writes in his journal, "The photos were bad, real bad. I didn't want to think about them" (127). Finally, when the medical examiner takes the stand, readers receive the most detailed account of Mr. Nesbitt's violent death. As Dr. Moody testifies,

> The bullet entered the body on the left side and traversed upward through the lung. It produced a tearing of the lung and heavy internal bleeding and also went through the esophagus. That also produced internal bleeding. The bullet finally lodged in the upper trapezius area. (135)

Such descriptions are clearly meant to incite shock, revulsion, and even horror in the reader. "Death," the doctor goes on, "was caused by a combination of trauma to the internal organs . . . as well as by the lungs filling with blood. He wouldn't have been able to breathe" (135). Lest the horrific nature of mode of death be unclear, the district attorney rhetorically asks, "You mean he literally drowned in his own blood?" (136).

Together with highlighting the ghastliness of violent crime, the new genre of secular crime literature also emphasized its inherent mystery. Although Steve is acquitted by the jury at the end of the novel, his innocence is far from clear. The narrator-protagonist testifies that he was not in the drugstore anytime on the day of the robbery and that he was certainly not involved in the crime (224). But, near the middle of the narrative, Steve also writes in his journal, "I walked into a drugstore to look for some mints, and then I walked out. What was wrong with that? I didn't kill Mr. Nesbitt" (140). This comment raises the question of whether Steve committed perjury; even more importantly, though, it also casts doubt on his assertion that he did not serve as the "lookout man" for the crime. Steve's remark can be read as an effort to minimize his culpability by rationalizing that, although he was involved, he was not the one who actually pulled the trigger. Myers's protagonist goes on to make this exact point: "Isn't that what being guilty is all about? You actually do something? You pick up a gun and you aim it across a small space and pull a trigger? You grab a purse and run screaming down the street?" (140). In the face of these and other passages, Steve's innocence is uncertain. Readers finish the novel neither convinced that the sixteen-year-old did play a role in the robbery nor that he did not. Myers has added to this mystery, pointing out that "I didn't acquit Steve, the jury did" ("Questions" 11).

At various points, even Myers's own narrator-protagonist is unsure if he is guilty or not. As the young man reflects in a journal entry: "I lay down across my cot. I could still feel mama's pain. And I knew she felt that I didn't do anything wrong. It was me who wasn't sure" (148). The jury's verdict, rather than offering clarity, only raises more questions. As the narrator-protagonist writes in his journal, "After the trial, my father, with tears in his eyes, held me close and said that he was thankful that I did not have to go to jail" (280). Mr. Harmon's choice of words here is significant, for he does not express relief that his son has been able to prove his innocence, only that he is not going to prison.

Monster also echoes more contemporaneous accounts of crime with its inclusion of supplemental materials that allow readers to examine the available evidence and decide whether the protagonist is guilty or innocent for themselves. Intermingled with Steve's film script and journal entries are photographs, video stills, mug shots, marginalia notes, courtroom sketches, and even fingerprints. Myers has explained his rationale for including these elements: "I wanted the reader, given the facts of the case and having the benefit of Steve's inner thoughts, to reach their own decision" ("Questions" 11).

Although *Monster* may include elements from modern forms of crime literature, it does not do so in the interest of mere sensationalism. Instead, such details are in the service of Myers's original—and more historically grounded—goal: to urge young readers to empathize and even identify with his sixteen-year-old protagonist. Myers's mission to humanize his main character is not predicated on his innocence. The fact that the young man may be guilty of the crime only further demonstrates the author's commitment to debunking existing beliefs that murderers are monsters. Steve might have been the lookout for the drugstore robbery that resulted in the killing of Mr. Nesbitt, but this possibility does not negate his humanity. On the contrary, Steve remains an amiable character—one that young adult readers continue to like, sympathize with, and even support. Commenting on this phenome-non, Myers has said that "most young people are relieved when Steve Harmon is found not guilty, but bothered by his possible role" (13). This response demonstrates the narrative's success in emphasizing ethical choices and moral decisions. As the author asserts in an interview, "Whether Steve's *legally* guilty or innocent doesn't make any difference: he is guilty. And to me, that's the essence of the book. Apart from the legal machinations, is he accepting moral responsibility for what he's done or is he just trying to avoid it?" ("*Booklist*" 1101; italics in original). The blood and gore in the novel do not distract from this objective; they augment it. Descriptions of Mr. Nesbitt lying on the floor in a "grotesque position" drowning in his own blood highlight the horrific consequences that may follow from a series of seemingly harmless decisions. Any repugnance that readers experience when encountering these passages is directed not toward Steve but toward an arena that Myers deems far more worthy of their revulsion: crime itself.

Fredric Jameson, in what has become an oft-quoted comment, once asserted that the late twentieth century was characterized by a sense of "historical amnesia." Whereas teachers, historians, and politicians could once assume a baseline of historical knowledge—such as the start and end dates of major wars, the names of significant civil and military leaders, and the chronological period of major domestic and foreign events—such information could no longer be assumed. According to Jameson,

> The disappearance of a sense of history, the way in which our entire contemporary social system has little by little begun to lose its capacity to retain its own past, has begun to live in a perpetual present and in a perpetual change that obliterates traditions of the kind which all earlier social formations have had in one way or another to preserve. . . . The information function of the media would thus be to help us to forget, to serve as the very agents and mechanisms of our historical amnesia. (*Postmodernism* 20)

Many men and women in the 1980s and 1990s did not know much about the past, and, in Jameson's view, were not very interested in learning. They were more focused on the present. For this reason, Jameson argues that the postmodern era signals "the end of history" (*Postmodernism* 73).

Since Jameson first articulated this argument, various historians, literary scholars, and cultural critics have called it into question. Samuel Cohen, in

After the End of History: American Fiction in the 1990s, for example, points out that numerous historically themed novels appeared during the final decades of the twentieth century and were among the most commercially successful and critically acclaimed narratives of their era, such as Toni Morrison's *Beloved* (1987), Thomas Pynchon's *Mason & Dixon* (1997), and Philip Roth's *American Pastoral* (1997). Morrison's *Beloved* was awarded the Pulitzer Prize in fiction while Roth's *American Pastoral* was a runner-up in a poll taken by the *New York Times Book Review* to identify "the single best work of American fiction published in the last 25 years" ("What Is the Best Work" par. 1).*

Given the preponderance of historically themed narratives as the twentieth century came to a close, Cohen proposes a modification to Jameson's theory. Rather than characterizing the postmodern period as one rife with historical amnesia, he argues that "these works reconnect the past to a present that is ironically keen on denying that connection" (4). In other words, they are historical novels that do not identify themselves as historical. They use settings, scenes, and elements from the past, but not in a direct or explicit way. As Cohen explains, "these novels don't just do history, they reflect historically on the making of the historical narrative, examining how the times in which we live shape the way we understand the past" (3–4).

Monster can be included in this category. The narrative has been credited "as the beginning of a postmodern trend toward a variety of forms, including metafiction, free verse, and unreliable narrators" in literature for young readers (Snodgrass 32). But the novel also contains a powerful historical component about our understanding of criminals. The fact that this feature is unspoken does not render it any less strong or central.

---

* Incidentally, the winner of this poll was Morrison's *Beloved* ("What Is the Best Work" par. 1).

"Just Because You Don't Have a Pulse Doesn't Mean You Can't Be Perky"

My So-Called Death, Young Adult Zombie Fiction, and Murder in the Posthuman Age

> When a dead man opens his eyes and looks about, moves his limbs, throws his arms on his breast, grinds his teeth, and tries to catch you, it requires strong nerves to witness the spectacle.
>
> ROBERT M'CONAGHY AND PETER ROBINSON, *The Trial, Confession, and Execution of Robert M'Conaghy* (1841)

By the dawn of the twenty-first century, literature in the United States had seemingly presented every conceivable type of murder. After centuries of featuring killings by family members, friends, coworkers, neighbors, and strangers, both fiction and nonfiction narratives had ostensibly exhausted all of the possible combinations of victim and perpetrator.

Then, the zombie emerged—or, perhaps more accurately, rose from the dead. As reanimated corpses with an insatiable appetite for the flesh of the living, books featuring this figure offer a variation on the common construction of killing. In a new twist on the portrayal of homicide, zombies are not murderous people, but murderous *dead* people.

Of course, zombies were not invented during the opening decade of the twenty-first century. As Marc Leverette and Shawn McIntosh have written, the living dead "have held a unique place in film and popular culture throughout most of the twentieth" century (viii). At least since the release of Victor Halperin's B-movie *White Zombie* in 1932, reanimated corpses have permeated American print, visual, and material culture.

While zombies may have been a feature of popular culture for several generations in the United States, they have been experiencing a heyday since the close of the twentieth century. Novels such as Max Brooks's *World War Z: An Oral History of the Zombie War* (2006) and Seth Grahame-Smith's *Pride and Prejudice and Zombies* (2009) have become fixtures on bookstore shelves. Likewise, zombie-themed video games, such as the *Resident Evil* franchise (1996–present), a first-person shooter game that pits players against a mob of marauding zombies, have created a new market niche.* Similarly, given the powerful imagery that the walking dead evoke and inspire, graphic novels have become another common locus of representation. The illustrated horror narrative *Zombies: A Record of the Year of Infection* by Robert Twombly was released in 2009 and became an instant fan favorite. Such fictional first-person accounts of the living dead have been accompanied by an array of nonfiction handbooks: *The Zombie Survival Guide: Complete Protection from the Living Dead* (2003), *Zompoc: How to Survive a Zombie Apocalypse* (2009), *U.S. Army Zombie Combat Skills* (2009), *The Zombie Survival Guide: How to Live Like a King after the Outbreak* (2009), and *The Zombie Combat Manual: A Guide to Fighting the Living Dead* (2010). In a powerful indication of the ubiquity of zombies in millennial print culture, these figures even appeared in the somewhat unlikely world of superheroes when, in 2005, the first issue of *Marvel Zombies* was released. Set in the future, the comic chronicles the aftermath of a highly contagious virus that has turned not only most of the world's citizens into zombies but also many of its most prominent protectors: Spiderman, the Incredible Hulk, Captain America, Wolverine, and Iron Man. The series ran until 2006, giving rise to its own line of merchandising as well as imitators.†

Zombies are equally ubiquitous in the nation's film culture. Movies about corpses rising from the dead have become a common facet of mainstream, feature-length cinema since the beginning of the twenty-first century. These films include ones that directly and self-consciously participate in the zombie genre, such as *Planet Terror* (2007), *Land of the Dead* (2005), and *Zombieland* (2009) in addition to titles like *28 Days Later* (2002) and *I Am Legend* (2007) that, while not explicitly about the living dead, feature zombie-like creatures. Finally, the new millennium has also seen the remake of several classic zombie movies, including George A. Romero's *Dawn of the Dead* (2004) as well as

---

*For more on zombie-themed video games, see Kryzwinska.

†For more information on *Marvel Zombies*, see the official website for the series at http://marvel.com/comic_books/series/998/marvel_zombies_2005_-_2006.

the release of cinematic adaptations of other zombie-themed media: by 2012, for example, the *Resident Evil* video game franchise had given rise to no fewer than five feature-length movies.

Far from a fringe cultural movement, print, visual, and material items about the living dead have been among the most commercially successful. Ruben Fleischer's *Zombieland* (2009) stars Hollywood A-list actor Woody Harrelson. In addition, as journalists Clark Collis and Chris Nashawaty note, "by the end of its first weekend, *Zombieland* had sunk its teeth into $24.7 million—a bloody box office feast" (37). Likewise, both Brooks's apocalyptic *World War Z* and Grahame-Smith's *Pride and Prejudice and Zombies* have sold hundreds of thousands of copies, earning them spots on the *New York Times* bestseller list. And *Resident Evil* has been one of the most popular video games of the era, selling more than forty million copies in thirteen years and morphing into a series of novellas, a line of action figures, and a comic book series (Mitchell "Capcom" par. 1). Finally, zombie-themed merchandise forms a visible segment of the nation's material culture. With the living dead featured on everything from board games, apparel, and action figures to posters, collectibles, and even tear-apart dolls, some stores—like the popular novelty shop Archie McPhee—have opened their own zombie department.

Given the "zombie mania" that has swept the nation, it should come as no surprise that a World Zombie Day was established.* A charity event that raised money to fight global hunger, the first "WZD," as it came to be known, was celebrated on 26 October 2008 and boasted more than sixty-five hundred participants in "46 cities in North America, Europe and Australia" ("World Zombie Day" par. 2). The pervasive presence of zombies in American print, visual, and material culture prompted Kyle William Bishop to assert that the new millennium has been witnessing nothing less than a "Zombie Renaissance" (5).† Echoing this observation, David Flint explores "how the living

---

* This event was preceded and, in some ways, even inspired by the zombie pub crawl held in Minneapolis on 9 September 2006. As McIntosh has documented, the crawl attracted "350 participants dressed as zombies in various states of blood and gore, shuffling from one bar to another" (15).

† This widespread interest in the living dead was not simply limited to U.S. popular, visual, and material culture; it also appeared in the intellectual and scholarly realm. As McIntosh points out, during the opening decade of the twenty-first century, the term "zombie" was "appropriated in computer lingo" to denote an operating system that is being run remotely, usually by a hacker—and it also appeared in "philosophical treatises on the nature of consciousness," primarily with regard to questions about mind/body dualism (1).

dead devoured pop culture" in his 2009 book *Zombie Holocaust*.* All puns aside, it seems undeniable that the zombie hordes had invaded.

Literature for young people has not been immune to this phenomenon. Since the final decade of the twentieth century, an array of narratives for young readers have appeared featuring the walking dead as main or at least minor characters.† Not surprisingly, horror writer R. L. Stine has been at the forefront of this trend. In 1998, he released *I Was a Sixth-Grade Zombie* (1998, #30), a novel in his Fear Street franchise. Then, the following year, Stine published *Zombie School* (1999, #40), a book in his wildly popular Goosebumps series.

Zombie-themed books have also come from some unexpected authors. In 1994, Francine Pascal published *Steven the Zombie* (1994), a title in the Sweet Valley Twins and Friends series. Likewise, in 2002, Pulitzer Prize–winning writer Paul Zindel published *The Gourmet Zombie* (2002). Less surprisingly, given the mass popularity of zombies, these figures have been a frequent subject in more commercially minded narratives for young readers. In 1998, Scholastic released *Scooby-Doo and Zombies Too!* (1998). The title was quickly followed by *Scooby-Doo on Zombie Island* (1998). Then, eight years later, a third book completed the trilogy: *Scooby-Doo and the Rock 'n' Roll Zombie* (2007). Most recently, Ken McMurtry's *Zombie Penpal* (2010), a Choose Your Own Adventure novel, joined this cohort.

In light of the strong association of zombies with suspense and horror, the mystery genre has become a routine home for the living dead. Narratives like R. A. Noonan's *My Teacher Is a Zombie* (1995) and Rob Roy's *The Zombie Zone* (2005) challenge young readers to play the role of detective with regard to the walking dead. Is the new fifth-grade teacher really a zombie in disguise? Or, but similarly, can the strange creature haunting the local cemetery really be a corpse brought back to life? Even David Lubar's *My Rotten Life* (2009),

---

*Flint's book is far from the only sociocultural examination of zombies. As Jerrold E. Hogle has observed, the number of academic books about the living dead has increased steadily, giving rise to what may be called "zombie studies" (2). Via titles like *Zombie Culture: Autopsies of the Living Dead* (2008), *Zombie Holocaust: How the Living Dead Devoured Pop Culture* (2009), and *American Zombie Gothic: The Rise and Fall (and Rise) of the Walking Dead in Popular Culture* (2010), zombies have become their own distinct area of academic study.

†Prior to this period, zombie-themed books were not altogether absent from juvenile fiction. In 1958, for example, popular juvenile science fiction author E. C. Eliott released *Kemlo and the Zombie Boys*. Likewise, in 1982, the seventy-first novel in the Hardy Boys series was titled *Track of the Zombie*. That said, books featuring the living dead were relatively rare, appearing only occasionally.

the first book in the "Nathan Abercrombie, Accidental Zombie" series, along with its sequel *Dead Guy Spy* (2009), can be viewed in this context: the bulk of the first book centers on the title character's quest to locate an antidote to the "zombie serum" that he has ingested, while the second novel focuses on the protagonist's spy work for the clandestine Bureau of Useful Misadventures.

As in literature for adults, the walking dead have been a fixture in graphic novels and illustrated narratives for adolescents. From Elise Primavera's zany *Fred and Anthony Meet the Demented Super-Degerm-O Zombie* (2007) to Paul D. Storrie's gothic *Nightmare on Zombie Island* (2008), these texts run the gamut from the silly to the scary. Indeed, while many of the narratives that feature the living dead fit most comfortably in the horror genre, a significant number are comedic. Reflecting Leverette and McIntosh's observation that in the modern era the zombie "was as hilarious as it was horrific" (ix), Paul Martin's *Runaway Zombie!* (2004) contains far more goofy fun than gothic fright. In a preview of the gross-out humor that permeates the book, the front cover shows a ghoulish creature whose eyeball is hanging out of its socket wittily announcing, "Time for some shut-eye!" J. J. Hart and Will Meugniot's *Zombie Monkey Monster Jamboree* (2006) follows a similar pattern, only with scatological humor. One of the characters, in fact, is called "Gas" owing to his chronic flatulence. Kirk Scroggs's *Grampa's Zombie BBQ* (2006) goes even further. Forming part of what Bruce Campbell has termed "splatstick"—a subgenre of horror films known for combining physical comedy with gross-out humor (see Bishop 187)—Scroggs offers the following comedic disclaimer on the back cover: "This book is oozing with gassy zombies, highly explosive hot sauce, toxic beef borscht, contaminated potato salad, and slimy avocado face cream." Finally, the humorous focus of Andy Griffiths's *Zombie Butts from Uranus!* (2004) is self-evident.

Novels aimed at adolescent readers are not the only category of children's narratives to feature the living dead. The unexpected realm of picture books also has been participating in the zombie renaissance. The alphabet book *Z is for Zombie* (1999) written by Merrily Kutner and illustrated by John Manders features a different monster for each letter. Kutner's 2007 book, *The Zombie Nite Café*, reprises this theme. Written in rhyming couplets from the perspective of a young boy, the narrative chronicles the ghoulish patrons at the eponymous restaurant. While the café's customers include an array of gothic monsters—Frankenstein, Dracula, the Boogeyman, and the Headless Horse-man, to name just a few—zombies play a prominent role. As the narrator relays:

> The owner rose up from the floor,
> Then vanished through a secret door.
> Another Zombie left his tomb
> And staggered right across the room
> To feast upon the dread buffet
> In the Zombie Nite Café.

A few pages later, when the two-headed waitress arrives to take the boy's order, she enumerates the café's specials; they include "Chicken McMaggots," "Flesh Wound on Wheat," and "Type 'O' Blood Pudding."

In some zombie-themed narratives, the presence of the living dead is a mere hoax or spoof. Kevin Alexander Boon has discussed what he calls this "zombie ruse" in children's and adolescent literature: "A surprising number of young adult and children's titles contain the word zombie. . . . It is common to discover by the end of many of these works that the zombies were not actual zombies at all but the result of misunderstanding or deliberate misleading" (37). As he goes on to note, Harry Harrison's 1991 narrative *Bill, the Gallactic Hero on the Planet of Zombie Vampires* "doesn't actually have any zombies in it" (37). What is more typical, however, is not the total absence of the living dead but the fraudulent co-opting of this identity. In the finale to Zindel's mystery *The Gourmet Zombie*, for example, readers learn that the killer is not actually a reanimated corpse. Rather, he is a living and breathing cook who wears a ghostly looking mask made of dough to conceal his identity. Likewise, just as in the conclusion of nearly every case that the Mystery Inc. gang investigates, the "zombie" in *Scooby-Doo and the Rock 'n' Roll Zombie* is not the walking dead; it is simply a villain wearing a clever disguise.

Such examples aside, the bulk of zombie-themed narratives do contain "actual" zombies. Whether intended for a young adult or an elementary-aged audience, these narratives link the living dead with their most common eth-nocultural origins: voodoo and black magic. Annelise Sklar offers a succinct overview of this phenomenon: "Zombies come to popular culture through Haitian folklore, where it was thought that a *bokor*, or Voudou practioner, could enchant a person into a coma-like state, steal their soul, and then revive the victim—now without a soul, memory, personality, or speech—to be a slave" (144). The bulk of juvenile narratives about zombies use this informa-tion as their starting point, locating the living dead within this socioreligious tradition. Strange things start to happen in Pascal's *Steven the Zombie* when the central character makes a voodoo doll of her elder brother for a school project about the history and culture of Haiti. The stories in both Roy's *The Zombie Zone* and McMurtry's *Zombie Penpal* center on the people and prac-tices of New Orleans. Not only are both books set in Louisiana, but their zombie characters are firmly connected to voodoo. In the opening pages of *Zombie Penpal*, for example, the central character's new friend in New Orleans writes to tell him that "Mammaw won't let me go into some stores here. They sell strange things like black candles and herbs and potions. She calls them Voodoo shops and says I must not visit them" (n.p.).

Other narratives that do not connect their zombies with the tradition of voodoo associate them with the occult. As one of the ghoulish figures in *Monsterville* explains, "Zombie delicacies contain a magic ingredient. . . . Eat these and you'll fall under the spell of the living dead" (25). Likewise, in an interesting combination of voodoo and the supernatural, the coach in *Zombies Don't Play Soccer* (1995) becomes a member of the walking dead after being placed under a spell by a witch: "The old woman had long stringy hair that hung over her wrinkled face. Her black dress almost reached the ground" (14).

"I . . . Did My Best Imitation of a Horror Movie Creature, Groaning 'Braiiinnnnssss' to My Pale Reflection": The Postmodern, Ironic, Self-Referential YA Zombie

Of the various zombie narratives that have appeared since the 1990s, how-ever, one stands out: *My So-Called Death*. Written by Stacey Jay and released in March 2010, the book is a murder mystery. *My So-Called Death* chronicles the experiences of fourteen-year-old zombie protagonist Karen Vera as she tries to discover which one of her fellow corpse classmates at DEAD High has been munching on the brains of her peers. As Karen sagely reflects in the wake of the first attack, "I had a strange feeling I'd be able to help find Kendra's brain before it was too late. I'd always been good at solving puzzles, and my gut told me that I already had part of this one put together" (41).

The debt that *My-So-Called Death* owes to popular culture is apparent from the title that Jay chose for her text. A pun on the short-lived but critically acclaimed television program *My So-Called Life* (1994–95), the novel is filled with current slang, a hipster attitude, and comedic references to well-known shows and celebrities. Discussing her outfit for the first day of zombie school, for instance, Karen muses that "purple was totally the new black, and the glitter was intentionally ironic" (23). Similarly, after seeing the gothic decor chosen by her roommate, Clarice, the protagonist describes that side of their dorm as "the inside of an emo vampire's lair" (26). Later, when Karen contemplates whether love interest Gavin McDougal reciprocates her feelings, she asks herself, "And just *how* cute did he think I was? Like puppy cute or Kate Bosworth in *Blue Crush* cute?" (108; italics in original). Throughout the remainder of the book, Karen displays her conversance with numerous other facets of pop culture, mentioning everything from John Hughes's film *Pretty in Pink* and VH1's program *I Love the 80s* to the Twilight series and Hello Kitty, which, in true hipster fashion prompts her to confess, "Say what you want about my taste being juvenile, but I love Kitty of the Hello" (42).

My So-Called Death also contains many self-referential comments about the zombie genre. When one character discusses the existence of brain-eating zombies who drool, her father humorously remarks, "'And I thought they were only in Romero films,' . . . earning a chuckle from the principal" (15). Not long afterward, Karen goes into the bathroom and reports that "I looked at myself in the mirror and did my best imitation of a horror movie creature, groaning 'braiiinnnnsssss' to my pale reflection" (19). Indeed, in a comment that typifies Karen's bubbly personality, the book's postmodern sensibility, and what Leverette and McIntosh would characterize as "the self-reflexive humor of a saturated [zombie] genre" (ix), she wryly quips that "just because you don't have a pulse doesn't mean you can't be perky" (9). In light of these and other passages, one reviewer aptly characterizes Jay's novel as "a cross between Stephenie Meyer and Joss Wheden" (qtd. on StaceyJay.com). Meanwhile, another reviewer is even more direct, deeming the book "Part *Buffy the Vampire Slayer*, part *Night of the Living Dead*" (qtd. on StaceyJay.com).

While Jay may borrow extensively from millennial popular culture, she does not do so when it comes to explaining the root or origins of her protagonist's zombism. Karen's identity as a member of the walking dead is not the result of voodoo or witchcraft. On the contrary, the fourteen-year-old former cheerleader is a zombie because of her DNA. Unlike "typical" human beings, Karen has inherited a gene that prevents her from dying. The young woman discovers that she has this trait when, in the book's prologue, she tumbles seventeen feet to the ground and splits open her skull on the pavement but does not die, at least in the conventional sense. As the protagonist herself explains, "My very short-lived career at Peachtree High ended that day I fell from the top of the stunt pyramid and died. But didn't. That day I found out I wasn't ever going to die a normal death" (5). On the contrary, the young woman lives on, but now as a zombie:

> "You mean . . . she's dead, but she's not?" Dad asked. . . .
>
> "No, she's dead," Principal Samedi said. . . . "Her heart will never beat again, her core body temperature will be much lower than an average person's, and her skin will be vulnerable to rot if she does not take the proper precautions." (9)

Amazingly, this turn of events does not surprise Karen's father. A university professor, Mr. Vera discovered while researching his ancestry that many of his relatives had a history of experiencing what he calls "extended life." As Karen relays,

> Back in Cuba, Dad's great-great aunt had been chased out of her seaside village for looking about twenty years old when she hit her sixtieth birthday. . . . There were others, including a great-great-great-grandfather in Spain and a ninety-year-old third cousin who could still pass for a man in his early thirties. (7)

For years, the Vera clan largely discounted her father's belief in this family trait. In the words of the protagonist, "Mom, of course, thought Dad was nuts and all the stories a bunch of bull-honkey" (7). Naturally, all that changed in the wake of the cheerleading accident. "Then she became a believer. Big time" (7), Karen says about her mother, but such sentiments also clearly reflect her own viewpoint.

Aware of his family's tradition of extended life, Mr. Vera acted fast when his daughter toppled to the ground. Jay's protagonist recounts these events:

> So while Mom hyperventilated . . . and the crowd gasped and wept . . . Dad scooped my brains back into my skull and hustled me to the car before the paramedics could arrive on the scene. Thank god he did. . . . I don't know what would have happened if normal people had figured out I was Undead. (7)

Karen's genetic inheritance places her in a distinct subcategory of humans, those known as the "death challenged." As the teenager quickly clarifies, however, death challenged is "just a politically correct term—like horizontally gifted (fat) or petroleum transfer technician (gas station attendant)—for *zombie*" (5–6).

The presence of this new type of genetically determined zombie does not stop the walking dead from coming into being via other methods. As Principal Samedi from DEAD High School—an acronym for "death-challenged education for adolescents and the deprogrammed"—who visits the Vera household in the days following Karen's accident, cautions, "'You'll also run the risk of being confused with black magically raised zombies.' She then went on to explain how black magically raised zombies are mindless, scary, red-glowing-eyed freaks who want to chow down on human flesh and not much else" (15).* Fortunately, according to the school principal, "sometimes, black magically raised zombies can have their soul returned to their body if their corpse was raised within a year of their death. And if the proper spells are employed before they develop a taste for human blood" (15). This process is known as being "deprogrammed," and upon its completion the individual remains a walking corpse but is purged of its mindless mental state and appetite for human flesh.

Whether an individual's zombidom arises from being death challenged or deprogrammed, Principal Samedi makes clear that the living dead cannot remain in the mainstream community: "When we become something that society cannot accept, we must find a new society" (9). Consequently, she encourages Karen's parents to allow her to attend DEAD High: "We are the oldest Undead boarding school in the central United States" (10). At the institution, the fourteen-year-old will not only be able to continue her education in conventional subjects like math and English but will also receive instruction in areas necessary to live as the walking dead: the way to care for zombified skin, what to do in the case of a maggot infestation, how to know when her dietary needs dictate that she should consume raw cow brains and when cooked ones are sufficient. The principal explains the importance of

---

*The name that Jay chose for this character alludes to the long association of zombies with voodoo. As Hans-W. Ackermann and Jeanine Gauthier have written, in the zombie folklore of Haiti, Baron Samedi is the figure who guards the cemetery and permits—or denies—corpses from being reanimated as zombies. With respect to this particular process of zombification, they explain that "the victim becomes ill, dies, and is interred. At night, the sorcerer goes to the victim's grave and asks Baron Samedi, the lord of the cemetery, for permission to open the grave. If Baron Samedi agrees, the corpse is removed. The sorcerer then awakens the corpse by holding the bottle with the victim's soul under its nose and feeding it a special drug" (474). However, the connection between Principal Samedi in Jay's novel and this figure from Haitian folklore is never made explicit. Instead, it operates in the background, adding to the history and culture of zombies that are present in the text for readers who either know the reference or seek it out.

zombie health, nutrition, and hygiene, saying "your physical body is now even more precious than it was before. . . . You could potentially live for hundreds of years, and you're going to have to learn to take very good care of your mortal flesh" (14). Thus, Karen quickly realizes that the living dead possess their own distinct culture. The epigraph to each chapter of *My So-Called Death* is an excerpt from one of Karen's zombie-themed schoolbooks or from popular corpse culture, and thus emphasizes this point. The following verses from a late eighteenth-century Irish zombie folk song form a representative example:

> Zombie Joe lost his toe and still went a courtin'
> Zombie Beth lost her breath, but still got up in the mornin',
> But Zombie Fred lost his head and now we're all a mournin'
> Mournin', mournin', we all fall down. (62)

"Because I Wasn't a Normal Person, I Was a Genetic Anomaly. A Mutation": Zombies and the Posthuman

The presentation of a parallel zombie world locates *My So-Called Death* within the existing body of cultural depictions of the walking dead in the United States. But the book's introduction of zombies whose condition is the result of a genetic mutation places it in dialogue with a different, and even more significant, phenomenon: the posthuman.* Although this concept first emerged during the early twentieth century, it attained great intellectual and cultural traction during the 1980s and 1990s. The posthuman, according to the *Oxford English Dictionary*, denotes "a hypothetical species that might evolve from human beings, as by means of genetic or bionic augmentation." In this way, posthumanism is commonly seen as blurring the line between human and animal or, more commonly, between human and machine. Stephanie Fae Beauclair, more commonly known as "Baby Fae," is perhaps the most

---

* In many ways, Daniel Waters's Generation Dead series can also be viewed in this light. The YA trilogy focuses on a growing cohort of what has come to be known as "living impaired" teens, who have mysteriously arisen from the dead. Referred to as "differently biotic," these young men and women are in dialogue with both the long-standing tradition of zombies and the subject of the posthuman. That said, the novels—which were published between 2008 and 2010—are largely concerned with romance: namely, the various dates, crushes, and relationships of protagonist Phoebe Kendall along with her two friends, Margi and Adam. Thus, while the Generation Dead series does engage with issues of life and death, it is not focused on the subject of murder in the same way— or to the same extent—as Jay's *My So-Called Death*.

famous example of the former phenomenon. In 1984, she became the highly publicized recipient of a xenotransplant—a procedure in which organs, tissues, or cells are transferred from one species to another. The girl was born with a grave congenital heart defect, and when a human donor could not be found, a baboon heart was chosen for transplantation. The procedure made headlines around the world, heralded both as marvel of modern medicine and as a poignant example of its misuse (see Pence).

Donna Haraway has been a leading voice for the impact that technology has had on conceptions of the body. In her now famous essay "A Cyborg Manifesto," Haraway notes the way in which men and women during the late 1980s and early 1990s were becoming not simply dependent on machines but codependent on them. Without their cell phone, fax line, or computer, for instance, many reported feeling lost, "naked," and even unable to function: "By the late twentieth century, our time, a mythic time," she concludes, "we are all chimeras, theorized and fabricated hybrids of machine and organism; in short, we are cyborgs" (150).

The new millennium has witnessed a growth in this trend toward the cyborgian amid the nearly ubiquitous presence of smart phones, iPods, and laptops. Men, women, and even children have become so connected to various forms of technology that William J. Mitchell has called this perpetually linked-in person "Me++," a pun on the computer programming language C++. Listening to their iPod while surfing the internet on their web-enabled cell phone, these individuals embody Haraway's concept of "a cybernetic organism, a hybrid of machine and organism, a creature of social reality as well as a creature of fiction" (149).*

Genetic engineering forms another powerful locus of posthumanism. As Elaine Ostry has remarked, "Biotechnology focuses on creating 'improved' children, designer babies, and on screening fetuses, thereby already determining much of a person before he or she is even born, or created by other means" (222–23). Using chromosomal analysis parents may soon be able to create their own "custom" babies. In the words of Francis Fukuyama, "Genetics will identify the 'gene for' characteristics like intelligence, height, hair

---

*Posthumanism, of course, can also emanate from the opposite direction, as machines move closer to a state of humanness rather than humans merging with animals and/or technology. Perhaps best exemplified via fictional examples like the Terminator, the Six Million Dollar Man, and the computer HAL 9000, these characters represent an evolutionary enhancement to humanness that can be placed on the spectrum of the posthuman. That said, the transformations that are taking place in the human body itself are most pertinent to this discussion.

color, aggression, or self-esteem and use this knowledge to create a 'better' version of the child" (76). The Human Genome Project, which commenced in 1990, could push this phenomenon even further. If it can discover the genetic source for debilitating diseases, the cellular cause for fatal illnesses, and the chromosomal processes by which the human body deteriorates, the venture could have a profound impact on both the quality and the length of human life. As Fukuyama reports:

> Some promoters of the Human Genome Project, such as Human Genome Science's CEO William Haseltine, have made far-reaching claims about what contemporary molecular biology will achieve, arguing that "as we understand the body's repair process at the genetic level . . . we will be able to advance the goal of maintaining our bodies in normal function, perhaps perpetually." (18)

In the wake of such advances, "long-familiar processes and events such as aging, disease and accident" would be "made aberrant and deviant" (Seaman 249). Indeed, as Fukuyama points out, "People's relationship to death will change as well. Death may come to be seen not as a natural and inevitable aspect of life, but a preventable evil like polio or the measles" (71). In this way, the posthuman is a harbinger of a "'postbiological' future for the human race" (Hayles 6).

My So-Called Death engages with both the promise and the perils of posthumanism by introducing individuals whose genetic composition bestows them with the extended life of zombism. Karen Vera and her fellow death-challenged zombies defy conventional mortality. As Jay's narrator-protagonist remarks in the wake of the cheerleading accident, "That day I found out I wasn't ever going to die a normal death. Because I wasn't a normal person, I was a genetic anomaly. A mutation. A defect" (5).

In presenting Karen's experiences as a zombie, Jay's novel spotlights many of the moral, social, and ethical problems associated with the posthuman. As Bart Simon has written about the hazards associated with this seemingly beneficial transformation to the human body, "Genetic technologies will alter the material and biological basis of the natural human equality that serves as the basis of political equality and human rights" (1). In its most modest form, posthumanism creates not simply a distinction between different types of corporeal bodies but a hierarchy among them, with the new, altered incarnations being seen as superior to existing men and women. To be sure, the inequities that emerge from the advent of genetically or technologically modified humans frequently form the basis for science fiction books, films, and television programs. Figures like the Six Million Dollar Man, the Bionic Woman, and even the Terminator are cast as clear improvements to the human form.

The problems associated with posthumanism emerge in the opening pages of *My So-Called Death*. If mortality is one of the most fundamental aspects of humanness, then being an undead zombie renders these men and women something different and even other. Principal Samedi explains how "conventional" individuals who lack the gene for extended life are fearful of the undead, seeing them as abnormal at best and abominations at worst:

> "Integration with living society is simply not possible for our kind. It isn't safe for us to reveal our true nature."
>
> "Because people are afraid. Intolerant of anything extremely different," Dad said, in his professor voice.
>
> "Exactly. Invariably, the Undead are hunted out and destroyed, no matter how civilized our behavior or how earnestly we seek to integrate ourselves into the human world." Samedi's words sent a little chill down my spine as visions of zombie-hating mobs danced through my head. (11)

When Mr. and Mrs. Vera are still hesitant to permit Karen to attend DEAD High, Samedi elaborates on some of the perils faced by the undead: "There are paranormally gifted humans who devote their lives to slaying the creatures" (15). Underscoring the rigid division that has emerged between conventional mortal humans and immortal zombie posthumans, she soberingly states that "there are others who believe any Undead who refuses to return to the grave deserves to be destroyed" (15).

Soon after arriving at DEAD High, Karen discovers that such stratification also exists among the undead. The distinction between individuals who are biologically death challenged, or "DC," and those who are deprogrammed, or "DP," is not insignificant; rather, it forms the basis for the hierarchy of the students at DEAD High. As Trish, Karen's closest friend at the school, explains, a clear social pecking order exists among the living dead, with those who are born undead enjoying a status above those who have been raised from the dead by black magic. The deprogrammed are second-class citizens in the zombie world, a position that is structurally reinforced at DEAD High: the DP students are required to work around the campus—laboring in the cafeteria, as Karen's love interest Gavin McDougal does, or cleaning the bathrooms, which is Trish's assignment—while the DC are not. Gavin explains the origins of this hierarchy: "The Death Challenged alumni who make the donations that run the school took a vote and decided they didn't want their money to go toward Deprogrammed tuition" (104). Karen protests the inequity of this arrangement, arguing that "the Deprogrammed are obviously not treated fairly" (103), a point she subsequently reiterates even more passionately: "There are two groups of people being treated differently for reasons that have more to do with what they are than who they are or anything they've done" (107). When Gavin shrugs her concerns off by saying "that's just the way it's always been," Karen utters her most pointed and politicized retort to date: "Well, that sounds a lot like what people said when they didn't want women or minorities to have the same rights as everyone else" (107).

Given the way in which deprogrammed zombies are relegated to a subordinate social status, death-challenged students commonly shun them: they rebuff their friendship and even avoid socializing with them. Karen makes this discovery during a conversation with Trish: "A horrible realization pricked at the end of my mind. 'Is that why people have been looking at us funny? Do the Death Challenged and the Deprogrammed not usually'—'No, not usually,' Trish glanced down. . . . [Her] expression was a little sad and a *lot* angry" (49; italics in original).

The tensions that arise from this division form the motive for the murders that take place throughout the novel. Trish discusses a long-standing belief among black-magically raised zombies: "People are saying that Deprogrammed kids could become stronger and faster than the DCs. That, with the right magic, we could be like superheroes compared to the genetically Undead. But only if we work this super-hard spell within the first two years of our deaths" (50). Using a supernatural means to level the zombie playing field sounds sensible enough, until Trish goes on to reveal its taboo ingredient: "This spell requires brains. . . . Not animal brains. . . . The brains of other Undead [human zombies]" (51).

When Kendra Duncan's body is found in a heap on the cafeteria floor, her brain freshly harvested, this abstract possibility becomes a concrete reality. As Trish says about the seeming occult motive for the cranial confiscation, "I'm pretty sure the spell called for eating them" (52). These details give rise to a horrid realization on Karen's part, namely, "that while Kendra was the first, she won't be the last" (52).

Her prediction is correct. In the very next chapter, Karen discovers the second victim, fellow freshman Penelope Sweetney, on the floor of the girl's bathroom. Jay's narrator-protagonist describes the gruesome scene in the stall in a way that echoes Julia Kristeva's account of abjection: "That was all it was— a mess. I couldn't think of it as a person. And I especially couldn't think of it as a person who'd had their skull opened and their brain removed with the little garden trowel lying next to them on the tile" (60). Even more frighteningly, the killer has not yet left the premises: after sneaking up behind Karen, the villain knocks her unconscious and then flees, leaving her brain mysteriously untouched. This event only seems to confirm that the attacks are the result of interzombie animosity. "You know, both Penelope and Kendra were De-programmed," Trish points out (76). "So you think whoever did this left me alone because I'm naturally Death Challenged," the narrator-protagonist sagely muses (76). When Karen's best friend becomes the next victim—"Trish was dead! Trish! *My* Trish was floating there [in the DEAD High pool] with her brain swiped from her poor, innocent skull" (113; italics in original)—this theory is confirmed.

When Karen and her love interest Gavin finally discover the identity of the assailant, however, the situation isn't exactly as they had suspected. The killer, DEAD High's English and zombie poetry teacher Mr. Cork, is not a depro-grammed zombie looking to increase his occult powers; rather, he is a death-challenged one who consumes human brains to bolster his failing health. As he tells Karen, "I am one of the first, child. One of the very first. . . . I walked the earth long, long before your parents' parents were born" (202). After centuries of being undead, however, Mr. Cork's physical well-being has deteri-orated. To rejuvenate his decaying flesh, he needs the restorative power not simply of cow brains but of the far more potent human ones. Mr. Cork selects his victims based on his belief that naturally death-challenged zombies are superior to those who are deprogrammed. He openly tells Karen that the deprogrammed "didn't deserve to live on after death" (200). The English teacher's animosity toward the nongenetically undead thus constitutes a form of "zombie eugenics." Cork sees himself as cleansing or even purifying the zombie community by ridding it of these "mongrel" members. As he tells the Deprogrammed zombie Gavin, "Of course you, little sir, are as much an abom-ination as the rest" (202).

"If You Were a Normal Girl You Would Totally Be Dead": The Prospect of Posthomicide and the Future of Murder Literature

My So-Called Death has significance beyond simply introducing the issue of posthumanism to a juvenile audience; the text also breaks new theoretical and cultural ground. As a murder mystery in which both the killer and his victims are zombies, the narrative invites readers to contemplate what it means to murder someone who is genetically unable to die as well as to commit further acts of homicide against these zombified figures. In the opening pages of the novel, Karen describes her cheerleading accident as a type of murder. The fourteen-year-old junior varsity member does not tumble from atop the pyramid because of her own misstep but rather because of the reckless behavior of a fellow classmate. When spectator Kevin Jenkins tells his buddy that "Karen Vera's not wearing underpants" (3), the two girls supporting the narrator-protagonist grow curious and glance up. This small act produces a domino effect: "Hips tilted forward as heads tilted up, hips tilting led to feet tilting, feet tilting led to knees bending, which, in turn, led to the complete and absolute sabotage of the entire pyramid" (4). As Karen reflects, "I didn't even have time to scream, just a split second to stare up into the sky, streaked with red from the setting sun, and wonder if Kevin Jenkins would feel properly guilty *for killing me*" (4; my emphasis).

This prediction is quickly complicated by the fact that the young girl possesses the gene for extended life. While Karen does die in some concrete ways—she loses her pulse, she has a funeral, and so forth—she also continues to live as an undead zombie. Throughout *My So-Called Death*, the narrator-protagonist walks, talks, eats, sleeps, and, of course, attends school. These details give rise to a paradoxical state: the young girl is dead but she is also alive. At the same time, and even more puzzling, she is also alive *because* she is dead. Karen herself comments on this oxymoronic situation: "There's just nothing more terrifying than falling to your death and having your brains splattered all over the pavement. Unless it's falling to your *undeath* and having your brains splattered all over the pavement" (6; italics in original). The fourteen-year-old cheerleader is able to enjoy her new life not *in spite of* her death but *because of* it. If her classmate hadn't "killed" her in the human world, then she wouldn't be "alive" in the zombie one. Consequently, Karen is simultaneously dead and undead.

This situation becomes even more complex after the brain harvestings begin. After all, Mr. Cork is committing murder against zombie figures who are, technically, already dead. Moreover, the seemingly lethal act of removing the brains of these corpse-kids kills them but—once again—does not. As Principal Samedi reveals in the wake of the first attack, they can still be saved: "Kendra Duncan has had her cranium fully harvested. If we don't find her brain within the next few days, she won't be . . . won't be returning to us" (38). Samedi makes an analogous statement after the second attack, correcting Karen's assertion that Penelope Sweetney has been killed: "She's not dead. We are going to find the person responsible in time to restore both Penelope and Kendra" (64). In this way, the zombified girls defy conventional notions of biological determinism: they are dead yet still alive, and then they can be killed (again) and yet still be brought back to life.

Soon after Trish's brain is harvested, the assailant attempts to kill Karen and Gavin by crushing the duo behind a row of bleachers. Jay's narrator-protagonist considers this act nothing less than attempted murder:

> Someone had tried to *murder* me, and Gavin too. Murder. Like, *for real* murder.
> (I go to the *Encarta World Dictionary* to reinforce how serious and real this is):
>   MURDER:
>   n. The crime of killing another person deliberately and not in self-defense or with any extenuating circumstance recognized by law.
>   v. To kill somebody with great violence and brutality, to put an end to or destroy something. (121; italics in original)

As before though, this claim is complicated by the fact that both she and Gavin are already dead and, thus, even crushing their bodies behind the heavy wooden benches does not prove fatal. As Karen says to herself, "If you were a normal girl you would totally be dead" (120).

Jay's novel thus pushes the question of genetic alterations to the human body, the creation of a new biological subset of humans, and the transcendence of conventional mortality beyond the posthuman and into the realm of what might be termed the "posthomicidal." The undead zombies in *My So-Called Death* engage with the question not only of what it means to be alive but, by extension, what it means to commit murder in a posthuman age. As a passage from Karen's textbook *Total Health for the Death Challenged* that appears as the epigraph to the first chapter of *My So-Called Death* asserts, "Many Traditionally Alive people assume such a mutation can only lead to disease or death, but for the Death Challenged, our genetic anomaly leads to an entirely new way of life" (5). If genetically undead individuals cannot die, then, by extension, they cannot be murdered. Consequently, in the same way that mortality has become passé for the death challenged, then so too has homicide. Although Jay's young adult novel is ostensibly a murder mystery, its posthuman zombies also render it a posthomicidal one: a narrative in which the act of murder has become invalid, defunct, and outmoded.

My So-Called Death illuminates another even more significant implication of posthumanism. Together with forming a site of collection for millennium meditations on death and dying, the undead zombies in Jay's narrative also provide a vehicle by which to examine the impact that these figures have on traditional notions of crime, killing, and corporeal violence. The rise of posthumanism and the increasing ability of humans to delay, defer, and even defeat death have ramifications that affect the entire genre of murder-themed literature. Will advances in medical science and genetic engineering render homicide a meaningless act, not just for individuals who possess a special genetic mutation but for anyone who has access to modern medical care? If so, will it be possible for authors like Stacey Jay to continue to write in the murder mystery genre or for readers to understand or even have an interest in such texts? While the possibility of a fully posthuman and, thus, truly posthomicidal world may be many generations away, it does raise intriguing questions about the future of not merely murder-themed literature but humankind as a whole. If individuals lose the ability to die, how will it change the way they live? Will life continue to be seen as important and even precious if it is permanent and unending?

Wade Davis, in a book examining the ethnobiology of Haiti, argues that the country's enduring belief in zombies offers "a confirmation of a fundamental conviction that the dead wield power in the world of the living" (57). Davis would likely agree that this sentiment is not limited to the island nation. Rather, beliefs in the power of the deceased—both in the afterworld and in the present one—permeate all times, places, and modes of writing. Stacey Jay's *My So-Called Death* reveals how the influence that the dead wield over the living extends to individuals who are seemingly the furthest removed from the end of the human life cycle and the realm of death: young people.

During an interview, Philip Pullman, the author of the critically acclaimed *His Dark Materials* series for young readers, was asked for his viewpoint about the oft-contemplated difference between narratives written for adults and those intended for children. He suggested that "at the best-selling end, adult literature is about childish things: Does my bum look big in this? Will the Arsenal win the Cup? But children's literature is about grown-up things. Where did we come from? Where do we go? What is consciousness?" (qtd. in Brennan 95). In this book, I both affirm Pullman's observation and expand on it. The analyses throughout the previous chapters reveal how many of the most popular fairy tales, adventure novels, detective stories, and young adult texts may commonly be seen as childlike, yet their themes are anything but childish.

In a memorable, if macabre, comment that appears in a nineteenth-century trial pamphlet, a condemned killer reflects that "when a dead man opens his eyes and looks about, moves his limbs, throws his arms on his breast, grinds his teeth, and tries to catch you, it requires strong nerves to witness the spectacle" (M'Conaghy and Robinson 15). This book takes an important step toward witnessing the spectacle of homicide in a venue that is simultaneously its most unexpected and, perhaps, its most instructive. Narratives for young readers are routinely seen as educating boys and girls about the roles and responsibilities that they will face later in life. Indeed, paraphrasing a comment made by Jack Zipes, Jackie E. Stallcup has written that "one of the major organizing features of children's books is the socialization process" (129). From offering information about how to be law-abiding citizens and productive workers to giving advice on how to become loving spouses and good friends or neighbors, books for young readers seek to acculturate children.

This project reveals that it is equally necessary for children to learn about violence, trauma, and murder. In the same way that a convicted murderer needs to muster the courage to confront death, so too must even the youngest of the nation's readers. By providing information about crime and killing, murder-themed books for children participate in what Ann Pellegrini has termed "necropedagogy," or the lessons that the living can learn from the dead. By compelling individuals to grapple with questions of trauma, mourning, and "the weight of identification," necropedagogy encourages the consideration of "moral claims about progress, the universal human, and the ordering of time itself" (Pellegrini 100, 98).

Ronald Doctor, in an essay about the social history of homicide, points out that "the story of the crime of murder is nearly always a cover-up" (79). Whether the act occurs in a fictional world or the real one, it is—to greater or lesser degrees—a mystery. Even in cases where both the victim and the killer are known, family, friends, and often police officers are left wondering why. Why did this terrible event occur? How could it possibly have happened? What lessons can be learned from it?

As Roger Lane has written, academic research can also be likened to detective work in many ways. From following textual clues and formulating an interpretive theory to gathering primary and secondary evidence and making a persuasive argument, scholars play the role of sleuth (Lane 1–2). The chapters in this project bring these two practices even closer together. By making visible the long-overlooked tradition of homicide in literature for young readers, they present new evidence in ongoing efforts to crack one of the most infamous unsolved cases of all time: the origins of the American obsession with violence and the motive fueling its fascination with crime and criminals.

Works Cited

"About the Society." American Society for Psychical Research. http://www.aspr.com/who.htm.

An Account of the Apprehension, Trial, Conviction, and Condemnation of Manuel Philip Garcia and Jose Demas Garcia Castillano. Norfolk, VA: C. Hall, 1821.

Ackermann, Hans-W., and Jeanine Gauthier. "The Ways and Nature of the Zombi." *Journal of American Folklore* 104.414 (1991): 466–94.

Alcott, William. *The Young Husband; or, Duties of Man in the Marriage Relation.* Boston: Waite, Pierce, 1846.

Alder, Christine M., and June Baker. "Maternal Filicide: More Than One Story to Be Told." *Women and Criminal Justice* 9.2 (1997): 15–39.

Allen, James. *Without Sanctuary: Lynching Photography in America.* Santa Fe, NM: Twin Palms, 2000.

The American Bloody Register, Containing a True and Complete History of the Lives, Last Words, and Dying Confessions of Three of the Most Noted Criminals That Have Ever Made Their Exit from a Stage in America. . . . Boston: E. Russell, 1784.

The Amityville Horror. Dir. Stuart Rosenberg. Perf. James Brolin, Margot Kidder, Rod Steiger. MGM, 1979. DVD.

Anderson, Hans Christian. *The Little Mermaid.* Copenhagen: Scandinavia Publishing House, 1987.

Anderson, Robyn. "Criminal Violence in London, 1856–1875." PhD thesis, University of Toronto, 1990.

Annals of Murder; or, Daring Outrages, Trials, and Confessions, &c. Philadelphia: John B. Perry, 1845.

Apel, Dora. *Imagery of Lynching: Black Men, White Women, and the Mob.* Camden, NJ: Rutgers University Press, 2004.

Arnoldi, Richard. "Parallels Between *Our Mutual Friend* and the Alice Books." *Children's Literature* 1 (1972): 54–57.

Asher, Robert, Lawrence B. Goodheart, and Alan Rogers. Introduction to *Murder on Trial, 1620–2002*, edited by Robert Asher and Lawrence B. Goodheart and Alan Rogers, 3–30. Albany: State University of New York Press, 2005.

Ashliman, D. L. "Rapunzel by Jacob and Wilhelm Grimm, a Comparison of the Versions of 1812 and 1857." http://www.pitt.edu/dash/grimm012a.html.

Associated Press. "Sale of Chicago Serial Killer's Art Draws Protests." *St. Petersburg (FL) Times,* 6 June 2004.

Awful Disclosures and Startling Developments, in Relation to the Parkman Tragedy. Boston: n.p., 1849.

Ayers, Edward L. *Vengeance and Justice: Crime and Punishment in the 19th-Century South.* New York: Oxford University Press, 1984.

Baldick, Robert. *The Duel: A History of Dueling.* London: Chapman and Hall, 1965.

Barrie, J. M. *Peter Pan.* 1904. New York: Penguin, 2011.

Barzilai, Shuli. "Reading 'Snow White': The Mother's Story." *Signs* 15.3 (1990): 515–34.

Batey, Mavis. *Alice's Adventures in Oxford.* Andover, UK: Pitkin Pictorials, 1980.

Baum, L. Frank. *The Wonderful Wizard of Oz.* 1900. New York: Barnes and Noble Classics, 2005.

Bederman, Gail. *Manliness and Civilization: A Cultural History of Gender and Race in the United States, 1880–1917.* Chicago: University of Chicago Press, 1995.

Bernard, Nicholas. *The Penitent Death of a Woeful Sinner; or, The Penitent Death of Jo. Atherton, Late Bishop of Waterford in Ireland.* . . . London: R. Ibbitson, 1651.

Bettelheim, Bruno. *The Uses of Enchantment: The Meaning and Importance of Fairy Tales.* New York: Routledge, 1977.

The Big Sleep. Dir. Howard Hawks. Perf. Humphrey Bogart, Lauren Bacall. Warner Brothers, 1946.

Bishop, Claire Huchet. *The Five Chinese Brothers.* 1938. New York: Putnam, 1989.

Bishop, Kyle William. *American Zombie Gothic: The Rise and Fall (and Rise) of the Walking Dead in Popular Culture.* Jefferson, NC: McFarland, 2010.

Black, Joel. *The Aesthetics of Murder: A Study in Romantic Literature and Contemporary Culture.* Baltimore, MD: Johns Hopkins University Press, 1991.

Blomberg, Thomas G., and Karol Lucken. *American Penology: A History of Control.* Hawthorne, NY: Aldine de Gruyter, 2000.

Blum, Harold. "Masochism, the Ego Ideal, and the Psychology of Women." *Journal of the American Psychoanalytic Association* 24.5 (1976): 157–91.

Boa, Kenneth. *Cults, World Religions and the Occult.* 1977. Colorado Springs, CO: Cook Communications, 1990.

Boon, Kevin Alexander. "Ontological Anxiety Made Flesh: The Zombie in Literature, Film and Culture." In *Monsters and the Monstrous: Myths and Metaphors of Enduring Evil,* edited by Niall Scott, 33–43. Amsterdam: Rodopi, 2007.

Boreman, Robert. *A Mirrour of Mercy and Judgement.* London: Thomas Dring, 1655.

Bottigheimer, Ruth B. *Fairy Tales: A New History.* Albany: State University Press of New York, 2009.

———. "Tale Spinners: Submerged Voices in Grimms' Fairy Tales." *New German Critique* 27 (1982): 141–50.

Bouthoul, Gaston. *Les guerres, traite de sociologie* Paris: Payot, 1951.

Boyz N the Hood. Dir. John Singleton. Perf. Cuba Gooding Jr., Laurence Fishburne, Ice Cube. Columbia Pictures, 1991. DVD.

Brandon, Craig. *The Electric Chair: An Unnatural American History.* Jefferson, NC: McFarland, 1999.

Brennan, Geraldine. "The Game Called Death: Frightening Fictions by David Almond, Philip Gross and Lesley Howarth." In *Frightening Fiction: R. L. Stine, Robert Westall, David Almond, and Others*, edited by Kimberly Reynolds, Geraldine Brennan, and Kevin McCarron, 92–127. New York: Continuum, 2005.

Brinton, Crane. "The National Socialists' Use of Nietzsche." *Journal of the History of Ideas* 1.2 (1940): 131–50.

Bronski, Michael. Introduction to *Pulp Friction: Uncovering the Golden Age of Gay Male Pulps*, edited by Michael Bronski, 1–21. New York: St. Martin's, 2003.

Brooker, Will. *Alice's Adventures: Lewis Carroll in Popular Culture*. New York: Continuum, 2004.

Brooks, Max. *World War Z: An Oral History of the Zombie War*. New York: Three Rivers, 2006.

———. *The Zombie Survival Guide: Complete Protection from the Living Dead*. Illus. Max Werner. New York: Crown, 2003.

Brown, Charles Brockden. *Wieland; or, The Transformation: An American Tale*. 1798. New York: Norton, 2010.

Bureau of Justice. "Homicide Trends in the U.S.: Trends by Race" Office of Justice Programs. http://bjs.ojp.usdoj.gov/content/homicide/race.cfm.

Burroughs, Edgar Rice. *The Mucker*. 1914. New York: Ace Books, 1974.

———. *Tarzan of the Apes*. 1914. New York: Penguin, 1990.

Burshtein, Karen. *Walter Dean Myers*. New York: Rosen, 2004.

Busby, Sian. *The Cruel Mother: A Memoir*. New York: Avalon, 2005.

The Cambridge Guide to Children's Literature. Edited by M. O. Grenby and Andrea Immel. Cambridge: Cambridge University Press, 2010.

Campbell, Patty. "*The Outsiders*, Fat Freddy, and Me." *Horn Book Magazine* 79.2 (2003): 177–83.

———. "Radical *Monster*." *Horn Book Magazine* 75.6 (1999): 769–73.

Capote, Truman. *In Cold Blood*. 1966. New York: Knopf, 1994.

Caputi, Jane. "The Sexual Politics of Murder." *Gender and Society* 3.4 (1989): 437–56.

Carroll, Lewis. *Alice's Adventures in Wonderland*. 1865. In *The Annotated Alice: The Definitive Edition*, edited by Martin Gardner, 3–127. New York: Norton, 2000.

———. *Alice's Adventures in Wonderland* and *Through the Looking Glass*. New York: Penguin, 2003.

———. *Alice's Adventures under Ground*. New York: Macmillan, 1886.

Cart, Michael. *From Romance to Realism: 50 Years of Growth and Change in Young Adult Literature*. New York: Harper Collins, 1996.

Carter, Angela. *The Bloody Chamber*. 1979. New York: Knopf, 1995.

Cavan, Ruth Shonle. *Juvenile Delinquency: Development, Treatment, Control*. Philadelphia: Lippincott, 1962.

"Chicago Leader in Criminology." *Chicago Tribune*, 26 Apr. 1909, 6.

Christianson, Scott. *The Last Gasp: The Rise and Fall of the American Gas Chamber*. Berkeley: University of California Press, 2010.

Christie, Agatha. *Murder on the Orient Express*. 1934. New York: HarperCollins, 2011.

Clark, Beverly Lyon. *Kiddie Lit: The Cultural Construction of Children's Literature in America*. Baltimore, MD: Johns Hopkins University Press, 2003.

Clark, Richard. *Capital Punishment in Britain*. Surrey, UK: Ian Publishing, 2009.

Clockers. Dir. Spike Lee. Perf. Harvey Keitel, John Turturro, Mekhi Phifer, Isaiah Washington. 40 Acres and a Mule Films, 1995.

Cohen, Daniel A. *Pillars of Salt, Monuments of Grace: New England Crime Literature and the Origins of American Popular Culture, 1674–1860*. 1993. Amherst: University of Massachusetts Press, 2006.

Cohen, Matt. Introduction to *Brother Men: The Correspondence of Edgar Rice Burroughs and Herbert T. Weston*, edited by Matt Cohen, 1–50. Durham, NC: Duke University Press, 2005.

Cohen, Morton. *Lewis Carroll: A Biography*. New York: Knopf, 1996.

Cohen, Samuel. *After the End of History: American Fiction in the 1990s*. Iowa City: University of Iowa Press, 2009.

Colburn, Don. "The Risky Lives of Young Black Men." *Washington (DC) Post*, 18 Dec. 1990.

Collingswood, Stuart Dodgson. *The Life and Letters of Lewis Carroll*. 1898. Detroit, MI: Gale, 1967.

Collins, Suzanne. *The Hunger Games*. New York: Scholastic, 2008.

Collins, Wilkie. *The Woman in White*. 1860. New York: Penguin, 2003.

Collis, Clark, and Chris Nashawaty. "Zombies A–Z." *Entertainment Weekly*, 16 Oct. 2009, 36–39.

Columbo. NBC. 1971–78. Television series.

Colwell, Miriam. *Young*. New York: Ballantine Books, 1955.

Cooper, James Fenimore. *The Last of the Mohicans*. 1826. New York: Penguin, 2005.

Cornelius, Michael G. Introduction to *Nancy Drew and Her Sister Sleuths*, edited by Michael G. Cornelius and Melanie E. Gregg, 1–11. Jefferson, NC: McFarland, 2008.

Craig, Patricia, and Mary Cadogan. *The Lady Investigates: Women Detectives and Spies in Fiction*. New York: St. Martin's Press, 1981.

CSI: Crime Scene Investigation. CBS. 2000–present. Television series.

Cummings, C. Michael. "Rise and Fall of Youth Cigarette Brand Over the Past 50 Years." Paper presented at the Conference on Tobacco or Health, San Francisco, CA, 20 Nov. 2002. http://ncth.confex.com/ncth/2002/techprogram/paper_4832 .htm.

Currier, Tammy L. Review of *Monster*, by Walter Dean Myers. Teenreads.com, 21 Apr. 1999. http://www.teenreads.com/reviews/monster-0.

Dadey, Debbie, and Marcia Thornton Jones. *Zombies Don't Play Soccer*. New York: Scholastic, 1995.

Daly, Jay. *Presenting S. E. Hinton*. Rev. ed. Boston: Twayne, 1989.

Daly, Martin, and Margo Wilson. *The Truth about Cinderella: A Darwinian View of Parental Love*. New Haven, CT: Yale University Press, 1998.

Daly, Maureen. *Seventeenth Summer*. 1942. New York: Simon and Schuster, 2011.

Davenport, Barnett. *A Brief Narrative of the Life and Confession of Barnett Davenport.* Hartford, n.p., 1780.

David, Alfred, and Mary Elizabeth David. "A Literary Approach to the Brothers Grimm." *Journal of the Folklore Institute* 1.3 (1964): 180–96.

Davis, David Brion. *Homicide in American Fiction, 1798–1860: A Study in Social Values.* Ithaca, NY: Cornell University Press, 1957.

Davis, Ivor. "Archdeacon Dodgson." *Jabberwocky* 5.2 (1976): 46–49.

Davis, Kenneth C. *Two-Bit Culture: The Paperbacking of America.* Boston: Houghton, 1984.

Davis, Wade. *Passage of Darkness: Ethnobiology of the Haitian Zombie.* Chapel Hill: University of North Carolina, 1988.

Dawn of the Dead. Dir. Jack Snyder. Perf. Sarah Polley, Ving Rhames, Jake Weber. Strike Entertainment, 2004. DVD.

DeForest, Etienne. *The Zombie Survival Guide: How to Live Like a King after the Outbreak.* OnDemand Publishing, 2009.

Dégh, Linda. "Grimm's *Household Tales* and Its Place in the Household: The Social Relevance of a Controversial Classic." *Western Folklore* 38.2 (1979): 83–103.

deMause, Lloyd. *History of Childhood.* New York: Psychohistory Press, 1993.

de Mexico, N. R. *Marijuana Girl.* New York: Universal Publishing, 1951.

Demurova, Nina. "Toward a Definition of Alice's Genre: The Folktale and Fairy-Tale Connections." In *A Celebration of Lewis Carroll: A Celebration; Essays on the Occasion of the 150th Anniversary of the Birth of Charles Lutwidge Dodgson*, edited by Edward Guiliano, 75–88. New York: Potter, 1982.

"The Detection Club Oath." http://www.sfu.ca/english/Gillies/Engl38301/oath.htm.

DiCamillo, Kate. *The Tale of Despereaux.* Cambridge, MA: Candlewick, 2003.

Dinges, Barnaby. "Black Youths Are City's Top Murder Risk." *Chicago Reporter*, Feb. 1990, 1, 6–9.

Dixon, Franklin W. *Track of the Zombie.* New York: Simon and Schuster, 1982.

Doctor, Ronald. "History of Murder." In *Murder: A Psychotherapeutic Investigation*, edited by Ronald Doctor, 9–91. London, England: Karnac Books, 2008.

Dodgson, Charles Lutwidge. "The Two Brothers." In *Lewis Carroll*, by Richard Kelly, 54. Boston: Twayne, 1977.

Doherty, Thomas. *Teenagers and Teenpics: The Juvenilization of American Movies in the 1950s.* Philadelphia: Temple University Press, 2002.

Donelson, Kenneth L., and Alleen Pace Nilsen. *Literature for Today's Young Adults.* 7th ed. Boston: Pearson, 2005.

Donnelly, Jennifer. *A Northern Light.* New York: Harcourt, 2003.

Donovan, Patricia. "America's Fascination with Murder." *University at Buffalo Reporter*, 6 Sept. 2007. http://www.buffalo.edu/ubreporter/archives/vol39/vol39n2/articles/SchmidMurder.html.

Doyle, Arthur Conan. *Sherlock Holmes: The Complete Novels and Stories.* 2 vols. New York: Random House, 1986.

Dragnet. CBS. 1951–59. Television series.

———— (aka *Dragnet 1967*). NBC. 1967–70. Television series.

———— (aka *L.A. Dragnet*). ABC. 2003–4. Television series.

Dreiser, Theodore. *An American Tragedy*. 1925. New York: Penguin, 2010.

Duncan, Lois. *Killing Mr. Griffin*. 1978. New York: Random House, 1990.

Dyer, Carolyn Stewart, and Nancy Tillman Romalov. "Part II: Reading Nancy Drew, Reading Stereotypes." In *Rediscovering Nancy Drew*, edited by Carolyn Stewart Dyer and Nancy Tillman Romalov, 89–94. Iowa City: University of Iowa Press, 1995.

Dyer, Richard. *White*. London: Routledge, 1997.

Eco, Umberto. *The Limits of Interpretation*. Bloomington: Indiana University Press, 1994.

Elder, Robert K. *Last Words of the Executed*. Chicago: University of Chicago Press, 2010.

Ellson, Hal. *Duke*. New York: Scribner, 1949.

————. *The Knife*. New York: Lancer, 1961.

————. *Tomboy*. 1950. New York: Bantam, 1951.

Enoch, Kurt. "The Paper-Bound Book: Twentieth-Century Publishing Phenomenon." *The Library Quarterly* 24.3 (1954): 211–25.

Erskine, John. *The Private Life of Helen of Troy*. New York: Popular Library, 1948.

Falk, Gerhard. *Murder: An Analysis of Its Forms, Conditions, and Causes*. Jefferson, NC: McFarland, 1990.

Fantz, Ashley. "Convicted Killer Fears His Last Moments." *CNN.com*, 2 May 2007. http://articles.cnn.com/2007-05-02/us/lethal.injection_1_lethal-injection-three-drug-cocktail-cocktail-of-lethal-drugs?_s=PM:US.

FAQ. Misc. section. S. E. Hinton.com. http://www.sehinton.com.

FBI (Federal Bureau of Investigation). "Murder Victims by Age, Sex and Race, 1995" (table 2.5). In *Crime in the United States 1995*. http://www.fbi.gov/about-us/cjis/ucr/crime-in-the-u.s/1995/95sec2.pdf.

————. "Murder Victims by Age, Sex and Race, 2000" (table 2.5). In *Crime in the United States 2000*. http://svp.soic.indiana.edu/svp/4232284/FID9/TABLES/02S0288.PDF;1.

————. "Murder Victims by Age, Sex and Race, 2004" (table 2.4). In *Crime in the United States 2004*. http://www2.fbi.gov/ucr/cius_04/offenses_reported/violent_crime/murder.html.

————. "Murder Victims by Age, Sex and Race, 2008" (table 2). In *Crime in the United States 2008*. http://www2.fbi.gov/ucr/cius2008/offenses/expanded_information/data/shrtable_02.html.

Fielding, Steve. *The Hangman's Bible: The Story of Every British Hangman of the Twentieth Century*. London: John Blake, 2008.

Fine, Benjamin. *1,000,000 Delinquents*. New York: Signet, 1957.

Fisher, Leona W. "Race and Xenophobia in the Nancy Drew Novels." In *Nancy Drew and Her Sisters Sleuths*, edited by Michael G. Cornelius and Melanie Gregg, 63–76. Jefferson, NC: McFarland, 2008.

Flint, David. *Zombie Holocaust: How the Living Dead Devoured Pop Culture*. London: Plexus, 2009.

Foucault, Michel. *Discipline and Punish: The Birth of the Prison*. Translated by Alan Sheridan. New York: Vintage, 1977.

Freud, Sigmund. *The Interpretation of Dreams*. Vol. 4 of *The Standard Edition of the Complete Psychological Works of Sigmund Freud*. 24 vols. Edited and translated by James Strachey. London: Hogarth, 1953–74.

———. *Totem and Taboo: Some Points of Argument Between the Mental Lives of Savages and Neurotics*. Translated by James Strachey. 1950. London: Routledge, 2001.

———. "The Uncanny." In *Studies in Parapsychology*, edited by Philip Rieff, 7–13. New York: Collier, 1963.

Friday the 13th. Dir. Sean S. Cunningham. Perf. Betsy Palmer, Adrienne King, Jeannine Taylor. Paramount, 1980. DVD.

Friedman, Susan Hatters, Sarah McCue Horowitz, and Philip J. Resnick. "Child Murder by Mothers: A Critical Analysis of the Current State of Knowledge and a Research Agenda." *American Journal of Psychiatry* 162(9) (2005): 1578–87.

Fleming, Thomas. *Duel: Alexander Hamilton, Aaron Burr, and the Future of America*. New York: Basic Books, 1999.

Fukuyama, Francis. *Our Posthuman Future: Consequences of the Biotechnology Revolution*. New York: Farrar, Straus and Giroux, 2002.

Fyvel, T. R. *Troublemakers: Rebellious Youth in an Affluent Society*. 1961. New York: Schocken, 1966.

Gabler, Neal. *Walt Disney: The Triumph of the American Imagination*. New York: Random House, 2006.

Gaiman, Neil. *The Graveyard Book*. New York: HarperCollins, 2008.

Gardner, Martin, ed. *The Annotated Alice: The Definitive Edition*. New York: Norton, 2000.

Gatrell, V. A. C. *The Hanging Tree: Execution and the English People, 1770–1868*. Oxford: Oxford University Press, 1994.

General introduction to the Modern Criminal Science series. In *Crime and Its Causes*, v–ix. Translated by Henry P. Horton. 1911. Montclair, NJ: Patterson Smith, 1968.

Gerhardt, Lillian V. Review of *The Outsiders*, by S. E. Hinton. *Library Journal*, 15 May 1967, 390.

Gibson, Mary, and Nicole Hahn Rafter. Introduction to *Criminal Man*, by Cesare Lombroso, 1–36. Durham, NC: Duke University Press, 2006.

Gilbert, Sandra M., and Susan Gubar. *The Madwoman in the Attic: The Woman Writer and the Nineteenth-Century Literary Imagination*. New Haven, CT: Yale University Press, 1979.

Giradot, N. J. "Initiation and Meaning in the Tale of Snow White and the Seven Dwarfs." *Journal of American Folklore* 90.357 (1977): 274–300.

"Girl Psychic Wonder Eugene [*sic*] Dennis Old Photo 1920's." http://www.worthpoint.com/worthopedia/girl-psychic-wonder-eugene-dennis-19961217.

Goetting, Ann. "When Parents Kill Their Young Children: Detroit, 1982–1986." *Journal of Family Violence* 3.4 (1988): 339–46.

Golding, William. *Lord of the Flies*. 1954. New York: Penguin, 2003.

Goldsby, Jacqueline Denise. *A Spectacular Secret: Lynching in American Life and Literature*. Chicago: University of Chicago Press, 2006.

Gordon, Thomas J., and Jerry J. Tobias. "Managing the Psychic in Criminal Investigations." *Police Chief* (May 1979): 58–59.

Gorey, Edward. *The Gashlycrumb Tinies*. 1963. New York: Harcourt Brace, 1997.

Gould, Stephen Jay. *The Mismeasure of Man*. Rev. ed. New York: Norton, 1996.

Grafton, Sue. *A Is for Alibi*. 1982. New York: St. Martin's, 2005.

Grahame-Smith, Seth. *Pride and Prejudice and Zombies*. New York: Quirk, 2009.

The Great Train Robbery. Dir. Edwin S. Porter. Perf. Gilbert M. "Broncho Billy" Anderson, A.C. Abadie, George Barnes. Edison, 1903.

Griadot, N. J. "Initiation and Meaning in the Tale of Snow White and the Seven Dwarfs." *Journal of American Folklore* 90.357 (1977): 274–300.

Griffiths, Andy. *Zombie Butts from Uranus!* New York: Scholastic, 2003.

Grimm, Jacob, and Wilhelm Grimm. *Hansel and Gretel: A Fairy Tale*. Illus. Dorothy Duntze. New York: North-South Books, 2001.

———. "Snow White." In *The Classic Fairy Tales*, edited by Maria Tatar, 83–89. New York: Norton, 1999.

Grisham, John. *A Time to Kill*. 1989. New York: Random House, 2009.

Griswold, Jerry. *Feeling Like a Kid: Childhood and Children's Literature*. Baltimore, MD: Johns Hopkins University Press, 2006.

Gruner, Libby. "Blog U: On Children's Literature and Academic Administration." *Mama Ph.D. Inside Higher Education*, 5 Oct. 2009. http://www.insidehighered.com/blogs/mama_phd/on_children_s_literature_and_academic_administration.

Gubar, Marah. *Artful Dodgers: Reconceiving the Golden Age of Children's Literature*. Oxford: Oxford University Press, 2009.

Gubar, Susan. *Racechanges: White Skin, Black Face in American Culture*. New York: Oxford University Press, 1997.

Guiley, Rosemary Ellen. *The Encyclopedia of Ghosts and Spirits*. New York: Checkmark Books, 2000.

Haapasalo, Janna, and Sonja Petäjä. "Mothers Who Killed or Attempted to Kill Their Child: Life Circumstances, Childhood Abuse, and Types of Killings." *Violence and Victims* 14.3 (1999): 219–39.

Hall, G. Stanley. "Corporal Punishment." *West Virginia School Journal*, Oct. 1899, 54–56.

Halloween. Dir. John Carpenter. Perf. Donald Pleasance, Jamie Lee Curtis, Tony Moran. Starz/Anchor Bay, 1978. DVD.

Halttunen, Karen. *Murder Most Foul: The Killer and the American Gothic Tradition*. Cambridge, MA: Harvard University Press, 1998.

Hammett, Dashiell. *The Maltese Falcon*. New York: Pocket Books, 1944.

———. *The Maltese Falcon*. New York: Pocket Books, 1947.

Hancher, Michael. *The Tenniel Illustrations to the "Alice" Books*. Columbus: Ohio State University Press, 1985.

Handler, Phil. "Forging the Agenda: The 1819 Select Committee on the Criminal Laws Revisited." *Journal of Legal History* 25.3 (2004): 249–68.

———. "The Law of Felonious Assault in England, 1803–61." *Journal of Legal History* 28.2 (2007): 183–206.

Hanly, Conor. "The Decline of Civil Jury Trial in Nineteenth-Century England." *Journal of Legal History* 26.3 (2005): 253–78.

Haraway, Donna J. "A Cyborg Manifesto." In *Simians, Cyborgs and Women: The Reinvention of Nature*, 149–82. New York: Routledge, 1991.

Harris, Sharon M. "Mary White Rowlandson [Talcott] 1637?–1711." In vol. A of *The Heath Anthology of American Literature*, 5th ed., edited by Paul Lauter, 437–39. Boston: Houghton Mifflin, 2006.

Hart, J. J., and Will Meugniot. *Zombie Monkey Monster Jamboree*. Boston: Actionopolis, 2006.

Haut, Woody. *Pulp Culture: Hardboiled Fiction and the Cold War*. London: Serpent's Tail, 1995.

Hay, Douglas. "Crime and Justice in Eighteenth- and Nineteenth-Century England." *Crime and Justice* 2 (1980): 45–84.

Hayles, N. Katherine. *How We Became Posthuman: Virtual Bodies in Cybernetics, Literature, and Informatics*. Chicago: University of Chicago Press, 1999.

Heath, Peter. Introduction to *The Philosopher's Alice*, by Lewis Carroll, 3–9. New York: St. Martin's Press, 1974.

Heilbrun, Carolyn G. "Nancy Drew: A Moment in Feminist History." In *Rediscovering Nancy Drew*, edited by Carolyn Stewart Dyer and Nancy Tillman Romalov, 11–21. Iowa City: University of Iowa Press, 1995.

Herman, Gail. *Scooby-Doo on Zombie Island*. New York: Scholastic, 1998.

———. *Scooby-Doo and Zombies, Too!* New York: Scholastic, 1998.

Herman, Judith. *Trauma and Recovery: The Aftermath of Violence—From Domestic Abuse to Political Terror*. New York: Basic Books, 1997.

Hernstein, Richard J., and Charles Murray. *The Bell Curve*. New York: Free Press, 1994.

Hibbard, Whitney S., Raymond W. Worring, and Richard Brennan. *Psychic Criminology: A Guide for Using Psychics in Investigations*. Springfield, IL: Charles C. Thomas, 2002.

Higgins, Jim. "Former 'Bad Boy' Taps into Youths' Minds, Struggles." *Milwaukee Journal Sentinel*, 26 May 2002, 1.

Hillman, Bill. Introduction to "Edgar Rice Burroughs Reports on the Notorious William Edward Hickman Trial." *ERBzine*. http://www.erbzine.com/mag17/1767.html.

Hinton, S. E. *The Outsiders*. 1967. New York: Speak, 1995.

Hipple, Marjorie. "S. E. Hinton." In *Writers for Young Adults*, 3 vols., edited by Ted Hipple, 2:113–20. New York: Charles Scribner's Sons, 1997.

"History of the Society for Psychical Research." Society for Psychical Research. http://www.spr.ac.uk/main/page/history-society-psychical-research-parapsychology.

Hixon, Martha. "Rewriting History." *Children's Literature* 38.1 (2010): 231–36.

Hoffmann, Heinrich. *Struwwelpeter: Merry Stories and Funny Pictures*. New York: Frederick Warne, n.d.

Hogle, Jerrold E. Foreword to *American Zombie Gothic: The Rise and Fall (And Rise) of The Walking Dead in Popular Culture*, by Kyle William Bishop, 1–4. Jefferson, NC: McFarland, 2010.

Holden, Carol E., Andrea Stepheson Burland, and Craig A. Lemmen. "Insanity and Filicide: Women Who Murder Their Children." *New Directions for Mental Health Services* 69 (1996): 25–34.

Holland, Isabelle. "What Is Adolescent Literature?" In *Young Adult Literature: Background and Criticism*, compiled by Millicent Lenz and Ramona M. Mahood, 33–40. Chicago: American Library Association, 1980.

Homicide: Life on the Street. NBC. 1993–99. Television series.

The Horrible Murder of Mrs. Ellen Lynch and Her Sister, Mrs. Hannah Shaw. Philadelphia: A. Winch, 1853.

Horrid Massacre!! Sketches of the Life of Captain James Purrinton. Augusta, GA: Peter Edes, 1806.

Hostettler, John. *Fighting for Justice: The History and Origins of the Adversarial Trial*. Winchester, UK: Waterside, 2006.

Howard, Jennifer. "From 'Once Upon a Time' to 'Happily Ever After.'" *Chronicle of Higher Education*, 22 May 2009.

Hudson, Derek. *Lewis Carroll: An Illustrated Biography*. New York: Clarkson N. Potter, 1977.

The Hunger Games. Dir. Gary Ross. Perf. Jennifer Lawrence, Josh Hutcherson, Liam Hemsworth. Lionsgate, 2012.

Hunt, Peter. *An Introduction to Children's Literature*. New York: Oxford University Press, 1994.

Hunter, Evan. *The Blackboard Jungle*. 1954. New York: Pocket Books, 1999.

———. *The Jungle Kids*. New York: Pocket Books, 1956.

I Am Legend. Dir. Francis Lawrence. Perf. Will Smith, Alice Braga, Charlie Tahan. Warner Brothers, 2007. DVD.

"Innocence and the Death Penalty." Death Penalty Information Center. http://www.deathpenaltyinfo.org/innocence-and-death-penalty.

Ireland, Robert M. "Privately Funded Prosecution of Crime in the Nineteenth-Century United States." *American Journal of Legal History* 39.1 (1995): 43–58.

Irving, Washington. *The Sketch Book of Geoffrey Crayon, Gent.* 1820. New York: Dodd and Mead, 1954.

The Island. Dir. Michael Bay. Perf. Ewan McGregor, Scarlett Johansson, Djimon Housnou. Warner Brothers, 2005. DVD.

"Jack and the Beanstalk." In *Anthology of Children's Literature*, edited by Edna Johnson, Evelyn Ray Sickels, Frances Clarke Sayers, and Fritz Eichenberg, 220–25. New York: Houghton Mifflin, 1977.

Jacobson, Josepha. "The Many Cuts that Slowly Finished the Bloody Code." *Times* (London), 11 Oct. 2005: law 11.

Jaffe, Rona. *The Best of Everything*. 1958. New York: Penguin, 2005.

James, Kathryn. *Death, Gender, and Sexuality in Contemporary Adolescent Literature*. London: Routledge, 2009.

Jameson, Fredric. *The Cultural Turn: Selected Writings on the Postmodern, 1983–1998*. New York: Verso, 1998.

———. *Postmodernism; or, The Cultural Logic of Late Capitalism*. Durham, NC: Duke University Press, 1991.

Jason, Janine, Jeanne C. Gilliland, and Carl W. Tyler. "Homicide as a Cause of Pediatric Mortality in the United States." *Pediatrics* 72.2 (1983): 191–97.

Jay, Stacey. *My So-Called Death*. Woodbury, MN: Flux, 2010.

Kadish, Sanford H., and Stephen J. Schulhofer. *Criminal Law and Its Processes: Cases and Materials*. 6th ed. New York: Aspen, 1995.

Kasson, John F. *Houdini, Tarzan and the Perfect Man: The White Male Body and the Challenge of Modernity in America*. New York: Hill and Wang, 2001.

Kaufmann, Walter. "Nietzsche, Friedrich." In *The Encyclopedia of Philosophy*, 508–14. New York: Crowell, Collier and Macmillan, 1967.

Keene, Carolyn. *The Bungalow Mystery*. 1930. Bedford, MA: Applewood, 1991.

———. *The Clue in the Jewel Box*. 1943. Bedford, MA: Applewood, 2005.

———. *The Hidden Staircase*. 1930. Bedford, MA: Applewood, 1991.

———. *The Message in the Hollow Oak*. 1935. Bedford, MA: Applewood, 1999.

———. *The Mystery at Lilac Inn*. 1930. Bedford, MA: Applewood, 1994.

———. *The Mystery of the Ivory Charm*. 1936. Bedford, MA: Applewood, 1999.

———. *The Mystery of the Ivory Charm*. 1964. New York: Grosset and Dunlap, 1974.

———. *The Secret at Shadow Ranch*. 1931. Bedford, MA: Applewood, 1994.

———. *The Secret of the Old Clock*. 1930. Bedford, MA: Applewood, 1991.

———. *The Secret of Red Gate Farm*. 1931. Bedford, MA: Applewood, 1994.

———. *The Sign of the Twisted Candles*. 1933. Bedford, MA: Applewood, 1994.

Kehr, Dave. "Masters of Animation, Old and Old School." *New York Times*, 1 Oct. 2009, AR12.

Kelly, Richard. *Lewis Carroll*. Rev. ed. Boston: Twayne, 1990.

Kerr, Howard, and Charles L. Crow. Introduction to *The Occult in America: New Historical Perspectives*, edited by Howard Kerr and Charles L. Crow, 1–10. Urbana: University of Illinois, 1983.

Kidd, Kenneth B. *Freud in Oz: At the Intersections of Psychoanalysis and Children's Literature*. Minneapolis: University of Minnesota Press, 2011.

Kill Bill. Vol. 1. Dir. Quentin Tarantino. Perf. Uma Thurman, David Carradine, Daryl Hannah. Miramax, 2003.

Klein, Kathleen Gregory. Introduction to *Diversity and Detective Fiction*, edited by Kathleen Gregory, 1–4. Bowling Green, OH: Bowling Green University Press, 1999.

Knelman, Judith. *Twisting in the Wind: The Murderess and the English Press*. Toronto: University of Toronto Press, 1998.

Knowles. John. *A Separate Peace*. 1959. New York: Scribner, 2003.

Knox, Sara L. *Murder: A Tale of Modern American Life*. Durham, NC: Duke University Press, 1998.

Koenen, Mark, and John W. Thompson Jr. "Filicide: Historical Review and Prevention of Child Death by Parent." *Infant Mental Health Journal* 29.1 (2008): 61–75.

"*Krabat*." Otfried Preussler. http://www.preussler.de/index1e.htm.

Kryzwinska, Tanya. "Zombies in Cyberspace: Form, Context, and Meaning in Zombie-Based Video Games." In *Zombie Culture: Autopsies of the Living Dead*, edited by Shawn McIntosh and Marc Leverette, 153–68. Lanham, MD: Scarecrow, 2008.

Kutner, Merrily. *Z Is for Zombie*. Illus. John Manders. Morton Grave, IL: Albert Whitman, 1999.

———. *The Zombie Nite Café*. Illus. Ethan Long. New York: Holiday House, 2007.

Laderman, Gary. *American Remains: American Attitudes Toward Death, 1799–1883*. New Haven, CT: Yale University Press, 1999.

Land of the Dead. Dir. George A. Romero. Perf. Simon Baker, John Leguizamo, Dennis Hopper. Universal Pictures, 2005. DVD.

Lane, Roger. *Murder in America: A History*. Columbus: Ohio State University Press, 1997.

Larsen, Anita. *Psychic Sleuths: How Psychic Information Is Used to Solve Crimes*. New York: Dixocery Books, 1994.

"The Last Public Execution in America." NPR, 1 May 2001. http://www.npr.org/programs/morning/features/2001/apr/010430.execution.html.

Leonard, Todd Jay. *Talking to the Other Side: A History of Modern Spiritualism and Mediumship*. Lincoln, NE: iUniverse, 2005.

Lesser, Wendy. *Pictures at an Execution: An Inquiry into the Subject of Murder*. Cambridge, MA: Harvard University Press, 1993.

Leverette, Marc, and Shawn McIntosh. Introduction to *Zombie Culture: Autopsies of the Living Dead*, edited by Shawn McIntosh and Marc Leverette, vii–xiv. Lanham, MD: Scarecrow, 2008.

Levine, Lawrence. *Highbrow/Lowbrow: The Emergence of Cultural Hierarchy in America*. Cambridge, MA: Harvard University Press, 1988.

Levitsky, Susan, and Robyn Cooper. "Infant Colic Syndrome—Maternal Fantasies of Aggression and Infanticide." *Clinical Pediatrics* 39.7 (2000): 395–400.

Lewis, Catherine F., Madelon V. Baranoski, Jospehine A. Buchanan, and Elissa P. Benedek. "Factors Associated with Weapon Use in Maternal Filicide." *Journal of Forensic Sciences* 43.3 (1998): 613–18.

Lieberman, Marcia K. "'Some Day My Prince Will Come': Female Acculturation through the Fairy Tale." In *Don't Bet on the Prince: Contemporary Feminist Fairy Tales in North America and England*, edited by Jack Zipes, 187–200. New York: Methuen, 1987.

Lief, Michael, Harry Caldwell, and Benjamin Bycel. *Ladies and Gentlemen of the Jury: Greatest Closing Arguments in Modern Law*. New York: Scribner, 1998.

Liem, Marieke, and Frans Koentaadt. "Filicide: A Comparative Study of Maternal

Versus Paternal Child Homicide." *Criminal Behavior and Mental Health* 18.3 (2008): 166–76.

Linders, Annulla. "The Execution Spectacle and State Legitimacy: The Changing Nature of the American Execution Audience, 1833–1937." *Law and Society Review* 36.3 (2002): 607–56.

"Lizzie Borden Bed and Breakfast History." Lizzie Borden Bed and Breakfast/ Museum. http://www.lizzie-borden.com/index.php/about-the-house/history.

Lloyd-Bostock, Sally, and Cheryl Thomas. "Decline of the 'Little Parliament': Juries and Jury Reform in England and Wales." *Law and Contemporary Problems* 62.2 (1999): 7–40.

Loach, Loretta. *The Devil's Children: A History of Childhood and Murder*. New York: Icon, 2009.

Locke, John. "Glorifying the American Goon." In *Gang Pulp*, edited by John Locke, 7–32. Castroville, CA: Off-Trail Publications, 2008.

Lombroso, Cesare. *Crime: Its Causes and Remedies*. Translated Henry P. Horton. 1911. Montclair, NJ: Patterson Smith, 1968.

———. "The Criminal." *Putnam's Magazine* 7.7 (1910): 793–96.

———. *Criminal Man*. 1876. Translated and edited by Mary Gibson and Nicole Hahn Rafter. Durham, NC: Duke University Press, 2006.

———. Introduction to *Criminal Man, According to the Classification of Cesare Lombroso*, by Gina Lombroso-Ferrero, xxi–xxx. 1911. Montclair, NJ: Patterson Smith, 1972.

Lombroso-Ferrero, Gina. *Criminal Man, According to the Classification of Cesare Lombroso*. 1911. Montclair, NJ: Patterson Smith, 1972.

London, Jack. *The Call of the Wild*. 1903. New York: Penguin, 2008.

Lott, Eric. *Love and Theft: Blackface and the American Working Class*. New York: Oxford University Press, 1993.

Louison, Cole. *U.S. Army Zombie Combat Skills*. Illus. David Cole Wheeler. Guilford, CT: Lyons, 2009.

Lovell-Smith, Rose. "The Animals of Wonderland: Tenniel as Carroll's Reader." *Criticism* 45.4 (2003): 383–415.

Lowry, Lois. *The Giver*. 1993. New York: Random House, 2002.

Lubar, David. *Dead Guy Spy* (Nathan Abercrombie, Accidental Zombie Series). New York: Tom Doherty Associates, 2009.

———. *My Rotten Life* (Nathan Abercrombie, Accidental Zombie Series). New York: Tom Doherty Associates, 2009.

Lundman, Richard J. "The Newsworthiness and Selection Bias in News about Murder: Comparative and Relative Effects of Novel and Race and Gender Typifications on Newspaper Coverage of Homicide." *Sociological Forum* 18.3 (2003): 357–86.

Lupoff, Richard A. *Edgar Rice Burroughs: Master of Adventure*. New York: Ace Books, 1968.

Lyons, Arthur, and Marcello Truzzi. *The Blue Sense: Psychic Detectives and Crime*. New York: Warner Books/Mysterious Press, 1991.

Ma, Roger. *The Zombie Combat Manual: A Guide to Fighting the Living Dead*. Berkley Trade, 2009.

MacLeod, Anne Scott. *American Childhood: Essays on Children's Literature of the Nineteenth and Twentieth Centuries*. Athens: University of Georgia Press, 1994.

Maddux, Rachael. "Listen Up: High-Brow, Low-Brow, No-Brow, Schmo-Brow." *Paste Magazine*, 28 Dec. 2009.

Malcolm, Janet. *The Journalist and the Murderer*. New York: Knopf, 1990.

Mallone, Michael. "Tough Puppies." *Nation*, 8 Mar. 1986, 276–80.

Malmgren, Carl D. *Anatomy of Murder: Mystery, Detective and Crime Fiction*. Bowling Green, OH: Bowling Green University Press, 2001.

Mandel, Paul. "Tarzan of the Paperbacks," *LIFE* magazine, 29 Nov. 1963, 11–12.

Mansfield-Kelley, Deane, and Lois A. Marchino. "Part I: The Amateur Detective." In *The Longman Anthology of Detective Fiction*, edited by Deane Mansfield-Kelley and Lois A. Marchino, 25–28. New York: Pearson, 2005.

Martin, Douglas. "Dorothy Allison, 74, 'Psychic Detective,' Consulted by Police." *New York Times*, 20 Dec. 1999.

Martin, Paul. *Runaway Zombie!* New York: Hyperion, 2002.

Marvel Zombies. Five-issue Comic Book Series. Written by Robert Kirkman. Art by Sean Philips. Covers by Arthur Suydam. Marvel Comics, December 2005–April 2006.

"Marvel Zombies." Marvel.com. http://marvel.com/comic_books/series/998/marvel_zombies_2005_-_2006.

"Mary Anne." *Brewer's Dictionary of Phrase and Fable*. 14th ed. New York: Harper and Row, 1989.

Masur, Louis P. *Rites of Execution: Capital Punishment and the Transformation of American Culture, 1776–1865*. New York: Oxford University Press, 1989.

Mayer, Frederick. *Our Troubled Youth*. New York: Bantam Books, 1960.

Mazzocco, Robert. "The Supply-Side Star." *New York Times Review of Books*, 1 Apr. 1982.

Mbembe, Achille. "Necropolitics." Translated by Libby Meintjes. *Public Culture* 15.1 (2003): 11–40.

McCann, Jesse Leon. *Scooby-Doo and the Rock 'n' Roll Zombie*. New York: Scholastic, 2007.

McCaskey, J. P. *Franklin Square Song Collection: Two Hundred Favorite Songs and Hymns for Schools and Homes, Nursery and Fireside*. Vol. 3. New York: Harper and Brothers, 1885.

M'Conaghy, Robert, and Peter Robinson. *Trial, Confession, and Execution of Robert M'Conaghy*. Philadelphia: n.p., 1841.

McGivern, William P. *Savage Streets*. New York: Pocket Books, 1961.

McGowen, Randall. "Civilizing Punishment: The End of Public Execution in England." *Journal of British Studies* 33.3 (1994): 257–82.

———. "A Powerful Sympathy: Terror, the Prison, and Humanitarian Reform in Early Nineteenth-Century Britain." *Journal of British Studies* 25.3 (1986): 312–34.

McGreal, Chris. "Romell Broom to Face Execution Next Week Following Botched Lethal Injection." *Guardian*, 17 Sept. 2009. http://www.guardian.co.uk/world/2009/sep/17/ohio-death-penalty-lethal-injection.

McIntosh, Shawn. "The Evolution of the Zombie: The Monster That Keeps Coming Back." In *Zombie Culture: Autopsies of the Living Dead*, edited by Shawn McIntosh and Marc Leverette, 1–17. Lanham, MD: Scarecrow, 2008.

McKee, Geoffrey R. *Why Mothers Kill: A Forensic Psychologist's Casebook*. New York: Oxford, 2006.

McKee, Geoffrey R., and Steven J. Shea. "Maternal Filicide: A Cross-National Comparison." *Journal of Clinical Psychology* 54.5 (1998): 679–87.

McKee, Geoffrey R., Steven J. Shea, Robert B. Mogy, and Carol E. Holden. "MMPI-2 Profiles of Filicidal, Matricidal, and Homicidal Women." *Journal of Clinical Psychology* 57.3 (2001): 367–74.

McMurtry, Ken. *Zombie Penpal*. Waitsfield, VT: Chooseco, 2010.

Media Awareness Network. "Violence in Media Entertainment." http://www.media-awareness.ca/english/issues/violence/violence_entertainment.cfm.

Meranze, Michael. "Review: The Hanging Tree." *Law and History Review* 15.2 (1997): 373–75.

Mertz, Maia Pank, and David E. England. "The Legitimacy of American Adolescent Fiction." *School Library Journal*, Oct. 1983, 119–23.

"Mickey Spillane." *Contemporary Authors Online*. Literature Resource Center.

Mitchell, Richard. "Capcom: Resident Evil Franchise Nears 40 Million Units." Joystiq, 8 May 2009. http://www.joystiq.com/2009/05/08/capcom-resident-evil-franchise-nears-40-million-units-sfii-sti.

Mitchell, Sally. *Daily Life in Victorian England*. Westport, CT: Greenwood, 1996.

Mitchell, William J. *Me++: The Cyborg Self and the Networked City*. Boston: MIT Press, 2003.

Monkkonen, Eric. "Homicide: Explaining America's Exceptionalism." *American Historical Review* 111.1 (2006): 76–94.

Monster. Dir. Patty Jenkins. Perf. Charlize Theron, Christina Ricci, Bruce Dern. Sony, 2003. DVD.

Moore, Michael S. "Causation and the Excuses." *California Law Review* 73.4 (1985): 1091–1149.

Morris, Frankie. *Artist of Wonderland: The Life, Political Cartoons, and Illustrations of Tenniel*. Charlottesville: University of Virginia Press, 2005.

Morrison, Toni. *Beloved*. 1987. New York: Knopf, 2004.

Mortal Kombat. Midway Games/Acclaim Entertainment. 1992–present. Video game.

"Most Frequently Challenged Authors of the 21st Century." American Library Association. http://www.ala.org/ala/issuesadvocacy/banned/frequentlychallenged/challengedauthors/index.cfm.

Motley, Willard. *Knock on Any Door*. New York: New American Library, 1950.

Motz, Anna. "Women Who Kill: When Fantasy Becomes Reality." In *Murder: A Psychotherapeutic Investigation*, edited by Ronald Doctor, 51–64. London: Karnac, 2008.

Murder!! Death of Miss Mack Coy, and the Young Tazer. Boston: Coverly, 1813.

Murder: Narrative of the Trial, Conviction and Execution of Captain William Corran. Newport, RI, 1794.

Murder, She Wrote. CBS. 1984–96. Television series.

Murder Most Foul! A Synopsis of Speeches of Ogden Hoffman, Thomas Phenix [sic], Hugh Maxwell, Judge Edwards, & c. on the Trial of Robindon, for the Murder of Ellen Jewett. Compiled by Richard Robinson. New York: R. H. Elton, 1836.

A Murderer Punished and Pardoned; or, A True Relation of the Wicked Life, and Shameful-Happy Death of Thomas Savage. . . . London: n.p., 1668.

"Museum Info." The Museum of Death. http://www.museumofdeath.net. *My So-Called Life.* ABC, 1994–95. Television series.

Myers, Walter Dean. "The *Booklist* Interview." *Booklist,* 15 Feb. 2000, 1101.

———. "Escalating Offenses." *Horn Book Magazine* 77.6 (2001): 701–2.

———. *Monster.* New York: HarperTempest, 1999.

———. "Questions for Walter Dean Myers." In *Monster.* New York: HarperTempest, 1999.

Nabokov, Vladimir. *Lolita.* 1955. New York: Knopf, 1989.

Nash, Jay Robert. *Murder, America: Homicide in the United States from the Revolution to the Present.* New York: Simon and Schuster, 1980.

National Association for the Advancement of Colored People. *Thirty Years of Lynching in the United States, 1889–1918.* New York: Negro Universities Press, 1969.

"Nationwide Murder Rates, 1996–2008." Death Penalty Information Center. http://www.deathpenaltyinfo.org/murder-rates-nationally-and-state.

Natov, Roni. "The Persistence of Alice." *The Lion and the Unicorn* 3.1 (1979): 38–61.

New Jack City. Dir. Mario Van Peebles. Perf. Wesley Snipes, Ice-T. Warner Brothers, 1991. DVD.

Nickell, Joe. Introduction to *Psychic Sleuths: ESP and Sensational Cases,* edited by Joe Nickell, 11–20. Amherst, NY: Prometheus Books, 1994.

———. "A Skeleton's Tale: The Origins of Modern Spiritualism." *Investigative Files* 32. 4 (2008): 17–20. http://www.csicop.org/si/show/skeletons_tale_the_origins_of_modern_spiritualism.

"Nietzsche, Friedrich." *Routledge Encyclopedia of Philosophy.* London: Routledge, 1998.

Nietzsche, Friedrich. *Thus Spoke Zarathustra: A Book for All and None.* 1883–85. New York: Random House, 1995.

A Nightmare on Elm Street. Dir. Wes Craven. Perf. Heather Langencamp, Johnny Depp, Robert Englund. New Line Cinema, 1984. DVD.

Noonan, R. A. *My Teacher Is a Zombie.* New York: Aladdin, 1995.

Olshaker, Edward. Prologue to *Witness to the Unsolved: Prominent Psychic Detectives and Mediums Explore Our Most Haunting Mysteries,* edited by Edward Olshaker, 19–26. Owings Mills, MD: Remiel Press, 2005.

Opie, Iona, and Peter Opie, eds. *The Oxford Dictionary of Nursery Rhymes.* Oxford: Oxford University Press, 1951.

O'Rourke, Meghan. "Nancy Drew's Father." *New Yorker*, 8 Nov. 2004.

Ostry, Elaine. "'Is He Still Human? Are You?' Young Adult Science Fiction in the Posthuman Age." *The Lion and the Unicorn* 28 (2004): 222–46.

The Oxford Companion to Children's Literature. Edited by Humphrey Carpenter and Mari Prichard. Oxford: Oxford University Press, 1999.

Palermo, George B. "Murderous Parents." *International Journal of Offender Therapy and Comparative Criminology* 46.2 (2002): 123–43.

Papke, David Ray. *Framing the Criminal: Crime, Cultural Work, and the Loss of Critical Perspective, 1830–1900*. North Haven, CT: Shoe String Press, 1987.

Paradiž, Valerie. *Clever Maids: The Secret History of the Grimm Fairy Tales*. New York: Basic Books, 2005.

Parry, Sally E. "The Secret of the Feminist Heroine: The Search for Values in Nancy Drew and Judy Bolton." In *Nancy Drew and Company: Culture, Gender, and Girls' Series*, edited by Sherrie A. Inness, 145–58. Bowling Green, OH: Bowling Green State University Press, 1997.

Pascal, Francine. *Steven the Zombie*. New York: Bantam, 1994.

Patmore, Coventry. "The Murderer's Sacrament: A Fact." In *The Poems of Coventry Patmore*, edited by Frederick Page, 56–57. Oxford: Oxford University Press, 1949.

Peck, Dale. "'The Outsiders': 40 Years Later." *New York Times*, 23 Sept. 2007.

Pellegrini, Ann. "'What Do Children Learn at School?' Necropedagogy and the Future of the Dead Child." *Social Text* 26.4 (2008): 97–105.

Pence, Gregory E. *Classic Cases in Medical Ethics: Accounts of the Cases that Have Shaped Medical Ethics, with Philosophical, Legal, and Historical Backgrounds*. New York: McGraw-Hill, 1990.

Perkins, Kenneth. *Relentless*. New York: Bantam, 1948.

Perkins, Rollin M. "The Law of Homicide." *Journal of Criminal Law and Criminology* 36.6 (1946): 391–454.

Perrault, Charles. "Bluebeard." In *The Classic Fairy Tales*, edited by Maria Tatar, 144–48. New York: Norton, 1998.

———. "Little Tom Thumb." In *Perrault's Fairy Tales*, translated by A. E. Johnson, 26–40. Hertfordshire, UK: Wordsworth Editions, 2004.

———. "Sleeping Beauty." In *Perrault's Fairy Tales*, translated by A. E. Johnson, 3–17. Hertfordshire, UK: Wordsworth Editions, 2004.

Perry, Barbara. "Defending the Color Line: Racially and Ethnically Motivated Hate Crime." *American Behavioral Scientist* 46.1 (2002): 72–92.

Perry Mason. CBS. 1957–66. Television series.

———. CBS. 1973–74. Television series.

Pickard, Phyllis M. *I Could a Tale Unfold: Violence, Horror and Sensationalism in Stories for Children*. London: Tavistock, 1961.

Pinkham, Paul. "Jacksonville Father Gets Life for Beating Daughter to Death." *Florida Times-Union* (Jacksonville), 26 May 2010.

Pitkin, Walter. *What's That Plane? The Handbook for Practical Aircraft Identification*. New York: Penguin, 1942.

Planet Terror. Dir. Robert Rodriguez. Perf. Rose McGowan, Freddy Rodriguez, Josh Brolin. Dimension, 2007. DVD.

"Plea Bargaining." In *Encyclopedia of Everyday Law,* edited by Shirelle Phelps, 365–68. Gale Cengage, 2003.

Plotz, Judith. *Romanticism and the Vocation of Childhood.* New York: Palgrave, 2001.

Poe, Edgar Allan. "The Murders in the Rue Morgue." 1841. *The Murders in the Rue Morgue.* New York: Modern Library, 2006.

Porges, Irwin. *Edgar Rice Burroughs: The Man Who Created Tarzan.* Provo, UT: Brigham Young University Press, 1975.

Potter, Harry. *Hanging in Judgment: Religion and the Death Penalty in England from the Bloody Code to Abolition.* London: SCM Press, 1993.

Prager, Arthur. *Rascals at Large; or, The Clue in the Old Nostalgia.* Garden City, NY: Doubleday, 1971.

Preussler, Otfried. *Krabat [The Satanic Mill].* Translated by Anthea Bell. New York: Simon and Schuster, 1991.

Price, William H., and Peter B. Whatmore. "Behavior Disorders and Pattern of Crime among XYY Males Identified at a Maximum Security Hospital." *British Medical Journal* 1.5539 (1967): 533–36.

Primavera, Elise. *Fred and Anthony Meet the Demented Super-Degerm-O Zombie.* New York: Hyperion, 2007.

"Psychic Detectives." In *Encyclopedia of Forensic Science: A Compendium of Fact and Fiction,* edited by Barbara Gardner Conklin, Robert Gardner, and Dennis Shortelle, 229–31. Westport, CT: Oryx Press, 2002.

Psycho. Dir. Alfred Hitchcock. Perf. Anthony Perkins, Janet Leigh, Vera Miles. Universal, 1960. DVD.

Puzo, Mario. *The Godfather.* 1969. New York: Penguin, 1983.

Pyles, Marianne S. *Death and Dying in Children's and Young People's Literature: A Survey and Bibliography.* Jefferson, NC: McFarland, 1988.

Pynchon, Thomas. *Mason & Dixon.* 1997. New York: Picador, 2004.

Rackin, Donald. *"Alice's Adventures in Wonderland" and "Through the Looking-Glass": Nonsense, Sense, and Meaning.* Boston: Twayne, 1991.

Ramsland, Katherine. "Existential Murder: The Nietzsche Syndrome." True Crime Library. http://www.trutv.com/library/crime/notorious_murders/famous/nietzsche_crimes/7.html.

———. "Serial Killer Art." True Crime Library. http://www.trutv.com/library/crime/criminal_mind/psychology/serial_killer_art/index.html.

Rascovsky, Arnaldo. *Filicide: The Murder, Humiliation, Denigration, and Abandonment of Children by Parents.* Northvale, NJ: Jason Aronson, 1995.

Rebel Without a Cause. Dir. Nicholas Ray. Perf. James Dean, Natalie Wood, Sal Mineo. Warner Brothers, 1955. DVD.

"Regional Murder Rates, 2001–2009." Death Penalty Information Center. http://www.deathpenaltyinfo.org/murder-rates-nationally-and-state.

Rehak, Melanie. *Girl Sleuth: Nancy Drew and the Woman Who Created Her.* Orlando, FL: Harcourt Brace, 2005.

Renier, Noreen. *A Mind for Murder: The Real-Life Files of a Psychic Investigator*. Charlottesville, VA: Hampton Roads Publishing, 2008.

Resident Evil. Capcorn, 1996–present. Video game series.

Resnick, Phillip J. "Child Murder by Parents: A Psychiatric Review of Filicide." *American Journal of Psychiatry* 129.3 (1969): 325–34.

Ressler, Robert. With Tom Shachtman. *Whoever Fights Monsters: My Twenty Years Hunting Serial Killers for the FBI*. New York: St. Martin's, 1992.

Rhine, J. B. *Extra Sensory Perception*. Boston: Boston Society for Psychic Research, 1934.

———. Foreword. In *A Handbook for Testing Extra-Sensory Perception*, by C. E. Stuart and J. G. Pratt, 7–9. New York: Farrar and Rinehart, 1937.

Robinson, Jean. "Could I Kill My Baby? Unjustified Infanticide Fears." *British Journal of Midwifery* 12.9 (2004): 582.

Rochman, Hazel. "Interview: Walter Dean Myers." *Booklist*, 15 Feb. 2000, 1101.

Roediger, David. *The Wages of Whiteness: Race and the Making of the American Working Class*. New York: Verso, 1991.

Rogers, John. *Death the Certain Wages of Sin to the Impenitent: Life the Sure Reward of Grace to the Penitent Together with the Only Way for Youth to Avoid the Former, and Attain the Latter. . . .* Ipswich, MA: Bartholomew Green and John Allen, 1701.

Rollin, Lucy. "Dreaming in Public: The Psychology of Nursery Rhyme Illustration." *Children's Literature Association Quarterly* 19.3 (1994): 105–8.

Rome, Dennis. *Black Demons: The Media's Depiction of African American Male Criminal Stereotype*. Westport, CT: Praeger, 2004.

Roth, Philip. *American Pastoral*. 1997. New York: Knopf, 1998.

Rowe, Karen E. "Feminism and Fairy Tales." In *Don't Bet on the Prince: Contemporary Feminist Fairy Tales in North America and England*, edited by Jack Zipes, 209–26. New York: Methuen, 1987.

Rowe, Walter. "Psychic Detectives." In *The Encyclopedia of the Paranormal*, edited by Gordon Stein, 585–97. Amherst, NY: Prometheus Books, 1996.

Rowlandson, Mary White. "A Narrative of the Captivity and Restoration of Mrs. Mary White Rowlandson." In vol. A of *The Heath Anthology of American Literature*, 5th ed., edited by Paul Lauter, 440–68. Boston: Houghton Mifflin, 2006.

Rowling, J. K. *Harry Potter and the Sorcerer's Stone*. New York: Scholastic, 1997.

Roy, Ron. *The Zombie Zone*. New York: Random House, 2005.

Royal Commission on Capital Punishment. *Report of the Capital Punishment Commission, Together with Minutes and Evidence*. London: Eyre and Spottiswoode, 1866.

Ryan, Pam Muñoz. *Esperanza Rising*. 2000. New York: Scholastic, 2002.

Salisbury, Harrison E. *The Shook-Up Generation*. New York: Fawcett, 1958.

Sartre, Jean-Paul. *Dirty Hands*. In *Three Plays*, 3–152. Trans. Lionel Abel. New York: Knopf, 1949.

Savitz, Leonard D. Introduction to *Criminal Man, According to the Classification of Cesare Lombroso*, by Gina Lombroso-Ferrero, v–xx. Montclair, NJ: Patterson Smith, 1972.

Sawyer, Jeffrey K. "'Benefit of Clergy' in Maryland and Virginia." *American Journal of Legal History* 34.1 (1990): 49–68.

Sayers, Dorothy. *Murder Must Advertise.* 1933. New York: HarperCollins, 1995.

Schechter, Harold. *Depraved: The Definitive True Story of H. H. Holmes, Whose Grotesque Crimes Shattered Turn-of-the-Century Chicago.* New York: Pocket, 1994.

Schick, Frank L. *The Paperbound Book in America: The History of Paperbacks and Their European Background.* New York: R. R. Bowker, 1958.

Schwartz, Lita Linzer, and Natalie K. Isser. *Endangered Children: Neonaticide, Infanticide, and Filicide.* Boca Raton, FL: CRC Press, 2000.

Scott, Gini Graham. *American Murder.* Vol. 1: *Homicide in the Early Twentieth Century.* Westport, CT: Praeger, 2007.

———. *American Murder.* Vol. 2: *Homicide in the Late Twentieth Century.* Westport, CT: Praeger, 2007.

Scott, Ron. "'Now I'm Feeling Zombiefied': Playing the Zombie Online." In *Zombie Culture: Autopsies of the Living Dead*, edited by Shawn McIntosh and Marc Leverette, 169–84. Lanham, MD: Scarecrow, 2008.

Scroggs, Kirk. *Grampa's Zombie BBQ.* New York: Little, Brown, 2006.

Seaman, Myra. "Becoming More (Than) Human: Affective Posthumanisms, Past and Future." *JNT: Journal of Narrative Theory* 37.2 (2007): 246–75.

Sebold, Alice. *The Lovely Bones.* New York: Little, Brown, 2002.

Seeley, E. S. *Street Walker.* New York: Beacon, 1959.

Seitz, Trina N. "A History of Execution Methods in the United States." In *Handbook of Death and Dying*, vol. 1., edited by Clifton D. Bryant, 357–67. Thousand Oaks, CA: Sage, 2003.

Seltzer, Mark. *Serial Killers: Life and Death in America's Wound Culture.* New York: Routledge, 1998.

"Serial Killer Art." Lowbrow Artworld—Serial Killer Art for Sale. http://www.low browartworld.com/serial_sale00.html.

Seven. Dir. David Fincher. Perf. Morgan Freeman, Brad Pitt, Kevin Spacey. New Line, 1995.

Shepard, Jon. *Sociology.* 10th ed. Belmont, CA: Wadsworth, 2010.

The Shining. Dir. Stanley Kubrick. Perf. Jack Nicholson, Shelley Duvall, Danny Lloyd. Warner Brothers, 1980. DVD.

Shortsleeve, Kevin. "The Wonderful World of the Depression: Disney, Despotism, and the 1930s; or, Why Disney Scares Us." *The Lion and the Unicorn* 28.1 (2004): 1–30.

Shulman, Irving. *The Amboy Dukes.* 1946. New York: Critic's Choice, 1986.

Siegel, Deborah L. "Nancy Drew as New Girl Wonder: Solving It All for the 1930s." In *Nancy Drew and Company: Culture, Gender, and Girls' Series*, edited by Sherrie A. Inness, 159–82. Bowling Green, OH: Bowling Green State University Press, 1997.

The Silence of the Lambs. Dir. Jonathan Demme. Perf. Jodie Foster, Anthony Hopkins, Scott Glenn. MGM, 1991.

Silverstein, Shel. "The Man Who Got No Sign." *Freakin' at the Freakers Ball.* 1972. Sony, 1999. Compact Disc.

Silvey, Anita. "The Problem with Trends." *Horn Book Magazine* 70.5 (1994): 516–17.

Simon, Bart. "Introduction: Toward a Critique of Posthuman Futures." *Cultural Critique* 53 (2003): 1–9.

Sims, Calvin. "Schools Responding to Beeper, Tool of Today's Drug Dealer, by Banning." *New York Times*, 25 Sept. 1988.

The Sixth Sense. Dir. M. Night Shymalan. Perf. Bruce Willis, Haley Joel Osment, Toni Collette. Hollywood Pictures, 1999.

Sklar, Annelise. "Can't Sleep When You're Dead: Sex, Drugs, Rock and Roll, and the Undead in Psychobilly." In *Zombie Culture: Autopsies of the Living Dead*, edited by Shawn Mcintosh, and Marc Leverette, 135–52. Lanham, MD: Scarecrow, 2008.

Smith, Erin A. *Hard-Boiled: Working-Class Readers and Pulp Magazines*. Philadelphia: Temple University Press, 2000.

Smith, Katharine Capshaw. Introduction to "Trauma and Children's Literature" Forum. *Children's Literature* 33 (2005): 115–19.

Snicket, Lemony. *The Bad Beginning*. 1999. New York: Harper Collins, 2001.

———. *The Composer Is Dead*. New York: Harper Collins, 2008.

Snodgrass, Mary Ellen. *Walter Dean Myers: A Literary Companion*. Jefferson, NC: McFarland, 2006.

Snow White and the Seven Dwarfs. Dir. David Hand. Perf. Adriana Caselotti, Harry Stockwell, Lucille La Verne. Walt Disney, 1937. DVD.

"Speaking with S. E. Hinton." In *The Outsiders*, by S. E. Hinton, 182–86. 1967. New York: Speak, 1995.

Spierenburg, Pieter. *A History of Murder: Personal Violence in Europe from the Middle Ages to the Present*. Cambridge, England: Polity, 2008.

Spinney, Robert G. *City of Big Shoulders: A History of Chicago*. Dekalb: Northern Illinois University Press, 2000.

Stallcup, Jackie E. "Power, Fear, and Children's Picture Books." *Children's Literature* 30 (2002): 125–58.

Stanley, Henry. *In Darkest Africa*. 1890. Torrington, WY: The Narrative Press, 2001.

"States with and without the Death Penalty." Death Penalty Information Center. http://www.deathpenaltyinfo.org/states-and-without-death-penalty.

Staunton, John A., and Francine Gubuan. Review of *Monster*, by Walter Dean Myers. *Journal of Adolescent & Adult Literacy* 45.8 (2002): 791–93.

Steelwater, Eliza. *The Hangman's Knot: Lynching, Legal Execution, and America's Struggle with the Death Penalty*. Boulder, CO: Westview, 2003.

Stern, Fritz, ed. *The Varieties of History: Voltaire to the Present*. 1952. New York: Random House, 1973.

Stern, Jeffrey, ed. *Lewis Carroll's Library*. Charlottesville: University Press of Virginia, 1981.

Stine, R. L. *Bad Dreams*. New York: Scholastic, 1994.

———. *Beach House*. New York: Scholastic, 1992.

———. *Call Waiting*. New York: Scholastic, 1994.

———. *I Was a Sixth-Grade Zombie*. New York: Parachute, 1998.

———. *Piano Lessons Can Be Murder*. New York: Scholastic, 1993.

———. *Zombie School*. New York: Scholastic, 1999.

Storrie, Paul D. *Nightmare on Zombie Island*. Minneapolis, MN: Graphic Universe, 2008.

Stuart, Charles E., and Joseph G. Pratt. *A Handbook for Testing Extra-Sensory Perception*. New York: Farrar and Rinehart, 1937.

Susina, Jan. *The Place of Lewis Carroll in Children's Literature*. New York: Routledge, 2010.

Sutton, Roger. "The Critical Myth: Realistic YA Novels." *School Library Journal*, Nov. 1982, 33–35.

———. "Problems, Paperbacks, and the Printz: Forty Years of YA Books." *Horn Book Magazine* 83.3 (2007): 231–43.

Szegedy-Maszak, Marianne. "Mothers and Murder." *U.S. News and World Report*, 18 Mar. 2008, 28.

Tabori, Paul. *Crime and the Occult: How ESP and Parapsychology Help Detection*. New York: Taplinger, 1974.

Taliaferro, John. *Tarzan Forever: The Life of Edgar Rice Burroughs, Creator of Tarzan*. New York: Scribner, 1999.

Tappan, Paul W. *Juvenile Delinquency*. New York: McGraw-Hill, 1949.

"Tarzan." Box Office Mojo. http://boxofficemojo.com/movies/?id=tarzan.htm.

Tatar, Maria. *Enchanted Hunters: The Power of Stories in Childhood*. New York: Norton, 2009.

———. *The Hard Facts of the Grimms' Fairy Tales*. 2nd. ed. Princeton, NJ: Princeton University Press, 2003.

———. *Off With Their Heads! Fairy Tales and the Culture of Childhood*. Princeton, NJ: Princeton University Press, 1992.

Texas Chainsaw Massacre. Dir. Tobe Hooper. Perf. Marilyn Burns, Edwin Neal, Allen Danzinger. Dark Sky Studios, 1974. DVD.

Thomas, Michael G., and Nick S. Thomas. *Zompoc: How to Survive a Zombie Apocalypse*. Swordworks, 2009.

Thompson, George N. *Confessions, Trials, and Biographical Sketches of the Most Cold Blooded Murderers*. 1837. Hartford, CT: S. Andrus and Son, 1844.

Toffoletti, Kim. *Cyborgs and Barbie Dolls: Feminism, Popular Culture and the Posthuman Body*. London: I. B. Taurus, 2007.

"Top Ten Most Frequently Challenged Books of 2010." American Library Association. http://www.ala.org/ala/issuesadvocacy/banned/frequentlychallenged/21stcenturychallenged/2010/index.cfm.

Torgovnick, Marianna. *Gone Primitive: Savage Intellects, Modern Lives*. Chicago: University of Chicago Press, 1990.

Torres, Tereska. *Woman's Barracks*. New York: Gold Medal, 1950.

Tribunella, Eric L. *Melancholia and Maturation: The Use of Trauma in American Children's Literature*. Knoxville: University of Tennessee Press, 2010.

Tucker, Nicholas. "Lullabies and Childcare: A Historical Perspective." In *Opening*

Texts: Psychoanalysis and the Culture of the Child, edited by Joseph H. Smith and William Kerrington, 17–27. Baltimore, MD: John Hopkins University Press, 1985.

Twain, Mark. *The Adventures of Tom Sawyer*. 1875. New York: Penguin, 2006.

———. "Pudd'nhead Wilson's New Calendar." In *Following the Equator*. New York: Harper, 1897.

28 Days Later. Dir. Danny Boyle. Perf. Alex Palmer, Cillian Murphy, Naomie Harris. Fox Searchlight, 2002. DVD.

Twombly, Robert. *Zombies: A Record of the Year of Infection*. San Francisco: Chronicle Books, 2009.

"Ubermensch." *Oxford Dictionary of Philosophy*. Oxford: Oxford University Press, 1994.

Updike, John. "Fiabe Italiane." In *Hugging the Shore: Essays and Criticism*, 655–62. New York: Knopf, 1983.

Van Dine, S. S. "Twenty Rules for Writing Detective Stories." *American Magazine*, Sept. 1928, 129–31. http://gaslight.mtroyal.ca/vandine.htm.

"Vasilisa the Beautiful." In *Favorite Folktales from Around the World*, edited by Jane Yolen, 335–42. New York: Pantheon, 1986.

Vernon, Alex. *On Tarzan*. Athens: University of Georgia Press, 2008.

"Victorian England." In Vol. 5 of *The Greenwood Encyclopedia of Daily Life*, edited by Joyce Salisbury, 333–38. New York: Greenwood, 2004.

Vronsky, Peter. *Serial Killers: The Method and Madness of Monsters*. New York: Berkley, 2004.

Wasko, Janet. *Understanding Disney: The Manufacture of Fantasy*. Oxford, UK: Blackwell, 2001.

Waters, Daniel. *Generation Dead*. New York: Hyperion, 2008.

———. *Kiss of Life*. New York: Hyperion, 2008.

———. *Passing Strange*. New York: Hyperion, 2010.

Waugh, Auberon. "Hanged for an Apple by the Bloody Code." *Independent*, 17 Nov. 1989, 19.

Weber, Eugen. "Fairies and Hard Facts: The Reality of Folktales." *Journal of the History of Ideas* 41.1 (1981): 93–113.

Webster, John. *The Duchess of Malfi*. London: British Library, Historical Print Editions, 2011.

Weinstein, Beatrice. "Women with Conscious Wishes of Infanticide." In *The Inner World of the Mother*, edited by Dale Mendell and Patsy Turrini, 285–98. Madison, CT: Psychosocial Press, 2003.

"What Is the Best Work of American Fiction in the Last 25 Years?" *New York Times*, 21 May 2006.

White Zombie. Dir. Victor Halperin. Perf. Bela Lugosi, Madge Bellamy, Joseph Cawthorn. RKO, 1932.

Wicks, Robert. "Friedrich Nietzsche." *Stanford Encyclopedia of Philosophy*. http://plato.stanford.edu/entries/nietzsche.

Widdecombe, Ann. Foreword to *Capital Punishment in Britain*, by Richard Clark, 7–10. Surrey, UK: Ian Publishing, 2009.

Wiener, Martin J. "The Sad Story of George Hall: Adultery, Murder and the Politics of Mercy in Mid-Victorian England." *Social History* 24.2 (1999): 174–95.

Wilcox, Tamara. *Mysterious Detectives: Psychics.* Austin, TX: Raintree Steck-Vaughn, 1977.

Wilkerson, David. *The Cross and the Switchblade.* New York: Pyramid, 1963.

Wilson, Antoine. *S. E. Hinton.* New York: Rosen, 2003.

Wilson, Buck. *The Lone Ranger and the Menace of Murder Valley.* Racine, WI: Whitman, 1938.

Wilson, Colin. *The Psychic Detectives: Paranormal Crime Detection, Telepathy and Psychic Archeology.* San Francisco: Mercury House, 1985.

Windling, Terri. "White as Snow: Fairy Tales and Fantasy." In *Snow White, Blood Red,* edited by Ellen Datlow and Terri Windling, 1–14. New York: Avon, 1993.

Wolffram, Heather. "Crime, Clairvoyance and the Weimar Police." *Journal of Contemporary History* 44.4 (2009): 581–601.

"World Zombie Day Is Back—And the Zombies Are Still Hungry!" *PRLog,* 25 Mar. 2009. http://www.prlog.org/10205152-world-zombie-day-is-back-and-the-zombies-are-still-hungry.html.

Wright, Richard. *Native Son.* 1940. New York: HarperCollins, 2005.

"XYY Trisomy." In *A Dictionary of Genetics,* edited by Robert C. King, William D. Stansfield and Pamela K. Mulligan, 479. Oxford: Oxford University Press, 2007.

Yablonsky, Lewis. *The Violent Gang.* New York: Pelican, 1966.

You've Got Mail. Dir. Nora Ephron. Perf. Tom Hanks, Meg Ryan, Greg Kinnear, Parker Posey. Warner Brothers, 1998.

Zimring, Franklin E. *The Contradictions of American Capital Punishment.* Oxford: Oxford University Press, 2003.

Zimring, Franklin E., and Gordon Hawkings. *Capital Punishment and the American Agenda.* Cambridge: Cambridge University Press, 1986.

Zindel, Paul. *The Gourmet Zombie.* New York: Hyperion, 2002.

Zipes, Jack. *Breaking the Magic Spell: Radical Theories of Folk and Fairy Tales.* 2nd ed. Lexington: University of Kentucky Press, 2002.

———. *Fairy Tales and the Art of Subversion: The Classical Genre for Children and the Process of Civilization.* 2nd ed. New York: Routledge, 2006.

———. Introduction to *The Great Fairy Tale Tradition: From Strapola and Basile to the Brothers Grimm,* edited by Jack Zipes, xi–xiv. New York: Norton, 2001.

———. "Who's Afraid of the Brothers Grimm? Socialization and Politicization through Fairy Tales." *The Lion and the Unicorn* 3.2 (1979/1980): 4–56.

———. *Why Fairy Tales Stick: The Evolution and Relevance of a Genre.* New York: Routledge, 2006.

Zombieland. Dir. Ruben Fleischer. Perf. Woody Harrelson, Jesse Eisenberg, Emma Stone. Sony, 2009. DVD.

Zusak, Markus. *The Book Thief.* New York: Knopf, 2005.

Index